FIVE MOONS RISING

LISE MACTAGUE

BELLA
BOOKS
2017

Bella Books, Inc.
P.O. Box 10543
Tallahassee, FL 32302

Printed in the United States of America on acid-free paper.

First Bella Books Edition 2017

Editor: Medora MacDougall
Cover Designer: Judith Fellows

ISBN: 978-1-59493-537-4

Other Bella Books by Lise MacTague

Depths of Blue
Heights of Green
Vortex of Crimson

Acknowledgments

Thanks as ever to my alpha and beta readers: Lynn, Christina, Nikki, Eden, and Fern and Shari. You guys are awesome, and I couldn't do this without you. It's a little embarrassing how many continuity errors and typos you run across, but I'm glad you winkle them out for me.

Speaking of all the mistakes I've made, many thanks to my amazing editor: Medora MacDougall. I'm very proud of this story, and I know it's only been made better because of your suggestions. I'd also like to thank the entire crew at Bella for making my book the best it can be.

This book was the last one I wrote while sitting across the table from Mary Lou, my writing partner, which makes me very sad. I'm going to miss discussing werewolf mythos with you, and hearing about the eight billion writing projects you have going at the same time. Your work, in its breadth and diversity, is inspiring to me. When I'm a grown-up writer, I want to be just like you.

To my family: Lynn, Whit, and CeCe, thank you for being there for me, for putting up with the "what if" ramblings and for turning road trips into extended plotting sessions. Thanks especially to Whit for being my Truck Physics Consultant on this one.

Finally, to my readers: I don't think you know how much it makes my day when I hear from you about my work. Your feedback is one of the things that gets me up in the morning and cranking out more stories. Thank you all, and I hope you like this story as much as I enjoyed writing it.

About the Author

Lise is the author of the science fiction trilogy: *On Deception's Edge*. She grew up in Canada, but left Winnipeg for warmer climes. She flitted around the US, living in Ohio, New Jersey, and Wisconsin, before most recently settling in North Carolina with her wife, step kids, and three cats. Lise crams writing in around work, family, and building video game props in the garage. Find out more about what she's up to, and find some free short stories, at lisemactague.com.

Dedication

For Fern. Thanks for backstopping me all these years, and in more than hockey. I couldn't ask for a better friend, and I'm not saying that just to cement this book in your heart as your favorite.

CHAPTER ONE

She barely kept her feet, hunched over as she was, trying desperately to fill her lungs with air. The large pillar kept her hidden well enough for now, but it wouldn't be adequate concealment for long. The stitch in her side was nothing compared to the knot of fire higher up along her rib cage. The bastard was damn fast. If she'd been almost any other human, she would be lying dead on the floor, a crater bashed into her rib cage. As it was, her torso bled slowly from half a dozen shallow puncture wounds. Whatever he was, he was covered in spikes. That had been a surprise. She was lucky it hadn't been worse. There was none of the grinding that would have accompanied broken ribs.

Sucking in a slow deep breath, she tried to focus on her surroundings through her agony. Beyond herself, she listened as hard as she could for the slightest whisper out of place.

The darkness of the loft pressed in on her and seemed to swallow all sound. All she could hear was her strained inhalations. She struggled to get them under control. If she could hear herself breathing, chances were the thing hunting her could as well.

Where is he? He'd gotten the drop on her, moving faster than she'd believed possible. According to her intel, he was little more than a run-of-the-mill demon, though of a type they'd never seen before.

It hadn't stopped him from clawing out his own little corner of the shadow-world.

Why did it have to be a demon? She hated demons the most of the creatures she was set to take down. Demons came in so many horrible flavors, not like the rest of the supranormals. Werewolves and vampires started out human, at least. Demons were so different they might have been from an alien planet, not that her superiors would confirm or deny that. Human values meant nothing to them; they simply didn't operate on anything near the same set of morals. Fortunately, there weren't that many of them. Hunting vamps and furries took up most of her days. Confrontations with demons and the fae were fewer and further between.

She hadn't dealt with fairies and changelings enough to get a handle on them. They'd been brought up in training, but she could count the number of interactions she'd had with them on the fingers of one mutilated hand. Demons on the other hand… Her theory on demons, not shared by her employer, was that they came from another dimension. Such ideas bordered on the mystical and were not accepted by the United States government, but their theories had so many holes and required such mental gyrations that they weren't any more reasonable. She'd never met a demon she could stand to share a room with. Her current quarry was no exception.

A brush of air across her cheek was her only warning. She dropped to her knees, one hand on the floor, the other slicing through the air, the katana an unthinking extension of her body. His hand thudded into the pillar where her head had been less than half a breath before. Masonry exploded and small bits showered down on her head. The katana bit, blade sliding deep into his thigh. A hiss that turned into a wordless shriek was her satisfaction.

Determined not to lose her advantage, she surged to her feet, turning the sword in both hands and lining up for another strike. As fast as she was, the demon was faster. He blurred away from her and disappeared back into the darkness, leaving her fencing with shadows.

There was no time to consider her next move. He was on the run and she had to track him down before he made it out of the building. Now that he knew she'd been set upon him, he could easily disappear and she could not allow that to happen. He couldn't be allowed to prey upon the unwary any longer. Countless scores of young runaways had already been sacrificed to his appetite.

Stalking through the empty loft after him, she was glad she'd at least marked him. Droplets of bright blue blood glowed and smoked on the concrete floor, corroding it, leading her onward. She peered deep into the gloom. Even enhanced as it was, her night vision was barely enough to keep her from running into the debris that littered the ground. He had a decided advantage in the dark. She pulled a compact cylinder from her pocket, holding it in her right hand as she stalked the darkness.

The droplets stopped and she looked ahead into the shadows. There was no sign of him, but from behind her came the barest rustle of spine upon spine. She grinned tightly, clamped her eyes shut, faced the other direction and pressed the button on the cylinder in her right hand. Light splashed across her corneas despite her precautions. If her calculations were right, though, the flash would have blinded the demon.

Another scream met her efforts and she dropped the cylinder, bringing her right hand up to grasp the end of the handle of the katana. In one smooth motion, Malice turned and raised the sword, getting her first good look at the thing. The demon cowered in front of her, hands over too-wide eyes that oozed thick blue blood. A spiny crest jutted aggressively from the top of his head. He was covered everywhere in spikes of varying lengths, even on the backs of his fingers. Her blood still stained the protrusions on one hand. His movements were jerky and quick, almost impossible to track.

"Don't," he choked, voice thick with pain. "For the love of the Seven Realms, Malice, please don't."

Malice gazed down at him. How many of his victims had pleaded with him in just the same way? They hadn't deserved their fate, but he certainly did. She brought the sword down in a smooth arc, cleaving through his neck and both up-raised hands. They hit the floor in a series of small thuds as his body slumped over.

Already, the acrid stench of his death threatened to overwhelm her.

Another reason to hate demons, Malice thought. They can't even die cleanly.

Not for the first time, she wished supranormal corpses simply disintegrated into ash, the way vampire ones did on human television shows. This wasn't *Buffy the Vampire Slayer*, for better or worse. She had no sidekicks to rely upon, no snappy banter; it was just her and her prey. Reality, as was so often the case, was much messier than fantasy. His body should corrode away to nothing over the next twenty-four hours, if her previous experience was anything to go by. At least he'd had the sense to make his lair in an abandoned factory building. She could leave his corpse and be relatively certain nobody would blunder across it. It wouldn't do for some luckless human to stumble across the body. They weren't supposed to know about the nightmares that congregated in the underbelly of society. The government made very certain to keep knowledge of the beasts from their constituents. Their presence was an inconvenient truth, which was where Malice came in.

Impassively, Malice stared at the blackening corpse for another moment before turning. She pulled a cloth from her pocket and drew it along the blade of her katana. Demon blood was so corrosive it would pit the metal if left there more than a few minutes. Satisfied the blade was clean, she dropped the cloth. Already, holes were being eaten through the fabric. It would dissolve completely long before his now-inanimate corpse would.

Through the abandoned loft and down four flights of deserted stairs, Malice kept the katana ready in her hand. Demons sometimes ran in packs. She wasn't sure about this one. His spiky exterior and impossible speed were brand spanking new. He could have had a dozen brothers and sisters with him, or he could have been the last of his kind. If there were others, they wouldn't catch her unaware. Malice hadn't survived as long as she had without keeping her head on a swivel.

Nothing moved in the shadows and she emerged into a dark courtyard. Light poles dotted the perimeter, and broken glass glittered in the light of the moon below each one. Folded in a neat pile in one corner was a black trench coat. Malice picked it up and slipped it over her shoulders, sliding the katana back into its sheath on her back. She pulled up her hood to disguise the sword's handle. With easy strides, she left the courtyard, never looking back at empty windows that seemed to follow her every move.

The area was mostly industrial and deserted at that time of night. Malice walked swiftly down silent blocks, past shuttered factories and storage facilities. Her truck was a few blocks away from her target's nest. She'd been trained never to get too close in a vehicle, and years of experience had only reinforced that training. Most supranormals had excellent hearing. She smiled slightly as she contemplated the other reason. If she didn't survive the mission, her superiors didn't want anything to connect her to them. She would be simply one more dead Jane Doe in a city full of them.

There were many reasons why she and her remaining cohort were stationed in major cities. The beings they hunted were drawn to large urban centers, full of humans who wouldn't be missed, full of easy meat. In the wash of humanity, another dead body wouldn't be a big deal. Malice knew that when she died, her body would spend its last days in a drawer in the morgue before being interred with the other John and Jane Does beneath the tall trees of Homewood Memorial Gardens. Unclaimed bodies went there, and there was no chance her body would be claimed upon her death. Her family would never know what happened; she would simply disappear from their lives. It was only a matter of time. It had only been, what, five years since she completed her training? Of her original platoon, six were already gone and that was of the sixteen who had survived their training and... enhancements.

Malice grimaced slightly and twitched her mind away from the scant memories she still retained of that time. Even what little she remembered was more than she cared to. They said that memories of physical trauma were never as sharp as the actual pain, but that didn't seem to apply to what had been done to her. Her bones ached, cold and sharp, and Malice brought her sister's face to mind. Cassidy's smile chased away the last vestiges of remembered agony.

Her truck was where she'd left it. The black Mitsubishi pickup gleamed under a lone street lamp. She extended her senses, but nothing seemed out of place. She emptied her pockets, pulling out more light grenades, a couple of knives and a Taser, and placed them in the toolbox in the truck's bed. Her katana had its place in a specialized holder in the box's lid. Satisfied that everything was secure, Malice headed home.

It was a long drive home, over forty-five minutes. At least with as late as it was, Chicago traffic wouldn't be the headache it usually was. She flipped on the radio and relaxed as pounding drums and heavy guitar riffs seemed to absorb the adrenaline that still coursed through her veins. It would be a while before she would relax completely. This night's takedown had been closer than most. *Still, not as close as some.*

Malice pulled off the side street and onto the Tri-State. Prudently, she kept her speed down. Traffic blew by her on the left as she made sure not to be the fastest one out there. If she was pulled over for speeding, she would have a hard time explaining the contents of her toolbox.

The wind whistled through her window, stripping the last bits of acridness from the inside of her nose. She breathed deeply, tucking a stray lock of hair behind one ear. Regs demanded that an operative with long hair club it back into a tight bun, but she preferred the ponytail. At just above her shoulders, her hair didn't always cooperate with a bun and the pony was easier. It wasn't like she had some sergeant waiting at home to get on her back about it, only her handler, and he certainly didn't go out on missions.

Slowly, the Chicago skyline passed by on her left, lights twinkling merrily at her through the stillness of the evening. It was a gorgeous autumn night, but late enough that traffic on the Tri-State was almost non-existent and she made it home five minutes earlier than she'd anticipated.

Her neighborhood wasn't that different from the one she'd just left. It was mostly warehouses and as quiet at night. She pulled up in front of one of the older buildings, three stories of weathered brick and frosted glass windows. It took up half the city block. Bending over, she felt around for the small button hidden under her dash. It was little more than a depression in the molded plastic, but it clicked loudly when she pressed it down.

The large metal door a few yards away raised, metal creaking slightly in protest. As soon as the door was barely high enough to drive under, she roared in, pressing the button again. The tortured squeal of the door reversing in its track echoed throughout the cavernous first floor. It reminded her uncomfortably of the demon whose existence she'd terminated scarcely an hour before.

The entire area was open and mostly empty. Large pillars marched along the interior and did much to break up the emptiness. Malice could have parked anywhere, but she pulled up next to a small area enclosed with chain-link fence. She opened the door and vaulted from the truck's running board onto the edge of the bed. Bending her knees, she picked up the toolbox in both hands. It was heavy, but nothing she couldn't handle. Since no one was around, she made no effort to hide her strength. The weight would have been too much for most men, never mind most women, but she handled it with little more than a grunt.

She knew she was on the short side. Oh sure, statistics might say the average height of a woman in the US was 5'3", but she always felt short when around other humans, though by the numbers she was exactly average. Even her baby sister was taller at 5'6", and that rankled. The day Cassidy had discovered Mary Alice was no longer the taller one still burned in her memory. As a moody teenager, that had done nothing to improve her attitude. That had been the day before she'd joined the US Army.

At least her strength was a hell of an equalizer. Some people thought they could mess with her, normal humans who didn't know any better. Little did they know that even the fastest and most ripped man had little chance against her, all thanks to Uncle Sam.

With another grunt, she stepped up on the side of the bed and dropped to the ground, bending her knees again to absorb the extra weight. Malice gasped aloud at the pain in her ribs. She'd forgotten about her injury. Adrenaline and a boosted metabolism had driven it from her mind. She set the box on the ground and took a deep breath. It didn't feel like she'd damaged herself any further, but she needed to be more cautious.

Against the chain fence was another toolbox, identical in appearance to the one she'd just removed. This one actually carried tools, and not ones meant for dispatching supranormals. Carefully, she lugged it to the end of the truck and balanced it against the bumper as she pulled down the tailgate. Placing the box on the bed, she gave it a good shove. It slid the length of the bed before coming to a rest against the cab with a muffled thump.

Satisfied, Malice headed over to the freight elevator on the other side of the enclosure. Wooden gates stood open, and the elevator car waited for her. Weariness dragged at her. It was all physical, the adrenaline finally waning. She knew from experience that her mind would continue to churn for hours yet. It was good to be home where she didn't have to worry about anything else.

Inside the elevator, she pulled the wooden gates closed before pressing the button for the top floor. A reluctant rumble accompanied the car as it moved between the floors before coming to a stop on the third floor. She opened the doors and stepped into the echoing loft. Almost home, she thought. Her quarters were all the way across the large empty space. If anyone ever tracked her to her home, she wanted as much warning as possible. Her distance from the elevator gave her some peace of mind, but she really wanted to unwind. A hot bath sounded divine, and it was still too far away.

Privacy screens created the illusion of walls, turning the cavernous space into something cozy and comfortable. Malice dropped her trench coat on the floor by the door. It wasn't really a door, more like a gap between the screens, but she couldn't help but think of it as such. *I should really pick that up.* She hesitated for a moment. *Nah.* There was no one to nag her. That was a good thing. *Why does that always sound like I'm trying to convince myself?*

A blinking light in the kitchen caught her eye. Her personal cell phone lay on the island, flashing mindlessly, the light gleaming off the stainless steel countertop. She had a message. Malice fished out her other phone, tossing the burner down onto the counter without much thought. Unlike her own phone, this one was built like a brick and could take a beating after being submerged in water for three days. Operational security dictated she leave her own phone at home on a run, but the burner was indispensable if she needed backup. She rarely did, but the few times she'd gotten in over her head, she'd been glad for it.

She had seven messages, as it turned out. Malice eyed the screen before sighing. That didn't bode well. Only a handful of people had the number and a reason to leave her a voice mail. Even if they all called at once, there wouldn't be seven messages. Malice left a very light impression on the human world. Tapping in her password, she brought up her voice mail and set it to speaker.

"Hi, Mary Alice." Her sister's voice filtered tinnily through the speaker. Malice smiled and pulled her shirt over her head, ignoring the twinge that went through her ribs. "Don't forget, we're on for lunch with Mom next Wednesday before she heads home. You can't get out of seeing her for much longer. I can't wait to introduce you guys to the new place I went with my classmates."

Cassidy's voice did more to relax her than even veterinary-grade sedatives could. These days her metabolism was too high for most drugs to have more than a fleeting effect upon her anyway. She smiled as her sister prattled on for another minute or so while she prodded her side with cautious fingertips. Satisfied that the worst she had to deal with were a few bruises and shallow cuts, Malice advanced to the next message.

"Mary Alice, it's Uncle Ralph. I miss you, kiddo. Call me." Despite the words, the voice was curt, almost impersonal, and Malice rolled her eyes. Her handler wanted to know how the night's activities had gone. He was always impatient. After five years of working together, he still thought he could rush her into debriefing. She needed to come down before she'd talk about it. He knew that, but it didn't stop him from trying to prod her into talking it out sooner than later. He would simply have to wait. Daylight would be more than soon enough to touch base.

"Hi, Mary." Her head snapped up at the voice that filtered through the phone's speaker. Her voice light and slightly breathless, the woman sounded nervous. "I had a great time the other night, and you said you'd call, but you haven't. I hope you don't mind me calling, but I got your number from your gallery."

Oh no, she didn't! Disbelieving, Malice slumped into one of the high chairs at the island. She stared at the phone. It had been a mistake to go on that second date with Ann; she'd known it when she agreed to it. The girl was nice and they'd had a lot of fun at her apartment. So much fun, in fact, that Ann's downstairs neighbor had pounded on the floor to get them to tone it down. But all it had been for her was an opportunity for some fabulous sex and to blow off some much-needed steam. Apparently, Ann hadn't taken the hint.

She picked up the phone and scanned through the other messages. They were all from that Ann chick. With a groan, Malice deleted them without bothering to listen further. She was going to need to change her phone number. That was no big thing—she did it periodically as a security precaution. But Ann had said she'd gotten her number from the gallery. Her hand tightened around the phone and it flexed slightly. She quickly relaxed her grip; it wouldn't do to crack another screen.

The morning was the earliest she'd be able to track down the gallery owner and find out what the hell had happened. If the answer wasn't satisfactory, she would have to take her sculptures elsewhere, somewhere that understood the value of discretion.

She glanced around the darkened kitchen, and then heaved a sigh of irritation. There was no point trying to unwind for bed. Her heart rate was back up and thudding in her chest. She was keyed up for more action, almost tingling with the need to hit something. If she wasn't going to be able to sleep tonight, then she might as well do something useful. It was time for a little workout. Maybe if she worked her body past the point of exhaustion, she'd be able to grab a couple hours of sleep before the sun came up.

CHAPTER TWO

"Ruri. Ruri…" The voice cooing in her ear sent shivers down her spine, and she grinned, face turned against the pillow. "Come on, baby. Wake up."

Determined to keep up the charade that she was still sleeping, Ruri kept her body limp. A tongue's warm tip brushed delicately against her earlobe, chasing shivers with delicious goose bumps. Ruri bit her lower lip to keep from gasping. A low chuckle told her she'd failed to sell the illusion of sleep. The tongue was replaced by teeth that grasped hold of her ear and tugged gently.

Unable to contain herself, Ruri let out a low groan and was rewarded by a warm hand sliding over her rump, cupping and kneading it. Agile fingers slipped between her legs and dipped between lips already soaked by arousal. She couldn't help but raise her ass to allow better access to her aching pussy.

"I know you're awake." A warm body draped itself across her back. Ruri cried out when fingers penetrated deep inside her in a single thrust. Teeth closed over the back of her neck. Pain and pleasure intermingled, and she couldn't stop the growl that rose in her chest. She pushed herself up on her elbows and rocked back to meet each thrust, intensity increasing until they strained at each other, battling for orgasm.

She wasn't going to come this way. Ruri knew it. The pressure to orgasm built until she couldn't take it anymore. Sweat covered her body in a thin sheen and her gums ached from holding herself back, keeping herself together.

"Stop," she grunted. Immediately, the fingers stroking her pussy were removed. Ruri looked over her shoulder in time to catch her lover licking the juices from her fingertips. She caught Ruri looking and winked, before exaggerating the motion of her tongue.

"Britt…" Ruri whirled around on her knees and tackled her lover to the bed. Brittney's long, white-blond hair splayed out on the rumpled navy blue sheets. She stared at Ruri with mischief in her pale blue eyes. Normally, Ruri would have paused to admire the beautiful color of her eyes, but she had other things on her mind.

She straddled Britt's hips, grinding their mounds together, and the mischief was chased off her lover's face by raw desire. Her eyes practically smoked from the passion of her arousal, and she undulated her hips against Ruri.

"That's it, Britt." Ruri leaned forward and took Brittney's breasts in each hand, plucking at the nipples and smiling as they pebbled even harder in response. She looked down into Britt's face and noticed with satisfaction that her eyes had shifted. They were electric blue, a color never seen in humans. Britt was getting close.

Ruri's whole body jerked when her lover closed both hands over her hips and dug in. Nails, hard and pointed from their transformation, dug into her skin, sending prickles of pleasure-pain rushing up her spine and pooling in her groin. The ache in her gums gave over to a sweet pain and teeth, pointed and sharp, burst free.

She leaned forward and placed her hands on either side of Brittney's shoulders and thrust her pelvis against the soaked mound of her lover. Brittney growled at the increased friction, and Ruri dug her own hardened nails into the comforter beneath them in response.

Below her, Brittney's teeth erupted and her head thrashed from side to side. Her breathing picked up pace until she was almost panting. Abruptly, Brittney stiffened and arched her back, howling as her release tore through her. Twin pops and the tear of fabric accompanied Ruri's orgasm as she absorbed the energy Britt released when she came. Her back arched and she stiffened too, throwing her head back and howling in triumph at the ceiling. A thousand points sparked to life along her skin, then twinkled out slowly. She sagged forward, cradling Britt to her chest.

Entwined, they lay on the bed, breathing slowly, returning to something that resembled normal.

"Not again," Brittney said. "That's the third comforter this month." She lifted a hand and waved it indolently through the air. Feathers floated down upon them.

"You have that effect on me," Ruri said. She blew out a puff of air and laughed as downy white feathers swirled about.

"Don't I know it." Brittney pulled slowly out of Ruri's arms and sat up. She stretched, running long fingers no longer tipped with claws through her thick mane of hair before letting her arms drop.

"So was that all you needed?" One nipple seemed particularly fetching, and Ruri reached out her hand, running her hand over the perfect globe of Brittney's breast before giving her intended target a slow squeeze.

Brittney bit her lip and inhaled, closing her eyes. When she reopened them, the orbs that had only just reverted to their usual ice-blue already held a rim of brilliance around the center. She gently removed Ruri's fingers and slid out of her reach. "Actually, it's not why I came to wake you up at all." She swung her legs over the edge of the bed and stood up. "Dean's looking for you."

Alarmed, Ruri sat straight up, whipping the still-drifting feathers into a small blizzard around her. "The Alpha wants to see me and you thought we should go at it for a while before you told me that?" She regretted her sharp tone as soon as Brittney turned her back.

"He said it wasn't a big hurry, only that he wants to talk to you before the meeting."

Ruri repressed a groan. Britt was pouting and she was right to be annoyed. She should have known Britt wouldn't jerk her around if it was important. They'd been sleeping together exclusively for almost six months and Brittney had never given her any reason to doubt her. She wasn't prepared to initiate mate-bonding with the other woman, not yet, but she harbored hopes they would soon get there. They had fun together and their chemistry was explosive, if destructive—as the eviscerated duvet showed.

"I'm sorry, Britt." Ruri softened her voice. "I shouldn't have snapped. You did the right thing."

"You're damn right I did." Brittney unbent enough to turn around and regard Ruri through a curtain of hair. Satisfied that Ruri was sufficiently remorseful, she smiled. "I guess you do deserve the cup of coffee I made for you."

"You made coffee?" Greedily, Ruri sniffed the air. Now that she wasn't distracted by thoughts of sex, she could smell the delicious aroma of freshly brewed espresso. They didn't drink regular coffee.

It wasn't strong enough for the caffeine to have much effect, so most wolven couldn't be bothered. A quadruple-shot of espresso would perk her up, however. "You're a lifesaver."

"I know." Brittney walked across the room, with a roll to her hips that made Ruri's mouth go dry just watching it. She picked up the cup and handed it to Ruri who slurped down an ecstatic mouthful.

"Mmm." She closed her eyes as the caffeine hit her system. "It tastes different than usual. Did you add one of your flavors to it?"

"Yep," Brittney said brightly. "Caramel macchiato. What do you think?"

"It's great." Determined not to piss off her lover for the second time that morning, Ruri forced herself to take another gulp. The flavor was too sweet for her taste, heavy and cloying, but she wasn't going to screw up again by seeming ungrateful.

"I'm glad you like it." Brittney reached down and collected her clothes from their neat heap beside the bed. "I'll leave you to it. I promised Raquel I'd look in on her this morning."

"Have fun." Brittney pulled on her clothes as she walked out the door, and Ruri craned her neck to catch one last glance of exposed flesh before it was gone. She needed to get ready herself. Dean might have indicated that their meeting wasn't particularly urgent, but it never paid to keep the Alpha waiting.

She cast another glance at the open door. Knowing that people passing by could see her lounging naked on the bed didn't bother her. Her people were comfortable with nudity, and many of them spent their days half to fully naked.

This was not going to be one of those days for her. With a shudder, she put down the overly sweet cup of espresso. From the dresser, she pulled a pair of cargo pants and a tank top. Underwear was a strange conceit of humans, one she never bothered with. Ruri pulled back her chin-length hair into a short ponytail and slipped on a pair of sandals.

The Alpha's quarters were on the first floor near the front of the building. The pack had been living in the old hotel for a few years now. It was perfect for their purposes; everyone was close to each other, but there were opportunities for privacy. Ruri smiled as she walked through the hallway toward the stairwell. When they'd first moved in, the place had been a pit, everything stained and dirty. And the smell! Even for a human, the smell would have been overpowering. For them, the stench had been almost unbearable.

Now, the paint was pristine and the old carpets had been ripped up, exposing the original hardwood floors. Those had been stripped and refinished until they gleamed. The pack had restored the place to its original turn-of-the-last-century glory.

It was the kind of project Ruri thrived upon. She loved fixing things. She was a mean carpenter, electrician, plumber, a jack-of-all-trades really. When she was happiest, it was because she'd stepped back from a successful project and was basking in the glow of a job well done. When she thought about it that had a lot to do with how well she got along with Britt. The woman had come to them barely six months before. She'd been turned against her will and was struggling with controlling the change. Ruri had taken her in and helped her along, and now she was a stable, contributing member of the pack.

At the stairwell, Ruri took a quick peek over the railing before vaulting over and dropping down to the landing below. She landed quietly, knees bending slightly to take her weight. She repeated the maneuver two more times, then jogged from the stairwell into the building's lobby. The restored chandelier glinted and Ruri gave it a satisfied glance. That project had also turned out well.

The Alpha's door sat behind a long front desk, which had originally been used for check-ins. Now it was a guard post of sorts. A tall man slumped in a desk chair, his feet up on the counter. He was so tall that even in the chair he gave the impression of towering over everybody in the room. Couches and easy chairs were grouped in various configurations throughout the lobby. Unlike the building, the furniture looked tatty and beaten up. Werewolves were hard on the furniture. Even now, two young men and a girl roughhoused together on one couch.

"Dean's waiting for me, Lewis."

The tall man yawned, exposing his teeth to her in an unsubtle attempt at asserting his dominance. Mentally, Ruri rolled her eyes. Poor Lewis simply couldn't understand how a female could be the pack Beta. Clearly, he thought himself better qualified for the task. Constant posturing came with the territory. There were some days where it got the better of her, but she was in too good a mood today to care.

"Can it, big man." She vaulted the counter and kicked at the back legs of the chair. Lewis and the chair toppled over in a clatter and a shout. Derisive hollers greeted his spill but were quickly quelled when he bounced back up and bared his teeth at the disrespectful younglings. The growl was impressive, Ruri had to give him that. She grinned broadly.

"Don't even try it," she said when he turned toward her. She looked him in the eye and stepped toward him until they stood chest-to-chest and breathed the same air. He couldn't hurt her. She was faster and nastier and they both knew it. Lewis kept his eyes locked to hers as long as he could before he looked away, sweat beading his brow. An uncomfortable whine trickled from his throat. Happy that she'd gotten her way, Ruri backed down and stepped out of his personal space envelope.

"He's in there." Lewis's voice was soft, his eyes still averted. He righted the chair and sat back down, his spine ramrod straight.

Ruri pushed open the door. The comfortable living room was empty, so she wandered through to the near bedroom. In there, a short man, broad through the shoulders with defined muscles flexing across his back and rump, paced back and forth. His skin was dark, except where lighter lines ran through it. Short dreadlocks covered his head and swayed with every movement. He'd had them for as long as she'd known him, almost seventy years now. Even when they hadn't been fashionable, Dean had held onto the locks.

"Ruri." He didn't turn to greet her, instead pulling up his pants over a well-muscled backside. He reached over and grabbed a cookie from the plate on the bedside table. A quiet moan of pleasure reached her ears.

"Britt?"

He laughed lightly. "She's a witch in the kitchen. Between the coffee and the cookies, I think I've died and gone to heaven."

Ruri shared his laugh. "She spoils us, Alpha."

"That she does." Dean turned around, and she got a good look at the scars that crisscrossed his chest and abdomen. She carried her own scars and pulled her hand down from where she unconsciously fingered the notch in her right ear. Her scars were nothing compared to his; the Alpha carried many burdens for his or her pack. Being Alpha had its advantages, to be sure, but in Ruri's mind they weren't worth the constant struggle, both within the pack and without. She was satisfied with her position as Beta and had never striven to reach any higher.

"So what's the deal?" She relaxed against the doorway, crossing her arms over her chest.

"We have another loner petition. MacTavish is passing through again."

"Already?" Ruri frowned. She'd never liked the lone wolf; he'd spent too much time in town the last time he'd passed through. "Wasn't he here just a few months ago?"

"A little more than that. Seven or eight, I think it was." He raised both hands in a mollifying gesture when her brows drew even closer together. Ruri was rapidly losing her post-orgasm relaxation. "He's heading back through the other way, I've been told."

Ruri huffed in irritation. She seriously wanted to bite something. "I don't trust him. I say you close your jaws around his neck and shake. I mean, right off the bat. Show him you mean business."

Dean tutted at her. "That's not who we are. We're more than just monsters in this pack." He crossed the room and placed his hands on her shoulders. His closeness radiated reassurance and Ruri leaned into his calming energy. "We'll treat him like any other lone wolf who's never offered us any problems." He grinned suddenly. "Besides, do you really think he wants to go up against this?"

Against her better judgment, Ruri acquiesced. Dean was a fine specimen for a human and was even more impressive in wolf form. He might be short, but he was built, which meant he was a huge wolf. When they changed, they kept their mass. A 180-pound wolf was a sight to behold. Not only was he big, but he was also clever and quick. Ruri was the only one faster than he was, but he had no problems outsmarting her. It wasn't that she considered herself to be stupid; by her own estimation, she was plenty crafty. However, Dean was usually five steps ahead—or more.

"Fine," she said. She leaned into him and inhaled, pulling his scent into her and allowing it to calm the last of her nerves. "But if he even looks at you sideways, I'm going to rip out his throat with my teeth."

"Of course you will," he said, cupping the side of her face and holding her to his neck. The move wasn't sexual or threatening. It grounded her and drove home how much he trusted her. It would have been the work of a bare second to tear out his throat from this close if she'd wanted to.

Finally, she pulled back. "When will he be here?"

"In a couple hours. Do what you feel is necessary to prepare."

"Yes, Alpha." She looked up at him for a moment, and then carefully averted her eyes. His dominance demanded that she submit. His personality was almost palpable, but she was dominant enough herself that her display of submission was subtle. The same instinct that had howled at her when Lewis had been insubordinate to her demanded it.

"Cookie?" He held up the plate to her, the corner of his eyes creased in good-natured amusement. He knew how much it cost her to submit, even so little. While she had no designs on the position of Alpha, she probably could have been one in a smaller pack. More likely, though, if she hadn't found Dean all those many years ago, she would be a lone wolf today. Either that or dead.

"No, thanks. Britt will have my head if I scarf half the cookies she made special for you."

"Suit yourself." He tilted the plate toward his mouth and snapped a sliding cookie out of the air.

Ruri shook her head as she headed out the door to find Dean's honor guard. As Beta, she was in charge of his security, though she shared the duties of bodyguard with a dozen different packmates. She would need the strongest ones. There was no point in giving MacTavish a reason to think there was any weakness he could exploit.

CHAPTER THREE

The man kneeling before them was rank with stale sweat and something darker. Ruri's lip peeled back from her teeth and she snarled silently at him. To either side of her she was flanked by wolven, four on one hand and three on the other. Of them all, she was the only one not in fur-form. Instead, she wore loose black pants and her black tank. Her main concession to the meeting had been to show up armed to the teeth. The weight of the machete at her hip was scant comfort. A human would have been surprised to find out there was no silver in the weapon. Of course, a human would have been surprised to discover her existence.

Silver's effect on wolven was an old wives' tale, but one Ruri was just as happy was out there. Silver made shitty weapons. Anything that would handicap humans from hunting them down was fine by her.

There was no magic bullet to killing wolven. The only trick was to do as much damage to them as possible in a short time, before they could heal from it. Their high metabolism gave them healing properties that were off the charts. As a result, clashes between wolven typically involved bloodshed, but rarely death.

Dean stood in front of them and stared down at the disheveled loner.

"Alpha," MacTavish said. His voice was rough, like he didn't use it very often. "I...beg leave to pass through your territory." The form of his request was ancient and bordered on ritual. Still, it was clear in the tension along every line of his body that he despised asking permission for anything, let alone begging for it.

Ruri eyed him closely and stiffened when he raised his head enough to peer at the people gathered along the edges of the ballroom. Most of the pack had turned out for the audience. That in itself was unusual. Typically, only a handful would be present; they weren't the most exciting events to watch. She supposed they'd heard about MacTavish passing through barely more than seven months before and wanted a look at the wolven outsider who was becoming a fixture.

When the loner dropped his gaze again, Ruri relaxed a bit.

"You know the drill, MacTavish." The Alpha's voice was low and commanding. As happened every time she heard him speak in that tone, goose bumps rolled along her skin. She fought the urge to expose her own neck. Beside her, the wolves shifted, and those watching from the ballroom's dance floor cast their eyes down almost as one. A flash of almost-white hair in the throng caught her attention. Brittney was out there, watching. Alone of those around her, she looked directly at the group on the low stage. Her eyes were hungry, almost feral. When she caught Ruri watching, she shook herself slightly and gave her lover a wink and a smoldering look. Even across the huge room, Ruri felt herself warm at the promise in Britt's eyes.

"I do." MacTavish clambered slowly to his feet. Standing, he was huge, much bigger than Dean. His unkempt hair and dirty skin detracted from the imposing figure he might otherwise have been. He peered up at the stage. Yellow eyes slid from Dean to Ruri before coming to rest on the wolven next to her. It was obvious to Ruri that he spent a lot of time in wolf form. Usually, wolven only betrayed fur-form characteristics while clad in skin if they were very old. Eventually, the accumulation of time as a wolf caused some characteristics to bleed over. Idly, she wondered if his ears were pointed. It was impossible to tell with the matted mop of long hair he sported.

The wolf MacTavish had locked eyes with whirled on its hind legs and buried wickedly sharp teeth into the haunch of the wolf to its left. Before the hapless wolven could do more than whine in surprise, the aggressor whipped its head to one side and the wolf went down in a screaming heap, hamstrung.

Dean whirled and advanced upon the aggressor at the same time as Ruri. As she moved forward, she tugged her tank top over her head.

Unbuttoning her pants, she paused in her tracks opening herself to her wolf. Stupidly, she stood there. Instead of the rush of adrenaline and fur she expected, Ruri felt nothing. Her wolf coiled at the base of her spine, asleep and refusing to wake.

On the stage, the wolves had erupted in a seething mass of violence. Fur flew and teeth snapped. Growls and snarls filled the air. Aghast, Ruri watched as the discipline of her hand-chosen cadre of bodyguards dissolved into chaos.

Dean ripped open his shirt and stood before them, hands curled, but no claws burst from his fingertips. Like her, he seemed to be having problems calling forth his wolf. He raised his head and howled his rage at the ceiling. The sounds that came from his throat were much less than wolf; they were wholly human. Against the backdrop of vocal violence on the stage, he sounded puny and insignificant.

MacTavish stepped up onto the stage like he was taking a stroll in the park.

"I do know the drill, *Alpha*." He sneered at Dean, the teeth in his mouth pointed and dangerous. "If I want something, I take it." He snapped his teeth together, the sound shocking Ruri from her stunned reverie.

Dean pulled away from the lone wolf, pulling back his arm to punch him, but his reflexes were slow and MacTavish caught his fist before it made contact. Slowly, he squeezed, but the Alpha refused to give in. Bones cracked audibly and Dean's nostrils flared. He gave no further sign on pain.

Wake up! Ruri screamed inside herself. She was rewarded by her wolf shifting as if in the midst of a dream. Ruri launched herself at MacTavish, drawing the machete from its sheath and aiming for his spine. She wasn't at mere human level, but she wasn't at full strength either; her reflexes were dulled. MacTavish leaned forward, the machete just missing him. He let go of Dean's hand, and then backhanded her across the face hard enough that her ears rang and stars spangled in her vision. She staggered to one side; the machete slipped from nerveless fingers. Deep inside, she could feel her wolf stirring. Fur rippled softly through her mind, but not enough to shift. *What the hell is wrong with me? With us?*

Around them in the ballroom, the watching crowd was silent in marked contrast to the ruckus that was only beginning to subside on stage. Fights for the position of Alpha were between the Alpha, the challenger and their seconds. MacTavish had no second and hadn't observed the proper forms for a challenge, but that hadn't stopped him.

Taking advantage of MacTavish's distraction over Ruri, Dean lunged forward and fastened both hands around the upstart's neck, squeezing for all he was worth. The muscles of his forearms stuck out in stark relief, his hands dark against the sallow flush of MacTavish's skin. MacTavish reared back, his face flushing as he struggled for breath. Try as he might, Dean couldn't hold on with his damaged left hand and MacTavish staggered free. The Alpha followed up with a hard right to the sternum and a kick to MacTavish's knee. A harsh crack echoed through the now silent ballroom and MacTavish went down.

Exhausted by his exertions, Dean stepped back. From his knees, MacTavish chuckled. Ruri couldn't believe he would be laughing at a time like this. He was getting his ass handed to him by a wolven who couldn't shift. If that didn't prove he wasn't worthy of the mantle of Alpha, then nothing would.

On the dais, behind Dean, three wolves prowled forward around the forms of their fallen enemies. Their jaws were streaked with blood and one of them moved forward with a pronounced limp. Another was missing the better part of one ear.

Dean kicked MacTavish under the chin, snapping his head back. The loner put a hand back to keep from falling over, but only laughed louder. The sound echoed through the large room. Many of the spectators looked uncomfortable. They had no idea how to act. Nothing about this situation was normal. It followed none of the rituals or dictates they lived by. Some of the watchers looked expectant, almost eager. A few moved forward and Ruri whipped her head back to the action on stage just in time to see one of the wolves launch itself through the air.

Two huge paws hit Dean between the shoulder blades, opening gaping rents in the skin on his back. He tumbled forward onto MacTavish.

Wake up, wake up! Wake! Up! Ruri screamed at her slumbering wolf. Her frantic fear and accompanying adrenaline spike finally got through to her wolf. All fur and teeth, her wolf rolled through her.

The pain was excruciating, as it always was. She could hear her bones break and reform and a terrible burn as fur erupted from her skin. She dropped to her hands and knees and struggled to keep her head raised, to watch the scene unfolding in front of her. Powerless to do anything but watch as her wolf completed its transformation, she stared with unblinking eyes.

With Dean on top of him, MacTavish turned his head and bit a large chunk of flesh out of the Alpha's shoulder. Dean had managed to keep silent so far, refusing to show weakness even as his hand had been crushed and his back flayed open. The bite was too much, even for him, and he screamed his anguish.

Ruri's jaw ached from the inability of returning his howl. Teeth shifted and poked through her gums. A salty wave of blood and fluid filled her mouth and she opened it, allowing the bloody mess to spew forth onto the floor. Liquid and more blood spattered the ground around her, artifacts of the speed of her change. She was almost there, just a little longer and she'd be able to help her Alpha…

In the middle of the stage, MacTavish pushed himself to his feet. He held Dean close, one arm around his neck, squeezing until the Alpha stopped struggling and went limp. With a terrible cry of triumph, MacTavish lifted Dean's still form over his head. He turned to face the silent audience. Maybe a quarter of the pack had moved closer to the stage and stood watching, faces rapt and eyes hungry. Ruri had to swallow a whimper when she saw a familiar shock of white-blond hair among them.

The whimper was ripped from her throat when the loner dropped the Alpha's body down upon his raised knee. A snap like a dead tree limb breaking echoed through the room. Even the group of pack members who clustered in front of the stage seemed taken aback by the brutality of the act.

Dean still wasn't dead. His fingers twitched and he drew a pained breath as he lay in a tortured heap on the floor. It was harder than that to kill a wolven, and MacTavish knew it. He stepped back and gestured at the fallen Alpha.

"Eat your fill, my brothers."

The three surviving wolves from Dean's protection detail slunk around him. There was a bare pause before they threw themselves at his prone form.

"The rest of you will submit!" MacTavish turned to face the room of quiet onlookers. His supporters turned to watch the gathered pack. First one, then another of Ruri's packmates went to their knees. Half the pack had submitted before MacTavish's wolves moved toward them. Raquel, one of Brittney's close friends in the pack, was still on her feet when Brittney stepped up next to her.

"You will kneel," Brittney said.

Raquel shook her head, chin raised proudly. Tradition allowed those who chose the time to leave; Raquel was clearly asserting her rights. Ruri was surprised so many of Dean's pack had chosen to stay, given the way MacTavish had beaten their Alpha. Her heart swelled with gladness that Raquel wasn't among them.

Brittney slapped Raquel across the face. Blood sprayed from the four deep scratches her claws ripped into her friend.

"Brittney!" Raquel held a hand to her face and stared at Brittney in disbelief. "We're friends!"

"Kneel or die," Brittney said, unmoved by her friend's pleas. She grabbed hold of a hank of Raquel's hair and yanked her head back.

Something happened to Britt, Ruri thought. That can't be her. She looked like her lover, but the warm fun-loving wolven was gone as if she'd never existed. Maybe the whole thing was a horrible dream. None of it felt real.

Another MacTavish supporter stepped up next to Raquel. With casual brutality, he closed his teeth over Raquel's exposed throat and tore it out. Pandemonium erupted in the ballroom. Wolven whirled and made for the exits, while others cowered on their knees, bent in half at the waist, faces pressed almost to the floor.

Ruri howled, her anger and frustration finally given voice. She needed to help. She had to do something. Her wolf demanded it as did she. Not far from the stage, one of MacTavish's wolves backed a pair of mated wolven into a corner. Mouse and Skippy were no threat to MacTavish. They were the gentlest pair Ruri knew, often stepping in to watch the pack's few cubs. Skippy stepped between their stalker and his mate. Mouse's frightened eyes met Ruri's eyes around Skippy's shoulder.

"Ruri!" she cried. "Help us!"

Ruri snarled and lunged forward, grabbing the back leg of the nearest wolf and twisting. Her wickedly sharp teeth shredded the skin around his hock. He yipped and whirled around, snapping back with teeth as sharp as hers. She'd been expecting the move and dodged out of the way. Ruri struck and fastened her teeth around his throat. A quick shake of her head and his neck was laid open. Blood fountained and she skipped back.

"Kill her," MacTavish roared, pointing at her. The two wolves turned away from Dean's bleeding form and advanced on her. There was so much blood. Even with a wolven's rapid healing and heightened metabolism, she was certain Dean couldn't survive the damage that had been done, but she had to give him as much of a chance as she could. Satisfied she had their attention, Ruri whirled on hind legs and hopped down from the stage. By the time she'd gone three steps, she was at a full sprint. The two wolves were right on her tail. Both were males—Francisco and Jamieson—from the smell. Both were solid, if new, members of the pack, or so she'd thought. Their betrayal hurt as badly as anything else she'd seen that afternoon.

She needed to get as many of MacTavish's wolves to follow her as she could. The others would have the chance to escape while she was being taken care of. The wolven chasing her were big and strong, but she was faster and had no doubt that she could outrun them. As she wove her way through the fracas on the dance floor, she nipped and bit at those who were attacking Dean's supporters. They joined the chase.

Ruri launched herself shoulder-first at the ballroom's swinging doors. They gave way beneath her weight and swung back into the path of her pursuers. She glanced over her shoulder to see that the wolves had paused to avoid the doors in their way. She whuffed a little in satisfaction and turned down a long hallway. Her claws scrabbled on the hardwood floor, and she cursed that they'd removed all the carpeting in the place. She was able to catch herself before she went over and bunched her legs under her, heading toward the back of the building.

There was no way she would be able to open the door that led out of the building. To do so, she'd have to shift back to human form and she definitely didn't have the time for that. There was just one way out in her current form. It was going to hurt, but she had no choice.

Two of the wolves were close enough behind her that she could hear their breathing and occasionally feel the heat of their breath on the back of her legs as one or the other tried to get close enough to hamstring her. Others followed close behind, unable to get past the wolves and close the distance because of the narrow hall. Ruri dug deep and put on an extra burst of speed she didn't know she had in her.

The hall opened into a brightly lit recreation area littered with exercise equipment. She slowed to dodge around an elliptical machine before vaulting over a treadmill. The far wall was glass with floor-to-ceiling windows. Ruri leaped over a set of barbells and landed on top of a weight bench. Her nails dug into the leather of the bench and she pushed off, leading with her shoulder.

Glass shattered around her, coming down in a crackling rain as she burst through the large pane. Agony bloomed along her body, and she stumbled when she hit the ground, rolling forward in a hail of glass shards. Smaller pains shot through her body as glass sliced cruelly into her skin, but she couldn't let it slow her down. Riding the crest of adrenaline and pushing the pain down, she surged back to her feet without missing a beat.

The wooded lot behind the old hotel promised shelter and safety. She would lose Jamieson, Francisco and the others in there. Then she would figure out how to take the Alpha's death out of MacTavish's hide. Slowly. Very, very slowly. Before this was over, he would suffer.

Her tongue lolled from her mouth in a canine grin that went away as she disappeared under the trees. Wolven still chased after her, but not enough to take the pressure off her people. She'd just abandoned dozens of her pack members to a rabid dog and his followers.

CHAPTER FOUR

"How's the pasta?" Mary Alice looked up from her plate at her younger sister's amused question. "Wouldn't it be better with real meatballs?"

Chewing busily on a mouthful of quinoa, Mary Alice swallowed before answering. "It's great. You should try some."

Cassidy shuddered dramatically. "No thanks, I'll stick to real meat." She attacked the steak on her plate with renewed vigor. She preferred her meat rare. Mary Alice had to suppress her own shiver of disgust at the red liquid seeping out of the hunk of meat. Her sister still gave her a hard time for going vegetarian, though it was going on five years now. How could she tell Cassidy she'd had no choice?

If Cassidy knew that her work involved hunting down those who viewed humans as food, she might think differently about the meat on her plate, too. Confronting beings higher on the food chain than she had forced her to take a long, hard look at her own eating habits. For all the energy that went into farming meat animals, they could have fed half the people starving in Africa. Not to mention the inhumane practices of factory farming. When she thought about it closely, she was always vaguely ashamed about humanity's treatment of the animals that sustained them.

"Leave your sister alone," the table's third occupant said to Cassidy, gesturing with the meatball at the end of her fork. "You could stand to put a little thought into what you eat. You won't have that figure forever, you know."

"Mom!" The sisters stared aghast at their mother.

"I didn't go vegetarian because I'm worried about my figure!" Mary Alice said for what felt like the thousandth time.

"What are you saying about my figure?" Cassidy demanded on top of her.

"Girls, don't yell at your mother." Sophia Nolan popped the meatball in her mouth and eyed them both critically as she chewed and swallowed. "If you didn't stop eating meat because of your looks, then why did you bother? And you look lovely, Cassidy, dear. But you won't always if you keep tucking it away like that." Cassidy sat straight up in her chair and opened her mouth to reply. When Sophia showed no sign of letting her get a word in edgewise, she shut it again. "I'm only telling the truth. After all, look at me." She put a hand to her temple before gesturing down to include the rest of her body.

It was all a play for compliments and Mary Alice knew it. She was pretty sure Cassidy knew it as well. Their mother looked fantastic for being just south of fifty. Many people mistook her for being at least ten years younger than she was, and not only salesmen. There wasn't a hair out of place on her head and not a gray hair to be found either. Sophia didn't have a whole lot of discretionary income. Their father's pension kept her in the rent-controlled New York apartment where Mary Alice and Cassidy had grown up, though the neighborhood had improved by leaps and bounds. Her work as a translator and workplace language trainer barely kept the rest of her expenses covered, but somehow she managed to get her hair done. Heaven forbid she should look her age.

"You look great, Mom." Mary Alice could hear the eye-roll in her sister's voice, though there was no sign of it on her face. "Dad was a lucky guy. I'm sure you have to beat the guys off with a stick."

"God rest his soul," Sophia said as she always did when anyone mentioned their father. "I have no interest in any other man."

"Too bad." Cassidy was quiet enough that only Mary Alice sitting next to her could hear. She only smiled sweetly at their mother's raised eyebrow and snuck a look over at Mary Alice.

Wondering what her sister was up to but refusing to give her the satisfaction of asking, Mary Alice wound a long strand of pasta around her fork and popped it in her mouth. The flavor of tomato and herbs exploded against her tongue and she closed her eyes, savoring it closely.

Even though it had already been a week since she'd almost been taken out by her target, food still tasted really damn good. It was amazing what a brush with death could do to increase your appreciation of the simpler things in life.

"So did you break things off with that Ann chick who was stalking you?" Cassidy's eyes glittered as she leaned forward to get the latest piece of gossip from her sister.

Mary Alice sighed. It had been a mistake to tell Cassidy about the woman, but it was hard not to tell her things. The fact that she concealed major parts of her life from her only remaining family members was hard enough. There was no way she could share a hard day at work with them, so when there was something she could tell her family, she usually did.

"No, I just changed my number." She felt a little ashamed for her cowardice, but it was one confrontation she didn't have to get into.

Cassidy rolled her eyes. "I wondered if that was why you were sending me yet another number change." She pointed her fork at Mary Alice for emphasis. "You really need to tell her. She found you once. What's to say she won't do it again?"

"Oh come on, Cass!" Her sister had a point, though she wasn't going to admit it. "I don't like hurting people. And besides, we had a good time while it lasted, but it was never going to be long term."

That Ann had been able to track her down still bothered her. She'd gone down to the gallery that showed her work in a fit of righteous rage which had dissipated quickly when she found out it was an intern who'd been talked into giving out the number. The poor young man felt terrible about it, and his dismay had been obvious as he stuttered and fell over himself trying to explain what had happened to Mary Alice and the gallery owner. While Missy had been prepared to fire him over the error, Mary Alice had relented. Whatever sob story Ann had given the poor guy must have been very convincing.

"If you don't settle down soon, I'm never going to get grandchildren," their mother said.

"I don't think kids are in the cards for me anyway, Mom."

It was an old argument, one she barely had to devote any energy to. Children would be a huge mistake in her line of work. Then there was her complete lack of anything resembling maternal instinct. If Mary Alice had kids, it would definitely be to their detriment. Some people weren't meant to reproduce, and she was just glad she hadn't found that fact out the hard way. Of course, there was no telling if she even could have kids. With whatever the government scientists had done to augment her, she had no idea how messed up her genes were.

"They never will be if you don't stop bouncing from one woman to the next," Sophia said. "You'd been out with her a few times, right? I thought maybe you two had something going. How long had it been since the last one? Six months? A year? You're such a pretty girl." She reached over and cupped the edge of Mary Alice's jaw. "If you wore even a little bit of makeup, you'd have women crawling all over you. And then I'd have some grandchildren."

Mary Alice shot Cassidy a glare. She hadn't told their mother any details about Ann or anybody else she'd dated. The only way Sophia would know anything was because her sister had narked on her.

"I just think it's kind of shitty." The offhanded tone of Cassidy's voice contrasted sharply with her words, and Mary Alice bridled slightly.

"Hey, who's the big sister here?" She sat up straight and mock-glared at her younger sister. "I'm the one who's supposed to give you crap for your poor choices, not the other way around. So spill, what questionable decisions have you made lately?"

"What makes you think I've made any questionable decisions?" Cassidy carved another strip off her steak and glanced at Mary Alice from the corner of her eye.

"Wait just a minute!" Her sister was being a little too coy. "You have done something. That's why you're giving me crap about Ann."

"No." Cassidy looked back down at her plate. "Of course not."

A waiter appeared out of nowhere before Mary Alice could get to the bottom of her sister's evasions.

"More wine, ladies?" He held up the bottle of red from which they'd already each had a glass. Cassidy grabbed her glass and polished off the last little bit at the bottom. Their mother nodded gravely.

"Yes, please," she said.

Mary Alice didn't say anything, instead holding her hand over her glass when he moved to pour her another. She drank very little, preferring not to have her senses or reflexes dulled. The weekly meals she shared with her sister were the only exceptions to her rule. A number of the members of her old unit had drinking problems and she didn't want to follow them into the bottle.

The waiter left and Sophia looked over her raised wineglass at Cassidy. "Don't think he saved you on this one. What have you been up to? You're avoiding your sister's questions a little too well."

"It's not that bad really, Mom. I promise." Despite her reassuring words, Cassidy took a deep drink of wine before placing the glass on the table. "I changed my major."

"Cass, really?" Mary Alice slumped back in the booth. "You said you were going to graduate next spring."

"I know, I know. But I just wasn't feeling it."

"This is the third time you've changed your major. You can't keep doing this. The money we got from the settlement won't last forever."

Part of the settlement from their father's car accident had gone to pay for Cassidy's college. The money was already gone, but her family didn't know that. Mary Alice was paying for Cassidy's classes using her GI Bill money. Because of the nature of her assignment, Mary Alice was never going to use the money herself. Her superiors had seen fit to make an exception and allowed her to apply the funds to her sister's tuition, but even that wouldn't last forever. It was too bad Cassidy seemed determined never to graduate.

"I won't change it again, I promise. I think this is actually what I'm meant to be doing."

"What is? What's your major now?"

"Finance."

Dumbfounded, Mary Alice stared at her sister. She'd enrolled at Northwestern University to pursue a degree in French literature and then had abruptly switched to fashion design. Now she was going for a degree in finance?

"Don't just stare at me," Cassidy said, her voice huffy. "Say something." An edge of warning lay beneath her words and Mary Alice knew better than to push her too hard. She kept her mouth firmly shut instead.

"Is that what you want to do?" Sophia asked. Her voice was carefully neutral, not condemning Cassidy's decision but not approving it either.

"It is." Cassidy's face lit up with excitement. "It's really interesting, and there's a chance for me to make some real money."

"If it's just about the money, you don't need to worry," Mary Alice said. "Things aren't that bad." They weren't yet, and she could always put the squeeze on her superiors. They wanted to keep her happy, and they couldn't afford to lose her. There were only so many of her compatriots left. The supranormal problem couldn't be properly handled by ordinary humans, not if they wanted to keep the public in the dark. If the voters found out what their government was conspiring to keep from them, a lot of legislators would be out of a job.

"Mom, it's exciting. So far, I really like my classes. All my core course credits will transfer, so I'm only pushing back graduation by three semesters. If I take courses this summer, I can graduate in December next year."

"If you say so," Sophia said. "You know there are lots of jobs in finance back home. You could move back after graduation."

Cassidy shrugged. "There are a lot of jobs here, too. I'll have to see what my options are, but there are a hell, I mean heck, of a lot more jobs in finance than in French or fashion."

She seemed genuinely enthusiastic, and Mary Alice forced herself to relax. "If it'll make you happy, then I'm happy."

Seeing relief chase tension from around her sister's mouth was reward enough. "Thanks, Mary. I knew you'd come around."

"Yeah, well." She carved one of her meatless balls in half with her fork and popped it into her mouth. She chewed and swallowed to give herself some time.

"It won't be so terrible a thing if someone in the family ends up making decent money," Sophia said. "Your father, bless his soul, had no head for it."

"That's for sure." Cassidy laughed. "The man was a union electrician, but never had any money. How did he even manage that?"

He played the ponies is how he managed that. Ponies, dogs, cars—if it raced, Jimmy Nolan had put money on it. Mary Alice and her mother had done what they could to shield Cassidy from the worst of Jimmy's failings. It felt like she'd been helping take care of Cassidy since she was seven years old. Still, it wasn't the time to bring that up. It probably never would be. In the face of her sister's cheerfulness, Mary Alice had no choice but to shake her head and laugh.

"All right, all right. If you think this'll work out for you, then I'm happy. I mean it."

"Thanks, Mary." Cassidy's face went somber. "Do you think Dad would be happy for me too?"

"Your father would be thrilled, sweet pea." Sophia smiled at Cassidy. "He would be so proud of both of you." She turned the smile on Mary Alice also. "Though I'm sure he'd be wondering when those grandchildren will be showing up."

"Mom..." Mary Alice did roll her eyes this time.

"It's not like we always wanted our oldest daughter to grow up to be a starving artist. The least you could do is give me a granddaughter to keep my mind off it, you know."

An inelegant snort issued from Cassidy before she could stop it. Instead of looking embarrassed by the noise, her sister smiled widely. "She's far from starving, and you know it. We've seen her place. It's pretty nice. Besides, that she's making enough from sculpting to be comfortable is amazing."

"I've been lucky," Mary Alice said. *And I'm being bankrolled by the government.*

"Lucky, nothing. Your stuff is really good, even though..." Her sister trailed off, reluctant to give voice to her true feelings about her sister's artwork.

"It's not your thing, I know." It was true. Cassidy preferred art that didn't look like the nightmares of a twisted psycho. Occasionally, she caught her sister looking over at her after seeing her latest piece. The look in her eyes seemed to ask if she was really that much of a nutcase. It wouldn't have seemed so strange to her if Cassidy had seen what she'd seen. Getting all that ugliness into fixed physical form helped her deal with it. She'd started doing it as therapy, but when her handler had found out what she was doing, he'd decided it made a far better cover for her than the job at the local credit union.

Mary Alice had been relieved. The huge difference between her cover and her real job had been difficult to take. It was next to impossible to act as if nothing was going on when she knew supranormal beings lurked beneath the underbelly of human civilization. They were always there, just waiting to take care of the unwary, to snatch them up and make their last living moments into hell on earth.

Actually, not all of them were like that, she knew. Many supras coexisted just fine with humans, and the vast majority of humanity was none the wiser. Those she dealt with were predators, serial killers, the deranged and demented. Idly, she wondered what it would be like to talk to a supra who wouldn't try to take her head off as soon as it saw her.

Still, any of them who saw her would try to kill her before asking questions. She was Malice, exterminator of supras. It didn't matter that the ones she was set upon were the ones who'd gone rogue, who threatened to expose their existence to a world who wouldn't thank them for opening their eyes. She imagined werewolf mothers and vampire sires teaching their spawn about the big, bad human who would assassinate them if they stepped out of line.

"Mary?" Cassidy's soft voice pulled her out of the dark pool of her thoughts. She reached across the table and took Mary Alice's hand. "I was only messing with you a bit."

Mary Alice gave her sister a tight smile and squeezed her hand. Her cell phone buzzed spitefully on the table, causing them to jump slightly. It vibrated again and Mary Alice reached for it.

"You know what that means!" Sophia smiled in triumph.

"I know, I know. I'm getting dinner."

"You sure are," Cassidy chimed in.

"I would have anyway." She thought Cassidy was going to stick out her tongue and decided to beat her to the punch. The immature move pulled a delighted laugh from her sister, and she grinned as she turned the phone over. A toothy death's head stared up at her and she kept the smile plastered on her face. *Uncle Ralph. What does he want?*

Bringing the phone up to her ear, Mary Alice kept her voice light when she spoke. "Mary Alice Nolan, how can I help you?"

"Mary Alice, it's Uncle Ralph. How are you doing, kiddo?" As always, her handler's voice was at odds with his words. Anyone listening in would wonder if he genuinely cared for her. Who knew, maybe he did, but Mary Alice could never buy the act at face value, not when he put so little effort into it.

"I'm well, and you?" She injected extra enthusiasm into her voice. "The weather's been great, I've got a bunch of new works started." He would know from her words that she had company, but that it was friendly.

"That's great. I'd love to see what you've got going on. Let's get coffee soon. You can tell me all about it." There it was again, the summons. She forced herself to remain open and unconcerned, but she could already feel her shoulders tensing as she wondered what her newest assignment would be.

"I'd love that. I'll see what's open on my calendar." He wanted to see her sooner rather than later, but she'd let him know he would have to wait a couple hours before she could get away.

"Good. See you soon." Ralph hung up, but not before letting her know it couldn't wait. That was as clear as if he'd hollered it at her.

She thumbed off the phone, wondering at the tension in his voice at the end. Looking up, she smiled at her family.

"Let me guess, you need to go," Cassidy said.

"I do. That was the gallery. They have a prospective buyer who wants to meet the artist and maybe commission something from me." She stood up and pulled on her trench coat. Sophia mirrored her, and then enveloped her in a big hug. For such a small woman, there was a lot of power in the squeeze around her rib cage, which barely twinged. Last week's injury was almost completely healed, the bruises faded to the barest yellow shadows.

Their mother kissed her on the cheek. "You know I kid about the grandchildren."

"No, you don't."

Sophia chuckled. "You're right, I don't. But don't worry about it. It will happen when it's meant to. God willing I'm still around."

"Thanks, Mom. When you heading back to New York?"

"My flight leaves at an ungodly hour tomorrow." Sophia quaked dramatically. "It simply isn't to be believed, but I need to put in a half day at work, so there you have it."

Mary Alice took a deep breath and offered before she could chicken out. "Do you need a ride to O'Hare?"

"I wouldn't do that to you." Sophia smiled broadly as if she really knew how little Mary Alice had wanted to make the offer. "I'll take a cab. It'll be fine."

Cassidy waited her turn before wrapping both arms around their mother. "I love you, Mom. Have a good trip. I'm glad you could come out for a visit."

"So am I." Sophia returned the hug with interest. "I'm glad I could get out before your midterms."

"Me, too. I don't know if I'd have been able to get away." She disengaged and wrapped Mary Alice up in a quick squeeze.

She was taller than Mary Alice, a fact that still irked her every single time they hugged. Little sisters should be just that—little.

"I miss you, Mary Alice." Cassidy's words were muffled but heartfelt. "When I graduate you'll be proud of me."

Mary Alice hugged her back. "I'm already proud of you. Call me if you need to." She slipped Cassidy's phone out of the inside pocket of her jacket and into the front pocket of her coat. She stepped back and kept her face neutral.

"I will." Instinctively, Cassidy's hand went to her jacket. She patted the front of it before putting her hand in. She quickly went through her other pockets, then started to rifle through her purse.

"Lose something?" Mary Alice asked.

"You little…" Cassidy held out her hand. "Give it back."

"I don't know what you're talking about."

Cassidy stepped forward and jammed her hands into the pockets of the trench coat. She fished around until she located the phone, then pulled it out. She waggled it in front of Mary Alice's nose.

"Just making sure you know where it is." Mary Alice bit her lip to keep from laughing, but she couldn't contain herself when Cassidy shot her an irritated look. Her sister's scrunched-together eyebrows never failed to amuse her.

"Children, that's enough," Sophia said. "Honestly. I don't know how you two manage without someone to referee. Maybe I should look into moving to town."

"That's okay, Mom." The words came out as an unintentional chorus, and the sisters shared a glance and grinned. As much as Mary Alice loved seeing her mother, there was no way she wanted to be in the same city. Chicago wasn't big enough for the Nolan sisters *and* Sophia.

Their mother sniffed and preceded them out of the restaurant. Cassidy mimed wiping sweat off her forehead and Mary Alice nodded emphatically in response. For once they were in complete agreement.

CHAPTER FIVE

The hotel looked empty. Ruri raised her head and tested the air. Traces of her former packmates still lingered, but they were old, probably about a week or so. None of the scents held the crispness of recent activity. There was no sign of Britt's scent, for which Ruri was relieved. Even the smallest reminder of her lover's betrayal still sent deep slices of agony through her chest. And yet, she prayed that somehow Britt hadn't been herself, that it had been someone else. If the wolven had appeared in front of her, Ruri wasn't certain if she'd have gone for her throat or tried to nuzzle her.

Carefully, ready to turn tail and disappear back into the bushes at any sign of movement, Ruri slunk out from beneath the shrub. On silent paws, she ghosted up to the back window. It was still shattered. No one had bothered to replace it or even to board it over. The broken pane yawned black where the other windows reflected the starry night sky.

She gathered her hindquarters and leaped, landing raggedly on the weight bench that still sat under the window. Her claws slipped on broken glass littering the seat and she skittered off it to land on the floor with a high yelp of pain.

Immediately, she pressed herself to the ground, unmindful of the shards there. Scooting backward, she cowered under the bench and waited for long, tense minutes. No one came to investigate the noise and she slowly eased her way out from her impromptu shelter.

Damn shoulder. It was still giving her problems, even a week later. Ruri had broken it on her way out the very same window. Healing was taking longer than it should have and she could only surmise that her sundered pack ties were responsible. She clamped her muzzle down on the mournful whine that threatened to escape her throat. The pack gave all wolven within it strength and community. She wasn't sure which she missed more.

Never letting down her guard, Ruri slowly roamed the hallways and rooms of the first floor. Traces of her former packmates still lingered in the corners. She inhaled deeply when she ran across them, trying vainly to reconnect with them. Mouse and Skippy. Her tongue lolled from the side of her mouth in a brief lupine grin. Those two were inseparable. A mated pair far down the pack's pecking order, they'd defended each other stoutly in all things just as they had that night.

The swinging door to the hotel's huge kitchen hung by one hinge. She could almost hear Consuelo and Beth yelling to each other as they whipped up the pack's latest meal. They'd been a unlikely pairing. Consuelo was almost as dominant as she was, and yet she allowed Beth to boss her around whenever they cooked. Ruri hadn't seen them in the ballroom; they'd probably been putting the finishing touches on lunch. She hoped they'd escaped.

In another corner, she caught a faint whiff of Wyatt. His shaggy black hair had always made her fingers itch to get a comb. He'd been a more recent addition to the pack. A street kid, he'd been turned by some lone wolf and then left to fend for himself. That he'd found them had seemed a miracle. Dean hadn't trucked with turning the unwilling. As Alpha, he'd never believed his responsibilities demanded he grow the pack using artificial means. He wouldn't turn anyone away who wasn't a threat to his authority. Ruri agreed with the stance, but she couldn't help feeling it had killed him and countless fur-sisters and brothers.

Dean. This time the whine did escape. She was in front of the doors to the ballroom and she sat back on her haunches to stare at them. Death was the predominant scent that assaulted her nose. Ruri sneezed and whined again. She remained still and perked up her ears. Still nothing.

She had to force herself on. Her wolf didn't want to go into the room and resisted mightily. Ruri shook her head roughly. She had no desire to go in there either, but she needed to see things for herself.

The ballroom was dark. A couple of chairs lay on their sides, and a table by the door was splintered down the middle. It looked as if someone had been thrown down on the top with brutal force. Aside from that, there was depressingly little sign of resistance or struggle.

Ruri skirted the open dance floor, keeping to the nearby furniture. The worst of the decay lay ahead of her on the dais. She caught the occasional fetid whiff and knew there were other carcasses scattered throughout the room. Not all the wolves in her pack had been content to accept the brutal change in leadership. Favoring her shoulder and without much grace, she scrabbled onto the dais.

Dean's body, or what remained of it, still lay at the front of the stage. The body had been picked almost completely clean of flesh. Even through the decay that filled her muzzle, she could still smell him. All she wanted to do was throw her head back and howl. Brutally, she quashed the desire. There would be time enough to mourn later—when she was safe.

At the back of the stage, the more complete bodies of Dean's bodyguards lay in human form. As the wolven always did, they'd reverted back to their human forms at the moment of death. Three of the corpses bore signs of bite marks; one had been left alone. Ruri cocked her head at the relatively pristine body. Bloat and decay made it hard to recognize, but under the smell of death, she could just make out who it was. Wyatt. They'd left him alone. Had he been in league with MacTavish? Surely, if he had been MacTavish's plant, they would have buried him. That they hadn't boded ill for MacTavish's treatment of the remaining members of the pack. *Is Brittney safe? Does it matter?*

There was nothing more to do here. She glanced again at her Alpha's corpse. Sorrow engulfed her and she struggled to breathe, wheezing around the knot in her chest. Her human half didn't like leaving him there, but her wolf was unconcerned. Dean would decay and become part of the world around them, as was right and natural. As it was, she couldn't do anything about it, not in fur-form and not without knowing where MacTavish was. She jumped down from the stage, trying not to land on her injured front leg. Leaving more quickly than she'd entered, she kept her eyes and nose out for the other corpses in the room, adding to the mental tally she was keeping against MacTavish. When his bill came due, she would make sure she was the one to collect and in full.

The rest of the hotel was as empty as the first floor had been. The only remnants of her former packmates were occasional items lying abandoned in a hallway or one of the rooms. Some rooms hadn't been touched, and they matched up with her fallen brothers and sisters in the ballroom.

Her room still had all its belongings, but it was anything but untouched. As she neared it, her nose twitched and she sneezed violently. Urine and excrement mixed in a nauseating stench. She nosed open the partially open door and looked around. Even in the darkness of the room, she could see well. Her wolven eyes took in the damage. Nothing she'd owned was still intact. It was torn, broken or shattered.

Just like me…

Everywhere she looked, urine painted the wall and floors. Someone, or more likely a couple of someones, had decided to relieve themselves on her bed and in the drawers of the dresser piled haphazardly atop each other on the floor.

She took a couple of steps into the room and something slid out from under her foot. A closer look revealed it to be pages from a book. In an act of particular malice, they'd taken the time to rip the pages from every single book she owned. The bookshelves had been toppled and were surrounded by a veritable mountain of paper.

The message was clear. She didn't belong there anymore. Not that she'd planned to go back to living in her old rooms, but there were some items she'd been hoping to salvage, most specifically the only photo she had of her human family. Ruri could bring it up in her mind's eye: six people, all sitting stiffly in their Sunday best, their expressions solemn. Her family had been happy enough, not that you could tell from the picture. At the traveling photographer's instructions, they'd held themselves very still for the minutes it took to get a decent exposure. The family had their problems, but back then everyone did, especially those who'd chosen to claw out their living on the frontier. The battered tintype photograph was all she had left of them. They had all died decades, if not a century ago, or so she could only surmise.

Now the photo was gone. She'd lost both families that day. There was literally nothing left there for her.

With one final look around, Ruri turned and left.

The cool, gray day had naturally turned into a chilly drizzling evening. Mary Alice glanced around. She knew she probably looked strange, a woman by herself on a bench under a lamppost in the middle of deserted park. Dead leaves littered the pavement in front of her, pasted to the concrete by the rain. There wasn't enough wind to peel them free, and for that she was glad enough. The river glinted at her through the trees, reflecting lights from the other side. She had no indication of anyone else in the park; everything was quiet and still. Occasionally, she'd catch movement as a raccoon or other wildlife rustled by in the undergrowth, but that was it.

Another rustle drew her attention, and she turned her head to glance at a nearby set of bushes. A coyote stood between two shrubs almost devoid of leaves. It watched her cautiously, recognizing another predator. There were probably others nearby. Mary Alice wasn't too worried. Coyotes would have to be very hungry indeed to risk attacking her. It would take an extremely large and coordinated pack to be truly threatening.

"Communing with nature?" A man's voice issued from outside the ring of light.

"Something like that." Mary Alice kept her voice light through the ease of years of practice. Truth was, "Uncle Ralph" made her acutely uncomfortable.

He stepped forward into the light, watching her as he moved in to sit next to her. As usual, a slight smile lurked on his face. She didn't like feeling like he was laughing at her, but she also wasn't going to give him the satisfaction of knowing he'd gotten under her skin.

A man of middle years, he had a gut that strained at his shirt. The cheap suit screamed federal agent to anyone with even rudimentary skills of observation. He didn't carry a badge and no longer belonged to any branch of law enforcement, but a lifetime of habits had been impossible to break.

"Coffee?" Ralph handed her a paper cup that steamed in the cool night air. The ubiquitous mermaid logo decorated the side.

"Don't mind if I do." Mary Alice accepted the offering and took a sip. The only time she drank coffee was with him. Her heightened metabolism made short work of the caffeine and it had very little effect on her. She still loved the flavor though. If she was going to have to put up with his company, she might as well indulge herself.

"There's been no fallout from your last takedown. That spiky bastard's body wasn't discovered. The city demo'ed the building yesterday, so you're golden on that one."

The smile on Mary Alice's face felt stiff. "I told you it would be fine."

"You still should have disposed of the body."

"I saw no sign of other residents. You know humans don't like to be near supras. The homeless population cleared out long before I took care of the sick bastard."

Irritated, Ralph waved his cup of coffee in her direction. "I didn't call you out here to rehash your latest crap judgment."

No shit, but it still doesn't stop you from harping on it. "I figured. So what's up that you couldn't wait to see me? I had to cut short dinner with my mom and sister, you know."

"Sorry." He wasn't really. She knew it and he knew she knew. Her continued relationship with her family was another bone of contention between them. All her counterparts had either completely severed ties with their families or hadn't had any family to begin with. Of course, most of her counterparts were either psychotic or neck-deep in substance abuse. If it wasn't for Cassidy and Sophia, Mary Alice was fairly certain she would be right there with them.

"The North Side lycan pack has a new Alpha."

She blinked at him, startled. Of all the news he could have dropped in her lap, this was some of the most unanticipated. That pack of werewolves was as stable as they came. A few other packs called the Chicago metro area home, but none were as large or as well established. She'd broken up more than a few packs over the years, but the North Side pack wasn't one she'd ever expected to have to worry about.

"What happened to Dean, their old Alpha?"

"I doubt he survived the transfer of power." Ralph's mouth twisted and he took a long draw on his coffee. "The furries moved out of the hotel, but I don't know where the new den is. I need you to track them down and check on the new Alpha. Let me know if he'll need to be taken out."

"And if the whole pack is affected?" It was a very real possibility. A lycan pack's Alpha was more than a leader or figurehead. The Alpha was a source of power, but more than that, he or she was the soul of the pack. Dean was about as decent a supranormal as could be found, which was why Mary Alice had never worried about the North Siders. He was strong, too. He wouldn't have gone down easily. If whoever had taken over was strong enough to keep the position, they could influence the pack in some very dark directions. Most of the members wouldn't be strong enough to strike out on their own and would fall in with whatever schemes the new Alpha had planned.

"If you think the pack is too far gone, you'll have to take them all out or scatter them at the very least." Ralph took another sip of his coffee and paused, wiping a dribble out of his stubble. "If you don't think you can handle them, let me know and I'll call in reinforcements."

"Sounds good." It would be a cold day in hell before she would submit to his version of reinforcements. Either she would end up with some black ops commando group who didn't know their ass from their elbows when it came to dealing with supras or he would bring in one of her former squadmates. The clueless commandos would be the better of the two options. She would never hear the end of it if she had to suffer help from one of the others.

"Good. Contact me as soon as you have something to report."

"Will do." Mary Alice stood, leaving the coffee behind. The first few sips had been good, but the news had soured her outlook and the coffee. She turned to leave.

"Oh, and Malice?"

Mary Alice glanced at him over her shoulder, one eyebrow lifted in silent query.

"Try to be a little more careful with your new phone number. That was sloppy as hell."

She rolled her eyes and walked away. Why the little shit insisted on baiting her, she didn't know. If she ever really lost it, she could tear him limb from limb, and he knew it. He'd been present for their creation and training; almost all the handlers had. A few of them hadn't lasted long and those they'd handled had disappeared without trace or explanation. Her hands twitched as she fantasized about breaking his neck. It wasn't the first time she'd indulged in the daydream, and it surely wouldn't be the last.

Now was not the time to be distracted by the little man. She had a job to do. Her pace picked up as she ran through her options. There was only one place to start: the pack's old den, the hotel. If that didn't pan out, there were other possibilities, though she hesitated to exercise them.

CHAPTER SIX

"I want to see Carla." Malice stared up at the hulking bouncer protecting the door. The man's head disappeared into his shoulders without the benefit of a neck. She'd rarely seen anyone so big, but she could tell by the way he held himself that the appearance of fat was deceptive. He might be grossly overweight, but there was muscle under the flab.

Beside her, a line of hopefuls waited behind a velvet rope to get into Faint. The nightclub was the preeminent nightspot in the area. It inhabited the space on the border between two neighborhoods in much the same way it straddled the line between the regular world and the shadow world. Normal people got to feel the frisson of fear that came with venturing into areas normally forbidden to them. Patrons of a darker sort didn't have to worry about the kind of scrutiny that would have come with living in a better area. The neighbors kept to themselves and did their best not to bring the cops down on their heads.

"She isn't in." The bouncer didn't even look at her. An obscenely long stretch limo pulled up to the front of the nightclub, and he moved toward it.

"She's in for me." Malice grabbed his arm and held on with little effort. The bouncer looked down, surprised, and tried to extricate himself from her grasp.

"What the hell?" His eyes darkened as his pupils dilated. The black swallowed iris and cornea alike, leaving only a thin outline of white around the pits of his pupils.

She pulled him down and spoke directly into his ear. "Control yourself." Mary Alice emphasized her words with a hard squeeze. That much pressure would have broken a human's arm, snapping at least one if not both of the bones in the forearm. As it was, he grunted in surprise and looked at her, this time really seeing who stood in front of him.

So far, those standing in line had only seen them in quiet conversation. If the vampire pushed it, she wasn't sure how far she would go, but she was willing to bet he wouldn't risk exposing the truth to such a large crowd.

"Malice." Her name was a hiss over his teeth. She could barely make out the tips of his canines where they'd extended through their sheaths. Interestingly, his pupils returned to their regular size. His extended teeth suggested he was interested in feeding, but he no longer considered her a threat. She would need to remind them all exactly what she was.

"In the flesh." She squeezed his arm again, twisting slightly. She could feel his bones shift and his eyes bled into darkness again. Far better to have him frightened of her than excited. "I will see Carla."

"Of course." His small smile exposed the tips of his fangs again. "For you...always." Reaching behind him, he unhooked the velvet rope that ran in front of the door. Malice could feel the weight of watchful eyes upon her. The hopefuls in line wondered who she was to gain access to the club. She wasn't on the list, and unlike them, she hadn't dressed to impress. The black cargo pants and tight sweater covered by the charcoal gray duster stuck out among the glitz and glamour of the would-be clubbers. Where they glittered and sparkled, she absorbed light.

The dark colors hid the stains she'd picked up when investigating and burying the lycan bodies she'd found at the hotel. Whoever had taken over the North Side pack had no interest in hiding his existence. Ralph wouldn't be happy about that. He also wouldn't be happy that she had no idea where the pack had gone.

She smoothed her hands over her thighs as she walked up the shallow stairs. The doors opened before her. Each was held by a young woman dressed in next to nothing. They smiled vacantly at her and

Malice suppressed a shudder. She was never certain how much the human employees at Faint knew about their boss.

Carla Sangre, born Angela Stepowitz, was what passed as the head of the supranormal community of Chicago. The daughter of a cobbler, she'd built up enough of a reputation as an artist that a mysterious benefactor had invited her to Italy to study. She'd come back a completely different person, no longer human, and had moved to Chicago. In one way or another, her presence had shaped the city for more than a century.

As Malice moved beyond the doors, a wall of sound washed over her and, beneath it, a seductive bass beat throbbed. Flashing lights and gyrating bodies caught her attention and she glanced onto the dance floor where humans swayed, jumped and danced to the music's frantic tempo. The energy they gave off was almost palpable. Malice inhaled, feeling their life force move through her. How long had it been since she'd danced? It was something she'd loved doing in high school. She and her friends had snuck into this or that club, not caring if they were caught. It had been somewhere to blow off steam, to hook up and to dodge the responsibilities of home and school, if only for a while.

On catwalks above the dancing throng, men and women lounged while gazing down on the seething mass of humanity. Malice would have been willing to bet that one and all owed their allegiance to Carla. Basking in the life essence that came from the dancers was likely a reward of sorts.

It was also an effective way to keep them in line. Vampires were only barely tolerated by her employers. Any vamp who was accused of drinking from an unwilling host would find her on their doorstep. Since supranormals didn't officially exist, they weren't entitled to due process. The slightest infraction was a capital offense and Malice was their executioner. There might be forty-some capital offenses for humans, but supras had to worry about at least twice as many. Or they would if they knew about them. Those weren't cataloged anywhere but had been handed down to Malice and her peers by their handlers.

From the catwalk, the vamps kept hungry eyes on their prey. As much as Malice knew about how they hunted, she still wasn't sure how they selected their hosts. Vamps who knew what they were doing invariably selected someone who was open to their advances. Was it a pheromone thing, or could they read minds? She preferred to think it had to do with body chemistry, but she suspected that was not the case.

She skirted the dance floor and headed around the club's periphery. Dozens of vampires inhabited the building and her skin prickled at their proximity. Keeping to the wall cut down on at least one avenue for attack. Eyes dark with menace followed her from all directions. They knew who she was. Malice never knew if they could feel her in the same way she could feel them. The cocktail that had been fed into her system had come from a variety of supras and she'd acquired her abilities from those she was tasked with taking down. Those abilities could have come from vampires, but her superiors would never tell. Whatever the cocktail had been, it had bordered on lethal.

On the edges of the club, the crowd was lighter, but she still had to work her way through the throng. Vampires moved out of her way without any prompting, treating her like she had a contagious disease. Humans were much less perceptive. She was still human enough that the sense of *other* given off by most supranormals didn't bother them. She had other ways to make sure humans respected her. She bared her teeth briefly and deftly split a group of human revelers who reeled across the hall, moving through the gap by force of will alone.

The music was quieter out here. The carpeted floor and thick crimson wall hangings absorbed much of the sound. She could still feel the bass through the soles of her feet, but her sensitive hearing was already acclimating. She practically felt her ears twitch at the first mention of her name.

"Shit, is that Malice?" The first voice held a mixture of fear and anticipation. Other murmured comments held combinations of dread, anger, respect and excitement to various degrees.

By the time she'd walked around to the back of the club, she was working hard to modulate her breathing and keep her heart rate down. She could show no weakness. To do so would invite an attack. None of Carla's vamps were bold enough to take her on in front of all the humans who packed the building, but it would only take the smallest fraction of a second to drag her into a side room.

The final obstacle en route to Chicago's vampire lord was a long staircase. It was carpeted like the rest of the club's back area and vamps lined the walls. It was this way every time she came in. Were they always there, just in case Carla might have some need for them, or did they gather because she was in the building? She gave no outward acknowledgment of their presence as she passed by. There was no sound on the stairs, neither rustle nor breath. The silence was oppressive and the vampires wielded it as a weapon. They never took their eyes from her and their heads turned slowly as she walked by them.

The door at the top of the stairs opened as she came close. No one was near it. Vampires could move so fast that human eyes couldn't track the movement, but her eyes weren't human, not completely. It was just another trick to push her off balance. Undeath occasionally forced the manifestation of various powers in some vamps and Malice wished she knew which one was gifted with telekinesis. Having no way of knowing, she instead made a mental note of the vampires who watched her quietly from the stairs. It could have been any of them.

The room through the doorway was dark, but her eyes had no problems picking out objects in the gloom. Her night vision might not be as good as a vamp's, but she certainly wasn't hampered by much short of pitch darkness.

A large elaborate desk crouched at one end of the room. Behind it was an enormous wingback chair that was just short of being a leather throne on wheels. Carla wasn't there. Malice turned slowly to survey the rest of the room. There was one vamp in the room; she could feel the creature like a barely perceptible pressure on her mind. It was definitely Carla, no other vampire she'd met could gentle their touch quite so much. Most vamps felt like the edge of a razor blade being dragged slowly across her skin. With Carla, the promise of pain was right there without any actual cutting.

"Carla." Malice kept her voice neutral.

"Malice." Carla drew out the last syllable of her name, hissing it softly into the darkness.

Malice completed her turn and finally saw her, lounging indolently on a chaise longue in the room's far corner. Carla sat, leaning on the chair's arm, her shapely legs drawn up beneath her, pushing the skirt far up her thighs and baring a swath of skin so light it practically glowed in the darkness.

"Come sit by me," Carla said. She patted the end of the chaise in invitation.

Malice licked her lips, then immediately wished she hadn't. She was sure Carla had seen the involuntary movement, small though it was. There was a lush promise to Carla, but the vampire had never moved on it before.

"I'm fine." Her voice was harsh, betraying more of her discomfort than she'd intended. Carla's lips stretched in a faint smile.

"Don't make me come to you." Her voice was playful and the smile widened further, revealing dimples that always surprised Malice. Goose bumps pebbled her arms. As playful as Carla sounded, there was steel just below the surface and that steel had razor-sharp edges.

Rather than sit right next to Carla, Malice chose instead to perch on the arm of the chaise. There was no way she would follow the vampire's orders. She didn't belong to the vamp, and she certainly wasn't going to act like it.

"So stubborn." Carla trailed her fingertips over Malice's thigh, her touch featherlight through her pants, but disturbing. The vampire's presence wrapped around her, whispering to her, speaking of things to come, things that would burrow down inside her and make her experience ecstasy like she'd never felt before.

Malice shook her head sharply to dispel the image of her hand on the back of Carla's head, of dark curls twining around her fingers as Carla knelt before her, mouth at the juncture of her thighs. "That's not what I came here for." Her voice was cold, but Carla grinned at her, eyeteeth in full extension. "Stop that."

"Stop what?" Carla's smile dropped easily into a small moue, lips pursed in a devastating pout. She slid her hand to the inside of Malice's thigh, her thumb brushing over her crotch. Against her better judgment and completely out of her control, Malice felt her pussy clench and she stifled a gasp. Of course Carla heard the change in her breathing. With delicate precision, she dragged her nails down the fabric covering Malice's mound. Heat raced through Malice's belly and pooled between her legs. She could feel herself getting damp and she closed her thighs. She hadn't even noticed they'd fallen open.

"I said stop." Malice glared down at Carla, who stared back at her, smiles and pouts gone. "You're trying to influence me. I won't have it."

"I am doing no such thing." Carla pulled back her hand from where it was trapped between Malice's thighs, but not before fluttering her fingers. Arousal shot through her, stoking the fire at her center. This time the gasp escaped her lips. "You don't seem that unhappy about it."

Cursing her traitorous body, Malice closed her eyes. Even so, Carla's eyes floated before her, the pupils so big she could fall into them, peering into her, seeing too much, weighing and sorting. "You can't take me against my will."

"Believe me, darling," Carla said, "if I wanted to take you, it wouldn't be against your will." Malice's eyes popped open in anger. Carla's voice had been light, and her eyes sparkled with amusement. Slowly, the pupils were dilating.

"I didn't come here to be mauled by you." At the gentle snort of amusement, Malice felt her face warm, but she pushed on. "I need some information and you're going to give it to me."

"You know the price, sweetling. Pay up, then we'll talk."

"Why don't we just call it even? I don't behead you for trying to push me into your arms. That's pretty damn close to taking the unwilling."

"If you insist," Carla murmured, "but I won't talk without payment. And feel free to behead me. The next Lord of Chicago is not likely to be as accommodating to your kind as I am."

Malice stared at Carla. A muscle jumped in her jaw. The vampire had a point. For a long moment she sat, not moving except for the angry tic at her jawline. Finally, she got up and crossed over to a long sideboard opposite the mammoth desk.

"You don't have to do it that way." Carla's voice floated over to her, barely audible. "I would really prefer it from the source."

Unbidden, excitement filled Malice again. Ruthlessly, she forced it down and picked up a crystal brandy snifter. With the knife from the top of her combat boot, she sliced a cut deep into the palm of her left hand. She hissed a little bit at the pain and the fog of arousal immediately dissipated, leaving her feeling completely clear-headed for the first time since entering the room. A crimson rivulet trickled down her hand and she held it over the glass, filling it with bright red blood. Deep though the cut had been, the flow of blood lasted only long enough to fill the snifter with a finger of liquid.

Carla sat up straight, all seductiveness absent from her pose. She watched the glass in Malice's hand seemingly to the exclusion of all else. Her nostrils flared at the metallic smell of blood permeating the air.

"Where did the North Side pack relocate?"

The vampire's gaze flicked from the glass to her face, then back. That couldn't have been fear flitting across her face, could it?

"For that information, you'll need to let me feed from the source," Carla said finally.

"That won't happen." Malice watched the vampire, who glared back at her, never moving a muscle.

"Then I'm afraid we have nothing further to talk about."

Carla's steady gaze unnerved her. Malice turned on her heel; she paced the length of the room, the rapidly cooling snifter of blood forgotten in her hand. The thrill of the vampire's quiet statement scared her more than the idea of actually being bitten, but she needed the information. Uncle Ralph expected results and if she didn't produce them, he would call in reinforcements. That hadn't happened yet, and she was determined that it wouldn't.

"You know that by trying to force me to host you, I have a green light to kill you, right?"

The slightly lifted shoulder conveyed Carla's unconcern. "No one is forcing you to do anything, Malice." This time Carla bit off the last syllable of her name, her only indication of irritation. "But I won't say anything without it. I've been waiting a long time to sample you directly. You're asking me to risk a lot. It's only fair that you should risk a little something of your own." This time it was Carla who licked her lips. Her pupils had swallowed her eyes until only the barest hint of white remained in the corners. "The new Alpha of the North Side pack is rapidly consolidating power. So far he's content to keep to his own kind. If he finds out where your information came from, he may change his mind."

"It's not like I'm going to have a conversation with him," Malice said. *Fuck. Am I resisting because I don't want her to feed from me, or because I do?* Malice kept pacing, stalling desperately. On her next pass, the vampire reached forward and placed a cool hand on her arm, halting Malice in her tracks. Without a word, Carla plucked the glass from her hand and lifted it to her lips, sipping at the blood inside.

"We don't want it to get too much colder." With a dainty finger, Carla wiped away the crimson residue on her lips, then stuck the finger in her mouth before drawing it out slowly while holding Malice with her eyes.

"Fine, then." Sternly, she told herself that she wasn't capitulating because she wanted to feel the vampire's mouth on her. The warm dampness between her thighs made a mockery of her mental admonishment. *Damn the vampire and her powers of persuasion.* Between one blink and the next, Carla was behind her, pressing her breasts against Malice's back. Her presence threatened to overwhelm Malice and with great effort, she pushed Carla out of her head. The vampire's presence lay over her mind like a blanket over a parrot's cage, clouding her thoughts and ensuring her compliance. With a twist, Malice moved away and held up one hand.

"Don't tell me you're changing your mind already, sweetling." Carla moved forward until Malice's hand pressed between her pert breasts.

"I know what you're trying to do." Malice tried not to think about how close her fingers were to the vampire's nipples. Her fingers twitched slightly against her will. "If you want what I can offer, you're going to have to take it honestly. I don't want you rolling me. I want to be aware during the…process."

"I never pegged you for a masochist." Carla's lips curled coyly. "It'll be so much better for you if you let me take your mind completely."

Let her take my mind completely? It was good to know that Chicago's strongest vampire couldn't roll her without her consent, but what about normal humans? If they could cloud human thoughts, even a bit, it didn't bode well for how the vampires were feeding. They were treading perilously close to the edge of taking without consent, if that was the case.

"You won't be taking anything until we talk. You receive your payment once I've received the information."

With one more pout at being thwarted, Carla turned and crossed the room back to the chaise longue, but not before leaning into Malice's hand on the way by. She could clearly feel Carla's stiffened nipple, straining through the fabric and into her palm.

"So, the North Side pack." Carla patted the seat next to her again. This time, Malice took her up on the invitation and settled next to her, back stiff. "Their Alpha is no more."

"I know. I saw his corpse. Or rather, what was left of it."

"It's too bad, really. Dean was an agreeable rival. He made sure our spheres of influence did little to cross. I'm not convinced that the new Alpha will be so collegial." Her fingers traced complex patterns on the top of Malice's thigh. She worked to keep her leg muscles from twitching at the attention but could do nothing to suppress the tension coiling in her abdomen.

"So who is this new Alpha?" To her surprise, her voice didn't waver.

"A lone wolf, or rather a former lone wolf. His name is MacTavish, but I don't know his first name. No one seems to. He's a brute and he's been through this way many times before. The last was six or seven months ago." Carla leaned her head on Malice's shoulder. The cool weight felt strange, though not altogether disagreeable.

"Seven months ago?" The time frame might be important, but Carla's body against hers distracted Malice from chasing the thought down.

"Mmm." The soft assent vibrated against Malice's neck. Carla nuzzled at the sensitive skin where her neck met her shoulder. "They've moved to the west side, near the Des Plaines River. He's moved them into an abandoned trucking hub by the airport."

"I need an address."

"Of course you do, darling." With one hand, Carla yanked down the neck of Malice's sweater, tearing it open and exposing her chest to the sternum. Malice could only watch as the vampire lowered her head to the top of her right breast. Carla shoved her bra straps aside with hasty fingers; then sharp pain pierced her breast.

"Oh god," Malice panted. The words were ripped from her, pain quickly turning to enjoyment. Her nipples ached, the tips pushing against the fabric of her bra, demanding attention Carla was only too happy to give them. Malice moaned when the appreciative vampire rubbed the pads of her thumbs over the proud protuberances, sending another shock of sensation coursing down her torso to join the tempest building in her belly.

She was close to coming, Malice realized, her hips twitching, thrusting in time with each gentle stroke of Carla's thumbs. Just like that, she'd lost control of the encounter. Dimly, she wondered why that was so important. *Just let go*, a voice whispered. *You know you want to.*

No. Without any thought beyond getting a grip on herself, Malice bit down hard on the inside of her lip. The pain cleared her head, as did the taste of salt and metal that bathed her tongue.

"Take your payment," Malice said harshly. "Nothing more." She captured Carla's hands in both of hers and drew them away from her breasts.

The vampire made a small noise of displeasure but kept sucking. Her tongue worked against the small wound in Malice's breast, lapping at the blood that pooled so quickly a small amount escaped. A thin scarlet rivulet trickled down her cleavage and stained the white sports bra.

With a shock that almost undid her tenuous self-control, Malice watched as the vampire unzipped the side of her skirt and slid her hand down the front. Carla's hips rose and fell in time with her sucking. Unable to pull her gaze away and more turned on than she could ever remember being before, Malice watched as the vampire brought herself higher and higher, finally coming silently but hard. Her teeth bit down harshly on Malice's breast and she gasped. Her pussy throbbed, demanding attention, to be stroked, filled and fucked. She bit down on her lip again, keeping her mouth clamped shut. Malice didn't trust herself not to beg Carla to take her.

The vampire's teeth disengaged and she lifted her head, looking down at Malice's chest. Instead of the round punctures Malice had expected, the holes were long, two rents that still sluggishly oozed blood. They had already started healing. She became aware of the wound on her palm and clenched it experimentally. It was a little sore, but she could tell it was closed. On a normal human, the cut would look three to four days old.

"I could have given you such pleasure, Malice." Carla's voice held a tinge of regret. She lifted her head and looked into Malice's eyes. Malice had the uncomfortable feeling the vampire gazed into the very seat of her being. "Why don't you let yourself go, just a little bit? You'd be so much happier if you did."

"I'm doing just fine, thanks."

"Are you? Really? Tell me the truth, Malice. Human sex just doesn't do it for you anymore, does it? You're looking for something else. Something more." The shock of the vampire's statement hadn't set in when Carla fastened her lips to hers. Malice tasted her blood on the vampire's tongue as it swept into her mouth. For the barest second, she accepted Carla, kissing her back with a passion she hadn't felt in far too long.

Abruptly, Malice stood up, practically dumping the vampire on the floor. Carla had been half in her lap by the time she regained her senses.

"Thanks for the information." Not sparing Carla a backward glance, she strode to the door. Once again, it opened without her touching it. The stairs beyond the office were empty. Malice took the steps two at a time, eager to be gone from the woman who was causing her such confusion.

When did Carla become the "woman"? she wondered. *Instead of the "vampire"?*

CHAPTER SEVEN

Something upstairs creaked and popped. Ruri tensed before realizing it was nothing more than the normal sounds of an old house settling. The abandoned bungalow suited her needs perfectly. The neighborhood hadn't been great to begin with, and had been half cleared out by the recession and never recovered. The area inhabitants had long ago trained themselves not to pay too much attention to their neighbors. So far no one seemed to have noticed her squatting in one of the street's many abandoned houses. The little nest she'd built herself in the corner of the basement had all the amenities of home with none of the comfort. Cinderblock walls on two sides were comforting, but nothing could substitute for her missing packmates. At night, when she missed them most, Ruri distracted herself by planning the complete gutting and remodeling of this house. As a strategy, it worked better some evenings than others.

Now that she was on her own, Ruri needed as much safety as she could provide for herself. Above the narrow cot she'd scavenged from the alley was a small window. It was the perfect escape route. She hadn't used it yet. If someone from the old pack tracked her down, she didn't want them to know about it. If it smelled like her, they'd set somebody on it for sure.

It was a boring life so far. She hunkered down in the basement until dark and only then ventured back out into the city. The solitude was the worst part. With little to distract her, Ruri's mind retraced the well-worn path of doubt and recrimination. Why hadn't she taken more notice of the sudden rash of newly turned and abandoned wolven? Dean hadn't seemed too concerned with their appearance, choosing instead to focus on integrating them into the pack. She should have known better. Security was her responsibility.

Had Wyatt been a plant? He'd proven himself so quickly and so eagerly. He earned his place as a member of Dean's bodyguard. If it had been anyone else, a wolven not so engaging who didn't look at her with a combination of hero worship and intense respect, would she have moved them into such an important detail so quickly?

And Brittney. What was there to say about Brittney that she hadn't already told herself a thousand times before? There was clear evidence of her betrayal. Ruri scrunched her eyes shut as if that could block out the remembered spray of blood as Raquel's throat was ripped open. Brittney was her biggest failure, and to her mind the linchpin in all the events that had gone wrong that day. Without their relationship, Britt wouldn't have had such easy access to Dean. She'd obviously drugged them, either in the coffee or the cookies or both. Without those limitations, Dean would have made short work of MacTavish. His coup would have been over even as it began. But no, Ruri had trusted the traitorous wolven, had loved her even. And where did it get her?

This isn't helping. It wasn't the first time, or the tenth time, or even the hundredth time she'd told herself that. That it was true didn't make the admonishment any more effective. She needed a distraction, needed to *do* something about what had befallen her pack.

Ruri glanced up at the westward-facing window. The sky was still light, but only barely. Carefully, Ruri stood up and stretched. Her shoulder still ached. At ten days since her injury, it should have been merely the memory of pain, but stiffness continued to plague her.

She rotated the sensitive joint, trying to work out the kinks. When she reached over to massage it, the inside of her arm brushed across her breast, sending tingles radiating from the sensitive nipple. Ruri closed her eyes in an unhappy combination of arousal and frustration. Her monthly heat was almost upon her. Her stomach dropped at the realization. How the hell was she going to deal with it now? Britt was with MacTavish. She swallowed a howl of anger; all that leaked out was a pitiful whine.

Carefully, trying not to move too quickly in deference to her injured shoulder, Ruri stripped her clothes to don fresher ones that didn't stink quite so badly. Even in her den, she couldn't relax. She had to be ready to go at the first sign of trouble. The smell that wafted off the soiled clothing tickled her sensitive nose, and she quashed a sneeze that promised to be explosive. She would have to wash them and soon. Fortunately, her other set wasn't quite so pungent. It wouldn't do to track down her pack in clothes they would smell a couple of miles away.

She wished she could shift to go after them. She'd been tracking them for days and had finally narrowed their new territory down to an industrial park in the northwestern suburbs. A wolf would be very out of place in that area. There existed next to no cover for her among the concrete parking lots, chain-link fences and squat factory buildings. The only green there was on small patches of lawn.

Feeling prepared, though not confident, Ruri crossed the basement and opened a small window. By now, it was completely dark. No one would see her as she slithered her way out of the basement. Thick plywood boards remained on the other windows and on all the doors. She'd left them in place so her presence wasn't trumpeted to the rest of the neighborhood. Away from the close dampness of her squat, Ruri inhaled, letting fresh air cleanse lingering mustiness from her nostrils.

By necessity and design, her current den was far removed from the hotel. Unfortunately, it was even further from the area to which she'd tracked her former family. There was no way she was going to take the bus. For one thing, she didn't think she could sit still that long, especially not with someone else in control of the vehicle. For another, being surrounded by humans, especially in her heightened state, wasn't a good idea. Finding transportation was her first goal.

Breaking into an easy run, Ruri scampered down the alley, keeping all her senses at peak awareness for anyone who might see her. She flitted from shadow to shadow, pausing only when she felt the presence of humans.

There! The old sedan parked behind a house a few blocks over from her den was exactly what she needed. It was old enough to be easy enough to hot wire and fairly nondescript, though the gold color was one not seen very often these days. She pulled on the handle— which didn't move. Ruri growled softly in frustration; since when did people lock their cars in this neighborhood? Who would even want to steal this pile? She bared her teeth in a grim smile at the irony.

Ruri pulled a thin strip of metal from the waist of her pants. She flexed it a couple times so it was somewhat straight then slid it down between the door and the window. After a little finessing, the lock popped open and Ruri slid in behind the wheel. She really was getting good at this. Her mother would have been so proud to see what she'd become.

Thoughts of her biological family washed through her with faint nostalgia. She couldn't bring their faces to her mind now, couldn't even remember how they smelled. The last one had died in the middle of the last century. The only photograph she'd had was gone, destroyed by her pack. They'd been poor, but proud. Years spent farming hadn't appealed to her and she'd left the family farm to head to the city. She'd never made it.

She knew the sadness was a side effect of the hormones bathing her system, though it didn't make the feelings any easier to deal with. Irritated, she hooked her fingers around the car's steering column and yanked at the ignition. The hard plastic dashboard parted like rotten cloth beneath her fingers and she bent over to peer at the exposed machinery. It was the work of a few moments to find the right wires and twine them around each other. The engine roared to loud and brash life. Ruri threw the car into reverse and peeled back into the alley. The car needed some serious muffler work. Lights in the house blinked on behind her and she turned onto the street with a squeal of tires.

She didn't relax until she was a couple of miles away. It didn't feel good to have to resort to thievery, but she needed to find out what the pack was up to. Crisp air rushed into the car through the open window. It carried the promise of new horizons and the mix of scents tugged at her. Ruri finally felt a little more like her old self. It wasn't as good as running beneath the stars in fur-form, but driving a car was a decent second to that sense of freedom. The only thing that would have made it better was a Corvette with the top down. Or better yet, a motorcycle.

Traffic was typical for Chicago. Even after the evening rush hour was technically over, she still ran into a couple of snarls that slowed her to a crawl. It was later than she'd anticipated when she finally arrived at her destination.

She'd followed her nose to this point. It had taken her days to track the pack. More than once she thought she'd lost the trace, but she'd always found it again, despite her rising panic. The previous night, she'd almost howled in triumph when she'd found scent traces of more than one of her former packmates. It was the first time she'd smelled more than one together, and she knew she was finally closing in on the new den.

Ruri parked the car at the side of the road and walked slowly toward the convenience store that stood at the intersection of two busy streets. She could smell wolven presence at the spot. Their scents overlapped one atop the other; they'd been coming and going for a few days now.

Most of the scents led in one direction, to the west. Wherever the pack was holed up, it was close enough that the wolven could walk to the convenience store. It narrowed the scope of her search considerably. They couldn't be more than five miles away, at the most.

With a spring to her step, Ruri trotted off after the trail.

The wind was cold, a reminder that the slow trudge to winter continued, no matter her current preoccupation. It tugged at the corners of Malice's trench coat though it didn't bother her too much. The thought tickled the surface of her mind, but she paid it scant attention, keeping her focus on the long, low building. It certainly looked abandoned. No lights twinkled at her from any of the windows in the plain cement facade. What few windows there were appeared to have been boarded over from the inside, though it was difficult to tell from so far away.

From her vantage point on top of a nearby factory outbuilding, she had a commanding view. Since there was nothing going on by the main building, she swept her binoculars over to investigate the perimeter of the adjacent property. That also came up empty. Malice breathed out a small huff of irritation. Mist wreathed her face momentarily before dissipating into the wind.

If she didn't see something soon, she would have to approach the building. The prospect of trying to sneak up on a building where a werewolf pack might have taken up residence didn't fill her with glee, but she needed to report something back to Ralph and soon.

This had better not be a red herring. If Carla had taken her for a ride, the vampire would find out why she'd earned her codename. Malice snatched the hand away from her chest when she realized she was caressing the top of her breast through her sweater's thick fabric. For a moment, she thought she could still feel Carla's mouth on her. The remembered pain awoke very real desire and once again wetness spread between her thighs.

A flash of furtive movement by the road caught her attention, and she swung the binoculars over to check on it. Just beyond the range of one of the few streetlights, a woman was doing her best not to skulk along the fence line that separated the property from the road. Shaggy blond hair hung to the woman's jaw and obscured her face. She was trying a little too hard to look like she was just out for a stroll, but no one would go for a walk in this place at this time of night. The nearest residential neighborhood was a few miles away; there was nothing out here except industrial wasteland.

The woman continued to slouch past the old trucking hub, never glancing toward the buildings. She might as well have been staring.

What's her part in all this? Movement further along the fence dragged Malice away from her contemplation of the strange woman. Three men chatted as they ambled through the large field that surrounded the hub. They moved with the easy grace and confidence of lycans, their limbs loose and their heads held high. When you were top of the food chain, you didn't worry about much. Malice smiled grimly. If they'd known she was there, they would have worried.

One man stopped in his tracks and lifted his nose to the sky. The other two, one short and weedy, the other broad across the shoulders with a shock of dirty blond hair, quickly followed suit. As one, they broke into a ground-devouring lope, heading right toward the woman.

She saw them approaching and shot into a sprint, arms and legs pumping madly, hair blowing back from her face. Malice had only the barest moment to see her face clearly, but there was no mistaking the terror on it.

Without thinking about it, Malice rose smoothly from her crouch and vaulted over the side of the building, fifteen feet to the ground. She hit the ground with a shock to her feet and rolled, coming up in one motion. Four figures streaked down the road, the men gaining on the woman. At the rate they were coming up on her, she wasn't likely to escape.

Malice took off running at an angle, calculating where the lycans would overtake their quarry. They panted almost upon the woman's heels. One went to all fours, then leaped on her, taking her to the ground in a tangle of limbs. The other two caught up a second later. She thrashed in the hold of the one who'd taken her down. He lay on top of her, trusting for his greater bulk to keep her pinned.

"Get the fuck off me!" Malice could barely make out the woman's voice. The wind whipped it away from her, but all she heard was fury and none of the fear she'd seen earlier.

"Holy shit, Jimmy." The smallest lycan bounced on the balls of his feet with excitement. "Mac is gonna be real happy."

"Yep." Jimmy grunted with the effort of holding the woman down. "She's in heat. I bet he won't mind if we take care of that. Here, help me hold her down."

The small lycan grabbed one of the woman's legs and leaned on it. The blond-haired one snagged the other and yanked it viciously to keeping her from kicking them while Jimmy held her down by the shoulders. The woman seemed to be doing her best to bite him, but he evaded her easily.

"Go ahead, kid," Jimmy said. "Take the first go."

The small lycan let go of the leg he'd been holding and Blondie grabbed it. Small knelt on the woman's thighs to keep them from moving. Reaching up, he hooked both hands around her waistband and worked on dragging her pants down her legs.

Malice was close enough to smell the woman's terror and to see that the small lycan had gotten the woman's pants halfway down her thigh. Without stopping to formulate a conscious thought, she whipped the katana out of its scabbard on her back and brought the blade around in one smooth motion.

Small's body slumped over and hit the ground, followed a moment later by his head.

Jimmy vaulted to his feet, using the woman to push off. Her torso thudded hollowly against the ground. Canines extruded violently from his jaw in a spray of blood, and he threw himself toward Malice. She backed away slowly, giving ground not because he worried her, but to give the woman room to get up if she wasn't unconscious. Blondie tried to flank her, but she kept him in front of her also.

The belligerent lycan stalked forward, eating up ground as she gave it. With muted pops, sharp claws tore through the tips of his fingers. Liquid dripped from his fingertips to splash softly on the concrete. His eyes shone phosphorescent green, glowing at her from the darkness.

He snarled at her and lunged, swiping fingers tipped by impossibly sharp claws toward her belly. With a smooth spin to his inside, Malice dodged out of his way, feeling the air whip by as he lunged past her. He came away with nothing except a square of fabric torn from the edge of her coat. That was closer than she'd wanted him to get, and she slid back a step to give herself a bit more room. Jimmy whirled around and stared at her, eyes widening in disbelief before he shook the cloth free from his claws and rushed her again.

This is just too easy. She was dimly aware of Blondie giving them space and never moving within reach of her katana. Malice stood her ground, waiting until the last possible minute before bringing the sword down on Jimmy's shoulder. The blade cut deep, nearly severing his arm and flinging out a geyser of blood that was startling crimson in the anemic light of the nearest streetlamp.

Jimmy stared at her, then slumped over, his eyes rolling back in their sockets. Blondie was halfway across the grassy expanse toward the shipping hub. He'd partially shifted and was pulling himself along on all fours to get even more speed. A soft scrape pulled her attention away from the fleeing lycan and she turned. The woman was no longer on the ground. She was already halfway down the street, sliding between two chain-link fences that were locked for the night.

As if she could feel Malice watching, the woman turned, meeting her gaze for a fleeting moment. The female's eyes glowed golden as she vanished into the darkness.

CHAPTER EIGHT

The basement was too confining. Ruri hadn't left it for too long, but leaving still felt risky. Since she'd been able to track the pack to their new den, the chances were good they could do the same in reverse, and they had many more resources at their disposal than she did. She needed to move, and soon, but first she had to recover her confidence. It had been badly shaken by the attack at the hands of three former packmates.

Fur rippled along the underside of her skin. It was getting harder and harder to deny her wolf. Her heat was upon her and the wolf wanted to mate. Needed to mate. Arousal wrung her center so hard it hurt and she gasped at the conflicting sensations. While she'd been lying face-first on the hard ground, there had been a moment where her wolf would have welcomed the assault. Ruri shuddered. She hadn't been touched that way by a man in decades, almost a century. The fear and revulsion of her human side had been enough to drive off the wolf, but she was paying for it now.

Dammit, Britt. This was all her fault. If she hadn't gone over to MacTavish, her heat would have been an event to be enjoyed, not this excruciating marathon of need and denial.

Her legs churned restlessly on the narrow cot and she slid her hand down the front of her pants. Her pussy was so very sensitive, she almost came simply from touching the outer lips. When her fingertips skated through copious wetness and plunged between swollen folds, she did come. Just the barest graze of her clitoris was enough to make her cry out, clamping her thighs around her hand and jerking helplessly as a wave of mindless pleasure crashed through her. She curled her fingers, making more deliberate contact with her clit and rocked her hips, pushing herself higher. Ruri came, again and again, until she lay wrung out on the bed.

She stared at the ceiling's dusty rafters. Cobwebs came slowly into focus as she emerged too quickly from her post-orgasmic haze. The edge to her craving was dulled, and for that she breathed a small sigh of relief. The respite was short-lived, however, and she gripped the bed in pointless denial. The edge of the metal bed frame groaned and bent under her hand. When the wave of need ebbed a bit, Ruri pushed herself up. She had to get laid. It had been a long time since she'd mated with a human, but it would have to do. She needed to come by someone else's hand. Her own wasn't going to do it, not now.

Ruri wrinkled her nose at the sour stench that rolled off her when she sat up. Something needed to be done about that. No woman, human or otherwise, would come near her when she smelled so rank. Slowly, carefully, trying not to touch anything that would bring the need back to the fore of her wolf's mind, she sponged herself down over the basement's drain. Her supply of water was getting low, something else that needed attending to.

At least her other change of clothes was somewhat clean. She'd scrubbed them down right after her disastrous trip to the new den. Jeans and a T-shirt weren't going to mark her out as prime material, but there was a certain type of woman who would be attracted to the look. It paid to know your quarry.

The boots were scuffed but would do. With a quick look in the age-spotted mirror over the sink in the small basement bathroom, Ruri shrugged. She didn't look particularly well. She was too skinny and her skin was dull, lacking luster. She looked like she'd contracted a fatal disease. If only she could trust herself to shift, the move from skin to pelt and back again would put some color back in her face. A steak would really help. Ruri promised herself she would stop for a couple of drive-through burgers on the way to the bar.

Her stomach growled and she cringed. It was a sign of exactly how badly she'd neglected her wolf when the thought of two much-overcooked, barely meat hamburger patties would elicit such a response.

Cassidy hung up the phone and looked critically around her small apartment. Mary Alice probably wouldn't be too heartbroken that she'd bailed on their weekly dinner. She was too busy to even answer her phone when her sister called, apparently.

The main living area wasn't too much of a pit, but she could stand to clean up a bit. The classmates coming over didn't need to see the week-old pizza box on the coffee table. She picked it up and knocked over a couple of soda cans. They didn't need to see those either. Puttering around the small living room picking up odds and ends didn't take long. It never took long to clean this place, unless she was doing a deep clean. Every now and then she realized how grungy the apartment had gotten and did her best to make it pristine. The carpet had seen probably half a dozen different student tenants and would never look great, but she could keep it from looking completely ratty.

I wish I had some decorations up. Those would have gone far to disguising the general shabbiness of the place. But decorations were mostly dust-catchers, and whatever she put up she'd also have to take down. There was no time for such things, not if she was going to do well in school and have a social life.

She stacked a couple of textbooks on the floor to clear the small table shoved against one wall in what passed for the dining area. Three chairs were pushed against the table, none of which matched. She needed one more, but that was going to make the area really cramped.

For a moment, Cassidy thought wistfully of her sister's place. The loft was huge, way more than she needed on her own, but Mary Alice had flat turned her down when she'd suggested moving in. Sure, she'd tried covering it by saying the place was too far from campus and nowhere near any convenient public transportation. Both those things were true, but it didn't change the fact that Cassidy could've had her entire Securities Analysis class over to study and still had room left over.

It was totally like Mary Alice, Cassidy decided. She was content to play the big sister role when it was convenient, but that was it. When Cassidy needed her, Mary Alice was nowhere to be found.

Should I bake cookies? Cassidy wondered. Normally she wouldn't bother, but they had a new addition to the study group, one she was pretty sure she'd be able to make some headway with. There was some cookie dough in a roll in the fridge. Usually she just ate it right from the pack with a spoon on nights she was up late studying, but it wouldn't take too long to bake.

Or is that sending the wrong message? If they did end up hooking up, there was no way Cassidy wanted Cal to think she was going to fall over herself trying to be some kind of domestic goddess. Her skills were decidedly lacking in that arena. Some chilled sodas would have to suffice. Still, Cal was very good-looking. He had that bright red hair which always seemed to be standing on end. Whoever had given him the undercut hadn't done him any favors. The first time she saw him yesterday, her fingers had practically itched to smooth down the hair that stood up almost in a crest.

He'd walked past her in the union, then had stopped and come back around. With that cheeky grin, he'd plopped himself down at her table and asked what she was studying for. When she'd told him, he'd nodded sagely and asked who her prof was. They agreed that McKittrich was a hard-ass, and he mentioned he'd aced the course last semester. The offer to help her study had been unexpected and she'd nodded dumbly at him, surprised that her fantasies were manifesting themselves in real life. He hadn't even minded when she mentioned the study group. He seemed nice enough, but she knew better than to invite a stranger over without anyone else there. But if things went well…she certainly wouldn't say no to some private time together. The longer she had to wait to see him again, the more certain Cassidy became that they would hook up.

"What's your address?" Cal had asked. He'd repeated the question when she stared blankly at him.

"My place is really small," she'd finally said.

"It's better than my place," he'd laughed. "Way too many roommates."

When she'd written down her address on a scrap of notebook paper and passed it to him, he'd winked, and then left.

The intercom by the front door buzzed sharply and she jumped. She'd been thinking of Cal's hair and chiseled cheekbones a little too long. Her cheeks colored and she was glad no one else was there. Having no roommates definitely had its advantages.

She pressed the button and leaned in until her mouth almost touched the microphone. "Who's there?" Hopefully whoever was at the other end would understand the question through the crappy speaker.

"It's Cal. Ready to get your study on?" At least that's what she thought he said. It was difficult to make out.

"Sure." Cassidy pressed the door release button, holding it down for a couple seconds. He was early, by almost two hours. Still, that gave them time to hang out just the two of them until the other members of their study group made an appearance. A thrill tingled its way down her spine. Who knew what could happen in a couple of hours?

She opened the door to the hall then looked down. If she'd known he would be this early, she would have worn something that showed a little more cleavage. It wasn't like there was that much of it, and what little there was, really needed to be displayed to its best advantage.

A couple of minutes later, Cal walked through the door, ginger hair standing straight up as usual.

"Hi," Cassidy said brightly, grinning at him across the living room.

He smiled back, lips tight. Four more people filed in behind him. She had no idea who they were; she recognized none of them from school. A woman and two men stood on either side of him while a second woman with white-blond hair shut the door behind them.

"Who are they?" Cassidy asked. Her excitement was gone, snuffed out as if it had never been. The air vibrated with tension. Something wasn't right. The blond woman threw the deadbolt and Cassidy jumped at the sound. "I think you should leave. I'll study on my own."

"That's not going to happen," one of the men said. His eyes seemed to be glowing red, which was impossible. She hadn't seen that. This wasn't happening, whatever it was.

Cassidy darted into the short hall to the bathroom and her bedroom. She slammed the bedroom door shut behind her so hard that one of her framed posters slid off the wall and hit the ground with a thump. There was a lock on the handle, thank god. The dresser slid more easily than she thought it should have. She wedged it against the door, and then took shelter in the closet, crouching under the hanging clothes. She needed help. Her heart pounded in her throat, making each breath into a shallow, shuddering thing.

The phone! She pulled it from her back pocket. Her fingers shook so badly she had to enter her pass code twice before the lock screen disappeared. The phone app opened much too slowly. They were at the door now. The handle fell off the door, bouncing on the dresser's top with a series of metallic clanks before falling to the floor.

Mary Alice was the last person she'd called and she mashed the redial icon madly until the phone indicated it was dialing. It went right to voice mail again, and Cassidy gave a strangled moan of frustration.

"Mary!" she whispered, trying to pull in enough breath to keep talking. "Oh god, you have to help me! They're here and I don't know what they want." The door crashed open, toppling the dresser and sending it sliding across the floor. She screamed, unable to stop herself and hating the high, thin sound of terror.

Cal strode through the doorway, both men with him. He grabbed the phone from her with one hand while yanking her from the closet by her hair. Cassidy grabbed at her scalp to try to relieve the pressure. He turned and threw her onto the bed. His eyes glowed brilliant white, and they burned into hers when he leaned over her.

"This is your sister's fault," he said. His words were garbled and he drooled slightly around pointed teeth that were much too large for his mouth. "We'd hunt her anywhere after what she did, but you'll do. I couldn't believe it when you were practically dropped in my lap at the union."

The man with the red eyes tossed a little square of fabric to him. "Make sure she's really the one we want."

Cal snatched the fabric out of the air without looking at it. He pressed it to his face and inhaled deeply, then bent toward her. He leaned in, sniffing the air next to her head in a curiously delicate fashion. The sniffing went on for a while, and he parted his lips, drawing her scent into his mouth.

"She's it. And even if she wasn't, you think MacTavish would care that much if we give him one more?"

Cassidy tried to crawl away from him, and he did nothing to stop her. She bumped into one of the other men who stood at the side of the bed. He grinned at her and his face blurred, stretching crazily. Fur sprouted around his eyes and Cassidy screamed again. This wasn't happening. It couldn't be happening. She chanted the thought like a mantra, but nothing changed.

"We're not going to kill you, little girl," said the third man on the other side of the bed.

"Not yet," Cal said. Ginger hair was spreading down the sides of his head and under his shirt. "You'll wish we had."

"Didn't anyone ever tell you not to play with your food?" said a voice in the doorway. The blond woman stood there, her eyes glowing electric blue. "We don't have much time, she called someone. Don't fuck this up."

"Yes, Britt." Cal turned back to her and grabbed her arm, pulling her toward him. They all ringed the bed now, staring down at her with eyes that gleamed in impossible shades. Fur-covered faces and hands tipped with claws reached out for her, holding her down, keeping her immobile as they shredded the clothes she wore.

One of them clapped a hand with too-long fingers over her mouth when she drew breath to shriek out her terror. What came out around the hand was indistinct and would never summon help. If only Mary Alice had answered the phone. But what could she do against these monsters?

Searing pain shot through her arm. Cal watched her, his mouth around her right forearm, blood oozing out between the long teeth buried in her flesh. Another bite, this one in the shoulder, pushed another scream from her throat. It felt like someone was holding a hot poker against her skin and refusing to let up.

The mattress sagged on one side and Cassidy stared in horror as a huge wolf climbed up onto the bed. Its tongue lolled out of the side of its mouth as it stalked toward her. Unable to process what was happening, Cassidy felt like she was watching the scene from the end of a long tunnel. When blackness closed in around her, she didn't fight it.

CHAPTER NINE

Uncle Ralph was not happy. His jowls quivered with the effort of not tearing into her in as public a place as the coffee shop.

"Look, I don't see what your problem is," Mary Alice said, her voice eminently reasonable. She smiled slightly. Anyone watching would have no idea she was in the middle of a heated argument. Uncle Ralph's red face was a little more obvious. "We know where the wolves are. We know they've attacked others. What more do you want to know?"

Ralph took a long pull on his coffee, and then exhaled slowly through his mustache. He massaged the back of his neck with one hand. "You managed to answer the least important question. Yes, we know the wolves are there, but you don't know how many are there or what their intentions are." He glared her down when she opened her mouth to speak, and she settled for taking a drink of her own coffee instead. "A bunch of furries attacking another furry doesn't tell us shit." He smiled stiffly, trying to look as natural as she was. "All it tells us is they have some territorial bullshit going on. They're furries, I mean, come on. When don't they fight over territory?"

"And since when have you heard about a female loner skulking around the edges of a pack, especially when she's in heat?" Mary Alice shook her head. "She should have been all over having someone to satisfy her, but she wanted nothing to do with them. There's more to it than there seems. I want to track down the female."

"For what? She's a tiny little goldfish in a pond full of barracudas. Don't worry about the goldfish nibbling on your toes while the 'cudas are trying to rip off your limbs."

Mary Alice had nothing further to say in the face of his insistence. She decided not to mention that she'd already taken the liberty of tracking the female to her general territory in a working-class neighborhood on Chicago's South Side.

Ralph pushed himself up from the table and looked down at her. The poorly concealed attempt to establish some dominance was wasted. Mary Alice simply stared back at him.

"Find out how many of them are left and what they're planning. Otherwise, you'd better bet I'll bring in Stiletto from Atlanta."

"That's fine, Ralph." This time, the easy smile was more of a baring of teeth than anything with even fake emotion. "You do what you need to do."

He stared at her suspiciously, then shook his head and stalked out of the coffee shop. Mary Alice waited the requisite seven minutes before exiting and heading in the other direction.

She walked down the busy Chicago sidewalk, barely aware of how the crowds opened up before her. Fishing her phone from her pocket, she thumbed on the touch screen and connected it back to the cell network. Protocols dictated that her phone never be connected to the network when she met with Uncle Ralph. In fact, she was to disable the phone fifteen minutes before the start of any briefing.

Almost immediately, voice mail notifications popped up on her phone. Had crazy Ann figured out her new number? She bit back an angry oath before bringing up her voice mail. If it was Ann, she was going to get that little flunky at the gallery canned, no matter how apologetic he was.

"Hey, Mary." Her sister's voice issued from the cell-phone speaker. "I need to cancel dinner tonight. I'm having some people over to study for midterms. I'll make it up to you, maybe we can do two dinners next week. I won't have to study my ass off then. So, yeah. Bye!"

That was no surprise. In fact Mary Alice kicked herself for not suggesting it. Cassidy had ducked out on their dinner for every midterm and final in the five years she'd been in university. Uncle Ralph and those lycans had taken up more of her thoughts than she'd realized.

The next message was also from Cassidy. Now that was weird, and the timestamp was maybe fifteen minutes after she canceled dinner. Her forehead creased into a small frown.

"Mary!" Cassidy's whispered terror came through loud and clear. "Oh god, you have to help me! They're here and I don't know what they want." Ragged panting filled Mary Alice's ear. A loud crash filtered through the phone's crappy speaker, loud enough that she had to pull it away from her ear. She held it back up to hear her sister's terrified scream be quickly muffled. The message ended.

There was one last message, also from Cassidy. Mary Alice stared at her phone's screen before pressing it with trembling fingers.

"Keep your nose out of things that don't concern you," said a rough male voice. "This is your own damn fault." The call disconnected and Mary Alice looked at the timestamp. This had been twenty minutes ago. Damn Uncle Ralph and his insistence on her phone being disabled when they met!

"Excuse me." A middle-aged woman twitched her shopping bags around Mary Alice's legs and she realized she was standing in the middle of the sidewalk. People flowed past her, some giving her dirty looks as they had to step around her.

Mary Alice broke into a jog, jostling through the crowded sidewalk, heading for her truck. She kept going faster, the sense of panic compelling her forward like a whip biting at her heels. When she couldn't stand it any longer, she stepped out into the street and sprinted along the parked cars. It was still half a block to her truck, but she made it there in record time. Shouts and cries rose in her wake; many of these people would never have seen anyone run so fast. Most humans couldn't approach her speed. If Uncle Ralph heard about this, she would catch it from him for sure, but she didn't give a rat's ass. Not if Cassidy was in danger.

Fumbling with her keys at the door of the truck, Mary Alice cursed herself for not having remote entry. The truck was from the nineties and had never been blessed with any modern convenience. The windows even rolled down using a handle, something which had never really bothered her before, but as she tried to force the key into the lock for a second time without success, she couldn't help but swear.

Once in the truck, she peeled out of the spot, not bothering with the seat belt. At least the car wasn't going to pitch a fit, not like her mom's newer-model sedan. Traffic was stop and go and she fumed as she inched closer to the light. If the sidewalk hadn't been full of so many weekend shoppers, she would have been tempted to cut across it.

How did they find her? It had to be lycans. Or maybe a group of vamps. No, not during the day. Maybe the demon she'd taken out a couple weeks back had been working with someone? She'd worked so hard to keep her work and family lives separate to avoid exactly this scenario. She hadn't been expecting to lose her dad, but one day he was just gone. If there was anything she could do to keep something from happening to Cass, she would do it. She would move mountains if it would keep her sister safe.

The light changed and she accelerated, leaving strips of rubber behind on the concrete. It didn't get her very far, but she felt a little better for it. At least now that she'd cleared the light, traffic was flowing.

The twenty-minute ride to her sister's crap apartment at the edge of campus was excruciating. Time passed very slowly for her under the best of circumstances, thanks to her improved reflexes and heightened awareness, but this ride was pure torture. Mary Alice was aware of every single minute that passed, second by unbearable second. The apartment had a loading zone out front and for once it was empty. She pulled in and jumped out of the truck, leaving it parked a couple feet away from the curb. People would bitch, but she didn't care.

Cassidy's apartment was on the fourth floor. She buzzed in at the intercom, but there was no response. Mary Alice pressed on the button again, really leaning on it. Still nothing. Feeling more frantic by the second, Mary Alice ran her fingers down the row of buttons. Seconds passed before a cacophony of voices issued from the speaker. Another couple of seconds ground by before she heard the buzz she'd been waiting for and the door clicked open.

Mary Alice burst through the door and headed straight for the stairs. She would usually have taken them instead of the elevator anyway, but not three at a time at a dead run. One of Cassidy's neighbors had to flatten himself against the wall of the stairwell as she flew by. He yelled something at her departing back. From the tone it was uncomplimentary, but she paid no more attention to the words than she had to him.

She paused when she exited the stairwell. For a dozen heartbeats or more, she stood frozen in the hall, feeling the air. There was no way she would go running headlong into a potential ambush; she'd been too well trained. Nothing she could see or hear should have put her on edge, yet she vibrated with wrongness. The air was too still. Something had happened. Something was definitely wrong.

On the balls of her feet, she stalked down the hall, past five closed doors, half of which were festooned with cheerily grim Halloween decorations. Grinning skeleton heads and yellow-eyed black cats seemed to watch her as she made her deliberate way to the hall's far end. Cassidy's was the last on the right. Mary Alice kept all her senses open to any signs of life. An apartment door would be the perfect place to launch an ambush. So would the wall. The supranormals she usually tangled with would have no problems coming through the cheaply constructed walls of this place. Ripping through drywall would be about as easy as tearing through a paper bag. Her training kept her focused, but what she really wanted to do was burst into her sister's apartment and kill anyone she found in there who didn't share her DNA.

Silence reigned behind the doors to the other apartments. That in itself was unnerving. The vast majority of humans knew nothing about the existence of supranormals. Most of them were happy in their cozy little world where they occupied the top of the evolutionary heap, but their primitive hindbrains recognized predators. Whatever was going on, the humans on this floor were terrified.

Mary Alice paused in front of Cassidy's door. She spread her fingers on the alligatored wood. Decades of paint rippled rough under her fingers where chips had been covered with more paint, then chipped again. She felt nothing, no vibrations, nothing to tell her anything about what she might find when she walked through the door. She heard nothing, but a faint metallic tang rode the air. It filled her nostrils as she stood there. The scent was as familiar to her as her own. It was half her own.

Blood. Cassidy's blood.

The door wasn't locked. The handle turned easily in her hand and she pushed it open, going down to her knees and rolling over the threshold in one motion. The living room was empty. Nothing moved in the apartment. There was no sign of Cassidy. A pile of textbooks sat on the coffee table. Everything else was pretty much as it had been every other time Mary Alice visited her sister.

Somehow, Cassidy's place looking as normal as it did made Mary Alice even more nervous. Her stomach swirled with acid, eating at her. Whatever had gone down here had been calculated.

The smell of blood was strong, but she didn't see any. She looked around and noticed the door to Cassidy's room was closed. The only damage was the missing doorknob.

From behind the door came a muffled moan, barely more than a sob. The last of Mary Alice's discipline was torn away. She crossed the room in two strides and threw open the door.

The room was untouched except for the blood on the sheets. Its brilliant red seemed to be the only color in the room. Mary Alice stared blankly, unable to comprehend the scene in front of her.

Cassidy was laid out on the bed, her arms spread, her legs crossed at the ankles. She was clad only in her panties. Scratches and crescent-moon-shaped bites marred her skin. The paleness of her flesh was streaked in crimson. Her chest rose and fell once in a choked gasp. Mary Alice was kneeling next to her on the bed before she realized she'd moved.

She reached out but snatched her hand back, not sure if she would do more damage and not wanting to hurt her. Cassidy's chest hadn't moved again, and Mary Alice pressed her head to her sister's rib cage. Her heart was beating; it was faint but steady. Blood oozed sluggishly from some of the wounds while others no longer bled.

The bite marks varied in size by a large margin. Some were human-sized and shaped; others were longer. Wolves had done this. She stared down at Cassidy's form, her worst fears confirmed. This was her fault. Her sister had just gotten caught in the crossfire.

The feeling of being in bed with someone she didn't know pulled Ruri from a well-sated doze. Whoever it was, they weren't pack. Ruri felt absolutely no connection and rolled away, careful not to jar whoever it was into wakefulness. The woman next to her murmured sleepily and reached out a hand. Ruri avoided it deftly, taking care not to jostle the bed. The knife-edge of need that had been riding her for days was finally and blissfully gone.

She smiled a little bit as the activities of the previous night came back to her. The woman had been an enthusiastic partner. They had fucked for hours in various positions and with various toys. Sex toys had been a new experience for Ruri. She'd never felt the need for such things, but then, she also hadn't coupled with a human for many years. The last time she'd done so, she doubted the sheer variety of toys she'd glimpsed in the bottom drawer of the dresser had even existed.

This was just what the doctor had ordered. Without the blinding need to mate clouding her thoughts, Ruri felt like she could finally move forward.

Carefully, she slid out of bed. The woman didn't move, for which Ruri was grateful. The last thing she wanted was to explain why she was leaving without even saying goodbye. She felt vaguely ashamed about using the human only for sex, but there was nothing she could offer a human except pain. Long-term couplings with their kind never ended well. Besides that, she knew nothing about the woman, not even her name. There was absolutely nothing aside from their compatibility between the sheets to indicate they might be well-suited to each other.

Even so, the opportunity to connect with another being was almost overwhelming, and she found herself watching the woman as she slept. Ruri knew what was going on. Her wolf was trying to forge a new pack. The beast didn't care that all Ruri had needed was some casual sex to take the edge off. She missed the company of others and yearned for more of it. Ruri couldn't fault her, but she wouldn't settle for a pale imitation of a real pack.

She pulled on her clothes quickly and slipped out before her wolf could become more insistent. Fortunately, a night of sex seemed to have made her more accommodating than usual. Not being taken over by the wolf was a constant struggle for every wolven. It required constant compromise. Some never bothered to learn that art, but Ruri wasn't one of them. She would control her beast, it wouldn't control her. Dean had taught her to master herself. A whine issued from her throat at the reminder of her former Alpha.

The apartment was dark, but not dark enough that she had any problems navigating the unfamiliar layout. As she headed out of the building, she grinned. A small river ran past the back of the property. She slipped through the trees and down to the water's edge. Rabbits by the dozen had made the place home; their scent was everywhere. Her wolf smelled them too and Ruri's jaw cramped as fur rippled across the underside of her skin. It was time to indulge her wolf. Ruri quickly stripped out of her clothes and opened herself up, letting go of her hard-earned control, one insubstantial fingernail at a time. Fur caressed her, teeth and claws gently scoring her insides. She closed her eyes and became one with the wolf.

Mary Alice sat next to the bed, trying to read a magazine and failing miserably. Every few seconds, it seemed, her eyes strayed from the page to check on Cassidy.

It had taken a bit of doing, but she'd managed to get her sister out of the apartment building without being seen. The humans on the floor had still been lying low without knowing why, which had helped immensely. It also helped that Cassidy wasn't a large woman and Mary Alice was extremely strong.

After getting home, she'd had the presence of mind to make a quick call to her contact at the CIA. Cassidy's apartment needed a cleaning crew. When they finished with the place, no one would have any idea what had gone on in there. While she was at it, she'd also asked TC to search her sister's phone and send messages to the members of her study group letting them know the session had been canceled.

It helped to have someone in the CIA supra-containment unit indebted to her. Since supras weren't considered citizens, the CIA was tasked with keeping them in check. It was an interesting rationalization. Personally, Mary Alice figured someone had decided the FBI was too much a band of boy scouts, and they'd tasked a group known for its ruthlessness to do what needed to be done.

TC hadn't seemed overly concerned when she asked that everything be kept under the radar. Ever since she'd pulled his brother out of a vamp nest, he'd been more than willing to do the occasional favor for her. She had the feeling she was about to stretch the limits of his gratefulness. Hopefully, it wouldn't be to the breaking point. It was certainly to her advantage that he hated Uncle Ralph as much as she did.

Bathing Cassidy had revealed the extent of her wounds. She'd been mauled savagely and from the varying bite shapes and sizes; there had been maybe a half-dozen of the animals. Even more concerning was that most of the marks on Cassidy's skin had already healed. Of the dozens of bites, only five now remained. Those were still as raw and angry as they'd been when she found her sister.

By all rights, Cassidy should have been shackled to the bed, but Mary Alice couldn't bring herself to do it. If she was going to follow the dictates of the regulations, she would already have contacted Uncle Ralph to report a civilian turned against her will.

Maybe she won't shift.

Mary Alice knew she was deluding herself. The rapid healing could only mean one thing. Cassidy was, in all likelihood, infected with the lycano-lupine virus. Her trainers and others of her platoon had flippantly called it the LOL virus, or just plain LOL for short. Mary Alice wasn't laughing now.

Already sweat sheened Cassidy's body, trickling down her forehead and onto her cheeks. Mary Alice stood and wrung out a washcloth over the bowl on the bedside table. She gently smoothed the cloth over her sister's face. Her hair was stuck to her skin. Cassidy moaned and turned her head slightly to one side. Mary Alice froze, her hand half-reaching toward her sister. It was the first movement she'd made since Mary Alice had brought her here.

She hovered over the bed for a long moment before settling back into her chair. To her disappointment, Cassidy made no other movements. What she really wanted was for Cass to open her eyes and talk to her, to tell her she was okay.

Maybe I should *turn her over to the government.*

The thought shocked her and Mary Alice slumped down in the chair. The government would love to have Cassidy. There was no question of that. Her sister would be quite the guinea pig. Unbidden, Mary Alice wondered how many lycans had been sacrificed in developing the serums that had been pumped into her. How human was she these days? Could she claim any more humanity than the beasts she tracked down for her masters?

Disturbed by the direction her thoughts were taking, Mary Alice stood up. She had to do something more than sit and watch. At the opening to her room, she paused and looked back. Cassidy looked so small in the middle of her king-sized bed. Did she dare go downstairs without restraining her somehow? Hating herself, she turned back and pulled a pair of cuffs out of a small duffel bag on the floor of her wardrobe. Bright blue fur lined them, an impulse purchase that had never been used for its intended purpose. Cassidy would give her such crap if she knew that she had them. Hopefully, she wouldn't come to while Mary Alice was getting a few things from the bottom level.

The sound of the cuffs clicking into place echoed loudly in the stillness and Mary Alice cringed. She strode from the bedroom, her strides eating ground, but it wasn't fast enough. She cursed the vast floor she had to cross to get to the stairs. Not for the first time, she contemplated knocking holes between the floors and installing a fireman's pole. The place was already hard enough to heat, and having a sizable hole in the floor wouldn't help. At least she didn't have to pay the gas bill. Good old Uncle Ralph, care of Uncle Sam, had her covered there.

It hadn't taken her more than a few minutes to get down to her weapon's locker and back up to her living quarters. She stopped in the kitchen to grab her laptop and brought it with her back into the bedroom. Between running through her exercises and doing some research, she should have enough to keep her occupied until Cassidy woke up.

CHAPTER TEN

Mary Alice ran through her katas again, the repetitive motions forging in her mind a fragile peace. Two days had gone by. Two days where she'd done everything she could, to no avail. Cassidy was still unconscious.

Mary Alice flowed, her hands moving from over her head, then down and through, slicing the air before pausing with both hands next to her hip. She carried the motion forward, swinging the practice sword over her head and turned, sweeping the wooden sword down. Her mind was empty except for the seamless motion from one form to the next. Two long days…

The practice sword wavered slightly in her hands and she pulled her thoughts away from Cassidy's long sleep. Her concentration didn't last long. Cassidy was frighteningly weak. She hadn't eaten anything beyond the little beef broth Mary Alice had been able to pour down her throat. Beef broth seemed to be what she tolerated best. The vegetable broth she'd tried first had sent her sister into spasms of vomiting. She'd thrown up far more than the pitiful amount Mary Alice had poured into her. Chicken broth had been a little more successful, but it hadn't helped much. At least with the beef broth she seemed to be holding on to her strength, and not losing it at such a frightening rate.

Her sister had never been especially athletic or physical; she'd always been slender. Now, however, her slenderness bordered on emaciation. Mary Alice didn't know how much longer she could last.

Mary Alice hesitated, up on one foot, the wooden katana over her head. Her body tilted to one side and she put her foot down to keep from toppling over. She lowered the practice sword and growled in frustration, pushing hair wet with sweat out of her face with her free hand.

"Mommy?" Cassidy's voice broke on the second syllable.

Mary Alice spun and crossed the room to her bedside. The wooden sword clattered to the floor as it fell, forgotten, from nerveless fingers. Her trainers would have kicked her ass for that one. The thought was inane, but she had a sudden mental image of Drill Sergeant Aoki staring at her, his face expressionless.

"She's not here, Cassidy." Her sister's hand was sweaty and cold. Mary Alice clutched at it, and then gentled her grip. "But I am." Shit, she thought. Mom. Thanks to whatever gods might be paying attention, Sophia hadn't yet tried to call her youngest daughter. She knew Cassidy was notoriously difficult to get hold of during exams, but that wouldn't last much longer. Another wrinkle was her friends; they wouldn't be happy with radio silence from Cassidy forever. Mary Alice needed to get back in contact with TC to get some cover crafted, or she'd have the cops on her doorstep when someone filed a missing persons report. Uncle Ralph wouldn't let that slide. She'd been so focused on Cassidy's physical state that she'd completely forgotten to cover all her bases. If this had been an operation, she would have long since been pulled off it and replaced. There was no excuse for such sloppiness, not if she wanted to keep Cassidy out of her employer's clutches.

"What happened?" Cassidy looked at her, the whites of her eyes so bloodshot that Mary Alice saw only red in them. "I don't feel good."

"Where do you hurt?"

"It's not that, really." Cassidy swallowed hard. Her voice was rough and Mary Alice let go of her hand to grab the glass of water that had been waiting. "It's everything else." She swallowed again.

"Take a drink."

Cassidy's hand shook when she reached for the glass. The long-sleeved T-shirt she had on rode up, revealing an angry bite mark on her forearm.

"What is that?" The pitch of her voice climbed quickly. "Oh god, Mary! What happened to me? I remember…"

"It's okay, Cass." Mary Alice put down the glass. "Just breathe. You're all right."

Cassidy's chest rose and fell rapidly; she was almost panting. Her eyes darted left and right as if looking for a way out. Mary Alice had seen the behavior before. Cassidy was about to make a break for it. She grabbed her sister's hand and squeezed hard, hoping the discomfort would snap her out of it.

Her sister's eyes snapped to Mary Alice, and her blood ran cold. Instead of Cassidy's usual dark brown eyes, ice stared back at her. Her eyes had turned a pale gray so light she would have been hard pressed to see the iris against the white, except for the red of her corneas.

"Cassidy!" Mary Alice's tone was one of command. Her sister would obey her; she would not shift. A sharp pain in her palm made her look down. Blood ran out from between their joined hands. Black claws tipped Cassidy's fingers.

Not relinquishing her grip, Mary Alice hopped onto the bed. She reached for Cassidy's other hand. In that moment, her sister went from a sick woman lying on the bed to a crazed bundle of teeth and claws trying to escape. It was only because of her finely honed reflexes and training that Mary Alice was able to grab Cassidy's other hand and throw herself back. Cassidy's teeth clacked together inches short of her nose. Instinct kept Mary Alice moving while her mind screamed at her not to hurt her sister. Cassidy and her mom were the only things she cared about, what kept her from telling Uncle Ralph to fuck himself before she disappeared into the Canadian wilderness.

She swung her knee into Cassidy's midriff and her breath came out in an explosive whoosh. Taking advantage of her sister's momentary immobility, Mary Alice let go of one hand and twisted the other, forcing Cassidy away from her. Muscle memory was the only thing she had to go on when she slid her arm around her sister's neck, catching it in the crook of her elbow. Tears streamed down Mary Alice's face, blinding her, as she tightened her grip. She dropped the other hand and cradled the back of Cassidy's head.

Her sister bucked against her, driving her feet into the mattress and pushing back. Sounds of ripping fabric rent the air and Mary Alice gasped, trying to see through her tears. Cruelly clawed fingers shredded the skin on her forearm, but she forced herself to keep the right amount of pressure on Cassidy's windpipe.

Cassidy's struggles faded slowly. By the time she was finally unconscious, the skin on Mary Alice's arm was in tatters. Blood dripped onto the white sheets. Mary Alice held Cassidy for a moment longer to make sure she wasn't faking unconsciousness. It would have been a cunning move, one that would never have occurred to her sister, but her sister's wolf half was another matter altogether. Her eyes filled at the thought and she sniffed deeply.

No time to dwell on that now. Mary Alice cradled Cassidy against her chest before laying her back on the bed. The only things that pointed to Cassidy being other than human now were the blood still dripping from Mary Alice's arm and the two foot-long gouges in the pillow-top of her mattress. The claws were gone. Mary Alice thumbed open one of Cassidy's eyes. The iris had returned to its normal brown.

What am I going to do? She sat on the edge of the bed and pushed a matted hank of Cassidy's hair back from her forehead. Regretfully, she pulled the cuffs out of the bedside table. She fastened them around Cassidy's wrist and to the bed. At least the frame was metal and not wood. As strong as her sister had gotten when her wolf tried to emerge, a wooden bed frame surely wouldn't have been enough to hold her. As it was, Mary Alice had severe doubts that the metal frame was up to the job. She needed something else to keep her safe and contained. Fortunately, Mary Alice thought she had just the thing in the workshop downstairs.

She would have to clean up quickly, put it in place and head back before Cassidy had a chance to wake up.

The small basement apartment suited Ruri just fine. She'd already known it would, but she gave it a quick once-over for the sake of the manager who hovered near the door. The man was nervous, though Ruri doubted he knew why. The human was sensitive to her; some humans were. They'd never understand why her presence made them so twitchy. Most of them would avoid her, but every now and again she ran across someone who bristled at the warning from their subconscious. She wasn't too worried; most humans could do very little to hurt her.

She smiled and the manager swallowed hard. Realizing her smile had been rather predatory, Ruri softened it into something more genuine.

"It's perfect," she said. "Here's the first month's rent and security deposit. I can have it immediately, right? That's what the ad said on Craigslist."

"Umm, yes." He reached out and plucked the envelope from her hand, taking great pains not to actually touch her. His hands shook and he covered for it by crossing his arms.

It had taken her a few days to search out the various stashes of valuables and cash that had remained in her old den. Most wolven didn't bother with banks. The hotel had been full of hiding places for money. So many wolves had been killed during MacTavish's takeover that she'd recovered enough cash to rent the small apartment. It was a shithole, but it had a window to the outside. Her old pack would never think to look for her among humans. They would expect her to hole up in an abandoned building as she'd first done.

Finally mating had allowed her to think clearly for the first time in days. Ruri had decided the best way to avoid her old pack was to go legit or as much as she could stand. She'd need a steady job. What skills did a 150-year-old farm girl from Minnesota possess that could transfer to today's employment market? Anybody who could give her a reference was long dead. She'd picked up a plethora of skills and knowledge over the years, but without a Social Security number, she couldn't even get through the first half of a job application. If worse came to worse, she could always look for a bodyguard gig or something requiring physical labor. With enough money, she could even invest in tools and maybe get a gig or two for some contract work. She had muscles to spare. Whatever she ended up doing, it would be under the table. She'd been born before Social Security even existed. Official documents would cost money she didn't have yet.

"Great." Ruri smiled at the manager. He mumbled something unintelligible and left, shutting the door behind him with a little too much force. "Oh well," she said to the empty apartment.

There was no furniture, of course. She would need to do something about that. There was one place where she could get all sorts of furniture for free, but the hotel was still a risky proposition. The rest of the North Side pack was very well aware that she'd stuck around. That mysterious woman had dispatched two of the wolven who'd attacked her, but the third had escaped. If she had any luck left at all, MacTavish would focus on the woman and leave her out of it. As much as it galled her to admit it to herself, she was no threat to his pack. At this point, she was pretty much beneath his notice.

Ruri shivered, the enormity of what almost happened settling on her. She leaned against the wall and slid down it until she sat on the cheap carpet. With her eyes closed, she tipped her head back until it thumped gently into the wall.

The feeling of helplessness gripped her again; her palms were uncomfortably damp and she scrubbed them on her jeans. Her wolf might have welcomed the chance to mate, but she hadn't. Being at the mercy of three who should have had her back made her clamp her teeth down on an anguished howl. Thoughts of betrayal inevitably led to memories of blond hair. Ruri pulled her traitorous mind away from *her*. She'd promised herself that she wouldn't dwell upon Brittney any longer. Time to move forward; Britt was her past. The blond wolven represented every stupid mistake she'd made that had cost her the Alpha and her pack.

Easier to contemplate than the betrayal was the appearance of her mysterious rescuer. Who had that woman been? Why had she intervened? The sword flashed again beneath the streetlights of her memory. The way she'd taken out two wolven without breaking a sweat disturbed Ruri more than she would have admitted to anybody. And she'd just let Ruri go. She'd felt the woman's eyes following her as she hauled ass away from the scene of her attack. Goose bumps rose on her skin at the memory and her wolf rippled in the back of her mind. Claws raked the underside of her skin. The wolf wanted out. She would rip apart whatever it was that bothered Ruri.

Ruri snarled, baring her teeth. Now was not the time to let the wolf out. Fortunately the full moon wasn't yet upon them. She would need to find somewhere to run on that night. There would be no denying the wolf then.

But her wolf had a point. She was vulnerable. As long as she was without a pack, she was exposed. Her injury and her heat had put her at a disadvantage. She needed to get back in fighting shape. Ruri pushed herself up from the wall. There was nothing for it. One last trip to the hotel would have to do. All she needed was a pickup truck, like the one she'd seen on her way to the pack's new den.

The old hotel building was quiet. Mary Alice watched it from a perch across the street. It wasn't surprising that no one from the neighborhood was squatting. Even though an abandoned building such as this one was usually a prime gathering spot for the city's homeless, it would be a long time before humans were brave enough to venture inside. The furries' prolonged presence had contaminated the place, and it wouldn't be fit for human habitation until their scent dissipated.

That didn't mean there mightn't be squatters of a more supranormal variety. In fact, it surprised Mary Alice that none of Chicago's supras had decided to make the place their home. Vampires, especially newly minted ones, would have loved a new place. It had been two weeks since the hostile takeover of the old pack, though it felt longer.

Whatever had happened was bad enough that everyone was giving it a wide berth.

She shouldn't even be here. Uncle Ralph had told her to get more intel on the pack, and she would. But she wasn't going to report back to him, at least not any more than it took to keep him off her back. She knew the furries were behind Cassidy's attack. The new Alpha had told her in no uncertain terms to back off. How he'd known to go after Cassidy, Mary Alice had no idea. Family made easy targets, and if they knew about Cassidy, they might know about Sophia as well. At least she was out of town and out of the pack's reach. There was no way Sophia could find out what had happened. If her mother knew someone had injured her baby girl, she would want to take them out herself. Mary Alice would have to keep her from rushing straight into their hands.

For a moment she wondered if that was part of the Alpha's plot. It was an awfully convoluted plan for a lycan, though. If she had been up against vamps, the tactics would make more sense. With a mental headshake, Mary Alice discarded the notion. The shifters were much too direct for a plan like that. Likely they would go after her mother in the same way they'd gone after Cassidy, whatever that had been.

Another hole in the plan gnawed at her. If her mother found out the truth about Cassidy's injuries, she would stumble upon a government cover-up decades in the making. She'd become a prime target for Mary Alice's superiors. They weren't above killing to silence inconvenient witnesses. In saving her mother from the pack, she'd be sentencing her to death from their government. Maybe the three of them should go on the run together.

Mary Alice snorted in amusement at the idea. Even if they didn't kill each other after too much time in close proximity, Uncle Ralph and his bosses would never let her go so easily. She was much too valuable to them, and Lord knew they had all sorts of leverage over her. When they were snapped up again, and they inevitably would be, Cassidy and Sophia would be locked away against her good behavior. And that was the best possible scenario.

That was a question for later. The priority staring her in the face was helping her sister. Once Cassidy was stabilized, she would make sure her mother was out of danger and take out the pack, in that order. After that, she would figure out where the leak was that had exposed Cassidy to the fucking furries.

Helping Cassidy meant finding someone to help her through the transition. For that, she needed a furry, preferably an unattached one.

Mary Alice had found signs of solitary lycan activity after the takeover when she'd last scoped out the hotel.

In the four, maybe five days since she'd found Cassidy, this was the first time she'd left her sister alone for more than an hour or so. The days were blurring together. Mary Alice couldn't have even said for sure what day of the week it was.

Leaving her sister unsupervised had Mary Alice distracted and the night was passing even more slowly as a result. Cassidy wasn't doing well. She couldn't control the shift. Any time she was angry or scared, which seemed to be at least every hour or so, the wolf came out but never completely. She lashed out with claws and teeth when she was frightened. Unfortunately, she was afraid most of the time. Mary Alice had taken to sedating her, but the solution wasn't a lasting one.

From her perch in the architectural detailing on top of the building, Mary Alice fretted. How much longer could she keep dosing her sister before Cassidy ended up with permanent damage? When would she have to hand Cassidy over to the government? No, Mary Alice would kill her first. At least her sister would die as a person and not as a thing to be experimented upon.

The moon rose over the hotel. It wasn't full, thank god. She had no idea what would happen to Cassidy at her first full moon. Even furries in full control of their beasts shifted that night. Cassidy half-shifted uncontrollably already, and she was extremely strong, both when she displayed wolf features and in human form. Mary Alice felt the pressure of time bearing down upon her. This was a deadline she had to meet, for both their sakes.

So there she was, hoping against hope that a furry would be stupid enough to return to this cursed place. She'd tracked the female she'd saved to the place she'd been holing up but had been too late. There had been no sign of the lycan, and her hidey-hole had already felt abandoned. This hotel was her last option before taking the fight straight to the rogue Alpha. She probably wouldn't survive that, but it was better than sitting around waiting for Cassidy to survive the change. Or not.

Mary Alice shook her head. No matter which plan she went with, there was too much that could go wrong, and too many of the outcomes left Cassidy dead or in the government's clutches. Death was preferable, but only in the way a car accident was preferable to a plane crash. The only way they could beat the odds stacked against them was to make everything work.

The faint sound of something creaking pulled her attention away from her worries. She scanned the street below, trying to pinpoint it. The street should have been busy—it was just off a highly trafficked thoroughfare—but not many people ventured down it if they didn't have to. She could hear sounds of traffic from her perch but had yet to see more than a couple cars driving through. Certainly, none of them had stopped.

Businesses lined both sides of the street, all of them shuttered for the night. It was well past their closing times. The sound hadn't come from any of them. Malice listened, imagining she was stretching her ears to catch the elusive noise. She couldn't rotate her ears like a wolf. Usually the idea of being anything less than human filled her with revulsion. Tonight, all she could think was that it would have been useful.

There still wasn't anything to see, but more sounds made their way through the usual city noise. Someone was inside the hotel. Maybe this was her lucky night. Or Cassidy's lucky night.

She slid down from her vantage point and sprinted over to the side of the roof where she'd climbed up. A rusted fire escape gave her quick and easy access to the ground. Though she wanted to race down it, she took her time, being careful to move silently. If she could hear whatever was in the hotel, then they would certainly hear her clattering down the iron stairs. Her heart pounded at her to move faster, but her practical side counseled patience. Years of training allowed the practical to triumph, but it was a very near thing.

The street was still empty, but Malice checked both ways before she darted across it. No parked cars lined the street, nothing she could use as cover if someone were to glance out the windows. It was a testament to humans' unease with the place that they were willing to forego prime parking spots and in Chicago no less.

Cautiously, she made her way to the back of the building. It would be best to enter through the busted-out window. Coming in through the front would alert anyone in there to her entrance. Trash and other detritus had begun to accumulate along the alley next to the building. Chicago's winds blew it along and deposited it where it pleased. The pack must have been diligent about cleaning up the junk; Malice hadn't seen much the last time she'd been here. In less than two weeks, there was already a significant accumulation.

The shattered window gaped black in the moonlight, shards of glass looking like the uneven teeth of a crouching beast. Malice hunkered down next to some bushes by the edge of the property. She had her choice of cover from which to watch the back, what with the untamed land that connected the hotel to the river. She could see why the furries had chosen it. From the hotel, they had plenty of access to places to run and hunt. Their new den area didn't have nearly the same luxury, and she wondered how the new Alpha was letting them blow off steam.

Noises still issued from inside. They weren't very loud and Malice doubted anyone passing by on the street could hear them. She wondered if they had anything to do with the incredibly beaten-up little pickup she'd passed in the alleyway. It could be that she'd stumbled upon some unusually brave human who had finally worked up the courage to loot the place. It would have been a goldmine for copper and other metals. From what she'd seen of the inside, the pack had put a lot of time and work into renovating the place. They'd had a sense of pride about it too; most of the updates were to bring the hotel back to its former glory. Someone in the pack had cared very much for their den.

Malice pulled a pistol from the holster under her arm. It wasn't an especially large gun, and it was strangely shaped. Most people wouldn't have recognized it. The weapon had little use outside her very small circle of colleagues. She chambered a dart and moved forward. This wasn't going to be a kill, not if she could avoid it. If it was indeed a furry, Malice needed it alive. If the noises were being made by a human, she would handle the scavenger using more conventional methods. For some reason, the idea of someone chopping up the hotel for profit offended her greatly.

On silent feet, she moved forward, taking care to avoid the shattered glass that still littered the concrete below the window. The window had been quite large, so it took her a while to navigate her way through it. Her thigh muscles tensed against the urge to move quickly, imprudently. Finally, she stepped over the sill and into the silent exercise room.

All was not as she remembered it. Another weight bench had been dragged up to the window and dumbbells were piled atop it. That seemed a strange item to loot, at least in its entirety. She cocked her head, trying to get a fix on the noises she'd heard, but there was nothing for the moment. Whoever was in here would be back, though. They'd moved the bench for a reason.

Malice moved to the corner of the room where she would be undetectable through the door. She crouched and deliberated. Should she set up here and wait for the person to come back? If it was a furry, she could lose it if it made a break for it. The window was too excellent an escape route. With the amount of noise that was being made, whoever was in here wasn't too worried about being caught. Either it was a supra or a very stupid human.

The risk of losing her prey was too great here, she decided. There was nothing for it but to press on. It was dark enough in the building that she had to work to make out shapes. Her night vision was beyond excellent by human standards, but if that was a furry who'd been making the racket, she'd be at a disadvantage if it detected her. Malice didn't have a choice. She needed to take care of Cassidy, and this was the only way, short of putting a bullet in the back of her sister's head, that she could think of to do it.

CHAPTER ELEVEN

The mattress was awkward to handle on her own. It wasn't heavy, but someone else to help guide it around the sharp corners of the stairwell wouldn't have gone amiss. Ruri had abandoned stealth for speed. If she was to get a few pieces of furniture before someone noticed, it was the best way.

Moving large pieces alone wasn't exactly conducive to stealth, anyway. Ruri had gone all the way to the third floor before she found a room with a usable mattress. It turned out hers was not the only room to be trashed and defaced, merely the worst of them. Maybe there were other members of her old pack out there. From the destruction and the bodies in the ballroom when she'd come back, she had assumed everyone else was either with MacTavish or dead. Now, she thought perhaps a handful had survived. The possibility filled her with more cheer than she'd felt since Dean had been murdered. Maybe she *could* rebuild her pack. Chicago was a huge city and they could be anywhere, and that was if they'd stayed in the area. Her wolf twined around her, filling her with warmth and approval. No matter how hard it would be, she had to try. She craved connection to her people and now that the possibility existed that she could rekindle it in a real way, she wouldn't give it up.

The door to the first floor was propped open and Ruri blessed her forethought as she pulled the mattress toward the opening. It got hung up on the carpet and she ducked to get a grip on the corner to jam it through. Something whistled over her head and pinged off the wall behind her.

Without thought, Ruri vaulted over the mattress and leaped, grabbing the top of the banister on the stairs. Her hands slipped on the slick wood and she scrabbled at it, trying to catch her grip. As hard as she struggled, she couldn't keep her hold and she slid down the wall. The mattress was yanked through the doorway and onto the bottom landing. A figure filled the doorway, stepping into the scant light from the frosted windows. It leveled a gun at her. Ruri threw herself to one side, the projectile passing so close it tugged at the fabric of her sweatshirt.

There was no thunder of gunshot, no acrid smell of gunpowder. As she ran up the stairs three at a time, she wondered what that could mean. Whoever was after her apparently wanted her alive, but why? Her breath caught in her throat. That it wasn't death in store for her frightened her. Death was final, but capture and possible torture could go on for eternity. Ugly rumors floated around about what happened to those who were captured by shadowy figures in black body armor. She hadn't checked too closely, but she didn't think there was any body armor on the person who was chasing her. That had to be a good thing, right?

Footsteps pounded up the stairs after her and Ruri cursed her weakened state. Days of malnourishment and the incomplete recovery from her shoulder injury worked against her. Her thighs burned and felt heavier with each stride. She couldn't afford to slow down, but her traitorous human body wasn't giving her much choice. The wolf scrabbled at the underside of her skin, demanding to be let out with sharp claws and teeth that worried at her bones.

She didn't have time to change. Even at her best, the change wasn't instantaneous. Right now, she didn't have the precious seconds it would take to shift from human to wolven. She pushed the wolf down as she ran, her pursuer drawing ever closer. Footsteps echoed behind her, pushing her until she couldn't run any faster. Ruri wasn't going to be able to get out of this through speed alone. She had to fall back on cunning.

The best way out was the roof. From there, she would have options, but she was under no illusions that she could beat her unknown attacker there. On the fourth floor, she stiff-armed her way through the door, which clattered noisily as it swung crazily behind her. Ruri dashed down the hall and ducked into the first room with an open door. She looked around wildly, scanning for somewhere to hide. The room was empty of furniture; whoever had been staying here had gone with MacTavish. Out of options, she fled to the bathroom.

The footsteps stopped when they reached the hallway. As she stood in the bathtub, tearing off her clothes, Ruri listened hard, trying to tell where her pursuer was. She went down on all fours and dropped the barriers in her mind. Her wolf rushed into her and she spasmed. Her teeth clenched on the howl of agony that threatened to burst free as her bones snapped and reformed, as muscles were rent and stretched beyond all recognition. The change was as fast as she could manage under the circumstances. From the way it was progressing, it would only be a matter of seconds before she was completely transformed. Her gums stretched and ruptured and long teeth forced their way into her elongated mouth. She panted at the exertion and spread her paws, claws seeking out purchase on the cold porcelain of the tub's bottom.

A soft click drew her attention and she whipped her head around in time to see the gun's muzzle pointing at her. Ruri growled a warning and gathered herself to spring at the stupid interloper who threatened her in her own den. She snapped her teeth and lunged. The sharp little pain in her side wasn't worth acknowledging; it wasn't even enough to slow her down. She snagged the side of the tub and used it to launch herself at the idiotic human with its puny gun that couldn't do more than annoy her. Two more pinpricks of pain followed in close succession, and she stretched forward, almost but not quite reaching her tormentor.

The human was at the end of a long passageway, and Ruri could feel herself stretching out as she slid down the tunnel. The human was just out of reach of her claws and she whined in frustration. She was slowing down and the human was watching her, not moving but somehow drawing ever further away. Her eyelids were heavy and she was being dragged down into the floor. She whined again, trying not to give in, but it was no use.

Malice stared down at the large wolf stretched out on the floor of the small room. Its chocolate brown pelt faded to a tawny golden color on its belly and legs; the same gold dappled its muzzle. Golden eyes had glared at her before rolling back into its skull from the powerful sedative overwhelming its system. One dart should have been enough to drop it; Malice had seen it work on bigger wolves. This one must be especially strong, that or incredibly driven.

The eyes still stood out in her mind. She'd seen them before, but where? Mary Alice watched the slumbering werewolf for a moment before remembering. This was the female who'd been attacked by the furries at their new den, the furries she'd dispatched for attacking someone unprovoked. At least she knew they weren't going to come looking for this one. The idea of taking one of the rogue Alpha's wolves would have been even better, a satisfying way of giving the middle finger to the new Alpha. Still, this was infinitely more prudent. All she had to do now was get the wolf back to her place before it woke up.

Lycan physiology was tricky. Even now, the female's incredibly high metabolism would be burning through the drug in its bloodstream. Malice stepped forward and gingerly lifted one eyelid. The female's golden eye was a tiny pinprick; it didn't even twitch at the change in light.

Malice pulled a couple of zip ties out of her pocket. Plastic ties of the variety the police carried would never stand up to the lycans' incredible strength. These were reinforced with flexible titanium-alloy cores and were incredibly expensive. Uncle Ralph bitched every time she requisitioned more. He preferred she simply dispatch supras indiscriminately. When she had her choice, she preferred not to, but she had recently come to appreciate his position. If she got her hands on the usurper, she wouldn't hesitate to end his sorry existence.

The zip ties secured the wolf's paws together, and she hefted the wolf over her back in a somewhat strange version of a fireman's carry. Of course, a firefighter would have looked strange also, if they had to worry about their cargo gaining consciousness and ripping their throat out with its teeth.

The wolf was heavy. Lycans retained their mass when they shifted and Malice thought this one must be around one hundred and thirty pounds. She was conscious of prominent bones beneath thick fur. Whatever this wolf's story was, it had been through a lot. Ruthlessly, Malice quashed the sympathy that rose unbidden within her. To her, the beast had one purpose. Once it accomplished what Malice needed it would be free to go its own way. Maybe.

By the time Malice got down to her truck, the wolf was already stirring feebly. Malice shoved it into the passenger side and belted it in. She opened the toolbox in the pickup's bed and rummaged through it until she located a small satchel. All she needed were the wolfsbane and a syringe. Once the herb was in the female, it wouldn't be able to fight off the sedative's effects.

Locating a vein in the wolf's forepaw, she pushed in the wolfsbane solution. The herb took effect almost immediately. The fur pulled back in a wave; limbs straightened and its muzzle receded back into its face. Within moments, a naked female sat trussed up in her pickup. Malice didn't have any clothing for it. She stared at it for a few seconds, trying not to notice its nudity. The female's skin glowed almost golden, despite signs of ill-health. Its ribs were too prominent and the muscles along its body stood out starkly under its skin. Pale purple mottling marred the skin on one shoulder. They looked like the vestiges of deep bruising only now healing completely. Her gaze dropped down to the female's chest before she looked away hastily, casting about the truck for something to cover it with, to no avail.

The trench coat! Malice whipped it off her back in a hurry and draped it over the female's body, hiding its disturbing nakedness. The missing corner rode up, giving her an uninterrupted view of the female's thigh. Malice tucked the edge around its leg, hiding the distracting expanse of flesh. Not wanting to leave anything to chance, she cuffed the female to the door. The handle probably wouldn't have held if the female had been aware, but now Malice would have some warning if it came to. The last trick was getting back to the loft with all possible speed, but without ending up catching the attention of an overly enthusiastic traffic cop.

The ride home was one of the worst trips Malice had ever experienced. Worse had been the drive a few days previous to get Cassidy back to her loft, but this one was a close second. The solicitousness she felt for her sister was translating to the female. What the female would be able to do for her sister, Malice wasn't exactly certain, but she knew it was far better equipped to help than she was.

Traffic was light at that hour and she managed to get home without getting pulled over or without having to fight off an enraged lycan in her truck while driving. For the first time in days, things were finally working out.

She pulled into the first floor and stopped by the elevator. The slumbering female didn't move when she opened the door. Malice tried to keep the trench coat draped around it as she carried the female in a bizarre approximation of a woman being taken over the threshold by her new husband. The thought was out of place and Malice shook her head, almost tripping as she stepped onto the freight elevator. She clutched her burden hard against her chest to keep from dropping her.

The feeling of a woman in her arms wasn't a new one, but she didn't know that she'd ever touched someone in this way. It felt like she was cradling the woman, sheltering her against harm. The feeling was laughable, really, though Malice was not amused. The woman— no, the female—was there for one purpose. She firmed her jaw and stood, holding it with stiff arms. It was a relief when they reached the top floor.

All she needed now was to secure the female's cooperation. She had some items that would help with that. She put the female down on the bed and cuffed it to the frame, then went to collect her supplies.

CHAPTER TWELVE

Ruri's head pounded. With each throb, she felt like it might burst open. *What happened?* She had only hazy memories of the previous night. There had been an apartment and the hotel figured prominently in what little she could remember. She didn't want to open her eyes. The last time she'd had a hangover had been decades before, but she thought she remembered it well enough to recognize the symptoms. Old memories told her it was only going to get worse.

Newer memories tickled at her mind. She couldn't feel her wolf. Usually the wolf stirred at her pain, wrapping herself around Ruri, offering comfort and warmth. The last time she hadn't been able to feel her wolf, Dean had been killed.

"Wolfsbane." The word came out of her mouth before she could stop it. Or rather, the word tried to come out. Her mouth was dry; it felt like she'd been licking cotton balls and the sound stuck in her throat. She coughed; then moaned. Her abused head didn't like that at all.

Keeping her eyes closed, she let her nose do the exploring. The area smelled old, like weathered timber and brick. The smells were muted, without any of the sharp edges and prickliness she associated with new things. Clean sheets made up the high notes, though the detergent was light, for which she was glad. Scented detergents made her sneeze. Given any opportunity, it seemed, humans tried to cover their own scent. The next layer was of blood and sickness. Someone hurt or very ill—or maybe hurt *and* very ill—had been lying close to where she was now. By the softness beneath her, she was in a bed on a very nice mattress. Likely whoever was sick had been on the bed, but they'd been moved and the sheets changed.

The top note she could smell was of wolf and nothingness. The scent of wolf was very faint, and when she recognized it, her eyes popped open in shock.

As she'd anticipated, light stabbed into her retinas and she squeezed them shut again, but not before getting a look at the exposed wooden beams above her head and the brightness of the place. Wherever she was, it had a lot of windows.

She heard movement next to the bed.

"You're awake." The speaker's voice was female, a little on the low side. It was also soft, for which Ruri was grateful. "Good, I was starting to worry." The tone didn't match the words. Her voice was soft, but the tone was brusque.

Ruri slowly turned her head and opened her eyes to bare slits. The light in the room was painful, but bearable. A woman sat in a chair next to the bed. At her ease, she lounged with one ankle crossed over her knee. Something about the way she sat belied the easy facade she was taking care to project.

"Who are you?" Ruri's voice was raspy. "Where am I?"

"You're in my home." The woman uncrossed her leg and sat forward, her elbows on her knees, hands clasped in front of her. "I'm sure you already know who I am." She smiled, lips thin. There was no trace of humor in her eyes. "Your people call me Malice."

Malice? That was impossible. Malice was huge, capable of taking down wolven, vampires, demons and who knew what other supras with her bare hands. Ruri realized she'd scrabbled to the edge of the bed, putting as much space between them as she could.

"Malice?" Her voice cracked again, this time in disbelief. "Impossible. You're no Hunter."

The woman stood and Ruri tried not to flinch. She certainly moved like a predator, each motion precise and purposeful.

"Here." She poured water into a plastic cup and handed it to Ruri, who just stared at her. "Drink something. After the drugs I pumped into your system, it'll help."

Ruri smacked her tongue against the roof of her mouth. It was still incredibly dry and water sounded heavenly. But why was Malice offering her water?

"Why aren't you killing me? Why even drug me at all?" No one knew what Malice looked like; wolven never survived the encounter. "Was that you, at the trucking company?" Slowly, never taking her eyes off the woman who claimed to be Malice, she reached for the cup. The water coated her mouth in coolness and slid down her throat. She moaned softly. It was the best thing she had ever tasted.

"Why would I kill you? You haven't done anything, at least not that I'm aware of." Malice stared at Ruri like she was insane. "And yes, that was me. Seems to me you didn't deserve what those furries had in mind for you. Are you objecting?"

Ruri shook her head vehemently before remembering her headache. She winced and stopped abruptly. "Then what do you want?"

Malice grinned again and this time Ruri had no problem believing she was who she said. The smile couldn't have been more terrifying if Malice had filed her teeth to points. The expression promised pain for someone.

"I need your help. Here." She tossed a bundle of clothing on the bed and turned to leave. "Holler when you're dressed."

With a start, Ruri realized she was naked. That was right, she'd shifted. She grabbed the clothes and pulled them on quickly. She wasn't particularly embarrassed by her nudity, but it did emphasize her position of vulnerability. The shirt was a little large for her. Malice hadn't seemed that tall, but she definitely had a fair amount of muscle packed onto her frame. The long-sleeved T-shirt gapped through the shoulders, though the arms were the right length. Ruri swung her legs over the side of the bed to pull on the pair of sweatpants.

"What the hell?" A black band wrapped snugly around her ankle. She probed it with a careful finger. It was almost as wide as her hand and bulky. Some sort of gel filled the gap between the wide band and her ankle. A red light blinked a warning at her and she jerked her fingers away.

Ruri yanked on the pants and stomped out of the bedroom, following the Hunter. The place didn't seem to have permanent walls. If she'd wanted to, she could have pushed the flimsy dividers over. Malice was waiting in the hallway and Ruri almost ran right into her.

"What the fuck is this?" Ruri yanked up her pant leg.

"Don't mess with it."

"That tells me nothing. What is it?"

"Come with me." Instead of answering, Malice walked off down the hall, leaving Ruri to fume soundlessly behind her before following along in her wake. Her pace was bruising and Ruri had to lengthen her stride to keep up. She was damned if she was going to run after the woman.

They stepped out between another gap in the flimsy walls and a huge open space yawned before them. They skirted the edge of the walled-in area. Malice stopped in front of a large metal box. It looked like it had been hand-welded together out of corrugated metal. As large as it was, she could have paced off each side in four long steps.

As they got closer, the smell of blood and misery overwhelmed her nostrils. The stench was strong enough Ruri could taste it, like wet ashes in her mouth. *What in the name of Luna is going on here?*

Malice stopped in front of a crude door and slid open a panel. "You're here to help her."

Ruri stepped back, her hand to her nose. With the panel open, the stench of injury and sadness overwhelmed her. On the tail of it, she got a strong whiff of wolf.

"What have you done?" Ruri scrambled to the door and peered through the small opening.

Someone had gone to the trouble to make the square metal box as comfortable as possible. It must not have lasted long. Strips of cloth littered the floor as did clumps of wadding. They'd been slashed into ribbons. Light filtered in through small windows cut into the top of each wall, making it almost impossible to distinguish the form huddled in the corner from its nest of fabric and foam. It lifted its head, hair hanging down in lank strands that swayed with the poor creature's palsied movement.

She turned her head to stare at Malice, horrified. "How could you—?"

A roar shook the metal box and Ruri felt as much as heard the form hurtling into the door. It struck with a hollow clang and enough force to set Ruri back on her heels. Red eyes glowed at her from the darkness and sharp teeth snapped where her fingers had been the moment before.

Malice reached over and slammed the hatch shut. Another scream in protest rose behind it.

"Who is that?" Ruri stared at Malice, unable to believe she was holding a wolven prisoner.

"That is my sister."

* * *

"Your sister?" the female asked again, her voice stretched thin in disbelief.

Mary Alice moved around the kitchen. She assembled Cassidy's noon meal. It was raw steak, but she'd discovered that Cassidy wouldn't eat it cold. She dropped the hunk of meat on a plate and shoved it into the microwave to defrost. If it was anything more than body temperature, Cassidy wouldn't eat it then either. She tried not to think of the implications.

"It is." Mary Alice closed her eyes against the despair that threatened to drown her. This was the worst Cassidy had been yet. Every day, she drifted further from humanity, and she didn't know how to bring her back. "Your old pack did this to her. It's a message for me to back off."

"I can believe that." The female flashed her a bitter smile that never touched its eyes. "MacTavish is as big a bastard as you'll meet. This sounds like his style completely."

"You need to fix her." The command came out more distressed than Mary Alice had intended. She was grasping at straws and she knew it.

"Fix her? She isn't broken."

"You saw her. She's out of control. I can't let her out like that. She'll kill someone. Then I'll have to kill her."

The look the female gave her brimmed with compassion. Mary Alice looked away. Her emotions were too close to the surface and desperation threatened to bubble over with the slightest hint of sympathy. She needed to be on an even keel if this had the remotest chance of working.

"Why should I do anything for you?" The female cocked its head in question. "You pretty much kidnapped me. I don't remember much, but some of it is coming back. You chased me through the hotel, didn't you?" It wasn't a question so much as a statement, and Mary Alice couldn't help but bridle at it.

"You'll help her because you're not leaving here until she's better."

The female laughed. "Once the wolfsbane wears off, you can't stop me from doing anything."

"Guess again. You know that bracelet you're so pissed off about? It has enough C-4 in it to blow your leg off. If you wander away from the building, it goes off. If I don't deactivate the automatic arming sequence every twelve hours, it goes off. If you try to take it off—"

"It goes off." The female finished the sentence for her with a bitter twist to its mouth.

Mary Alice smiled. "And don't even think about shifting to escape the bracelet. The gel on the band will make sure it stays put." The lycan reached down and gently fingered the band before bringing its fingers up to its nose and inhaling. "Satisfied?"

The female turned golden eyes on Mary Alice, piercing through its curtain of hair.

"Satisfied? Not hardly." It got up and walked out of the kitchen.

"Don't go too far or else…"

"I know, I know. It goes off!"

Mary Alice hoped the female would take her at her word. It wouldn't do to lose it right away. Tracking it down had been relatively easy, but who knew when she would get another opportunity like this one. If the golden-eyed female died, Cassidy was likely as good as dead, too.

The microwave beeped and Mary Alice removed the plate. It was barely warm to the touch. She poked at the meat with one finger. It was lukewarm and the iron tang of meat and blood rose from it to fill her nose. Red juices covered the plate on either side of the hunk. She stared at the meat, a little disturbed by how hungry she was getting. She hadn't eaten meat for years, and yet she couldn't completely escape the craving. It felt like a part of her, and the more vegetables she ate, the more she denied the darker parts of herself. Or so she hoped.

Since their modifications, at least a couple of her unit preferred meat almost exclusively. Most of the rest of them were more omnivorous, though most liked their meat on the rare side. She was the only one who'd gone completely veggie, and she didn't lack for temptation.

With a start, Mary Alice realized she'd been standing there for a long time, spacing out over a chunk of nearly raw meat. The strain was starting to get to her. She walked out of the kitchen, heading back to the box. Enough was enough. The female could start as soon as Cassidy finished eating.

CHAPTER THIRTEEN

Ruri hesitated in front of the metal door and stared at it. It wouldn't have been out of place on a bank vault. Where had the Hunter found it? The whole box was beyond comprehension. She was acutely aware of Malice's presence behind her. Her captor's motives were easy enough to decipher; she'd come right out and told her. Ruri had no reason to believe she was hiding anything. Her desperation was obvious; her body practically screamed it. However, she wasn't sure exactly what Malice expected of her. The transition from human to wolven wasn't an easy one even in the best situation. Even with the best pack support structure, many still didn't survive. The circumstances here were far from ideal, and she was fairly certain her life was forfeit if she couldn't deliver.

This wasn't going to get any easier. The faster she got in with the poor woman, the faster Ruri could see if she was salvageable.

"Open the door."

Malice moved around her without a word or a glance. She produced a key on a chain from around her neck. The large padlock on the outer door had confused Ruri at first. There was no way the woman—Cassidy was it?—would be able to get the door open, not with the bar across it. As Ruri thought about it some more, realization dawned on her. The lock wasn't for Cassidy's sake; it was for Ruri's. Not that Malice had anything to worry about, Ruri thought bitterly. The Hunter had her in a bind. No matter how she turned around the situation in her mind, Ruri couldn't figure a way out of the explosive ankle bracelet.

With a metallic clank and the squeal of metal being forced over the concrete floor, Malice muscled the door open. Ruri was confronted by the dark opening. The outline of Cassidy's body was barely visible in her nest. Ruri was doubting the wisdom of starting now. If only she'd been content with waiting until the wolfsbane wore off completely. She edged into the box and tried not to jump when Malice shoved the door closed behind her.

Rather than intruding on Cassidy's space, Ruri hunkered down by the door and waited for the tormented wolven to register her presence. Her form was completely still under the tattered scraps of blanket, and Ruri was sure Malice's sister knew she was there. Ruri was too dominant to expose her belly to appease another wolf, but she didn't need to provoke her either.

"What are you waiting for?" Malice hissed the question through the slot in the door.

"You're not helping," Ruri murmured back. "Leave me alone and let me deal with your mess."

Cassidy stirred at the sound of her voice, though Ruri had pitched it low to keep from disturbing her. She lifted her head and sniffed the air before turning to watch her. Ice-blue eyes glowed at her from the dark and Ruri had to work to keep from gasping. Her eyes had been red the last time Ruri had seen her. Wolven eye color didn't change. What was going on here? And that blue. She knew the blue of those eyes as well—better—than she knew the golden of her own. *Britt*.

Mostly bare shoulders were revealed as she shifted further. Cassidy had been wearing a shirt at one time, but by the looks of it, she'd done her best to claw it off of her. *Interesting*. It looked like she probably hadn't managed a complete transformation yet. The shirt would have been little more than a memory if that had been the case.

Cassidy slowly emerged from her cocoon. She never took her eyes from Ruri's face. Ruri was careful not to look at her directly. This was no time to provoke an attack. Cassidy didn't seem threatening, merely wary to the point of skittishness. Ruri settled herself into a sitting position, her legs crossed. She was more vulnerable like that, but less threatening. Would Cassidy be able to smell her wolf?

The loose pants Cassidy had once been wearing were just as ravaged as the shirt. They hung from her in long strips. Ruri caught a glimpse of a long crescent-shaped wound on her upper thigh. The relative darkness inside the box made it hard to tell without Cassidy holding still, but Ruri thought there were at least two more bite marks. No wonder the woman had so many issues.

The scent of wolf rolled off Cassidy as she ventured closer, but it was muddled. There was nothing clean about the smell. It was layered, not just with different smells of wolf, but with pain and despair. There was no sense of focus or purpose; Cassidy was losing herself.

She dropped to her knees in front of Ruri and leaned in, taking a deep whiff right next to Ruri's left ear. She whuffed a couple of times, tasting the air. There was nothing threatening about her now, a far cry from the aggressive and tortured thing that had snapped at her and Malice when they'd observed her through the door. For long heartbeats, Cassidy hovered over Ruri. Abruptly, with only a tired whine as warning, Cassidy lay down on the floor and put her head in Ruri's lap. Apparently her wolf had recognized Ruri's. With great caution, Ruri put her hand on Cassidy's head, smoothing greasy hair back from her face. Malice's sister moved with her hand, leaning into the contact, but not for very long. Her breathing grew more and more regular. Bare minutes after she curled up, Cassidy fell asleep.

In sleep, she reverted completely back to her human form. Fingernails replaced the wicked claws on her hands and her jaw subtly reformed as canines disappeared back into her gums. Her face lightened, and as Ruri stroked her hair she realized how alike Malice and her sister were, at least in looks. It was funny, she hadn't realized how pretty Malice was until she saw similar features in repose. They both shared a slight dusting of freckles across the nose and a stubborn jaw. Cassidy's nose was turned up a little at the end while Malice's was a much more aggressive Roman nose. Cassidy was cute where Malice was striking. Malice's brown eyes were almost black and looked like they'd seen too much.

This was not the time to be mooning over Malice's looks. Was there even a good time? Ruri couldn't think of one. Sleep was obviously a good idea if she was thinking about the Hunter that way. Ruri shifted onto her side. It wasn't the first time she'd had to sleep on the floor, and she really didn't mind it. Her wolf had no qualms about sleeping on the ground, and normally Ruri didn't either. The metal floor of the box was a little chilly, and Ruri wished she could call up her wolf for the warmth of her pelt. Since she didn't have that luxury right now, thanks to Malice, she curled around Cassidy.

Having contact with another wolven lulled her to sleep far more quickly than she'd managed in days. Ruri's last thoughts before she dropped off were of the multiple bites she'd seen. Cassidy was in a great deal of trouble, and Ruri didn't know if she was up to the task.

It wasn't easy for Mary Alice to see what was going on. The female and her sister were curled up together right in front of the door. That was some progress at least. She was pretty sure Cassidy hadn't gotten any real rest since she was turned. Mary Alice had been infusing her evening meal with sedatives, but more so she could clean out the box and get some sleep without worrying that Cassidy was somehow going to tear her way out while Mary Alice wasn't able to watch over her.

Not for the first time, Mary Alice considered installing a camera in the box, but she quickly discarded it. Watching her sister like that felt like crossing a line, one she wasn't sure could be crossed back again. If she was going to do this, she needed to be there for Cassidy, and she couldn't do that from behind a TV screen.

Unsure what else to do, Mary Alice leaned against the door and slid down to the floor. The only sounds from the other side of the door were the occasional rustle as Cassidy or the female shifted in her slumber. She allowed her mind to wander. Eventually, her own breathing slowed and she drifted off to sleep as well.

She came back to awareness all at once, unsure of what had woken her. As a child, she'd always woken up groggy and disoriented. Her time in the service and her training as one of the government's guinea pigs had broken her of that habit. She was completely aware of everything around her, and she sat without moving a muscle while she worked her way through that awareness.

The sun had moved around the side of the building and was coming in through the far side of the long loft. Hours had passed while she'd been sitting there, asleep. Stiffness in her back and neck confirmed what the sun told her. Mary Alice slowly rolled her head back and forth as she continued trying to sort out why she'd awoken.

There was no answer in the loft, not that she could see or hear. Carefully, she stood up, her legs protesting the move after being in the same position for hours. If something were to attack her now, it would have quite the advantage. Fortunately, her advanced metabolism and rapid healing combined to pass the stiffness along with only a couple of deep knee bends.

She glanced into the box and was gratified to see her sister and the female curled up together on the nest of torn cloth Cassidy had built. "Built" was a strong word. It implied a sense of purpose, and Cassidy seemed to be driven by little more than blind instinct. She certainly hadn't recognized Mary Alice for a few days. That she'd taken to the female both reassured Mary Alice and sent a pang of anguish through her. It had been her idea to find a furry to help her sister, but at the same time it was killing her that she couldn't be the one to help.

Suddenly angry, she lifted the bar off the door and pulled it open. It squealed in protest as usual.

"That's enough," she called. Both women's faces had turned toward the door when she opened it. "You…" Mary Alice trailed off when she realized that she didn't know the female's name. "Come. I want to talk to you."

"Mary?" Cassidy's voice was shaky and Mary Alice looked at her. For the first time in too long, her eyes weren't glowing at her from the darkness of the box. "Don't take her away from me. Please?"

"Sweetie, I have to talk to her." She spread her hands, trying to make Cassidy understand. "She's not going far."

The female had frozen halfway to her feet. She turned and looked at Cassidy, then whipped her head back around.

"Close the door." Her eyes glowed ever so slightly golden in the dark. "Now!"

Cassidy exploded from the nest and the female moved against her, standing her up and pushing her back.

"Close it," she hollered, voice guttural.

Cassidy howled and threw herself against the female, trying to reach the door. Her eyes blazed in the darkness, this time a brilliant emerald.

For a second, Mary Alice hesitated. She needed to speak with the female to find out what if anything she'd discovered. But Cassidy's contorted face snarling at her over the female's shoulder as she struggled to hold her back made up her mind. With a flick of her wrist, Mary Alice slammed the door shut and jammed the bar back in its holder. A second later a heavy body hit the door and Cassidy's barely recognizable face snapped at her from the small opening. Snarling lips revealed long teeth. Those same lips thinned and shaded toward black as she watched.

Abruptly, Cassidy's face disappeared from the window. All Mary Alice could hear was loud growling that gradually subsided. A low voice spoke in soothing tones. When the growls completely abated, Mary Alice looked through the window. The female and her sister were curled up on the makeshift nest in the corner.

The female looked up at her. "We need some food."

Numb, Mary Alice nodded and turned to leave.

"Cook it," the female called out after her. "She needs to be reminded of her humanity. She's spent too much time feral. If we're going to have any luck with her, we have to bring her back."

"Got it," Mary Alice said. The female's words resonated in her head as she made her way back to the kitchen, her heart leaden in her chest. "If" wasn't as promising as "when," but it was better than nothing. She tried to believe what she was telling herself, but the reassurances rang hollowly in her mind.

She tried to think through what needed to be done, but focus didn't come easily. The female hadn't said what kind of food she should make, just that it should be cooked. Cassidy hadn't been able to tolerate vegetables of any kind, so she decided to stick with meat. Hamburgers were easy, and she'd purchased plenty of ground beef along with the steaks. It was easier to hide pills in the ground beef, though injecting steaks with sedatives had worked well when Cassidy proved too canny for the pills hidden in the meat.

Soon the kitchen filled with the smell of cooking meat. Her stomach growled, reminding her how badly she'd been neglecting herself. She stood in front of the stove and stared at the sizzling meat. What exactly was she going to do with the female? Whether she could fix Cassidy or not, at some point Mary Alice was going to have to deal with her. The female had done nothing wrong except to be in the wrong place at the wrong time when Mary Alice's desperation had fixed upon her.

A noise pulled her from her thoughts, and she jumped before placing the sound. It was her phone. Uncle Ralph's ringtone barked at her. She'd thought it was pretty funny to set his ringer to the sound of barking dogs, but now it felt like he was hounding her. She turned back to the burgers and flipped them over to sear the other side. Screw him, and screw Uncle Sam. This was all their fault.

CHAPTER FOURTEEN

Ruri stroked Cassidy's hair and murmured soothing nonsense to her. She wasn't sure how much human speech the girl understood at the moment. The interior of the box was rank. Urine and feces overlaid the scent of desperate wolven. Malice must have been doing something to clean it out; she didn't see any sign of scat, but whatever it was wasn't enough. The smell was enough to drive anyone around the bend.

Her sensitive nose detected the smell of cooking beef even over the stench, which sent her stomach to growling. A slight sense of fur through her fingertips let her know the wolfsbane was wearing off. The wolf wouldn't help her get out of the situation, but she would help her deal with Cassidy.

She lay there, holding Cassidy, and allowed herself to drift. It was a little strange to do so when her wolf was all but gone. Usually, she used these times to connect with her wolf, but the wolfsbane had put her out of reach, if barely. Ruri could almost feel her, like she'd been lying on a patch of grass and had just gotten up, leaving only body heat behind.

This space inside her head was even emptier for the destruction of her pack bonds. She was finally getting used to that sensation, but the absence of her packmates still felt like the loss of a limb.

"I have your food." Malice's exhausted voice pulled Ruri out of herself.

Ruri extracted herself from the soft circle of Cassidy's arms. The woman didn't so much as stir; apparently exhaustion was rampant in the Hunter's home. She made her way to the door.

"She's out. Why don't you open the door and we'll leave her a plate." Ruri made sure to whisper. She didn't want to risk waking Cassidy.

Malice must have lifted up on the door, because it barely made any noise when it opened. Judging by how badly the concrete was scuffed after only a few days of dragging the door back and forth over the floor, it took more than a little muscle. Ruri filed Malice's strength away in the back of her mind. She didn't miss the way Malice turned her body and split her attention between the two threats in the room. She was ready for an attack by either of them. That was also interesting. Unless she missed her guess, Malice had received a great deal of training. No one knew a whole lot about the Hunters. They'd appeared a few years ago without any warning. Chicago wasn't the only city that had one. Lone wolves from other cities had their own stories of the mysterious humans who were a match for them. Here was a chance to find something out about them. She'd have to keep her ears pricked.

She padded quietly out the door and past Malice, trying not to tense in response to her captor's anxiety. Malice handed her a plate, which she took without comment, though the beef smelled divine. It was rare, practically swimming in red juices, just the way she liked it. Better yet, it was barely seasoned. Unless she missed her guess, the only seasonings were salt and a little pepper. She'd never understood what made humans want to drown the flavor of their meat in heavy sauces.

"Can I get a fork and knife?"

Malice blinked at her like she was surprised at the question. It took her a moment to process it, and then she turned and walked back toward the enclosed portion of the loft. Ruri decided she was meant to follow her and came along in her wake. It amused her to walk close enough to Malice to discomfit her. By the set of her shoulders and the quick glances she threw back at Ruri, she didn't like anyone behind her.

You brought me here and made sure I couldn't leave, so deal. When Malice slowed down enough for Ruri to draw up next to her, she smiled slightly in triumph. There might be some cracks in the woman's facade after all.

Her stomach growled loudly enough to echo in the large open area. Ruri looked down at it and glanced up quickly enough to catch the quirk of Malice's mouth. It wasn't quite a smile, and it disappeared when she caught Ruri watching her, to be replaced with a dark scowl.

That's fine, Ruri thought. I don't need to make nice with you. I just need you to let down your guard long enough to get out of here.

"Here," Malice said when they reached the kitchen. She pulled a knife and fork from a drawer and handed them to Ruri.

"I'm going to sit on the chair, just like a real person," Ruri said. "Try not to be too shocked."

"Huh" was all the response she got for her efforts. Malice pulled a stool away from the island in the middle of the kitchen and sat, watching Ruri the entire time. Slightly irritated that her sally hadn't engendered much response, Ruri deposited her plate on the tabletop and sat as far away as she could get and still be at the same table.

Her mouth watered and she dug into the pile of ground beef in front of her, trying not to drool. After her last crack, it wouldn't do to slobber all over herself. The meat was fantastic. Malice really knew how to cook and to a wolven's taste, no less. Her stomach let her know how long it had been since she'd eaten this well.

"This is really good," she mumbled around a mouthful of meat. "Aren't you going to have some?"

"No." Malice stared at her hands. "I'm a vegetarian."

"What?" Ruri scooped up another hunk of beef. "This is too good for you to be prey—I mean vegetarian. You know just how this is supposed to taste."

"Yeah, well. I don't eat meat, and I'm certainly not prey."

"Your loss."

"If you're done grilling me on my eating habits, maybe you'd like to tell me about my sister."

The mouthful of meat, so juicy and appealing mere seconds earlier, turned to rubber in her mouth. Determinedly, Ruri chewed her way through it and swallowed before deliberately putting down her knife and fork. There was meat juice on her chin, she discovered to her chagrin. Not willing to be rushed, she reached for a napkin from the holder in the center of the island. After thoroughly cleaning her face, Ruri turned and contemplated Malice.

"You know I'm not responsible for what happened to her, right?"

"I know." Malice met her eyes levelly. "But I expect you'll do your best for her, or I won't be resetting that bracelet. If I get any inkling you're slacking on me, I *will* leave you to your own devices."

"Yeah, I got that." Ruri's voice heated with her irritation. Her wolf rubbed along the underside of her skin, fur spiky and sharp, not the soft warmth she displayed when she was happy. At least the wolfsbane was really starting to work its way out of her system. She should be able to shift in a couple hours, she estimated.

"Good," the Hunter said. "I'm well aware of who did this to me and why. I don't blame you for getting her into this mess, that's all on me. You're just the lucky one who gets to help me get her out of it."

"If I can get her out of it, and that's a big if. A really big if." Ruri dragged her fingertip through the cooling puddle of meat juice next to the uneaten beef. "She wasn't meant to survive this. I've never seen anything like it."

"What do you mean?"

"What do you know about how wolven are made?"

Malice cocked her head at the unfamiliar word.

"You call us werewolves." Ruri cringed inwardly at the word. "Were" was an Old English word for man. Her people were distinct from humans, not some sort of freakish hybrids. Still it was better than the derogatory *furry* she'd heard Malice use. That one was fourteen levels of wrong.

"Oh," Malice said. "Then more than you think."

Malice didn't elaborate. When Ruri looked over at her and noted the way the cords in her neck stood out, she decided not to push the matter.

"When a wolven bites a human, the essence of their wolf is shared with them."

"We know it's a virus. The bite injects lycan DNA into the host."

Who is we? Ruri went on as if Malice hadn't said anything. "Sometimes, a human is bitten by two different wolven. When that happens, the two wolf essences compete in the human's body. Whichever one wins is the one that completes the transformation. Wolven almost always inherit traits from the one that bit them. When there's more than one bite, the wolven exhibits traits from the wolf that wins out."

"So how does that relate to Cassidy?"

"As far as I can tell, your sister was bitten by at least five wolven. Right now, the wolves are battling it out in her body. That's why her eyes are changing color. You may have noticed the little fur she's been able to manifest is in different colors also."

"I'd wondered about that." Her voice was calm, but agitation rolled off Malice in waves, raising the hair on Ruri's arms. Cautiously, she shifted in her seat, presenting Malice with her shoulder, creating as small a profile as possible should the Hunter choose to strike.

"So the question isn't will your sister stay human. She will be wolven, but only if she survives the battle inside her. Even for a human bitten by one wolf, coming through the transformation isn't a sure thing. When they're bitten by two, it's a lot harder. I've never seen anyone who was bitten by more than two." She gentled her voice. The Hunter had her sympathy over the loss of a family member. "I've certainly never heard of anyone surviving being bitten by more than two."

A loud crack reverberated through the room. The edge of the island where Malice was sitting tore free in her hands. Splintered wood groaned in her grip.

"I'll do what I can for her. I've shepherded more than one wolven through the process. Our best bet is to remind her of her human side." Ruri cocked her head to one side, wondering how Malice would take what she was about to lay upon her. The Hunter was doing the best she could for her sister, Ruri had to believe that. "She's wallowing in her own filth right now. That box needs to be disinfected."

"I hose it down whenever she gets enough sedative in her to knock her out," Malice said, her voice defensive.

"It's not enough. Her nose is even more sensitive than yours is. If you can smell even the faintest trace, for her it's like living in a dung heap."

"Fine. You control her, and I'll swab out her…" Malice's lips twisted as she tried to come up with a good word. "…room," she concluded quietly.

"Good. The next thing is that you can't sedate her anymore. She won't be able to come through this if she doesn't know what's going on. The wolves can't work through what they need to if they're always blitzed out."

"Got it."

"And you need to know there are no guarantees, even under the best of circumstances. Cassidy is in real trouble here."

Nostrils flared and chest heaving, Malice nodded. She stared at the wood in her hands as if uncertain how it had come to be there. Carefully, she put the chunk down on the island.

"I have to go," she said after a moment. With abrupt intensity, she pushed herself away from the island and stalked off.

Ruri watched her leave the room. A little while later, she heard a door open and close. It sounded far away and it definitely wasn't the door to Cassidy's box. Left alone, she wondered what she was supposed to do. She didn't want to get back in the box with Cassidy until her wolf was completely back with her. Without Malice there, she wouldn't be able to get past the lock let alone close the door behind her. As much as she hated to see a wolf caged, she knew Cassidy was wild now. The wolves battling for dominance within her were almost completely overwhelming her human side. She wouldn't be able to do much more than respond to the constant adrenaline that surged through her system, demanding she shift. That wouldn't happen until one of her wolves proved victorious. Cassidy's entire world right now was of internal conflict so intense she couldn't help but lash out. The next time Ruri went back into the box, she wanted her wolf to be with her. The presence of another wolf who wasn't trying to dominate Cassidy should soothe her enough to allow her some peace. At least that was the idea.

The meat on the plate was cold now, but Ruri decided to finish it anyway. A gleaming, stainless steel microwave sat next to the stove, but she chose not to use it. Better the beef be cool than overdone. Reclaiming her knife and fork, she dug back in to the meat, trying to wrap her head around the enormity of the task in front of her.

CHAPTER FIFTEEN

Sounds intruded on her from outside the box. Sharp noises, noises that hurt her ears and made her want to burrow into the cloth mounded around her. She shifted, pricking up her ears to make sure there was no immediate threat. Rather, she tried to prick up her ears. They didn't move. Confused, she stuck her head beneath one paw and stopped. No ears. No paws. The ears were round and almost useless. Her paws had these worm-like things at the end of them. She held one in front of her face and stared, fascinated, as they wriggled around before her eyes.

Where's your dirt, worm-things? she wondered.

Another sharp sound jerked her head up and she looked around, alarm shooting through her. She tried to tuck her tail between her legs, but that didn't work either. If only the new one was there. That one made her feel safe and warm. She'd been wrapped in shades of blue and tranquility. They were of each other. They were...not quite one, but they were of the same.

The other one. The hair raised on her body and she whined quietly to herself. The sound was somehow comforting and she did it again. The other one had trapped her in here with only the stench of her own filth for comfort. The other brought food and rage. That one was spiky and red, shading to virulent purple. She was anything but comforting. The food she brought tasted strange and part of her whispered it was the reason she slept so much, but when it came she was so hungry. Always so hungry. No sooner had she finished eating than she was overtaken by that terrible gnawing at her belly all over again.

Dull pain twisted her innards. Not food this time, something worse. She whimpered again, though this time it brought no comfort. She knew what was coming. This was her world. She bit down with teeth that already ached. The skin around her face and not-paws itched abominably and she rubbed them against each other, looking for some relief.

Pain. It became her world as her muscles seized and twisted within themselves. They wanted to move, to shift and change. Her body had already given the order, yet her muscles didn't comply. She trembled on the edge of changing, on the edge of relief. If she could only get past whatever it was that blocked her. She was being drowned in scalding water.

Unable to take it anymore, she leapt up and ran at the door, with its crack of light that promised freedom but never gave it up. It shuddered under her, creaking and straining, but going nowhere. Again she ran at it, determined that this would be the time. This time she would get to freedom. She would find the new one and be at peace. She would find the other one and bathe her face in the other's lifeblood as it pumped hot and wet from the ruined mass of her neck.

That's not right. She slid down the door, skin still aflame, muscles in cramping knots of useless flesh. The howl that burst from her throat died as suddenly as it had come into being. *Mary Alice.* Not the other at all. Sister.

Cassidy. I'm Cassidy. The pain was subsiding, her contorted limbs relaxing into their normal, foreign shapes. *Why is this happening to me?*

What did her sister know? She must know something. Cassidy made a note to confront her about it the next time she saw her. If she remembered. Exhaustion dragged down her eyelids, promising numbness, if only for a while. Her back leg twitched slightly and she kicked out, settling it in its proper place before curling up. She needed answers next. Answers and freedom to run.

Mary Alice trotted down the stairs two at a time. She needed to get away from that female before she ripped its head off its body. A couple of large splinters in her palm itched like the dickens. It was no more than she deserved for losing her cool and ripping the board out of the island, so she ignored them. She couldn't kill the female; she needed it too badly. If Cassidy had any chance at all, then Mary Alice wasn't going to ruin it for her, but she still wanted to destroy something. If the Alpha of the North Side pack had been in front of her, Mary Alice would have ripped him apart with her bare hands and thoroughly enjoyed it.

Only one thing could take the edge off now. She opened the door on the second floor landing and emerged into another huge room. Unlike the one above her that was mostly empty except for her living quarters, this one was filled with scraps of metal and large forms that were indistinct in the semi-darkness, even to her eyes. She swung up the large breaker switch by the door. Fluorescent bulbs slowly flickered to life, marching to the end of the room and bathing the area in cold light.

Her sculptures danced for a moment until the lights stabilized and the shadows firmed up around them. Heading to the far corner, Mary Alice meandered her way around the large works and raw materials that took up the place. Many of the pieces were ones she meant to take apart at some point. Most of them weren't worth saving. The ones she thought were of any value were either at the gallery or in the small enclosure to the left of the door. That enclosure was only half full. Her standards were exacting, and she could noodle away on a sculpture, tinkering and adjusting until it was perfect. Anything less than perfection wouldn't see the light of day until she achieved it. If perfection was out of reach, then she pulled the piece apart and repurposed what she could into a fresh work.

Repurposing was exactly what she needed now. Some controlled and extremely focused destruction was just the ticket. A long workbench ran most of the length of the far wall. She suspected it was original to the space. Its wood was almost black with age and countless layers of crackled varnish, and its sturdy six-by-six timbers gave it a solidity she never saw in modern furniture. When she worked, she often felt as if the workbench was the only thing grounding her to this life.

She put on a pair of safety goggles and picked up a small sledgehammer. A particularly stubborn piece she'd been trying to get right for weeks sat in the middle of the bench. It was on the small side as her pieces went, only about four feet tall. Four curved shapes reached upward, almost meeting in a point, clawing forever at something barely beyond their reach. Mary Alice hated the piece, had hated it almost since she started it. The promise of it had been so clear in her mind when she'd begun, but she hadn't been able to bring it anywhere near what she'd envisioned. The shapes were too squat, too uneven. Lifting the hammer above her head, she brought it down on the base, right where one of the imperfect pieces was anchored.

A sharp clang rang through the space, bouncing crazily off the weird surfaces. Again, she lifted the hammer and brought it down, and again the metal rang but refused to break. Over and over again, she raised the hammer above her head and swung it down on the defective mess in front of her. She screamed at it until her eyes overflowed with tears. She couldn't see anything, but she continued to blindly swing the hammer until her arm ached and she slowly came back to reality.

The sculpture lay in a pile in front of her; jagged metal forms bent and twisted in upon themselves. The goggles had steamed up and she could barely see through them. She pulled them off and scrubbed the back of her hand over her eyes. A small sound, a scuff of rubber on concrete, snagged her attention and she whirled toward the threat, sledgehammer raised over her head, ready to strike.

The female stared at her with shocked eyes. It turned, trying to present a smaller target, but it didn't flee. Mary Alice knew lycans tended to align themselves along a continuum of dominance and submission and she caught herself wondering where along that line the female fell. It wasn't important; she lowered the hammer.

"I heard a noise," the female said, its voice low and soothing.

"And you thought you'd rush in to save me?" Mary Alice sneered at her, desperate for someone else to hurt as badly as she did. "How noble of you, to come rushing down here to save your own skin."

The female's face hardened, and it drew itself up, its posture stiffening from sympathy to righteous anger. "If I have to save myself by saving you, whose fault is that?" Its voice was cutting in its contempt. "I didn't ask to be here. You're the one who dragged me here and made sure I couldn't leave. If you have a problem with the way I am, you should kick me out. I'd be fine with that. More than fine!"

Mary Alice clenched her fist around the hammer, and then forced herself to loosen her fingers. Carefully, she laid the hammer on the bench and stepped away from the female. That answered her question on the female's level of dominance. It was anything but submissive, that was for certain sure. It was also smart. There was no way Mary Alice would risk losing it, and the female knew it. To lose the female meant losing Cassidy. She would need to watch it closely. Already, it was reaching for power in the dynamic between them.

"You're here to stay until Cassidy is better." It took more effort to keep her voice steady than she should have needed. Her training had imparted a level of stoicism to her that she hadn't had beforehand. She'd been a rebellious teen, but boot camp had knocked most of that out of her. "Get used to it."

"Are you all right?"

The quiet question threatened to undo Mary Alice completely. The last thing she expected from the female was compassion, not when she'd kidnapped her and held her against her will.

"I'm peachy. Thanks for asking. How could things get any better than this?"

"Losing family is hard."

"I haven't lost anyone."

"Even if she comes through this, she won't be the same. Your sister is gone." The compassion was almost gone, drowned under brutal bluntness. "The sooner you *get used to it*, the more help you'll be in bringing her back." The female emphasized the mocking words, throwing them back in Mary Alice's face. She stalked closer to Mary Alice, getting close enough that she felt the heat of her body, though they weren't touching.

Her face heated and Mary Alice clung to her temper with everything she had. The female was toying with her, trying to break her down with pity, then bludgeoning her with reality. It wasn't going to work.

"You better hope she's not gone," she said, her voice barely more than a whisper. "If she goes, you'll follow right along behind her."

The female stood in front of her a moment longer, their bodies separated by less than an inch, their faces so close they breathed the same air. Just when she thought she was going to have to shove the female back, to get her out of her space, the female backed down.

"This is what I mean. You're too aggressive right now, too primed for a fight. Your sister needs calming energy, and you bring anything but that. She'll respond to your agitation, which is only going to fuel the wolves within her."

"I'm fine."

"You're anything but fine. Until you can rein yourself in, I can't let you near her."

"Let me?" Mary Alice thought she was going to burst a blood vessel as roaring filled her ears. The pulse in her neck pounded and her fingers twitched, wanting a target, something to rend to very tiny pieces.

"Do you want her to survive or not?"

"Of course I do." Mary Alice ground the words out past clenched teeth.

"Then do something to bring yourself back under control. You're no use to anyone in this state."

Mary Alice picked up the hammer and threw it hard at the far wall. It struck with a crack and powder rained down from crushed brick. The female stared at her, impassive, though the tool had passed within inches of her left ear. Without another word, she turned and wended her way between the scrap metal and waiting sculptures. The door to the stairwell closed behind her, leaving Mary Alice alone, chest heaving as she tried to breathe through the lump that had taken up residence in her throat.

It pained her to admit that the female was right, but the dent in the opposite wall was more than enough proof that she was losing it. The female had only vocalized what she'd already suspected but couldn't admit, not even in the quiet spaces of her own mind.

There was only one way she knew to get through this. She pulled the goggles back down over her eyes and picked up a torch. It was time to see if she could recreate the sculpture she'd just destroyed. Maybe this time she could get it to match the ugliness in her head.

CHAPTER SIXTEEN

Ruri stalked quietly back up the stairs. Malice had shaken her, though she didn't think the human knew it. For a moment, Ruri had seen her own death staring from Malice's eyes. If she'd wanted to, she could have crushed Ruri's head with that hammer. Ruri doubted she would have lost much sleep over her death. The only thing she would have mourned was the loss of someone to help her sister.

She opened the door back into the echoing vastness of the top floor space. Even though the floor one story down had been filled with scrap and what looked to her eyes like strange and spiky junk, it had seemed more vital and lived-in than this area.

The wolf had approved of the work area, oddly. Anything could have been hiding in there; it was that big a mess, but she'd felt more at ease than she did up here. Ruri reveled in the feeling of her wolf's fur just below her skin. She smiled and stood still, luxuriating in being reunited with her other half.

After reassuring herself that the wolf was definitely back, Ruri kept going. She needed to see if she could shift, and thinking of doing so in the middle of a wide-open space left her feeling too vulnerable, like eyes watched her from the shadows. She wandered through the makeshift rooms that made up Malice's living area. The kitchen was nice, with top-of-the-line appliances. The walls were basically temporary dividers, but they felt like they had more permanence here. Ruri could tell that Malice spent a lot of time in the kitchen.

Off the kitchen was a small living area. The overstuffed couch faced a television and DVD player. There was a thin layer of dust on the TV, and Ruri suspected it saw little use. The couch had an imprint where somebody spent a fair amount of time. A stack of books stood neatly next to that end of the couch, most of them creased and dog-eared as though they'd been read and reread many times. For a moment, Ruri was tempted to sit on the couch and shift. The couch would probably be ruined as a result and she was angry enough at the Hunter to contemplate it.

The bathroom was as unimpressive as the kitchen had been impressive. The space was barely bigger than a broom closet. The only way someone would fit on the toilet was if their legs were inside the temporary shower. The shower was a head hanging straight down from the ceiling sixteen feet or more above. A curtain could be pulled around for a modicum of privacy. Ruri wondered why Malice even bothered since she obviously lived by herself. The curtain would do very little to retain heat and she shuddered at the idea of showering in there. To one side was a large metal tub, which was even more disturbing than the shower. She could only imagine that it must be filled from the spigot in the ceiling, then the whole thing dumped out into the drain after bath time. As baths went, Ruri hadn't seen one this primitive since she'd left home. And they called the wolven animals.

Finally, Ruri made her way back to the bedroom where she'd first awoken. The room was spare, little more than a bed, one dresser and a wardrobe. It struck her as she looked around the depressing room that she hadn't seen much in the way of personal effects. The closest she'd come had been the stack of books next to the couch. Malice had no family photos, no pieces of artwork. There weren't even crappy posters of kittens with inspirational sayings on them. If the Hunter left one day and didn't come back, no one would have known anything about her from her living quarters. Ruri wondered if the impersonal nature of her living arrangements was purposeful or unconscious.

The bedroom was as good a place as any to try shifting. Fortunately, there was no carpeting in here, just a couple of bland throw rugs that did little to warm the place up or bring any character to the space.

Ruri shucked her clothes, tossing them on the bed. She moved the throw rugs out of the way and got down on the floor, one knee up and one down, her weight mostly on her hands. She closed her eyes and tried to let go of herself, to let the wolf come into her completely. When she was angry or afraid, the wolf naturally wanted to take charge, to protect her from whatever caused her trouble. Shifting was so much harder to do without external influences. It was one of the hardest things to teach the newly changed, even harder than keeping the wolf at bay when it was trying to respond to a threat.

Ruri emptied her mind of human concerns. She still buzzed with adrenaline from Malice's almost-attack, but not enough for the wolf to respond. Her mind wandered along strange paths, the strangest of which was her sadness over the emptiness of Malice's living space. She shed the thought quickly. What did she care if Malice was a sad, lonely person? The woman was holding her against her will. And what was she going to do about Cassidy?

The wolf surged into her, concern spiking to anguish at the thought of losing a potential new packmate. The last of the wolfsbane held her back and Ruri could feel the wolf straining below her skin by the thinnest of margins. Her skin prickled all over like fur was about to start sprouting but couldn't. It was like having a sneeze trapped in her sinuses but without giving her the satisfaction of erupting. Ruri growled with the effort of trying to let her wolf come forth while forcing her to the surface of her skin at the same time.

The image of Cassidy curled up among torn sheets in the corner of that metal box popped into her mind. The growl in her chest deepened and became more guttural as her wolf responded violently to it. The prickling intensified and Ruri's jaws cramped, then burst with fluids as long teeth forced themselves into her mouth. She lifted her head and opened her mouth, trying to give the extra teeth more room as her jaw lengthened to accommodate them. Suddenly, the change was on her in full force. Fur forced itself through her epidermis in an effluvial surge. She grunted in momentary pain as her bones snapped and her joints popped, muscles elongating and shrinking as they flowed into different forms.

Moments later, it was over. She panted, tongue lolling from her mouth as she adjusted to the shift. It had been more intense than normal. Almost violent as the pent-up energy her wolf brought had blown through her all at once.

Ruri gave herself a brisk shake, flinging from her fur the last of the fluids brought on by the rapidity of the shift. The human probably wouldn't be happy that they now painted half of her bedroom. She grinned a lupine smile, tongue lolling from her mouth, satisfied with the way her scent now almost completely covered up the little of

Malice's scent she could make out. The human smelled almost like nothing.

A low rumble welled up in her chest and ended in a questioning whine as she grappled with the implications. Vampires smelled like nothing at all. They existed as an absence of smell in the rich landscape of scents the wolven contended with when in wolf form. An experienced wolven could pick out a vamp by its scent-void. Malice was close to that, but there was enough there that Ruri knew she wasn't a vampire. What she was, though, Ruri couldn't decide. The wolf didn't like that. Malice didn't smell like predator or prey but like something altogether different. Some strains of her faint scent were definitely human, but others smelled familiar, and others were distinctly alien. Maybe her home smelled so empty because Malice didn't leave much scent trace behind.

A new smell wafted over to her. Cassidy's ever-changing scent caught the wolf's attention and she pricked her ears up. The underlying scent of the girl didn't change, but the wolf scent skittered and altered unexpectedly. She had work to do, she remembered. There was a young wolven to bring into the pack. She left the room, toenails clicking on concrete as she made her way through the rooms and out the front entrance.

The metal box was just as upsetting as she remembered and Ruri whined when she saw it. She heard movement in the box in response. Slowly, she circled it, trying to determine where she could get as close to Cassidy as possible. It sounded and felt like the girl was curled up in the corner closest to the door.

Ruri turned in a tight circle before lying down on the cold cement. It was chilly enough to seep into her bones even through the wolf's thick pelt. It didn't bother her, but she was aware of it. She leaned against the wall of the box and felt an answering presence on the other side. Cassidy was leaning into her, separated only by the thick metal walls of her prison. It was a good sign. The girl responded to Ruri's wolf. Hopefully she would have the strength to respond to her own wolf, once one finally came to dominate the others.

Content simply to lie there and offer quiet support to the suffering changeling, Ruri nosed at the bracelet on her leg, snuffing it carefully. Malice hadn't lied. The ankle bracelet was still there; it hadn't fallen off when she changed. It felt easily as snug as it had when she'd been in human form. The acrid smell of bitumen tickled her nostrils and she sneezed, covering the bracelet with slobber. It was a good look for it, she decided. She shifted her head so she wouldn't have the smell constantly assaulting her nose.

There was nothing to do now except to wait and let Cassidy get used to the wolf. When Malice recovered from her anger and showed her face again, Ruri would get her to open up the box. She yawned hugely, enjoying the way it stretched the muscles of her face and jaw, then settled in.

Mary Alice opened the door from the stairwell into gloom. She'd been down in the studio for hours. It had taken a bit, but she'd finally been able to lose herself in the work of creation. After that, she'd been in the zone and had lost all track of time. When she finally came out, it was dark. The windows on the west end of the room were slightly lighter, but they wouldn't be for long.

There was enough light to see by and she made her way to her quarters. If she hadn't known better, she would have thought she was alone up there. For the first time in days, no sounds came from Cassidy's box, no shifting or scratching, no whining and howling. There was also no sign of the female.

Mary Alice flipped on the lights as she moved through the rooms. There was no lycan anywhere. She found her first sign in the bedroom when she stepped in a puddle of iridescent goo. It slipped underfoot and only her excellent balance and reflexes kept her from going down. The wolfsbane had worn off. Apparently the female felt good enough to shift. Mary Alice hadn't expected her to be able to do so for a few hours yet. The female was stronger than she'd bargained for, not that it could be helped now.

She couldn't help but smirk a little. The message was clear. The female held her in enough disdain to shift in her bedroom. She couldn't fault her, not really. Uncertainty shivered through her. The ankle bracelet should have held up to the transformation, but it wasn't like she could test it. What if the female had slipped it? She could have taken off. Had she taken Cassidy with her?

Panic rose on the tails of uncertainty and Mary Alice shoved it down before it could overwhelm her. The important thing was Cassidy. She jogged through her home to the box. To her relief, the door was still barred, twin padlocks in place. The only key was still on the chain around her neck. A figure was curled up against one corner and it lifted its shaggy head at her approach. Twin ears lifted and rotated toward her; golden eyes glowed at her from the darkness.

The wolf flowed to its feet and gave itself a brisk shake before trotting over to her. It stopped just out of reach and regarded her. Mary Alice stared back. She knew better than to break off the stare. There was no way she was going to signal that she was anything other than in charge here. They stood, locked in their silent contest of wills before the wolf finally glanced to one side. Her tongue hung from the side of her mouth and she seemed to be laughing. Mary Alice got the distinct feeling she was being told she hadn't won the contest, but that the female had allowed her a dignified way out. Mary Alice mentally revised her estimation of the female's age. She'd assumed she was close to the age she appeared as when human, but there was a maturity to her wolf that she hadn't seen very often in her work.

The wolf gave Mary Alice a respectful berth and stopped in front of the door, looking back at her. When Mary Alice made no move to join her, the wolf tilted her head and looked up at the bar, then back at her. She expelled air through her nostrils in a whuff that couldn't have been anything but impatience.

Mary Alice realized the female wanted into the box. She shook her head to clear her distraction and pulled the key from around her neck. It took short work to open the locks and pull the bar off the door. She opened it enough for the wolf to get through, but no wider. She peeked her head around the corner in time to catch the wolf curling up around her sister.

A beep from her watch reminded her it was time to reset the ankle bracelet. The female seemed to be complying so far, so Mary Alice would live up to her end of the bargain. She closed and locked the door before heading back over to the stairwell. The terminal from which she monitored and controlled the anklet was with her work gear on the first floor. It hadn't seemed prudent to leave it in close proximity to the female. Sure, it was secured by a bio-lock, but her severed hand would open it just as easily as if her hand was still attached to her wrist.

As long as everything continued as it had been, the female would stay in one piece.

CHAPTER SEVENTEEN

The next few days, they settled into a routine. It wasn't exactly comfortable, but the female seemed content to do what she could with Cassidy and she tried to stay out of her way. Not that Mary Alice could help but try and observe what was going on, but the female had been right. Her presence did seem to agitate her sister. With some regret, she kept her interaction with Cassidy to a minimum.

The occasional sign of hope did a lot to reassure her. Cassidy was now eating cooked food and Mary Alice would overhear occasional murmured snippets of conversation between her and the female from inside the metal box. They knew when she was close, however, and the conversation quickly dried up if she tried to eavesdrop. She asked once, what the female was telling her sister. She hadn't been prepared for a lecture she received as a result. The female disapproved mightily of the fact that she'd made no real effort to clue Cassidy in as to what was going on. After that, Mary Alice didn't ask. If the female wanted to give her sister werewolf history lessons, she wasn't going to argue, not if it got Cass through in one piece.

One thing the female insisted upon was giving Cassidy her own space. When Mary Alice tried to pin her down on why she wasn't spending all her time with her sister, she only received a vague answer about not wanting the wolves vying for dominance within Cassidy to be unduly influenced by her presence.

Mary Alice had tried to get a more concrete answer from her, but the female was adept at avoiding her prodding. Mostly, Mary Alice spent her days in the second floor studio, trying to keep herself calmed down to the point where Cassidy could tolerate her presence. The evenings she spent in her living quarters, carefully avoiding the female.

She was sitting on the couch, trying to get past the fourth chapter of her very battered copy of Stephen King's *The Stand* when the freight elevator groaned to life. The female was curled up in front of the couch in wolf form. Her head lifted and ears pricked up at the sudden noise. She liked to spend her time out of the box in Mary Alice's general vicinity. Mary Alice wasn't sure why, but the female's presence wasn't something she bore easily. She felt ill at ease with her. It was probably the guilt talking, but then why was she constantly thinking of golden eyes peering out from beneath a veil of blond hair?

"Get out of here." Mary Alice vaulted over the back of the couch without waiting to see if the female complied. The scrabble of toenails on concrete let her know she'd headed out of the room.

Mary Alice reached under the end table and detached the pistol she kept secured there. The .45 automatic was reassuring in her hand. The hollow-point rounds she kept in it would take out most supranormals that could attack her here.

Is it the furries? Did they track me down, finally? Maybe vamps. The gun wouldn't be enough to slow down a full-grown vampire. She could bring a newling to its knees with a few well-placed shots, but a vampire that had come into its own would barely notice the bullets.

She darted from the living room into the kitchen and slammed open a drawer. It was full of combat knives; her cooking knives lived in a wood block on the counter. She grabbed the biggest one she could get her hands on and rushed through the opening that passed for her front door.

By the sound of it, the elevator was passing the second floor, coming right up to the top without stopping. Mary Alice would be able to get the drop on somebody in only a few places in the third floor's vast echoing emptiness. She chose the space to the right of the elevator. It was probably the most obvious, but it also had the advantage of being the closest. The last thing she wanted was anyone to get too close to the metal box where Cassidy was being held. She'd built it to keep her sister from hurting herself, but now it held her, trapped and unable to flee.

Her palms prickled and sweat made her shift her grip on her weapons as she waited for the door to grind open. They clanged as they reached their widest point and she threw herself around the corner, pistol at the ready.

"What the hell, Malice?" Uncle Ralph's gruff tones barked at her from within the elevator's depths.

"What the hell, yourself." Mary Alice skidded to a stop just before the opening. "What are you doing here, Ralph?" She peered at him, and then slowly lowered the gun.

"You haven't answered your phone in days." He stepped out of the elevator and strode toward her living quarters. For all of his bulk, he moved pretty quickly.

Mary Alice darted forward, making sure to stay on his right side so he wouldn't veer off toward the area where Cassidy's box was concealed behind the temporary walls of her home. "I've been busy."

Uncle Ralph raised an eyebrow at her and Mary Alice tried not to blush. The excuse had been transparent when it came out of her mouth, and she knew it. "Well, I have."

"What could possibly be more important than tracking down those fur-freaks?" He stomped into her home, making a beeline for the kitchen. "If they continue to make my life difficult, you can bet I'm going to make yours impossible."

She paused at the doorway for a moment; then hurried to catch up with him. To the best of her knowledge, he'd never been in her home before, and yet he seemed to know the layout very well. Ralph puffed a little bit as he poured himself a glass of water.

"You have anything stronger?"

She shook her head.

There was a rustle of movement behind them and Mary Alice's stomach plummeted. The female was going to expose her. And why not? She'd been holding her captive for days now. There was no way she could expect any kind of loyalty from the beast, though she'd hoped the female would feel some responsibility toward Cassidy.

"So that's why you've been so busy." Approval dripped from Ralph's voice and Mary Alice turned her head.

The female stood in the doorway, clad only in a sheer T-shirt and a pair of Mary Alice's pajama pants. They hung low on her hips, accentuating their curves. As usual, it was chilly in the loft, which was perfectly illustrated by the female's nipples straining against the shirt's flimsy fabric. She rested her weight on one leg, watching the two of them for a second before languidly strolling into the kitchen.

"What's going on, baby?" The female snaked an arm around Mary Alice's waist and snuggled herself into her side.

The female's warmth and the way the pajamas molded every dip and curve of her ass derailed Mary Alice's thoughts. All she could think of was how well they fit together and how good it felt to be touching someone.

"Baby?" The word was whispered in her ear and Mary Alice shivered. Goose bumps broke out along her right side and cascaded over her skin.

"Um, yes?" She licked her lips nervously. This was awkward; she didn't even know the female's name. Uncle Ralph was staring at her expectantly and she was caught flatfooted.

"Oh, for crying out loud." The female's voice was slightly pouty. "I'm Ruri."

"Y-yes. This is my Uncle Ralph." Mary Alice wanted to slap the smirk off his face and she reflexively wound her arm around the female's waist to keep from swinging at him.

"It's good to meet you, Ruri." Ralph gave her a little half wave. "I'd greet you properly, but you're not exactly…" His hand sketched the outline of her curves in the air.

Mary Alice tightened her arm around Ruri's waist, and then stepped forward, hiding her from his prying eyes. "Now you know. It's time for you to go."

"Have a nice day, Ruri." Ralph leaned around Mary Alice to get one last look.

Mary Alice grabbed him by the elbow and dragged him out of the kitchen and through the front door.

"It's very nice that you've gone and gotten yourself a girlfriend, Malice." Gone was the irritating smirk. In its place was a penetrating gaze. "You still have work to do. Don't be so caught up with fucking her that you lose sight of the bigger picture. And whatever you do, she can't find out what you do."

"Thanks for the advice," Mary Alice snapped. "I've got it taken care of."

"Good. Then you won't mind emailing me your full report on all the events related to the North Side pack. I want it in my inbox tomorrow."

"No problem." Her voice was stony and she made no effort to soften it. Their relationship had always been contentious, but he was treading in some dangerous waters. He had no idea how close she was to telling him to fuck off. Him *and* Uncle Sam.

"That's a good girl." With stunning audacity, Ralph reached out and patted her on the cheek.

Mary Alice closed her eyes and leaned back. Ralph gave her another smirk and stepped onto the freight elevator. She stood in front of the door as it closed and listened as the ancient cables creaked and groaned their way to the first floor. She waited until she heard the front service door slam, then finally let herself relax, slumping and leaning against the wall next to the freight doors.

That was too close. She needed to get Cassidy taken care of, and soon. But first, she needed to get that report to Ralph and quell some of his suspicions. That would get him off her back for a while at least.

Ruri perched on the edge of one of the stools at the kitchen island. She'd heard every word of the conversation between Malice and her so-called uncle. If he was her uncle, then she was Malice's mother. It seemed impossible that the woman could even have a mother, but Cassidy had to have come from somewhere, so she supposed Malice must have as well.

A small smile played around her lips when she remembered the gooseflesh she'd raised when she whispered in Malice's ear. She was glad to know she could incite emotions in Malice other than rage.

Malice walked back into the room and stopped awkwardly at the threshold. Ruri looked at her steadily. She wasn't going to help her with this. Malice was the one who had kidnapped her. Let her do the heavy lifting in their conversations. Ruri's entire body warmed, and unbidden, she relived the feel of Malice's arm around her.

"Is your name really Ruri?" Malice's voice was hesitant, as if uncertain about how the question would be received.

"It really is." She smiled, showing more teeth than really necessary. "Surprised to find out the animal has a real person name?"

Malice's face fell, and Ruri realized it had been as open as she'd ever seen it. She kicked herself for missing that.

"It's okay," Ruri said. "I'm sorry, that was shitty."

Malice lifted one shoulder and let it fall. "So is kidnapping you and holding you here against your will."

"There is that."

"So can I call you that? Ruri, I mean."

"I guess so." It was Ruri's turn to shrug, though inside she was heartened. If Malice saw her as more than an animal, there was a better chance she would survive this nightmare with her hide intact.

"You can call me Mary."

Without her enhanced hearing, Ruri would have missed the whispered offer. "Mary? That's a…pretty name." There was no answer and Ruri flailed around for something else to say. Something was there, chemistry, a small spark, perhaps, and she didn't want to lose the tenuous connection. "It doesn't suit you."

She was rewarded with a crooked smile, half amusement, half something else she couldn't identify. Malice moved all the way into the room and took one of the stools across from her.

"It's my first name. Middle name's Alice. So, Malice. Get it?"

"I guess. Who stuck that one on you?"

"My platoon when I was in training. They thought Malice was funny because it didn't really fit me back then. Mary was a much better fit. But things change. Enough that it was issued to me as an official code name when the time came."

Ruri tilted her head, watching Malice closely. "So who was the asshole?"

Malice smiled. "That's certainly an appropriate description. He isn't really my uncle."

"Really?" Ruri let her mouth drop open in exaggerated surprise. She was rewarded by a tight grin. "He didn't smell anything like you. Your sister smells more like you, even with her…issues. Even with your issues." She delivered the last under her breath.

Malice gave no indication that she'd heard the final sentence. She simply looked to one side and sighed heavily. "Really. He's my handler. I get my assignments from him."

"So that's how it works? You get assigned which of us to kill based on the say-so of an overweight white guy who looks like every cop drama's stereotypical schlub detective? That's *very* reassuring."

"I don't know where he gets his intel. He reports to someone else, that's all I know about our command structure. It's highly compartmentalized."

Ruri opened her mouth to ask another question, but snapped it closed when Malice's cell phone rang. By the eye roll at the sound of the ringtone, she wasn't thrilled with whoever was calling her. She still answered the phone, however.

"Hi, Mom."

It took an effort of monumental proportions not to laugh out loud. Her lips quivered, but Ruri thought she'd done a pretty good job of keeping a disinterested look on her face. From the dirty look Malice shot her, she hadn't succeeded.

Malice turned away and spoke quietly into the phone. "I'm good. How are you?" She paused, listening to the answer on the other end. "I was surprised, too. I thought she was getting serious with that finance major, but then she up and leaves for a service trip to Honduras right after midterms? Hopefully she'll get some perspective and get it together."

That was interesting. Malice did a very good job of not letting on that anything out of the ordinary was going on in her home. It could have been any other day where she wasn't entertaining one wolven in the kitchen with another locked up in a box not thirty feet away. Did Malice's family not know anything about what she did? Unbidden, a small kernel of compassion for the Hunter bubbled up within her. What would it be like to keep a secret like that hidden from those she was closest to?

Ruri certainly didn't know. When she'd been turned all those years ago, she hadn't even tried to go home again. Flashing teeth and glowing eyes in dark woods filled her mind, driving out the sympathy she was feeling. She snatched her thoughts away from the memory, one that hadn't intruded on her in fifty years or more.

She'd stayed away from the family homestead. What had happened had been clear to her, and she certainly wasn't about to endanger her family if she too was going to become a wolf. Instead, she'd skulked alone in the woods until her first full moon. Prints in the snow had confirmed what she couldn't remember, and Ruri had known she could never go home again. Keeping her family safe was only half of it. The looks of disgust and fear on their faces if they'd ever found out the truth about her would have killed her.

"Let's wait until she comes home and ask her about it," Malice said to her mother. "Besides, I don't know what kind of phone service she'll have in the rainforest. I think we're going to have to wait to grill her." She listened again, face impassive. "Okay, Mom. Look, I need to go now."

The answer on the other end was excited enough for Ruri to make out the tone, though she didn't understand the words.

"Yes, I have someone over," Malice said, her voice raised in exasperation. "No, she isn't going to give you grandchildren." She cringed in response to something her mother said. "Yes, I'm sure. I have to go, Mom. Really. I love you and I'll talk to you later." She hung up the phone without waiting for an answer.

"So that was your mom?" Ruri asked, face bland.

"You know it was." The look Malice shot her was wicked. "Surprised to find out the big bad werewolf hunter has a mother?"

Ruri nodded, acknowledging Malice's point. "A little. Though it shouldn't come as too much surprise since you have a sister also."

The thawing that had begun between them cooled instantly. Ruri kicked herself for bringing up Cassidy. No sense in reminding the Hunter who she was. If she was going to survive this, Malice had to see her as an equal, not a monster. This wasn't the way. Time to change the subject. There was more than one way to end a hunt.

"So 'Uncle Ralph'? It's a command structure, is it?" Ruri watched the Hunter's face carefully. She didn't want to spook her, but she needed to know more about her and her strange profession. "What do you even do? It seems like five years ago, all the supras in the area started trotting your name out like you're some kind of boogeyman. 'Better be good or Malice will get you.'"

From the way Malice blinked, she was surprised. "They knew I was around that quick?"

"You made quite an impression, especially after you cleared out that nest of vamps who were running kids for tricks."

"That was my third month on the job." Malice smiled again, this time looking pleased with herself.

"So why are you out here?"

"I'm here because someone needs to take out your trash." The smile was gone and in its place was implacable resolve. "Like the trash who did that to Cassidy. You supras don't do very well at policing yourselves. You each have your little corner of the world and you don't care what the others do as long as they don't infringe on your territory." Malice slid off the stool and paced the length of the kitchen. "How many of you knew what those sick vamp freaks were doing with those kids, but none of you bothered to do anything about it? You think because you can do so much more than 'normal' humans can, you don't need to be held to the same standards of behavior. Someone has to protect humanity from your shit."

Ruri slouched down in the seat, unprepared for the storm she'd just unleashed. "We're not all like that."

"Aren't you?" Malice sneered at her and Ruri wondered if she realized how inhuman she looked right now. "Where were you when Cassidy was being mauled?"

"Where was I?" Ruri threw herself off the stool and into Malice's face. "I was probably in the basement of an abandoned house trying to heal and mourning the loss of *my* family."

"Your family? Which of them were your family? Don't you dare compare your loss to mine!"

"Loss, what loss? You've lost shit, Malice. You still have a sister, despite all your best efforts. They were *all* family. Every last one of them, even the ones who went with MacTavish. So don't come crying on my shoulder. You still have a chance. I don't. I'm alone."

Tears streamed down her face in scalding waves, and Ruri had to sit before her knees gave out. Her back slid down the side of the island until she hit the floor with a thud. She clenched her hands into fists just as claws burst through her fingertips. Her jaw ached and she inhaled a deep, shuddering breath, trying to get her wolf under control. The wolf paid her no mind, trying to shoulder its way out of her body. Canines sprouted and her mouth filled with iron and salt. Ruri whined, high and pained at the eruption of the teeth and the loss of her pack. The wolf twisted and snapped inside her, trying to get through the last of her barriers.

An arm settled hesitantly around Ruri's shoulders, quieting her wolf for a moment. She stiffened and Malice twitched her hand back. Panicking that she might withdraw altogether, Ruri grabbed her wrist and held it.

"Please," she said quietly. Malice hesitated for a moment longer before settling her arm again. Ruri was only too aware of Malice's body pressed against hers through the too-thin T-shirt. Trying to keep her mind off the disquieting feelings swirling inside her and kicking up a curl of traitorous heat in the pit of her stomach, Ruri greedily absorbed her warmth. She kept her hand on Malice's arm and pulled it more snugly around her. She was still crying, but it was different now. Pain shared was pain halved, her mother used to say. It was a saying she hadn't really understood until she'd been part of a pack. That was gone, and Malice most assuredly wasn't pack material, but for the moment it felt good to pretend.

CHAPTER EIGHTEEN

The contact wasn't unwelcome, but Mary Alice found herself unable to relax completely, though some part of her desperately wanted to. The only times she was this close to a supra were moments before dispatching one or her interactions with Carla. The latter didn't feel so bad, if she was to be completely honest with herself; sometimes they even felt really good. *That's not real*, she reminded herself harshly. Carla had the power to roll her mind, to make her feel things she didn't want to.

But this, what she had right now, this felt right. Ruri was offering something she hadn't realized she needed so much until it was right in front of her. It had been maybe a week since she'd discovered Cassidy in her apartment, but it felt like she had been laboring under the burden of her sister's attack for months.

She should have pulled her arm back, but the desperation in Ruri's eyes matched her own. Instead Mary Alice—Malice, destroyer of supras—held on to her as she cried softly.

Eventually the lycan's tears subsided into quiet sniffles. She seemed content to cuddle up against Mary Alice's side, secure in the shelter of her arms. However, now that she'd stopped crying, Mary Alice was getting twitchy.

"Ruri is a pretty name." The statement popped out without conscious thought. It was true, it was pretty and it suited the blond werewolf. On the surface it was innocuous enough, but there was an edge to the name. "Is it short for anything?"

"Not that I know of. My parents were from Iceland. I think one of my grandmothers was also called Ruri." She gave one final sniff and wiped her eyes on the back of her hand. "They wanted something that reminded them of the old country. While other settlers from Iceland called their kids more American-sounding names, my parents had other ideas."

"Settlers?"

"That's what I said. They were some of the first to come over and establish a farm on the frontier."

The frontier? Who even talked about the frontier anymore, unless they were talking about space? How old was Ruri, anyway? They'd been told lycans likely had prolonged life spans, though nothing like the near-immortality experienced by very lucky—or very ruthless—vamps. However, it had been offered as a theory rather than a known fact. Not surprisingly, lycans did poorly in captivity and tended to die when held for any period of time. The pressure of Cassidy's situation bore down on her all over again. She couldn't keep her in that box forever because she would waste away, but if Mary Alice let Cassidy out in the shape she was in, Malice would have to kill her.

"I've been in this country a very long time." Ruri shifted again, enough for Mary Alice to feel her breasts moving against her side. Another flash of heat sparked in her groin.

"I guess." She closed her eyes. This was not good, so not good. "How long is that, exactly?" The question was blurted out from a confused need to keep Ruri's barely clothed form from her mind while not letting go of her any sooner than she had to. Visions of her naked in Mary Alice's bed intruded no matter how hard she tried not to go there.

"Long enough." The openness was gone from her face. Ruri's eyes were opaque, like tiger's eye marbles. A ring of brilliant gold sprang to life around the center of her irises.

Mary Alice watched, fascinated as the gold bled to consume Ruri's iris. She'd never seen a lycan's eyes change in quite that way. There had been a time or two when she'd ambushed one and their eyes had shifted in the space between moments, but this was a slow bleed.

"If you're not going to make a move, then I will."

Mary Alice blinked. The hunger in Ruri's voice surprised her. Her response surprised her almost as much. She tightened her arms, pulling Ruri to her, and stared into her beautiful molten gold eyes. "I...can't." Shame flooded her. How could she even contemplate sleeping with a supra?

What about Carla? a traitorous voice whispered from the corner of her mind. *Admit it, you wouldn't mind if she tumbled you onto your back and fucked you sideways.*

That's different, she shot back. Carla had mind powers, Ruri didn't. There was no explanation for what she felt now. It was wrong. Worse than wrong.

But why? Surely there were worse things, like taking someone's sister, penning her up and experimenting upon her until she died. "Like I would ever." Mary Alice sneered at the female and let her go, pushing her away as she did.

"Come on, Mary, you need this as much as I do. Let go of yourself for a little bit. You'll feel better. I'll feel better. What's wrong with that?"

Stung by the accuracy of her comment, Mary Alice stood up. Ruri had to scramble to keep from being dumped on the floor.

"Don't flatter yourself. I have better things to do than spend my time whoring around with a mongrel." She spun on her heel and headed for the door.

"Clearly," Ruri yelled at her back. "Which is why you smell like you need a good fuck right here and now."

Mary Alice raised her hand behind her and proudly saluted the lycan with her middle finger. She held it until she was through the doorway and down the hall. There was no sound of pursuit, but she still broke into a jog, then to a run. She took the stairs three at a time and burst through the door into her studio. With a heave that would have sent a lighter door through its frame, she slammed the metal door. The resounding clang echoed hollowly through the stairwell.

She leaned back against the door with a frustrated shriek, almost a howl. Why did the damn wolf have to be so right? She needed to be touched, to touch, to let someone else inside her walls for long enough to be held by something other than her own sheer force of will. A nice uncomplicated fucking would have done the trick, and if Ruri had been anything other than the lycan she was holding captive, she would have taken her up on it.

In fact, she would have her fingers buried deep in the woman's pussy right now. Her center clenched in response at the thought and she let out a strangled whimper. She could feel the wetness between her thighs demanding to be satisfied. With feverish haste, she ripped open the front of her pants and gasped with relief when her fingertips skated through slick folds to graze the tip of her clit.

She clenched her eyes shut against the sensation shooting through her core, and then opened them just as quickly. Golden eyes held hers. *There's no way I'm attracted to one of them.* Mary Alice was glad she hadn't said the words aloud to hear how hollow they sounded. How could she be feeling this way for a monster? The female was something who would as soon tear out her throat as look at her; that was what she'd always been trained to believe. Not far below the surface of each supra was a ravening beast, worse than an animal. So far all she'd seen below Ruri's surface was a woman who'd had her family torn from her and was determined to rebuild it.

Her fingers had stilled and she drew them over herself again, chasing release. The whimper that came from her throat was nothing compared to what she was sure Ruri could have pulled from her.

"Goddamn...fucking...human!" Ruri tasted blood in her mouth. Her gums were shifting as the teeth within them lengthened. What had gone wrong? Malice had smelled of arousal, warm and moist. Ruri's wolf paced restlessly beneath her skin. She needed to be calmed, and sex would have been a quick way to take the edge off. The wolf liked Malice, saw something in her that reminded her of them. There was something wolf-like in the way Malice protected her sister at all costs. Her pack was small, but she held it as surely as any Alpha Ruri had ever met.

When she'd propositioned the Hunter, the scent of arousal swirling between them had swelled until she had to stop herself from panting, to draw it over her tongue and into her nasal passages. It had been fine until the spike of fear had shot through Malice's scent, acrid and sharp. Ruri wrinkled her nose at the memory of the smell. The wolf's pacing increased, her fur rubbing spikily on the underside of Ruri's skin. She wanted to be let out, but Ruri wasn't about to allow that to happen, not when she wasn't sure what the wolf would do.

She leaned her head back and rested it on the back of the worn couch. Staring sightlessly up at the exposed girders of the ceiling far above her head, Ruri wondered what the fear was in response to. The woman had an explosive device shackled to her ankle, for crying out loud. If anyone had a right to be frightened, it was Ruri. And yet, she couldn't quite bring herself to fear Malice. Mary Alice. Ruri snickered.

The Hunter's real name was unexpected. It was feminine and…pretty. The farm girls she'd known as a child had similar names. Malice was anything but a farm girl. She was impressive to be certain, but scary?

Ruri shook her head. The woman would blow off her foot if she wasn't useful to her. How long would she survive as a lone wolf with three legs? Not long, there was no question. And yet, Malice was diligent about making sure she didn't get close to missing the deadline for resetting the device. Surely she wouldn't let it go off if Ruri did everything she could for the sister, even if it didn't work out.

Certainly, she wasn't going to risk losing her limb, and throwing that odious man off their scent had been part of that. If Malice got herself injured or killed and couldn't deactivate the device, Ruri would also pay. The fear that had threaded through Mary Alice's attraction to her had been nothing compared to the terror that had obliterated all other scents when the lift had started up.

The ache in her gums subsided, replaced by the need to move around and stretch her legs. There was no way she could leave the building. What she really needed was a run and a kill, since it seemed sex was currently out of the question. While she didn't think Malice would really blow her leg off, she wasn't prepared to test it by leaving.

At least this was something she could do herself. She slipped a hand down the front of the loose pants and smiled bitterly. She was dressed for the activity.

The space between her thighs was so hot she wondered that she hadn't already combusted. Ruri clamped her legs together, rocking against her hand. The delicious friction against her clit was good, but not nearly enough. With her other hand, Ruri roughly squeezed one erect nipple through the sheer fabric of Mary Alice's shirt. She bit her lip at the pain and the answering bolt of pleasure in her belly.

"Dammit, Malice," Ruri whispered. Her eyes drifted shut and she could see the human's sober face behind her eyelids. It didn't take much to imagine Mary Alice with her eyes intent on her, dark with pleasure. The wicked look she'd given her earlier had promised another side to the Hunter, one that could be very fun to explore. "Take me, Mary," she breathed.

She slipped first one finger, then another inside of herself. The pressure had built to levels impossible to deny. Sweat trickled between her breasts and she tweaked then flicked her nipple, gritting her teeth at the delicious combination of discomfort and euphoria. Her canal was slick and her fingertips slid over that rough spot at the front, once, twice, again and again.

"God, yes!" Her hips jerked of their own volition, driving her fingers deeper inside her until they could go no further. "Malice!" She came in a rush of fluid around her fingers, howling her captor's name at the ceiling.

She imagined Malice's arms pulling her close, but phantom arms were as close as she would ever get to being held by the Hunter. Sated for the moment, her wolf slumbered, curled comfortably around her center, and Ruri sobbed for the bonds she couldn't build.

"Ruri, oh god, Ruri!" Mary Alice hissed the words through clenched teeth, her back braced against the door and her knees locked to stay upright. She threw her head back, barely feeling it when it thunked solidly into the unyielding metal surface. The fingers flying over her clit paused for a second before redoubling their efforts.

She had her eyes tightly shut, despite—or maybe because of—the golden eyes that watched from behind her eyelids. They blazed brighter and brighter as she got closer to the brink of orgasm. Finally, when she came in a shout of triumph, they seared her vision, so much so that she expected to see the afterimage when she slowly came back to reality and opened them.

This wasn't where she'd started out. Or it wasn't the same position she'd started out in. Her knees must have given out when she came and she hadn't even noticed. She sat in a heap, back against the door. Wondering at the strength of the orgasm, Mary Alice stretched slowly. She was relaxed in a way she hadn't been in quite some time.

She froze. Upstairs, Ruri was howling her name in anger.

CHAPTER NINETEEN

Cassidy shifted in her box. She burrowed into the scraps of cloth in the corner. Unhappiness filled every corner of the place, but for once it wasn't all hers. Her sister and the new one were miserable. The angular scents of anger and fear made her nose wrinkle and she sneezed.

How could she even smell those things? Emotions were something you felt and could maybe pick out on someone else's face and in their body language. The smells were so vivid, her other senses seemed almost dull by comparison. They had colors and texture, which confused her because she couldn't see them, and yet there they were. Anger was all oranges and reds swirling together unpredictably, never stopping, never slowing. Fear was different. It smelled just as spiky and seemed red, but darker. It moved, but not like anger. It almost stuttered along, barely shifting, then changing between one moment and the next.

Beneath it all was one she couldn't identify as easily. It was mellow and low, lush and full in shades of green and blue. She had to taste that one for a while before identifying it. The anger and fear got in the way. When she figured it out, she wanted to chuckle but couldn't remember how. Mary or the new one was turned on, or they both were.

Mary Alice had sex, Cassidy knew that, but she never really thought about it. The thought was strange and not one she wanted to contemplate too closely. It was almost as bad as thinking about her mom making love. She shuddered once under her blanket of torn cloth, then again for real when the fabric brushed against skin that felt strange naked. There should be something over it, but not those clothes. They restricted her, kept her from moving freely.

The new one—now Cassidy could envision her having sex. The urge to present herself to her was growing stronger as the days went by, though sometimes she dreamed of the other presenting herself to her. Cassidy didn't know what was going on. She'd had the occasional female friend that she'd fooled around with, but she certainly wasn't the staunch lesbian her sister was. For the most part, she preferred men. Women were fine, fun even, but usually what she wanted was to be taken by a man. And yet here she was, contemplating taking a woman.

The scent of arousal was getting stronger, slowly overtaking the smell of anger. Cassidy whimpered, the feelings of lust she was feeling intensified and she could do nothing about them. She didn't dare touch herself, not with fingers tipped with wicked claws. Bringing herself to release wouldn't satisfy the relentless need she felt burning within her anyway.

Frustration burst from her in a scream that went on and on. Gooseflesh rippled across her skin and muscles writhed beneath, but nothing happened. She was so tired of being on the edge. Either way she went, it needed to stop.

Her throat felt shredded and Cassidy realized she was still screaming. She closed her mouth, swallowing the scream, drowning it inside herself once again.

On the heels of her name, so close that it almost overlapped it, Mary Alice became aware of another scream. This one lingered, and it couldn't possibly be Ruri.

"Cassidy." She whirled and ripped the door open in one motion. The stairs flew by under her feet and she hit the door at the top of the stairs at a full sprint with her hand held out. It sprang open from the stiff-arm and slammed into the wall. Bits of masonry rained down and she dimly realized the handle had likely split the bricks behind it. The steel door was warped where she'd hit it, but that wasn't important. What was important was getting to her sister.

She skidded to a stop in front of the box. The door was open. The locks had been ripped off it and were in scattered pieces on the floor.

The door was still intact and leaned crazily away from the opening, still partially attached to the hinge and bolt that had held it in place.

Ruri was down on her knees in the far corner with Cassidy wrapped up in her arms. Thankfully, she wasn't screaming any longer. Mary Alice had heard enough of Cassidy's howls to last her a lifetime. Her sister's arms were wrapped around herself and Mary Alice could see where her nails had torn the flesh of her shoulders. Those same shoulders shook with heaving sobs.

Her arrival hadn't been subtle. Ruri looked back over her shoulder. She shook her head and tipped it away, indicating Mary Alice should leave. There was no way that was going to happen, but maybe she didn't need to loom quite so dramatically in the entrance.

She lifted the door and tried to swing it closed quietly. Whatever Ruri had done to get through it had bent it and it no longer closed completely. One hasp had been torn off its hinge and lay ten feet away, the padlock still attached to it. How would she lock her sister in now? How would she keep her safe?

Why couldn't she help Cassidy?

There was no way she would allow Ruri to cut her out of taking care of her sister. At a loss for what else to do, Mary Alice carried a wooden chair over from the kitchen and dropped into it, her eyes on the gap where the door didn't quite meet up with the box. She settled in to watch for as long as she needed to.

Ruri knew very well Malice still lurked just beyond the door. She hadn't meant to upset her, but the presence of both of them seemed to be upsetting Cassidy. The poor not-quite-wolven trembled in her arms, her emotions a quivering knot of smells that tickled Ruri's nose. She was in quite the state. Not unexpectedly given her distress, her wolven features had come to the fore. Sharp teeth protruded from her gums, matching the sharpness of the nails from her fingertips. Her body was covered with a sparse coat of what could generously be described as fur. It varied greatly in coverage. Some places it was almost nonexistent and in others, especially around the back of her neck, genitals, and the base of her spine it was almost opaque. The fur shifted in color from white through shades of gray and brown. In a couple of patches it was a dark charcoal that was nearly black. Her eyes had changed also, this time to emerald green.

The scream had verged on a howl and Ruri wondered if Cassidy was trying to find her packmates. She had none; the closest she had was her sister.

There was a sharp pain on her shoulder, and Ruri looked down to find it bleeding slightly and Cassidy watching her with those emerald eyes. She grinned up at her. *You little…* Cassidy had just nipped her.

Ruri leaned forward and clashed her teeth together right in front of Cassidy's face. The snap was loud enough to reverberate in the small space and Cassidy shrank back, turning her face away. *Good.* There was no way she was going to let a sick wolven play dominance games with her. If she'd made it through the transformation in a normal pack, Cassidy would have started at the bottom of that pack's dominance structure. Until she figured out what she was about, she would stay there. It was usually impossible to tell how dominant a wolven was until after the transition was complete and the new wolf had figured out which end was up, so to speak. It took a while to learn the limits of the new body.

Ruri smiled. She had chafed at being counted among her pack's lowest when she first turned. Many of the scars along her back and flanks had come from that period. Each one had been a lesson, a painful and humiliating one, but one she'd taken to heart. She'd quickly won her way off the bottom rung, but it had taken her decades to reach the level of Beta. Cassidy would have to navigate her own path through the hierarchy of whichever pack took her in.

A soft "oof" in her ear clued her in to the fact that she'd tightened her hold around Cassidy. Ruri loosened up without letting go. Cassidy would go on her way soon enough, but it didn't have to be now. It couldn't be now, not when she had yet to go through a full transformation.

Slowly, Cassidy's agitation ebbed. Her anxiety melted away and she fell into an exhausted slumber. Her hands and ears twitched in whatever dreamscape she ran through. Ruri envied her, in some ways. For a moment she considered curling up around the troubled wolven, but decided against it. She had to face Malice sometime. With deliberate care, she eased herself out from Cassidy's grasp. Cassidy whined slightly and sniffed the air as if looking for her but didn't wake.

The door to the box was mostly closed but not latched. It would take a lot of work for the box to lock again, Ruri had seen to that. Perhaps she'd used a little more force than truly necessary to rip the hasp off the door, but in that moment all her frustration had boiled over at once. Frustration at Malice's refusal, anger at being trapped like an animal, rage at what happened to her pack. Finally it had a focus, and the hasp hadn't stood a chance. Neither had the door.

She lifted it carefully to avoid waking Cassidy. Ten feet in front of the door, arranged in a sulky pose on a chair from the kitchen, was Malice. The human's anger no longer really worried Ruri, though she wasn't sure exactly why. Something had changed, and she stood for a long while as she contemplated her captor.

"What happened?" Malice asked, her voice pitched barely loud enough to carry to her ears.

Ruri held a finger to her lips and smiled wryly inside at the flicker of irritation that skittered across Malice's face. Taking care not to let any of her amusement show, she turned with exaggerated caution and closed the door to the box.

Malice sat back and pulled her ankle over her knee before crossing her arms and settling further into the chair. She never broke eye contact with Ruri.

That was what had changed. Malice was scared of her. She was trying a little too hard to appear unconcerned, but Ruri knew better. Fear skittered along beneath a layer of sex and arousal. What had Malice been up to? The same thing she had, it seemed. Ruri sashayed forward, her hips rolling provocatively before stopping in front of Malice. She propped her hand on one hip and stared back at the Hunter.

The human looked away first, another spike of fear streaking through her scent.

"Hell if I know." Taking pity at the stricken look in Malice's eyes, Ruri leaned forward and took her hand, pulling her out of the chair in one yank.

Instead of flying into her arms as she'd intended, Malice stopped suddenly, like she'd somehow doubled her gravity. "We can't leave her unsecured."

"She's asleep. She'll be fine for a few moments." Ruri walked away, toward the living room, confident Malice would follow.

"Did you really have to bust down the door?"

The look Ruri shot over her shoulder was one of intentionally mild reproof, but Malice still flushed an embarrassed red.

"No keys, remember?"

"Yeah, I know. I'll give you a key when I fix it."

"I don't think we have that much time." Ruri perched on the arm of the sofa. She looked out the large windows that dominated most of the far wall. The glass in them was frosted, but one was tilted open and she could see outside. It was a crisp autumn day from the blue of the sky and the chill of the air inside the large room. She didn't have to watch Malice to know she was upset. Fear and shame trickled into her nostrils again, and she wondered if she would ever smell happiness from the woman.

"What do you mean?" Malice asked quietly.

"She's starting to go into heat." At Malice's blank stare, Ruri released a loud sigh. "Your government doesn't know nearly as much as it thinks it does. We wolven, the women I mean, go into heat. It's a period of fertility, sort of the opposite of your period."

"So?"

"So she's going to go into it in a couple of days, three or four at the most. If we can't get her to shift before then, we'll probably lose her. The wolves fighting within her will try to come forth at the same time to mate. The call will be undeniable, and if one hasn't come out on top…" She trailed off, not sure how to continue. She'd only heard stories of two-sire wolven; she'd never seen one herself. No one talked about what happened when the change went bad. They just mourned the never-wolven and moved on. One thing the stories did agree on was that they didn't have much time, and the onset of the first heat in females seemed to be a major milestone that couldn't be missed, second only to the first full moon.

"Then we delay the heat. Surely you know how to do that."

"And then? The full moon is a week away. Even if I could stop her heat, which I can't, the moon will force her."

The shame melted out of Malice to be replaced by exhaustion. She slumped against the chair back and stared at the ceiling, though Ruri doubted she really saw it. "So we're just giving up?"

"I didn't say that. All I'm saying is we're running out of time. She's gotten better than where she was when you first brought me here, but she's still stuck. I'm going to have to try some more…drastic methods."

"Drastic." It wasn't a question. "I don't like the sound of that. Drastic always has the possibility of going off the rails."

"It's a possibility, yes." Ruri wasn't going to deny that, but she had as much to lose here as Malice did. Cassidy was starting to feel, if not like pack, like something close to it. She carefully didn't examine what her relationship with Malice felt like. "But possibility means it isn't graven in stone. If we don't try we will probably lose her when she hits her heat. If she manages to survive that"—Ruri held up her hand when Malice perked up at the qualifier—"which would be nothing short of a miracle, then we *will* lose her at the full moon."

Malice sat back in the chair in defeat. "What are you thinking?"

"I want to take her out on a run."

CHAPTER TWENTY

"A run?" Mary Alice stared at the werewolf. She realized her mouth was hanging open and closed it with a snap. "Are you insane? There's no way that is ever going to happen." The last thing she needed was to expose Cassidy to the outside world before she learned to control herself. Not to mention, the explosive anklet would need to be modified.

"It's not crazy," Ruri said with quiet dignity. "We need to pull one wolf out before Cassidy either goes into heat or deals with the pull of the full moon. To do that, we need something that will convince the wolves fighting each other within her to go all in. When one of them comes to the fore, then that's the one who will complete the transformation."

There it was again. This wasn't the first time Ruri had referred to the wolf half of the werewolf as if it was a separate entity. Her training hadn't included much discussion of lycan psychology; it had focused almost entirely on physiology. Mary Alice knew dozens of ways to take a lycan down, but she didn't know what made them tick. It wasn't anything she'd seen as a shortcoming until Cassidy's attack. Now she wished she knew more about them in general and Ruri in particular. Ruri? No, she'd meant Cassidy.

"You make it sound like you aren't the wolf," Mary Alice said when she realized the silence had gone on too long. "How can you be separate from the wolf? It's not like you go somewhere when you shift to wolf form."

"It's true, I don't." Ruri smiled crookedly at her. Mary Alice hadn't noticed before how one side of her mouth pulled a smidge higher than the other. Of course, she hadn't seen Ruri smile a whole lot either. It was adorable and Mary Alice found herself wishing she could see it more frequently.

Stop that, she said to herself. Then aloud: "What do you mean?"

"It's hard to explain. I am the wolf and she is me. We're the same, but we aren't." She shrugged, her blond hair bouncing slightly around her shoulders. "I'm not even sure if everyone experiences it the same way, but most of the wolven I know talk about their wolf sides as separate from their human sides. I can feel her in me when I'm human, just as I'm sure she feels me. I think part of it is that we're so different, our human and wolven halves."

"I still don't understand." It sounded like Ruri experienced some sort of multiple personality-type thing. She cursed herself again for her lack of understanding about general psychology. None of this made sense and she didn't have the background or the vocabulary to get a decent handle on it.

"We have different priorities. When I'm in full wolf form, everything is so simple. I only have a few things to concentrate on and none of the complications of human life. The wolf sees things in very stark terms and she doesn't tend to dwell. You know what being human is like." There was that crooked smirk again. "It's full of complications and even when you think you know what's going on, you second-guess it. Things come back to gnaw on the back of your brain, even if it's something that happened years ago. The wolf lets all of that go. For me, anyway, it's easier to think of her and her instincts as a separate part of my personality, though she isn't, not really."

"So Cassidy will be like that?"

"Most wolven I've known are like that. The problem is Cassidy has five different wolves howling at her right now, each one with a different primal urge or directive to compete for her attention."

"Wow. I thought maybe if she…" Mary Alice couldn't finish the sentence. If what Ruri was saying was true, then her assumptions had been totally off base. Not only off base, but dangerous, both to Cassidy and to the public.

"Maybe if she tried really hard she'd be able to figure things out through sheer force of will?" Ruri's smile was bitter. "She probably thinks the same thing, or she did. The hardest part of becoming wolven, of going through that first transformation, is realizing you can't force the wolf. You have to let go and give in. The wolf moves through you and you are the wolf, but you can't force it to do anything, not really.

"Did you know that a lot of new wolven can hold it together for a while after they get infected? Eventually they start losing time as the wolf forces its way out. Those are the ones who probably won't make it. Either they lose themselves completely in the wolf and are never seen again in human form, or their minds can't handle it and they sort of shut down and waste away."

"And Cassidy's problems are different?"

"Hell yes, they are. She never had the option to ignore the wolf, not with five of them inside her howling at each other and her for dominance."

It had seemed to Mary Alice that Cassidy had been getting better over the past few days. She'd become less desperate and had calmed down, but Ruri's information cast that development in a terrifying new light. Despite her cautiously growing optimism, desperation boiled over within her again. It pushed at her, drove her to consider what she knew was beyond all common sense.

"We can't make this run happen during the day."

The look Ruri shot her was equal parts exasperation and irritation. "Really."

The flush that rose to fill her cheeks with heat was her own fault, and Mary Alice knew it. "Yes, really. I'm not going to let you bust this." The words were condescending, and she knew it, but she hated being embarrassed.

"Thanks for the concern. I wonder how we managed to survive so long without accidentally betraying ourselves to pitchfork-wielding mobs. It's so great to have you to keep me from making a terrible mistake."

Ruri's eyes sparked with irritation. Her hands were on her hips where she still sat perched on the sofa's arm. The embarrassment that had burned so strongly within her disappeared when Mary Alice realized how sexy the lycan looked when she was angry. Energy swirled around her, and though she was still skinny enough that Mary Alice was sure a stiff wind would blow her over, she suddenly wondered if she could actually take Ruri in a fight. Being presented with an equal made her mouth go dry and heat kindled again in her center.

"I'll think about it," Mary Alice said, pushing herself off the sofa. She had to get away from the lycan. The urge to reach out and slide her fingers through Ruri's hair was almost irresistible. Besides, there was still work to do. Uncle Ralph needed that report and wouldn't get off her back until she provided it. Protecting Cassidy required more than merely making sure her transformation happened. It would mean nothing if the world was waiting for her when she finally came out.

Ruri watched Malice's retreating back with disbelief. How could she up and leave in the middle of their conversation? She thought she'd finally made some progress with the human, and she just left. And after insulting her, no less. Who did Malice think she was?

The answer to that was clear, at least. Malice thought she was in charge, and while the damned device was on her ankle, she was. That wouldn't last forever. Ruri wondered if Malice had considered what might happen after. Would she really go through with allowing the bracelet to detonate and take Ruri's leg if Cassidy didn't survive? She still didn't think so, but Malice seemed more erratic. That could be to her advantage, potentially. Erratic meant mistakes, but the wrong mistake meant Ruri would be short a leg. On the other hand, it might mean Ruri being able to win her way free.

And if Cassidy did survive; what then? Malice hadn't realized yet that Cassidy wouldn't be around whether she made it through the shift or not. Wolven didn't tend to stay with their human families, not when they were likely to be hunted down and slaughtered upon discovery. Malice already knew her sister's secret, so things might be different, but Ruri didn't think so. The bonds of other wolven held so much more tightly than those of human families; that was simply the way things were.

What would Malice do if Ruri managed to save Cassidy? Surely she didn't think the insult of caging a wolf would go unanswered. Her wolf shifted within her, mute agreement in the way she wrapped Ruri's core self with soft fur and reassurance.

Yet, before Malice had left, she could have sworn the woman's pupils had widened in what she was almost certain was arousal. It was hard to tell from her scent, given the anger that had poured off her after she'd made the asinine statement about going on the run at night. What right did Malice have to be angry over her response? She was the one who'd been insulted.

Strangely, the wolf hadn't reacted to the change in emotion. Usually, that part of her was ready to take on any show of aggression. Her wolf didn't tolerate such things; it was part of what had made her so successful at the pack's higher levels. Malice didn't seem to elicit the usual reactions from the wolf, however. If anything, what she felt from the wolf in regard to Malice was rough affection.

Even now, when the wolf agreed that Malice needed to pay for their imprisonment, Ruri didn't get the feeling that she wanted to kill the human. She needed to be punished, certainly, but nothing permanent. Perhaps a strong nip to the ears and a gentler one at the flank. Ruri swallowed hard at the phantom sensation of closing her teeth around the nape of Malice's neck. It was unmistakable; she could almost feel warm skin between her teeth.

This simply would not do. What Ruri needed was a nice long run with a kill at the end of it. Apparently, she needed fresh air in her nostrils and hot blood on her tongue almost as much as Cassidy did.

Some air would do her a lot of good, but the anklet was set to go off as soon as she left the building, or so she'd been told. Maybe she could get to the roof. First things first, however. It was time to rattle Malice's cage a little harder.

A quick glance inside the box let her know that Cassidy still slept soundly. Ruri knew Malice had left the floor, but she hadn't been paying attention to see if she was in her sculpting studio downstairs. She couldn't hear any of the sounds she'd come to associate with Malice's sculpting work—not the partially muffled clangs as she hammered metal into place nor the squeal of a grinder. Usually she could hear something, but not this time. Still, Ruri stuck her head in the second floor. The only sign of Malice was the almost dissipated cloud of pheromones by the door. Malice had apparently brought herself to orgasm there just as Ruri had been doing the same one floor above.

She shook her head. They were obviously on the same page, so why didn't the Hunter accept her advances? Surely that would have been better than masturbating alone on the cold concrete floor.

Ruri had never been to the first floor, but that was all that was left, aside from the roof. She found Malice in a fenced-in enclosure. There were a few of them down there, but this one had a laptop and some filing cabinets. Malice sat hunched over the laptop, clicking away at the keys. She stopped to stare off into space every now and again. Content to watch her, Ruri stood at the enclosure's gate. The woman's muscles rippled under her skin even when all she did was type. She was certainly easy enough on the eyes. Her wolf rippled under her skin in agreement and urged her closer, close enough to smell her skin and feel her warmth. Ruri resisted the urge to bathe in Malice's presence.

"Do you want something, or are you going to hang around all day?" Malice never looked at her.

Ruri was struck all over again by how well developed Malice's senses were. She hadn't been trying to sneak up, but she knew she moved quietly. In fact, she had to work to be heard; her default mode was silent.

"I'm going to head up to the roof," Ruri said. "I need some air."

"I don't recall agreeing to that." Malice still didn't look up from her computer screen.

"I don't recall asking." Ruri knew it was juvenile to imitate Malice's tone, but she couldn't help herself. Something about the woman made her push back. Ruri would not—could not—look weak in front of her.

"You're supposed to be taking care of Cassidy. We have a deal, remember?"

"Is that what you call it? A deal?" Ruri's voice rose with her incredulity at Malice's characterization of their situation. Her wolf paced within her, no longer content to bask in the human's presence. Reminded of their captivity, she wanted out. Ruri shoved her down. "You ambushed me, drugged me and dragged me here where you threaten me physically to keep me from leaving, and that's a deal?"

The look Malice snuck over her shoulder was guilty, but only for a moment. Irritation replaced it so quickly that if Ruri hadn't smelled her shame, she wouldn't have believed it was there.

"I need to get this work done to keep Uncle Ralph off my back and you need to watch Cassidy."

"You watch Cassidy. Drag the blasted laptop up with you and get your work done. She's in that stinking box where you've left her for days. If she wakes up, maybe you should try talking to her. Explain why her own sister is caging her."

"It's for her own good."

"So tell her that. Have you even tried explaining the situation to her?"

"I tried back when she first woke up. It didn't seem to matter."

"She's calmer now and might actually be able to process what you're talking about. I'll be down in a while. You need me to get this air as much as I need me to." It was true, talking to Malice had ramped her agitation through the roof all over again. She needed to present a calm front to Cassidy, not anything resembling aggression for the wolves within to see as a threat to attack.

"But—"

Ruri looked her in the eye and let some of the wolf out. Her eyes would have bled golden, and she could hear Malice's intake of breath at the change. The muscles in her jaw ached as they hovered on the edge of shifting, though it wasn't exactly unpleasant. She clenched her teeth, dancing right on the edge of starting the change.

When she left the room, Malice said nothing. Ruri made her way past the other enclosures without really wondering what was in them. There would be time enough to look around later. For now she had to get up where the air moved, where new scents could clean out the rank stench of anger, fear and despair that infected her nostrils. She would be all right up on the roof. If there had been a chance that the device would go off, Malice wouldn't have made her objection about permission.

Ruri broke into a jog up the stairs. She couldn't wait to get out from under Malice's roof.

CHAPTER TWENTY-ONE

The moon was fuller than Mary Alice would have liked. It had waxed over halfway and she silently cursed it. Not only was each slice counting down to Cassidy's painful death, but it was lighter in the park than she would have preferred. Aside from that, Ruri's choice had been a good one. Pulaski Woods was vast and would be deserted at this time of night.

Her truck idled in front of the turnoff from the main path, with Ruri and Cassidy ensconced in the cab. Ruri had said that the chain across the service road should be easy to shift off the concrete post to which it was attached. Mary Alice eyed it doubtfully; it seemed pretty secure, though one side seemed like it might have some give.

She gave the chain an experimental tug, trying to move it out of the metal clip holding it in place. There was a gap at the top where the links might fit through it, if she could get the right combination of angle and force applied.

For a few minutes she struggled, working the chain higher millimeter by millimeter.

"Here." Ruri grasped the chain on either side of her hands. With a swift jerk and a tortured squeal, the stuck link popped free.

"I could have gotten that." Mary Alice covered up the surge of adrenaline that had coursed through her body at the unexpected contact.

"Clearly." Ruri's eyes caught the moonlight and flashed golden at her.

Mary Alice could tell she was being laughed at. She had a brief mental flash of a wolf, lips stretched in silent laughter, tongue lolling out of its mouth. "You're supposed to be watching Cassidy."

"Relax, she's still there. The bit of wolfsbane I gave her is taking the edge off. She'll be ready to go soon enough, though. Maybe we should get a move on." Her words might have been breezy, but tension lurked in her voice. She turned sharply on her heel and marched back to the truck, not waiting for an answer.

Mary Alice followed in her wake, fuming as she always seemed to after talking to Ruri lately. *How does she keep getting the last word on me?* Every time she thought she'd sewed up the conversation, Ruri would get in one final dig. And she was always watching, weighing her. It was enough to drive someone crazy.

"What?" Mary Alice asked. She could have sworn Ruri had watched her all the way to the truck. The lycan must have eyes in the back of her head to pull that one off. She was tired of being observed.

"We'll need to drive on a fair way. I'll tell you when to turn. How well can you see in the dark?"

"Well enough."

"Good, you'll want to keep the headlights off, at least until we're under the trees. There probably won't be any cops on patrol, but we don't want some helicopter crew on a flyby to find us out."

"Yes, ma'am." The bite in her tone was intentional. Once again, it failed to elicit the response she hoped for. The laughing wolf filled her mind again. Mary Alice put the truck in gear and peeled away with more force than necessary.

They sped past open grassy lawns, but she was forced to slow down when they reached the trees. The paved road meandered back and forth along the bottom of a bluff as the trees got thicker and thicker around them. Finally, she had to turn on the running lights to make out the road's twists and turns.

"So soon?" Ruri murmured from next to her.

She could have done without having Ruri crammed right up against her. The lycan's constant touch and the warmth of her presence were distracting in the extreme. Almost as addling was her smell. The earthiness and hint of spice she'd come to associate with Ruri filled her nose. She'd lobbied to have Cassidy between them on the truck's bench seat, but Ruri had pointed out that an out-of-control almost-lycan at her elbow might not be the best thing for her driving. If Cassidy lost it on the drive, Ruri would have the best chance of getting her under control. Not that Cassidy seemed like much of a threat. The most movement she'd made so far had been to pluck at her sweatpants as if unsure what they were for. She seemed extremely out of it, and Mary Alice wondered exactly what Ruri thought she would accomplish tonight.

"If you want me to drive into a tree, you'll keep up the comments," Mary Alice muttered back.

Ruri said nothing in return; her undivided attention seemed to be on their surroundings. The longer they went without her promised turnoff, the more nervous Mary Alice became. She kept glancing at every gap in the bushes that crowded the road, bare branches reaching toward them in the dim illumination of the running lights. There was nothing every time. She forced herself to relax with little success. Minutes ticked slowly by and the road kept winding in front of them. Cassidy had started moving more purposefully, and she worried about what might happen if the herb wore off before they got out of the truck.

"Here." Ruri sat up and pointed to a small gap in the trees that was coming up much too fast.

The turnoff was overgrown and she had to hit the brakes harder than she would have liked. She still had to throw the truck in reverse to get far enough back to make the turn. Cassidy shifted next to Ruri and reached for the door.

"It's okay, honey," Ruri said, rubbing Cassidy's thigh in small circles.

Mary Alice hoped it was soothing, though it didn't seem to be. Cassidy's eyes glowed emerald green in the darkness of the cab. It couldn't be much longer now.

The road sloped upward, taking them up a switchback so densely forested that branches scratched along either side of the truck. The first sounds of scratching made Mary Alice jump, and she glanced over at her sister, worried she was about to claw her way out. It sounded too much like nails on metal for her own peace of mind. Satisfied that it was only the surrounding trees, Mary Alice coaxed as much speed out of the truck as she comfortably could. The running lights were no longer up to the job, and she switched on the headlights. Branches, to which a few leaves still desperately clung, cast crazy shadows upon the gravel and grass in front of them, creating a constant sense of movement and chaos.

"Stop here," Ruri finally said.

She was so tense that she started a bit when the lycan spoke. It was not a moment too soon as far as she was concerned. Cassidy's nails had lengthened, and it was hard to tell in the dark, but there seemed to be fur on the back of her hands.

"It's about time." She set the parking brake and looked over at Ruri, who stared back at her.

"Get out and get our door open." The rending of cloth accompanied Ruri's hissed orders. Cassidy was tearing the pants off her legs with one hand, and Ruri had her hand clamped around the other arm.

There was no time to argue about her tone. Mary Alice threw herself out the door and dashed around the front of the truck. When she opened the far door, Cassidy tumbled out and caught herself on all fours. She raised her head to drink in the air. Ruri piled out behind her and Cassidy looked back. The ruined pants were little more than a belt around her waist. She seemed to have torn the sweatshirt clean off.

With a peculiar sideways crabwalk, Cassidy shuffled to the edge of the road. She shook like a tree in a high wind.

Movement from next to the truck caught Mary Alice's eye. Ruri was stripping down without wasting any time or effort. Muscles shifted under her skin. She couldn't help but watch, repelled but strangely attracted at the same time. Ruri was a perfect physical specimen. She'd put on some weight during her time with them. Just the right amount of muscle rippled along her torso, topped by pert breasts that weren't too large. Mary Alice thought they might fit her hands perfectly.

A strangled gurgle pulled her focus from the lycan and back to her sister. Cassidy was turning in small circles, still on all fours. There was more fur on her body than Mary Alice remembered seeing up to now. Her bones cracked loud enough that she could hear the dry snaps from where she stood.

She felt fur under her palm and looked down to see a large golden wolf next to her. It nuzzled her hand, drawing the palm along the side of its face. It bent its head to do so; its back was as high as her waist. Ruri sniffed at her hand and gave a small whuff of recognition before moving on to where Cassidy still struggled.

Her sister seemed to be stuck in some transitional stage. Her face had elongated and the emerald eyes no longer looked so alien. Sharp teeth protruded over lips that still seemed to be thinning and stretching. Ruri nosed her along, urging her toward the trees. Reluctantly, Cassidy allowed herself to be propelled forward.

"You need to be back in…" The lycans had already disappeared into the woods. "Four hours," Mary Alice concluded quietly. Ruri already knew that. She hoped Ruri's wolf could tell time. She had decided to disable the proximity sensor for this trip, but the timer was still on and running. If they weren't back home by 2 a.m., Ruri was going to lose her paw.

For the first time, Mary Alice wished she could shift and follow along on the hunt. Cassidy had left her behind; there was no way she could protect her where she'd gone. All she could do was hope Ruri would care for her sister.

The coolness of the woods closed around Ruri, welcoming her home in its shadowed embrace. Ahead, Cassidy stumbled, not quite comfortable on all fours. Her legs bent awkwardly, not quite shifted, but no longer fully human. Ruri nipped at her heels, urging her onward. They needed to get away from the road. As overgrown and out of the way as it was, the road still represented danger. When they got into the thickest part of the trees, they would finally be safe.

Cassidy turned and snapped at her, teeth meeting sharply in front of Ruri's nose. The display was impressive, but Ruri was having none of it. She slid to one side and reached in to nip Cassidy's shoulder. The other wolven whined and tried to catch her, but Ruri was too fast and Cassidy's teeth caught nothing.

The muzzle that protruded from Cassidy's face should have looked wrong, but it didn't. She was somewhere between her human and wolven forms. All she needed was a bit of a nudge and she would complete the change. Her body would finally be able to devote some energy to healing and not to the struggle that still waged within her. Eyes that had glowed emerald in the truck were now angry crimson.

She leaned her shoulder into Cassidy, forcing her onward, one stumbling step at a time. They needed a clearing in the deepest part of the woods and there was one further along. Time was running out. How many more chances would she have to coax Cassidy's transformation to fruition? Would she be able to get tonight's work done in time?

A whine rose in her throat and Ruri let it out. Her wolf didn't like to think in designated chunks of time; that was a human conceit. She thought in terms of sun and moon rise and in the speed of the wind as it swept past her, wafting along the smells of the woods with it.

The light breeze ruffled her coat like gentle fingers tugging at her fur. *How would it feel if Malice touched me like that?* The thought was as unexpected as it was unwelcome. Ruri was doing her best to get in Malice's head. There was no room for the Hunter in hers. There was some attraction there, but it had more to do with a lack of viable options, not true chemistry, no matter what her wolf thought. Besides, she had bigger problems.

Cassidy had slowed down again. When Ruri leaned into her this time, she simply leaned back. The woman was smaller than she was. It should have been the work of less than a moment to get her moving once more, but she was stronger than she looked. Ruri huffed as she dug nails into the loamy ground to get Cassidy moving, to no avail. She wasn't going to wear herself out, not so soon into their allotted time, but Cassidy had to get going. Try as she might, there was nothing for it. Cassidy would go no further.

There was more than one way to skin a cat. Cassidy had all her weight on her, and Ruri pushed off in the opposite direction, letting the struggling wolven fall over behind her. With a quick glance to see if Cassidy followed, Ruri took off. She flowed over downed logs and between trees, dead leaves swirling in her wake, always with half an eye behind her. As she'd hoped, Cassidy had been unable to resist the chase and she trailed behind Ruri. She wasn't as slow as Ruri had expected; she barely had to hold back at all. Bit by bit, Ruri increased her speed until she ran all out. She bounded and stretched over the forest floor, spinning to avoid thicker patches of undergrowth, her lips stretched in a wide wolven grin. This was what she'd been missing, the chance to go where she pleased. The wolf gloried with her, overjoyed to be back in her own skin with room to run.

A tug at her tail overbalanced her, and she only had a moment to glance back and catch Cassidy right behind her before she tumbled off into the underbrush with a startled yelp. The trees had thinned out. Apparently they'd found her clearing.

Cassidy paced forward on all fours and loomed over her. Patches of skin shone in the moonlight, broken up by patches of fur, some of which were lighter and others darker. Her head blocked out the moon. Ruri stared up at her, tense and ready to run again if she had to. *What is she up to?* If Cassidy had given herself completely over to the wolves, there was no telling what she might do.

CHAPTER TWENTY-TWO

Ruri hadn't survived this long by waiting for ill to befall her. She feinted to one side and rolled the opposite way when Cassidy moved to stop her. The momentum of her roll brought her feet under her, and she sprang up, heading to the far side of the clearing. A couple of downed trees gave her the cover she needed as she threaded her way between their bare boughs. Cassidy didn't know the area, but she did and she would use that to her advantage.

Behind her, Cassidy put up a heck of a racket clambering over the dead trees. She didn't know her body, not this way. As fast as she was, she wasn't particularly agile.

Ruri waited for her, tongue lolling and testing the breeze with her nose. The speed Cassidy had displayed was unusual. The between-form was one most wolven couldn't hold for long; it was mostly a transitory form. Some wolven could shift partially, but they were usually the strongest in a pack. Dean had been able to take on between-form, though he hadn't liked to. Not only had he found it ostentatious, but it wasn't overly practical. It seemed to have all the disadvantages of each form and none of the advantages. Ruri should have been able to outrun Cassidy back there, but when she'd almost been caught, she was running at full speed. What this meant for Cassidy, she wasn't certain. There was so much about her that might be attributed to the circumstances of her transition.

The wolf shook her head, ruffling the fur around her neck. Cassidy was as she was. Wondering why was a foolish conceit. There were bigger worries now.

She wouldn't be caught unaware again. When Cassidy emerged from the pile of downed trees, Ruri tensed again, ready to move in whichever direction was wisest. It didn't matter from which direction Cassidy tried to approach her, she was ready.

The breeze tickled her nostrils, bringing with it Cassidy's scent. The wolven didn't smell aggressive; excited perhaps, but there was nothing to suggest she needed to be worried. Still, Ruri didn't relax. If she had one wolf to contend with, she could have trusted her nose, but Cassidy was dangerous precisely because her wolf could still change. Things weren't going as she'd expected. Somehow she'd lost control of the situation.

Cassidy spread her arms, gripping the ground with deadly claws that dug long furrows into the earth. She lowered her front and looked up at Ruri, eyes bright and questioning. Every line of her body suggested she wanted to play. If she'd had a tail, it would have been raised over her back and wagging slightly. When Ruri didn't respond beyond a careful shift of her weight, she pushed herself lower.

If Cassidy's wolf wants to play, I might as well work with it, Ruri thought. Taking care not to let her head get lower than Cassidy's, she imitated her pose. Unable to completely lose the tension that tugged at her body, she felt her legs shake slightly. *I'm not going to be able to hold this for long*, she realized. She bounded forward and snapped her teeth together right by Cassidy's ear. The sound of her bite was loud even to her, and she darted away, startled by the noise.

Cassidy followed right along behind her, chasing on her heels. It wasn't what she'd meant to do, but once again there was no sign of aggression from the other wolven. She dodged around a tall tree stump that was roughly broken off a little higher than her shoulder and Cassidy mirrored her, planting herself in the way. Ruri dodged away, digging toenails into the ground and pivoting smoothly. Cassidy grinned and started forward, then stopped suddenly. She stood stock still, every muscle shaking, her claws chewing up the turf in rough gouges. Her sides heaved as she panted. Each breath shuddered in and out of her in billowing clouds of vapor.

It was chilly, the dry leaves around them speaking of autumn's relentless advance, but it wasn't cold enough for breath to be visible. Something was happening. Cautiously, Ruri inched forward.

Ice blue eyes stopped her in her tracks. Cassidy looked up at her with no sign of recognition. The eyes were familiar. No, she wouldn't think of that, not right now. Not when they finally had some sign of progress.

The shaking of Cassidy's muscles got progressively more violent before they shifted beneath her skin again. More cracking rent the air, each one a sharp report. The struggling wolven whined each time a bone snapped and re-formed. This was it. This was what Ruri had been waiting for. Her new sister was finally being born.

A strangled howl clawed its way from Cassidy's throat. New fur threaded its way down her shoulders before it suddenly stopped. She froze.

Ruri moved forward—her sister needed her help—but this was one trial she had to weather on her own. The only support Ruri could give her were the bonds of the pack. She would protect her packmate from all comers. As she came closer, she noticed that the new fur coming in was so pale as to be completely colorless. There was only one wolven she'd known who had fur that light. Between the color of Cassidy's eyes and the white of her fur, there was no denying the identity of at least one of the wolven who'd attacked her.

Britt... She didn't stop the howl that burst from her throat. Her wolf poured out its grief for a packmate lost, one whose betrayal had been breathtaking in its totality. The howl rose and fell before rising again. There was no hiding from it any longer. She would have to kill the wolven who had caused so much agony.

That pain wasn't complete. Cassidy still shuddered in front of her. More fur shaded in among the white, this time in dark brown. It progressed more slowly, sliding down her back before slowing again and fading back to white.

Ruri watched, fascinated. The wolves that had been fighting for dominance within Cassidy seemed to be waging a final battle. They were tenacious, wrestling back and forth as Cassidy trembled and whined. The change wasn't smooth or quick. Instead it came in fits and starts. Each time it ebbed and flowed, a strangled howl was torn from her tortured packsister, some cries sounding almost human, others that were definitely wolf. Each cry was lower and more distinct than the one that preceded it. Ruri paced back and forth, keeping one eye on Cassidy and the other on the trees around them. This was taking too long; her packsister was too exposed.

A figure separated itself from the shadows to her right. Ruri swiveled to stare at it. It moved on two legs, not four, and she'd darted halfway across the clearing before the wind brought Malice's scent to her. She slowed and walked the rest of the way. Malice gave no indication that she'd noticed her, instead staring where Cassidy now lay on her side, twitching.

Ruri walked around the human and beneath the hand that hung at her side, allowing it to slide over her head and rest on the highest point of her back. The wolf welcomed Malice's touch, and she was able to relax a bit. Malice gently clenched her hand in Ruri's thick fur. They stood there together for a moment, and Ruri moved forward. Malice walked beside her, matching her step for step back to where their sister lay.

By the time they returned, Cassidy was half-furred and her muscles continued to ripple and twitch slowly beneath her skin. There were no more sounds of bones snapping, but Ruri thought she could hear them creak. Cassidy lay in a puddle of fluid and blood, the remnants of her human skin and tissue that hadn't been repurposed for the change. At their approach, Cassidy looked up. Her face was completely wolven now and a long tongue lolled from her mouth from the force of her panting.

One red and one electric blue eye stared at them from a brindled face. Two ears twitched slightly in recognition. She tried to push herself up but stumbled to one side. The way she looked behind her made Ruri think she had probably been overbalanced by her tail. That took some getting used to, she recalled.

Cassidy's body looked strange as it was only partially furred. With an audible pop, her back legs settled, the knees shifting the last little bit until they were perfect. It was the final tweak and Cassidy shuddered one last time. Fur cascaded over the rest of her body, and before more than a couple of seconds had passed, she stood proudly before them. Ruri couldn't help but stare.

The fur on her body was wet and spiky, clumped together by fluids from the change. The way Cassidy shifted her weight to one side clued Ruri in on what was coming next. She stepped back and avoided the arc of liquid as Cassidy shook herself dry. Malice wasn't so lucky and ended up with fluid halfway up the front of her shirt. She glanced back at Ruri, her eyebrow raised. Clearly she expected Ruri to have tipped her off. The wolf was highly amused at Malice's discomfiture and didn't bother to hide the lupine grin that stretched across her face.

A low rumble from the clearing pulled her attention back to her packsister. She stood still, the moonlight highlighting the edges of her fur. Cassidy was a perfect specimen of wolven. Her muscles rippled impressively beneath luxurious fur, promising great strength and speed. Her chest was broad and deep and her shoulders high. Her fur was thickest over the nape of her neck and haunches, but her tail was truly a wonder to behold. She held it like a banner for the wind to ruffle through. For the first time since Ruri had met her, she seemed to be full of energy and in complete control. They would see how true that control was when it came time to shift back to her human form. It was unlikely that Cassidy's wolf would go without a fight.

"Cassidy?" Malice's low voice broke the spell in the clearing. She was crouched, one hand reaching toward her sister. "Is that still you?"

Ruri looked over at Malice and was conscious of Cassidy doing the same thing. She already had a feel for what the other wolven was up to. They'd bonded very quickly and Ruri could almost feel her to one side. It wasn't like having an extension of herself, but more like the way the sun felt on her fur. She could have closed her eyes and pointed Cassidy out with her nose, no matter where she was, as long as they were in relatively close proximity.

Cassidy flattened her ears to the sides of her head and tilted it to one side. An uncertain whine rose in her throat. She stood still for a moment before dancing backward into the comforting embrace of the trees behind her. Even to Ruri, only her mismatched eyes and the lightest parts of her pelt were visible in the shadows.

Malice's face was impassive when she stood, but grief poured from her. Wet ashes filled Ruri's nose, and her throat ached from the depth of Malice's anguish. She wanted to howl out the sadness of the one beside her.

The wind picked up for a moment, scattering dead leaves and bringing a new scent to her nose. Ruri's head snapped up at the scent of a third wolven. She turned in a tight circle, scanning the trees for more trace, all senses open for the intruder. Her ears twitched left and right, alert for any sound that didn't belong. She flicked her eyes from one spot to another, trying to pierce the deepest shadows. Cassidy scooted out from under the trees and dropped into a crouch next to her, mirroring Ruri's movements. They stood haunch to haunch; there was no way anyone could sneak up on them.

"What's wrong?" All traces of grief disappeared from Malice, subsumed by the smell of single-minded focus. "Is someone else here?"

In answer, Ruri lifted her chin and inhaled before letting out a long howl. The mournful sound had one purpose: to warn away whoever was out there. She wasn't sure how well they'd do against another pack, but she only smelled one other wolven. Unless there were others out there, they could take on whoever it was. Cassidy joined in, her voice rising to complement Ruri's. The timbre of her howl was lower than Ruri's and she shivered. There was a very real chance Cassidy would end up being much more dominant than she was. Her voice was even lower than Dean's had been, and he'd had a bell-like toll that had carried for miles when he'd wanted it to. He'd been able to rally the pack, no matter how far they'd ranged while hunting. Cassidy promised to be able to do at least that.

They both jumped when Malice lifted her voice with theirs. It wasn't wolven, but neither was her howl entirely human. There was depth and menace to it that she'd never encountered in another human. Unlike their howls that warned the interloper away, Malice's specifically promised violence. It danced a ragged knife-edge of rage and despair.

Anguish rose within Ruri in response to the agony in Malice's lament, and it swallowed her howl. She couldn't spare a glance for the human who stood with them, her hand wrapped in the fur at the nape of Ruri's neck. Across the clearing a four-legged shadow separated itself from the trees. It slunk closer until it stood in a patch of moonlight.

The strange wolven was tall, definitely much higher in the shoulder than either of them. Chocolate brown fur shaded to caramel at the tips of the wolven's ears and muzzle and along the length of its tail. The breeze brought the scent clearly across to her. This was no stranger.

Lewis. Her rival from Dean's pack stood before them, eyes glittering in the dark before fading back into the forest. She stood, waiting for an attack that never came. The three of them stood tensely for long minutes until Ruri was certain they were no longer in any danger.

There wasn't much time left. From the moon's position in the sky, they'd already used up an hour of their allotment. Her wolf protested at the strictures of their schedule but settled down when Ruri decided on a nice long run. She nudged Malice's thigh with her nose.

The human flinched a bit at the cold wetness and looked down. Ruri angled her head toward the edge of the clearing. It was time to take Cassidy for a run, to let her wolf stretch its legs so they'd have a prayer of getting her back into human form for the ride home. The large cage in the back of Malice's truck was Cassidy's other option to return. Seeing her in full wolf form, Ruri was doubtful they'd have much luck getting her into it. Best to track down some game and get Cassidy's wolf a quick kill to satisfy it.

Malice seemed to understand. She released her grip but not before tightening it momentarily. She seemed to regret letting go. Ruri felt a similar reluctance, like Malice was a packmate who had moved beyond her ability to sense them.

She bumped Cassidy with her shoulder and loped past her into the trees. Her packsister followed easily on her heels. They would have to range a way to find game that hadn't been frightened to ground by the sounds of Cassidy's shift.

CHAPTER TWENTY-THREE

The breeze swirled past Cassidy in a riot of colors and smells. It seemed as if every color corresponded to something new in her environment, and she wondered how she'd never noticed it before. She felt like for her whole life she'd been listening to a symphony without noticing the string section was missing. Tugging at the edge of her senses, another awareness lurked. It should have frightened her, but it didn't. Instead, it pulsed just beyond the edge of her knowing, a steady point of light. Somehow she knew it would never let her down.

Ahead, Ruri's golden form loped steadily, avoiding obstacles more quickly and smoothly than Cassidy thought possible. She kept up well enough but had problems when a rock or branch seemed to sprout in her path. They were really hauling ass, and she marveled at the speeds they must be hitting. It was impossible to put a number on it; exactitudes seemed beyond her grasp. They'd run long enough that her muscles had warmed up, but not so long that they cried out for her to stop. They could keep on much longer in her estimation.

Another rock sprang up in her path, and she dug her toenails into the forest's dirt floor, trying to slide past it just as Ruri had. She caught on something and instead of squeezing fluidly past the small boulder, she slipped right into it. Stars spangled briefly across her vision but were gone in a flash. Where had Ruri gone? *There*, whispered the wolf. *We can catch her if you just let me...* It overlapped her thoughts, leaving no room for human rationality, her worries and fears, those constant companions she'd never really thought about until now. All that existed was the two of them, the forest around them silent as a cathedral yet full of life and Ruri, somewhere ahead.

A golden tendril unfurled in front of them and they followed the unmistakable thread of the werewolf's scent. It was amazing how much more easily movement came when they were they and not her and she. Cassidy felt the wolf's approval as her own and basked in the glow of accomplishment when they came upon Ruri, who had paused for a moment in a small forest glen.

It wasn't even large enough for the moonlight to truly penetrate, but the shadows weren't as deep here. Not that it would have mattered too much. Their vision pierced all but the deepest gloom.

Ruri twitched an ear at them, and they knew it was a question. Were they all right to continue? They panted back a laughing assent. If they needed to, they could run for days. They didn't know how they knew, they had yet to be tested, but the night's run felt so easy. Ruri wasn't winded either, and Cassidy wondered how much the other werewolf could handle.

Less than we, the answer whispered back from her wolf half before it blurred with her again. Rather than wait for Ruri's lead, they threw themselves down a small game trail. A new scent demanded their attention. It floated warm and red above the dead leaves that covered the forest floor. It skipped ahead of them, slowly becoming more and more distinct until they could make out the small form of a terrified rabbit skittering ahead. Fear shed from its body in spiky yellow flares. The scent coated the inside of their nostrils and excitement woke in their breast. It pounded through them, driving them forward. They could no more deny it than they could stop the sun from rising. Cassidy had a small moment of remorse for the poor thing's terror, but it was quickly subsumed by her wolf and its enthusiasm.

The rabbit skittered ahead of them, always a nose ahead of their claws, never quite close enough to sink their teeth into. They bounded after it, but catching the little creature was as difficult as catching smoke beneath their paws. For all that they'd felt they could go on forever, Ruri finally caught up to them collapsed at the foot of a huge gnarled tree. Its branches provided them with cover, the trunk with support. They panted, trying to catch their breath as the red trail of the rabbit dissipated in front of them.

She laughed at them, her tongue lolling from her mouth, but they were still too exhilarated from their hunt to take offense. There would be other hunts, the wolf promised as much. Those would be successful. Cassidy burned to experience the kill at the end of the chase. It would be her just reward, after all.

Three hours and more had ground by. Seated on the edge of the truck's bed, Mary Alice kept up her vigil. There was nothing to see from where she sat, and it was the best view her truck had to offer, tucked as it was beneath the trees. She could wish there was less foliage on them. It wasn't even Halloween yet, and most species except the maples and the occasional other were still partly leaved. Then again, even without the leaves the trees were so dense that there wasn't much to see.

Would Ruri and Cassidy be back soon? They had to be. She still had to disable the timer from the anklet. Now that Cassidy had made the transformation, she would have to make good on her promise to release the lycan. It wasn't the first time her mind had come around to this point tonight. The first thing she'd felt upon seeing Cassidy's wolf form had been loss. She'd thought it had been for the loss of her sister to the virus that mutated her, but now she wasn't so sure. Cassidy was still around, after all. So what if her sister hadn't recognized her in the clearing; she'd been through a lot.

And yet, what would she do if Ruri no longer wanted to be around her? *Cassidy*, she corrected herself hastily. What would she do if Cassidy no longer wanted her around? It was fairly obvious that Ruri wouldn't want anything to do with her. She already couldn't stand to be close to her.

Then why all the staring? another corner of her mind whispered back to her. *Why does she keep watching?*

So maybe losing Cassidy wasn't the only thing.

And there she was again, back in the same corner she'd talked herself into three times already. It was past time to examine the tangled mass of feelings the lycan inspired in her. There was nothing else to do. She snorted and pushed herself off the truck's tall side. Leaves crackled under her feet as she paced back and forth.

Of course Ruri wouldn't stick around. Mary Alice was the one who had kidnapped her and kept her trapped in one place. Lycans didn't survive long in captivity, she knew that, and not only from her training, but it was something she'd witnessed countless times in the years she'd been doing Uncle Ralph's dirty work. Lycans might have a den, but they also ranged far and wide, some returning only on occasion. Some might spend more time in the den than others, but even they had to get out regularly.

How would I fit into their world? The notion danced lightly across her thoughts, as if too worrisome to leave a deep impression. Likely if she hadn't been paying attention, it would have stolen silently through without her notice. Mary Alice spun on her heel and stomped the other direction. There was no way she could live with a pack of lycans. The idea was beyond contemplating, it was so ridiculous. Beyond the logistics of having their executioner living among them, there was no good reason she should want to.

And if it's the only way to keep Ruri...and my sister? But it wasn't. It couldn't be. There were always more options. Her sister would remember her. As for Ruri she would have to...

Let go.

Mary Alice closed her eyes, unprepared for the rush of panicked grief she felt at the idea. Her breath was being stolen from her, whooshing out of her lungs. If someone or something came up on her now, she'd be dead for certain. Standing in the middle of a gravel road with her head down and her hands on her knees was no way to take on the supranormal menace.

"Malice?" Ruri's voice came from behind her. "Are you all right?"

Determined not to let the werewolf get the drop on her, she spun around and stopped dead in her tracks. Ruri was completely nude, her skin shining coolly in the moonlight. Mismatched glowing eyes drifted at her side, resolving slowly into Cassidy's crazy coat as she stepped onto the road. It was amazing how well her coat melted into the trees. It might as well have been made for the dappled moonlight that filtered through the spotty canopy.

"I'm fine." Of course she wasn't all right, but what else could she do except pretend? "I was worried about you two. We don't have much time left."

"Uh huh." Ruri strode steadily toward her, showing no sign of discomfort at the small stones that rolled beneath her bare feet.

Spots of moonlight floated across her skin, highlighting the dip of her collarbone, the hollow of one hip, here a nipple, and lower... Mary Alice licked her lips almost against her will. She decided that Ruri's skin couldn't possibly be as smooth as it looked, but her fingers itched to check.

"Earth to Malice." Ruri's voice verged on the edge of outright laughter.

She jerked her eyes up to meet the werewolf's. Ruri had stopped about five feet away, close enough that she could see every luminous inch of her skin, but not close enough to touch. Cassidy sat by her feet, her amusement unmistakable in the tilt of her head and the way those odd eyes twinkled disconcertingly at her.

"Well, what are you waiting for? Let's get Cassidy shifted and back in the truck. We have maybe forty-five minutes before the timer's up." Her response was cold, and she knew it, but she couldn't help herself. All she wanted was to take Ruri somewhere for an extended fuck, and she hated herself for it. Not only was the timing atrocious, but she shouldn't have been feeling the attraction in the first place. As much as she tried to push Ruri away, she was inevitably drawn back to her. Discipline was the key, but she'd had precious little of that since finding Cassidy torn and bloody.

"And whose fault is that?" Ruri stared back at her, refusing to let her eyes go.

Mary Alice looked away first. "It doesn't change the facts."

"Well, okay. But have you ever tried to get your sister to do something she didn't want to?"

"Cassidy?" Mary Alice scoffed at the idea. "She's fine, a little stubborn maybe. She always comes around to reason eventually."

"Eventually?" Ruri cocked a mocking eyebrow at her. "We don't have eventually, remember. Your sister may be one of the most stubborn individuals I've ever met, and I've only been dealing with her for a few days."

"Then why are we dicking around?" Mary Alice closed the gap between them in two long steps. Ruri held her ground, drawing herself up to her full height. "Get her to change or get her in the cage."

"The cage won't work. She's immensely strong. She'll rip through it in a second, and that's if she consents to being locked in there in the first place."

"What do you want from me?" The frustration was more than she could bear. Mary Alice could hear her voice rising, and she clenched her fists, digging her nails into her palms, trying to stay focused. The cords on her neck trembled from the strain of holding herself together, but she couldn't afford to lose it. She wasn't sure if she was about to break something or burst into tears.

A warm body leaned against the front of her legs, forcing her to fall back a step. The fur along Cassidy's back raised in mute warning. Her sister wasn't growling, not yet, but her top lip curled to reveal very large, very sharp teeth. Again, Cassidy had chosen Ruri over her. Anguish overwhelmed her, every fiber of her being focusing on dragging breath into her lungs.

A cool palm on her cheek refocused her from the feeling of drowning on the inside to the mess she had to deal with on the outside. She stared into Ruri's golden eyes; the werewolf leaned across the wolf who stood between them.

"I want you to ask her to change," she said as if nothing had happened. As if Mary Alice wasn't teetering on the edge of control. As if Cassidy wasn't slipping further and further from her. "I doubt she'll submit to being ordered around. She certainly won't to me." A wry smile told Mary Alice how much that rankled, though Ruri tried to put a good face on it.

Her despair thawed slightly, and Mary Alice sprang upon it, smothering it until only a small kernel of it remained. As hard as she tried, that refused to dissipate. These days it never quite did. It was her constant companion—that and her rage.

She inhaled deeply, finally filling her lungs completely. After holding it for a moment, she let her breath out slowly and looked down at Cassidy's brindled form, really taking it in for the first time. Her coat was a riot of shades, from white to black to chocolate brown and seemingly all the shades in between. Or most of them, anyway. She saw no sign of golden tawniness in Cassidy's fur and heaved a breath of relief. If Ruri was to be believed, that meant there was nothing of her DNA in Cassidy's mix. However, it certainly appeared as if more than one wolf's DNA had won through. Between the odd eyes and the stripes of color that marked her sister from the top of her shoulders to the base of her tail, there was some definite mixing. She'd never seen a lycan with the variation or pattern that were in Cassidy's pelt. Had Ruri been keeping something from her?

She shook her head. *It doesn't matter now.*

"I don't have time for this," she said aloud. The longer they stood around, the more chance there was that they wouldn't get back home on time. Cassidy looked back at her, unconcerned now that her anger was banked. "Cass, I need you to change back for me."

The sigh from Ruri was pure irritation and Mary Alice looked over at her. The werewolf rolled her eyes and shook her head.

What? Mary Alice mouthed at her only to receive another eye roll in return.

At her feet Cassidy yawned hugely, then casually paced closer to the edge of the road before sitting down. Her tail cleared a slow swath in the accumulation of dead leaves where dirt met the thin strip of grass before the trees.

That's right, Ruri had said to ask. It was Mary Alice's turn to roll her eyes. This was Cassidy to a tee. It had been years since she could order her around by virtue of being the older, and therefore wiser, sister. Even as kids, it had been easier to ask and cajole. If a gentler tone could get them back in the truck, it was worth it.

Mary Alice squatted and settled on her heels. "What do you say, Cass? We need to head home, so I need you to change back." One of Cassidy's ears twitched, briefly swiveling to face her, but aside from that, there was no sign her entreaty had worked. She extended her hand toward Cassidy. "Come on, Cass. Please? I don't want to go home without you."

The promise to leave her behind hung in the air between them. The only other sound was Ruri's sharp intake of breath.

"What, you didn't think I'd let your leg get blown off, did you?" How could Ruri think she'd actually do that? Aside from the fact that Malice had threatened to do just that at almost every turn. "Of course you did, why wouldn't you? The first thing I'm doing when we get back is removing that fucking anklet. You don't need it. I don't know if you ever did." The last was said to herself, though she was sure both werewolves heard it.

Across from her, Cassidy bounded to her feet before bracing them beneath her. She dropped her head and tucked her tail between her back legs. Every line of her body sang with tension.

Ruri knelt next to her, one arm around her shuddering shoulders. She murmured into Cassidy's nearest ear, which pricked up, quivering. For a moment everything was still, as if Cassidy and the world around them held their collective breaths. The first crack of bone heralded the reversal of her sister's transformation. It was much quicker than the tail end she'd seen of Cassidy's shift into wolf-form. Bone cracked and reformed so quickly it sounded like someone playing with a sheet of bubble wrap. There was none of the fluid expulsion that marked the shift from human to wolf. Instead the hair seemed to withdraw back into her body until Cassidy's naked form crouched in Ruri's protective arms. She panted as if she'd just sprinted the last leg of a marathon.

"Not so fast next time," Ruri said, hugging her arm around heaving shoulders. "Let's get dressed, and we'll be ready to go."

Time indeed. Mary Alice glanced at her wrist, where numbers on her watch face glowed dimly at her. She would have to break the speed limit to make it back in time. They didn't have far to go, but it was all surface streets. If she was lucky, there wouldn't be a cop around to catch her blowing through any red lights. They had some wiggle room, but not as much as she would have liked.

"Looks like." She should have been relieved. But if it was over, why did she have the feeling this had been the easy part?

CHAPTER TWENTY-FOUR

The drive back had been awkward, to say the least. To combat the pervasive silence in the truck, Mary Alice had finally flipped on the radio and let the local heavy metal station's pounding drums and crunching guitars wash over her. Usually that kind of music helped her relax and create a focus for her aggression. This time it had the opposite effect. By the time they pulled up in front of the brick warehouse she called home, she practically vibrated with anxiety. The clock in the battered dash of the truck said she had fifteen minutes to spare, but she was pretty sure it was five minutes slow. Or was that fast? At that moment, she doubted herself.

Fumbling under the dash for the opener took far too long, but her questing fingertips finally found the button and she jammed her finger down on it.

"Pull it in next to the first cage," she said as she slipped out the door. There was no time to wait for an answer. Surely Ruri could drive stick; if she'd been around since there was such a thing as the frontier, surely she'd picked up how to drive a manual transmission. She knew Cassidy couldn't. That was one lesson she'd never successfully imparted to her younger sister.

The door was open far enough that she could duck under it, though she had to bend at the waist to do so. The dull chunking of the opener's mechanism echoed dully through the cavernous first floor, following her as she sprinted for the furthest cage from the entrance. The biometric lock sprang open after accepting her palm print, and she rushed to the laptop. Ever the pessimist, she'd set the computer to sleep instead of shutting down. Even so, it still took too long to come back to life. The timer popped up on the screen with one click of the mouse. Ten minutes. Apparently the clock on the dash was slow. Just like that, the timer was reset for another twelve hours. Ruri would be safe now.

Or rather, she would be soon. Mary Alice dropped into the rolling office chair. As usual, it protested her rough treatment by dropping an inch, and she readjusted it without thinking. It shouldn't take much to shut the timer down completely. The shutdown was simple enough, but she still double- and triple-checked it to make sure it wasn't set to detonate. That wasn't enough to be certain, however. She refreshed the software to be positive. It definitely seemed to be disabled.

"Will I live?" Ruri's voice sounded from behind her. Mary Alice had been concentrating so hard on deactivating the explosive device that she hadn't heard the truck pull into the building.

"You're all good." Mary Alice turned around. Her smile faded when she saw how Cassidy was hanging on the other lycan's shoulder.

"Fantastic." Ruri turned to go.

"Hold on." She stood up and gestured at the chair. "Take a seat. Let's get that damn thing off you."

"For real?" Ruri asked, her voice high with surprise.

At her nod, the lycan moved into the small enclosure. Her arm was around Cassidy's waist and more than half-supporting her, much to Mary Alice's alarm.

"What's going on?" She moved toward the two of them before stopping just out of reach. Not sure how to help, she hovered there uncertainly.

"She's exhausted." Ruri lowered her gently to the chair. Cassidy seemed loath to give up her grip.

"I'm fine," Cassidy said, opening her eyes into the tiniest cracks. "I'd like to sleep for a week, but aside from that I feel…great!" A smile lit her face and she allowed her arm to drop.

"Good! That's really, really good." Mary Alice pointed Ruri toward desk. "Put your foot up there. I'll get some tools."

The implements she needed were one cage over. This one had a more conventional combination lock on it, and she spun the dial. The tools were pretty basic, not like the ones she had up on the next floor. Those had a specific purpose. These were the ones she used when tinkering with her truck or on her weapons. The tools she'd used to secure the anklet were close at hand, and she snagged them and hurried back to the other cage.

Ruri had her foot up on the desk and Cassidy was considering the anklet through a slitted gaze.

"It'll just take a second," Mary Alice said, ignoring the questioning look her sister sent her way.

"Are you sure you know what you're doing?" Ruri shifted her weight from her heel to the balls of her foot, like she was getting ready to make a dash for it.

"Of course. I put it there, didn't I?" She dropped the tools on the table and Ruri jumped. "Hold still."

Removing the anklet was easy enough, though Ruri twitched her way through the entire maneuver. When it was done, she stood stock still, as if uncertain what to do.

"You're free to go," Mary Alice said.

"I know."

"What do you mean, 'free to go,'" Cassidy said on top of Ruri's acknowledgment. "You were holding her here? What the hell, Mary?"

"I did what I had to." Her voice was stiff, and she knew it. The decision hadn't been an easy one, but it had been the best course of action. She wasn't going to argue about it with the person who had benefited most from it. "Cassidy, you're tired. You should get some rest. Use my bed."

"If you think—" Cassidy cut off when Mary Alice turned her eyes on her. She said nothing, simply looked at her, daring her to push it.

"Go to bed."

"We're going to talk about this," Cassidy said, pushing past her sister and storming out into the middle of the first floor. "Coming, Ruri?"

The other werewolf trailed after her. She had no more words for Mary Alice, only another long look. She seemed on the edge of saying something, but after opening her mouth a couple times to start, she gave up and left instead.

That was fine with Mary Alice. She didn't want to deal with the emotional turmoil the woman's presence stirred up. At least Ruri hadn't walked out the front door. She wouldn't have blamed her if she had, though. She knew she had no right to hope Ruri would stick around, and yet an optimistic corner of her held out faith that she might.

Email. She needed some distraction, and since she was at the laptop, she might as well clear out some of the crap that had accumulated in her inbox over the past couple of weeks. The first few were spam, and she gleefully relegated those to inbox oblivion. The next one almost followed, but at the last minute she stopped. The sender's email was vaguely familiar, though it wasn't one she saw frequently. Who was TBear2697@gmail.com? The cursor hovered over the email as she debated whether or not to open it.

Why the hell not. No one ever got a virus just from opening an email. Her mind made up, she clicked on the subject line. "I saw this and thought you could use a laugh." That was helpful.

The opening was brief and it contained a link.

"Hi Malice. This made me laugh my ass off and I know you could use a pick-me-up. Hope you enjoy as much as I did." The signoff line was simply TB and a winking smiley.

Malice. It could only be Al-Hasan. She opened the link, which brought her to a BuzzFeed page. "Twenty-Three Kittens Guaranteed to Make You Squee!" the headline blared. Below it, the post's images began to load.

As cute as the kittens probably were, Mary Alice had no interest in them. They were secondary to what was really going on. She reached for a piece of scrap paper and a pen. It was a cipher, though admittedly a simple one. The CIA had been using BuzzFeed lists as a way to pass messages for a few years now. The site was practically ubiquitous. She didn't know how they did it, but somebody from their staff had obviously put this one together. It was simple enough to decode; the key was in the title. She counted twenty-three words in to the list, including the photo captions, and wrote down the first word, then counted another twenty-three words from that one.

It only took a few minutes to uncover the message, but she stared at it, palms sweaty and cold, before running the cipher again. She licked suddenly dry lips as she prayed the message would change this time. Maybe she'd shifted a word. To her mounting horror, the results were the same.

Not good, she thought. "Not good at all." The last was said aloud as she willed herself into sudden action and threw herself out of the cage and toward the stairs.

"What exactly is going on here?" These were the first words out of Cassidy's mouth when they got to the third floor. Ruri could feel her anger as well as smell it. Cassidy was a blaze by her side. She might have been tucked into one corner of Malice's worn couch, but it felt like she was pacing the length of the floor. "How does Mary know so much about what's going on?"

That was what she was worried about? Ruri knew Malice had skimped on explaining the situation to her sister. Ruri had been living in this world for so long she'd forgotten what it was like to live outside it. It must be even more complicated for Malice, having one foot in the human world and one in theirs. Surely Cassidy had known something was different about her sister, but then perhaps not. Ruri wondered if she'd been brave enough to return home after the truth of her change was apparent, would her parents have noticed anything was off?

"And for that matter, how does she know you?" Cassidy was staring right at her now. They hadn't bothered to turn the lights on. Enough light filtered in through the multiple rows of windows to make it unnecessary. Her eyes glowed, one point of red and one of blue. They betrayed her wolf's agitation, though she didn't feel to Ruri like she was on the cusp of changing.

"The second part is easier to answer," Ruri said carefully. "She didn't know me. She didn't give me much choice in helping."

"What do you mean by that?"

The shame of being caught and trapped filled her again, and Ruri pulled in on herself. She should have been able to get away. Hell, she never should have been caught in the first place. If she'd been paying a little more attention that night, she wouldn't be where she was now. She'd thought her old pack had been what she needed to worry about. She hadn't been on the lookout for anything else. It was an arrogant mistake and one which had cost her.

A warm hand on her shoulder brought her back to Cassidy.

"What did she do to you?" Her voice was deadly quiet. It promised violence, but Ruri couldn't tell where it was directed. Cassidy's energy was unsettling. Ruri rubbed her hands down the outside of her arms. Goose bumps refused to be quelled, and her own wolf shifted in response. Cassidy made her nervous.

"You need to get your wolf under control."

"You don't need to tell me what to do." Despite the sharpness of her response, Cassidy closed her eyes for a moment. Her breathing slowed and when she opened her eyes, they were almost back to their normal brown shade. The only sign of her continued irritation were the sparks of red and blue that gleamed deep in the shadows of her gaze.

"Malice wanted to make sure you were taken care of." It sounded like an excuse. She was actually making excuses for the woman who kidnapped her. This was quite the case of Stockholm syndrome she'd picked up, and yet she knew where Malice was coming from. She would have done the same for one of her packmates. She would have done far worse if it had meant keeping her pack together and saving Dean. Lewis… He was still out there.

"Who's Malice?" Cassidy cocked her head to one side as if she were listening to something else, but Ruri didn't hear anything. "And who's Lewis?"

She hadn't realized she'd said anything aloud. "Malice is what we call your sister. It's like a code name. Lewis is a member of my old pack."

There it was, footsteps pounding up the stairs. Cassidy had picked on that a good three seconds before she had. Her hearing was extraordinary, and Ruri wondered what other depths were hidden within her new wolven sister.

"Code name? Why does she need a code name? She's my sister. She's Mary. All she does is sculpture and sleep with one girl after another. There's not much more to tell."

"Is that so?" The footsteps were almost to their floor; they turned as one to watch the doorway. The door from the stairwell hit the wall with a crash that reverberated through the mostly empty space. "And she tells you everything she does?"

"She doesn't have to. She's boring. Incredibly boring." The emphasis on the repeated word reminded Ruri how young Cassidy actually was. For all that she'd assumed authority as easily as pulling on a cardigan, she was little more than a girl. Ruri doubted she was much past her twentieth birthday.

"You need to ask her about it."

Malice burst through the doorway and stopped in her tracks, staring back at them as they watched her without blinking.

"Mary, what did you do to her?" Cassidy stood up in one motion and crossed the floor to her sister. "And why is she calling you Malice?"

"There's no time for that." Malice grabbed her sister's arm and jerked her head over at Ruri. "We're getting you out of here. Now."

"Like hell we are." Cassidy jerked her arm back and pulled herself to her full height. She was taller than Malice and glared down at her sister.

"I don't really have anywhere to go," Ruri said. "I doubt they've held my apartment this long."

The look Malice shot her at the mention of the apartment was incredulous. Ruri supposed a wolven needing an apartment sounded somewhat incongruous. Wait until they found out she'd been thinking of getting a day job. Not that there were many positions out there that she was fit to take. She was a farmer's daughter with a knack for middle-management and no marketable experience.

"We'll be fine here. You have the room to put us up." Cassidy sat back down on the couch, eyes flashing. Her eyes dared Malice to try again.

"It's going to be a lot more crowded here in a day, two at the most." Malice dropped the angry mask, allowing them both to see the fear that lurked beneath it. It was raw and real, and Ruri found herself on her feet, needing to be with her. "Please, Cass. We have to go."

"What's wrong?" Ruri's voice was soft, but Malice heard it easily enough. She turned anguished eyes on her.

"They're sending one of my old squadmates. One of my counterparts." She licked her lips and grabbed the back of her neck as if trying to massage some of the terrible tension out of her own shoulders. "She won't understand."

The bottom dropped out of Ruri's stomach. Malice hunted down the worst of her kind without flinching. Ruri had seen her scared, that was true, but scared for Cassidy was different than being frightened by an outside threat. There had been reports that Malice wasn't the only one like her out there, but Ruri had always assumed it was the kind of story that sprang up around her type. There were those who couldn't believe one human could be so dangerous to them, so it was only natural to assume that more like her existed out there somewhere. And now Malice had confirmed she wasn't alone.

"Cassidy, I think we should listen to her." She took Malice's upper arms and held them. Would the human accept a hug? Her wolf wanted to give her comfort the same way she would offer solace to a pack member. "Do you have somewhere in mind?"

"Yes." The relief that was written across her features drove home again exactly how frightened she was. "I have a safe house across the city. It's small, but should be fine for you two."

"Fine." Cassidy leaned on the doorframe watching them. She was the image of relaxed nonchalance. "But you're going to explain everything on the way. Both of you." All pretense of unconcern gone, she pinned both of them with a hard stare. "If I don't like what I hear…"

She didn't have to finish the threat. Ruri swallowed hard and looked down. It was going to be a long night.

CHAPTER TWENTY-FIVE

"How much further?" Cassidy's question struck Ruri as funny and she worked to swallow a laugh. What came out was a smothered giggle that both sisters ignored. In fact, Malice ignored Cassidy's question completely. This was starting to have all the hallmarks of a terrible road trip. Would someone make a movie about them? Hilarity threatened to escape once again forcing Ruri to bite her tongue.

On her right side, Cassidy leaned back against the seat, discontent evident in her stiffness.

"You holding up all right?" Ruri swallowed her giggles. She knew what it was like when the wolf wanted to stretch its legs, but there was no venue to do so.

"I'm fine," Cassidy grumbled back. She kept her voice low, as if Malice might not be able to hear her. "I just need to work the kinks out."

"Open the window. Let the air wash over you." She nodded emphatically at Cassidy's doubtful look. "It helps, trust me." The new wolven would have to trust her sooner or later, but sooner would be better. Plenty of pitfalls abounded; the danger wasn't gone simply because she'd survived her first transformation.

Cassidy grasped the crank of the window and gave it a quick turn. It broke off in her hand. The crack of plastic was loud enough that Malice jumped and glanced over at them. She jerked her eyes back to the road.

"Really, Cassidy?"

"It wasn't on purpose!" Cassidy tucked the broken piece behind the seat. "I didn't know I was going to do that."

"She's a lot stronger than she used to be," Ruri said. "She needs time to acclimate. You should have seen some of the damage I managed after my first shift."

"We don't have time for her to get up to speed," Malice replied. "She needs to do better."

"It's always 'do better' with you, isn't it Mary?" Cassidy put a foot on the dashboard and jiggled her leg impatiently. There was a creak as the dash protested and Malice shifted her eyes again.

"You have a tendency to take your time with things."

"And you rush into them. Not thinking things through got you in all that trouble in high school, remember?"

"I've changed a lot since high school." Malice heaved a sharp sigh, almost a huff. The defensiveness seemed strange from the woman who liked to project an air of complete control. Her sister clearly knew which buttons to press.

Ruri placed a hand on Malice's thigh. "You can't expect her to be able to rush through this. The process will take as long as it takes." What was with the peacekeeping role she kept jumping into between these two? Hopefully the sisters would work out their differences sooner than later. The biggest danger Ruri saw at the moment was the sparks the women were striking off each other.

Malice said nothing and went back to concentrating on the road. They'd been driving for almost twenty minutes, and with no indication of when they would arrive at their destination, her wolf was getting restless as well. She shifted and scored the underside of Ruri's palms with her claws. Ruri flexed her hands and the wolf subsided, though grudgingly.

The warm arm that Cassidy draped across her back was surprising, but more than welcome. The sense of connection calmed her and the wolf more than almost anything else would have. She leaned into the support it offered.

"Maybe this would be easier if I knew what was going on." Cassidy leaned her head on Ruri's shoulder. Anxiety, sour and sad, drifted off her in a small cloud. It explained her aggression, and since Malice wasn't being very forthcoming, Ruri decided it was on her to clear things up, at least as well as she knew them.

"You are wolven." She grinned at the quizzical tilt of Cassidy's head. "Humans call us werewolves."

"What?" Cassidy scoffed openly at the idea. "Those are only in stories, right?" Her voice trailed off, going from statement to poignant question with one quiet word.

"Then how do you explain what happened last night?"

"I've been sick. Hallucinating, even." It was rationalization at its worst, and Cassidy must have realized it. Ruri watched as frustration chased itself around her face to be replaced with resignation.

"Just starting with what we know for sure. You're wolven, but you're without a pack. Technically that makes you a lone wolf."

"Do you have a pack?"

"Not anymore."

Cassidy squeezed her shoulder at the flare of pain. "Doesn't that make you a lone wolf too?"

"I suppose so." She hadn't thought about herself in that way, but it was true. The past few days, her constant misery and disquiet had been overridden with the presence of the two women. As miserable as she'd been being cooped up, it had felt a bit like being back with her pack again.

"We can't both be lone wolves, not together. Aren't we a pack?"

"It's not that simple. There's more to being pack than both of us being wolven."

"Why do you call yourself—us—wolven? Why not just use werewolf?"

"Werewolf is what humans call us. We aren't defined by them. They have no capacity to understand what we are. You want to piss off one of our people, you use that term. It refers to wolven who try to live among humans, who turn their back upon the pack." She glanced over at Malice, who seemed to be ignoring their conversation. "We certainly do not use the term 'furry.'"

"So where do I come in?" Cassidy looked at her palm, then the back of her hand. She was probably noting the things that had changed slightly. Her fingernails would be harder, the pads on her palms and fingertips a little more prominent.

"I don't know exactly, but I know it has something to do with what happened to my people." Ruri took a deep breath to calm her wolf's agitated pacing. She still didn't like thinking about it. On the other side, Malice placed a comforting hand on her thigh. *How does she know?*

"A lone wolf took out my Alpha and half the pack. I escaped and he took the rest of them with him. Loners aren't to be trusted. Most of them want into a pack, but there's usually a good reason they're on their own."

Malice broke in, her voice flat. "It was me." The steering wheel creaked alarmingly under her hand again. "Your old pack was sending me a message after I took out two of their lycans. They were going after Ruri."

Cassidy nodded. Something seemed to have clicked for her.

"It's a damn good thing you were there," Ruri said. "I don't know what would have happened if you hadn't."

"I couldn't allow someone to be attacked like that. Not even…"

"Not even one of my kind, was that what you were going to say?"

"No. I meant not even when it compromised my mission." That seemed less than likely, but Ruri held her tongue. Malice certainly sounded like she believed what she said. There would be time to get to the bottom of the Hunter later. A flare of heat shot through her center at the unwitting euphemism. Her wolf rubbed approvingly along the inside of her skin, right where their thighs were plastered together. It was not the time, nor did it ever seem likely to be. Ruri ignored the wolf and inched her thigh away. For a few seconds, there was no contact and the riot of conflicting emotions and hormones subsided slightly. The reprieve was short-lived, and before she knew it, their legs were touching again, creating a touch point for the maelstrom of emotion the Hunter woke within her.

"One of the werewolves who attacked me said he was paying you back," Cassidy said. She still stared out the side window, but her eyes didn't look like they saw any of the scenery speeding by. "He said it was all your fault."

"It was." A muscle flexed in Malice's jaw. "I never should have allowed you to move to this city. You'd have been safer back home."

"There was no way that was going to happen, so don't even…" Cassidy turned to regard the two of them closely. Ruri got the feeling she hadn't missed the flare of attraction she'd had for the Hunter. "So I think I get what led up to me being inside that box. I don't understand how Ruri got dragged into this."

"Malice decided you needed someone to help you through the shift, so she kidnapped me."

"I thought that was what you were getting around to." Cassidy leaned around her and slapped Malice's knee. Her palm made contact with a resounding smack. It must have stung, but there was no sign of it from the human. "Mary, what the hell were you thinking?"

"I was thinking that Mom has already lost a husband, she didn't need to lose a daughter, too."

"That's a low blow. Don't bring Dad into this."

"It's true."

"I don't care. Don't think you can use our family history to excuse your behavior."

The truck wheeled onto the exit ramp without slowing down. The intersection at the bottom of the ramp flew toward them before Malice stomped on the brake. They screeched to a sudden halt, but for no more than half a second before Malice yanked the wheel to the right. Ruri crashed into Cassidy, the lap belt keeping her hips from sliding, but doing nothing to keep her torso immobile.

"Mary!" Cassidy's indignant squawk of outrage was swallowed by the screech of tires as they accelerated away from the corner. There was no opportunity for conversation as Malice squealed them from one stop to another and around corners at breakneck speed. Ruri held on to the edge of the bench seat and tried not to be flung about too wildly. She was all too aware of the heat of the bodies on either side of her, both waking in her an eerie disquiet, though for very different reasons.

Finally, Malice let the car come to a rest. The sleepy residential neighborhood they were in teetered just this side of being rundown. There was none of the scent of disuse and decay Ruri had learned to live with in the house she'd squatted in after MacTavish's takeover, but the edges of the area seemed frayed. Here a fence gate swung on one hinge and there a trash can lay knocked over and forgotten at the edge of a curb. Uncollected bags of leaves sat on the curb in front of some homes, but just as many had foregone raking, leaving the lawns dotted with ragged patches of brown and yellow.

Trees had once marched along each side of the street, but no one had bothered to remove the stumps after they'd been cut down. Leafless saplings straggled down the parkway. It was impossible to tell if they were dead or merely dormant until spring.

It was early yet, not much before six in the morning. The sun wouldn't rise for almost an hour, but a few people were out and about. Across the street, a woman walked a small dog. She watched them as she passed by, doubtless curious about the noise that had accompanied their arrival. Malice waved tightly to her out the window. A car passed by, probably someone on the way to work. Unless Ruri missed her guess, this was very much a working-class neighborhood, the kind that thirty years ago would have been filled with men heading out to their factory jobs at this time of day. She wondered where they worked now.

"We're here."

The announcement struck Ruri as somewhat unnecessary when she realized it had been meant for Cassidy. Malice's sister undid her seatbelt and opened the door as Malice did the same. The truck was suddenly and blessedly tension-free. Ruri took a deep breath and exhaled before exiting in Cassidy's wake. Malice pulled something out of the back of the truck and headed up the walk. She ignored the front door in favor of heading around the side of the small red brick bungalow. The paint on the house's trim was discolored and starting to crack. Dead leaves lay trapped, tangled in grass too long for raking. At one time, the little house had probably been cozy and full of life, but these days it simply seemed neglected. Cheerful red brick was overshadowed by a cracked sidewalk and general disregard. It fit into the neighborhood perfectly.

It wouldn't take much to get the house back to its original state. Some paint and replacing the walk would go a long way. Ruri's fingers twitched as she considered what it might take. The bones of the house were solid. There were a few stair step cracks among the bricks, but repointing wouldn't take long at all.

Malice disappeared around the corner of the house, Cassidy close behind. They were arguing again. Ruri couldn't hear their words over the rising wind. By the glances she'd been getting from both of them, they were talking about her. Malice wouldn't apologize for what she'd done, of that Ruri was certain. She didn't expect her to. It had been a logical decision, though not necessarily the sanest one.

Cassidy's part in all of this was the big question. Why was the new wolven sticking up for her? A bigger question was why was Ruri letting her? It felt natural, but there was no reason it should have. If anything, their positions should have been reversed with Cassidy looking to her for direction. She was the closest thing Cassidy had to a sire. Britt might be one of the wolven who was responsible for her change, but she was little more than a donor. Her contribution was evident in the patches of white fur and the one electric blue eye, but that was it.

Ruri rounded the corner and stopped. There was no sign of the sisters. She broke into a jog and hastened around back. Malice was wrestling with a key in the back door's uncooperative lock. Cassidy had one hand on her elbow and was going at her. The door finally opened and Malice stepped inside, Cassidy close on her heels. Both sisters were angry; stiff backs said as much. Ruri lingered outside the door, she could already hear raised voices inside. If they couldn't figure out their differences, she would step in. Not that she wanted to. She had to.

"Why won't you just tell me?" Cassidy's voice was exasperated. She was so close on Mary Alice's heels that her foot kept clipping the back of her shoes.

The house was dark and still, and there was no sign anyone had been there. Anyone coming in the front door would be in for a nasty surprise. That the door was still intact was a good sign that no one had tried to get in that way. Still, the rooms needed to be cleared before she could leave the two werewolves there.

Cassidy was like a mosquito, buzzing spitefully in her ear as Mary Alice tried to do her job and protect her. Mary Alice pulled her katana from where she'd concealed it along her leg. Time to get to work. She couldn't afford to let down her guard, especially not now.

"Whoa, what is that?" Cassidy's eyes were round, flecks of red and blue flickering in their depths as she registered a threat.

"It's what's going to keep us safe if anyone got here before us." Arms extended, leading with the katana, Mary Alice ghosted through the kitchen. She dismissed the door to the basement. The bar was still across it, and it was unlikely anything would come bursting through. The kitchen's corners were empty. They held nothing but the few pieces of cheap mismatched furniture she'd scavenged from curbsides and garage sales.

The door opened and closed behind her as Ruri finally joined them. She was all eyes, clearing the room much as Mary Alice had. Her eyes flickered from one area of potential threat to the next, all without betraying her nervousness. She might have been taking a stroll through the park at midday. Cassidy could learn a lot from this one. She would have to if she was going to survive the rest of her kind and keep her nose clean to avoid catching the government's attention.

Cassidy had whirled at Ruri's entrance and a low growl rose from her throat before she subsided. Red and blue were more than scattered specks now. They collected around her irises.

"Soothe your wolf," Ruri said quietly as she sauntered past them, the words barely reaching Mary Alice's ears. "But not too much."

Satisfied she had someone at her back who could cover them, Mary Alice slipped into the short hallway. A small living room opened up at her left. She looked back and caught Ruri's eye before inclining her head to the side. The werewolf nodded and moved into the room. Mary Alice crept along past built-in china cabinets that gleamed dully in the light filtering through the front windows. The sky was lightening, but the streetlights still shone out front and gave her more than enough illumination to see by.

The banister was a bit of a barrier to her line of sight, and she shifted her grip on the katana. If an attack was going to come, this was where she would have launched it. A supra might choose somewhere else, but someone with her training would take advantage of the high ground. She didn't think Uncle Ralph knew about the house. She'd planned it as the first leg of an escape route if she ever needed to get out of town. There was never any telling exactly how much the government knew, though, and until she was satisfied the house was empty, she would act as if the man himself waited up those stairs.

Cassidy trod on the back of her shoe again, and she bit back an acid comment. Her sister was diverting her focus, threatening to derail it. While it was gratifying that she'd chosen to stick with her and not the other lycan, this was typical Cassidy timing: unfortunate.

"Go to Ruri," she hissed as she turned the corner. The stairs yawned dark and empty above her. Just the upstairs to take care of, then the basement.

The first stair creaked slightly under her weight, but she made sure to spread it out, and it wasn't more than a small sound. Old houses were that much harder to sneak around in, especially one like this with only the barest furnishings. There wasn't much in there to absorb stray noises. She was halfway up when she realized the stairs were creaking behind her. There was nothing to do but grit her teeth and continue clearing each room. Cassidy's presence couldn't be allowed to distract her from the task at hand.

The second floor held two small bedrooms tucked under the eaves, both of which were blessedly empty, though the light was on in the back bedroom.

"Was someone here?" Cassidy cast her voice low, and she shifted to place her back against the wall. She had some instincts of self-preservation, it seemed. Hopefully she would pick up more, and soon.

"The light is on a timer," Mary Alice said absently. "I don't want the neighbors thinking the place is empty. I come by once a week at least to pick up junk mail, allow myself to be seen, though never from close up. There's no sense in encouraging anyone to make friends. If you and Ruri stay inside most of the time, everyone should go right on thinking what we want them to."

"You've done this before, haven't you?"

Mary Alice raised one shoulder; then let it drop. The less Cassidy knew, the safer she would be. The thought was a nice one, but she was uncomfortably aware it wasn't much more than a pretty fiction. She headed back for the stairs and didn't bother trying to hide her presence. The only place anyone could be waiting for them was the basement. If someone was down there, they already knew she was home and that she had company.

"How long have you been doing this stuff?" Cassidy asked, her voice sharper.

"Long enough."

Ruri was waiting for them at the bottom of the stairs. Her eyes held a dozen questions as she met Mary Alice's eyes, most of which Mary Alice wasn't prepared to answer. She nodded slightly; upstairs was clear.

"What do you do, exactly?" Cassidy's hand on her forearm slowed her down for a second, but she gently brushed it off. The longer she could delay this conversation, the better. Her sister wasn't going to be happy, but there was no point in rushing the confrontation. Besides, the basement still had to be cleared.

"She's a Hunter," Ruri said. "She executes us."

CHAPTER TWENTY-SIX

The drive back home was quiet and lonely. As much as Mary Alice had been praying for some silence, it wasn't as welcome as she'd expected. Cassidy hadn't looked at her once, not after she realized that Ruri had meant Mary Alice executed beings like them. A couple of weeks previous, Cassidy would have been horrified at the mere idea of her killing anybody. It was another sign of how quickly she was acclimating to her new circumstances that she hadn't mentioned anything about the executions. And yet, Cassidy was still refusing to talk, just as she'd expected. At least Ruri didn't look at her as if she was a monster.

Her laugh was bitter and tasted like ashes. If anyone was the monster, it was them. She was the human; she was the one who was still pure. Or so the army had said before starting them on the regimen of injections, supplements and surgeries that had transformed their cadre before each other's eyes.

Many of the lovers she'd had since the procedures loved her muscular body. They exclaimed over the definition of her abs, how the muscle seemed to slide effortlessly beneath the skin of her legs, how her upper arms bulged impressively when she flexed. She'd gloried in it, for a while. She was stronger and faster. Her reaction speed was lightning quick, allowing her to keep up with the vampires, werewolves and worse that roamed Chicago's streets. There wasn't much that could outrun her and so far nothing had outsmarted her in battle or not for long, anyway.

The transformation had been arduous and long and had made her into the perfect weapon against supras. Nothing had prepared her for the isolation. Without Cassidy and their mother, Mary Alice was certain she would have killed herself years ago. They'd been trained in compartmentalization, about closing off parts of their lives to those around them. It should have been easy, given the constant trouble she'd been in during high school. There had been a time when she couldn't wait to leave home. When it became clear college wouldn't be an option for her, she'd walked into the nearest recruiting station and signed up with the Army. By the time she was done with special training, home was a distant if fond memory, one she couldn't wait to get back to.

Mary Alice had discovered she had to close herself off from her body as well. The glory of the chase couldn't be matched, and when she wasn't stretching her body to its utmost limits and feeling adrenaline pounding through her limbs, she felt hollow. The world was a cold place, verging on colorless, but when the thrill of the chase rode her, everything was crisp and real. Sex helped a little bit, both in the feeling of closeness and in the adrenaline, but the comfort was fleeting.

Family had been what kept her sane. *Had.* It remained to be seen what role it would play in future. She'd managed to keep Cassidy alive, but now she was driving her sister away.

What am I going to tell Mom? The thought was too perilous to contemplate, and Mary Alice pushed it away as she pulled under the door to the first floor. There was much to do before Stiletto got there and little time to dwell on problems that weren't of immediate concern, let alone something that was still an unformed possibility.

That she would rather dwell on the arrival of someone who would probably insist Cassidy be put down rather than talk to her mom about what happened wasn't lost on her. Still, one had to choose one's battles. And if you couldn't choose the battle, it paid to have some say over the terrain.

There wasn't much that needed to be cleaned up on the first floor. She tossed the halves of the explosive anklet into a chest filled with other explosives-related odds and ends. It would be easy enough to explain there, and Stiletto would have to root through a lot to even wonder about it. No, the more damning bits of evidence were on the third floor. What was she going to do with the giant metal box?

Almost at the top of the stairs, Mary Alice had a flash of inspiration and backtracked to the second floor. TC's message had been spare on the details. All she knew was that one of her old squadmates was on her way, called in by Uncle Ralph. When Stiletto would be there, or why Ralph had seen fit to bring her, she had no idea. She was already on borrowed time, but how much remained to be seen.

The door brought back memories of the last time she'd been there, her back pressed to it and fingering herself as she burned for the werewolf upstairs. The werewolf who was no longer upstairs. There was no point in dwelling on that either.

The first things she needed were the metal cutouts she'd bashed off this same box only days ago. It seemed like that had been months ago. Cassidy's makeshift prison had started life as an installation piece, something different from what she normally did. It was terrible, made even more so by the need to lock her sister up inside it. Mary Alice promised herself that when she had the time, she would take the metal out and scrap it. Nothing good could come of it now.

It took a few trips to get the pieces up the stairs to the box. After another couple of trips, she had the welding equipment upstairs. Two hours later, she had a large metal art installation back on her hands. The box now had a plausible explanation for being there. The presence of lycan pheromones was another question. She opened the windows and hoped the wind would take care of the smell. Uncle Ralph might not have noticed them, but Stiletto certainly would.

The breeze filtering through large loft windows rapidly cooled the sweat that had accumulated as she'd worked on the box. Mary Alice rubbed her palms over the gooseflesh on her arms and headed for bed. It had been a long day and she hadn't slept for over twenty-four hours. She was accustomed to operating on varying amounts of sleep, but it wouldn't do to push things much further. She needed to be at the top of her game when company arrived.

The bed called to her and she took enough time to strip off her clothes. Thinking better of leaving them in a pile next to the bed, she snagged her bathrobe. The bedclothes would smell as much of lycan as her clothing currently did. They had to be taken care of. Lethargy dragged at her, slowing her and weighing down her eyelids. It was as if having given herself permission to head to bed, her body was actively resisting the last-minute chore she was putting it through. Finally everything was in the washer and she stumbled back to the bedroom, eyes closed for most of the walk back. Without bothering to put new sheets on the bed, Mary Alice let the bathrobe drop to the floor and rolled herself up in the quilt.

As exhausted as she was, sleep proved elusive.

"I can't believe she didn't tell me any of this." Cassidy leaned back into Ruri's comforting arms. The tears had stopped, but their damp tracks still remained. "How could I have been so blind? I knew she didn't always tell me everything that was going on in her life, but this…This is everything!"

"What would you have done if she'd told you?" Ruri asked. She understood very well why Malice had been less than forthcoming with her family. What would it have been like to know that their loved one was putting herself in harm's way every day? As far as she was concerned, it was a kindness to keep it from them, especially considering what had happened when the two worlds had actually intersected.

"I don't know." To her credit, Cassidy seemed to be seriously considering the question. She scrubbed the tear tracks off her face and inhaled deeply. "It would have seemed pretty crazy. But if she'd proved it, we would've believed her."

"Then what? Would you have been able to keep quiet about what she was doing? No one knows about us, at least not officially."

"I suppose." The questions weren't sitting well with Cassidy. She kept shifting her weight. It was like she was sitting on a rock, which was unlikely on the hardwood floor.

"You wanted her to make an exception for you." Ruri held her close for a second longer then let Cassidy go. "You're the reason she couldn't make an exception. You and your mom."

Cassidy rose to her feet in one motion and started pacing the length of the small living room. She slowed to peer out the windows each time she passed. "I know. And yet."

They were getting nowhere. It was time for a change of subject. "You're nervous. What's up?"

"I'm not sure. The wolf feels like we need to run, like someone's closing in."

"It's normal to have problems keeping your wolf down at the beginning. You need to work off some extra energy, that's all." Ruri wasn't feeling threatened. She was a little unsettled, that much was true. They hadn't had a chance to sit and breathe since the previous morning, and the way Malice had burst in and uprooted them again didn't bode well. But there was no immediate danger that she could sense. What she did sense was an absence. The absence of her packmates still ached, and the absence of Malice even more so.

"I would like to go for a run." Cassidy turned away from the window with a rueful grin. "I don't think I've ever said that before in my life. I hated P.E. in high school, and I've never been into sports. Mary was the sporty one. Until she was kicked off the basketball team her senior year, that is."

"I don't know this area, so I can't say where it would be safe to do that. We should wait until night, anyway. It's dangerous to go out as wolven during the day." Ruri got to her feet with the same economy of movement as Cassidy. The girl was learning quickly. "That doesn't mean we can't go look around and get the lay of the land."

"Yes, let's!" Cassidy darted across the room toward the front door.

"Don't!" Her strangled shout had the intended result and Cassidy skidded to a stop. "Look." She shouldered her way past her and indicated the rolled plastic around the doorframe. The end of a small wire was taped to the top corner of the door. It led to a piece of copper with wires coming out of it and jammed into the plastic. A familiar scent rose off it and scraped lightly at her nasal passages.

"Is that a booby trap?"

"It sure is. I'd recognize that smell anywhere. It's C-4. I had it strapped to my ankle for long enough."

"Jesus." Cassidy backed slowly away from the door. "She's crazy."

"Of course she isn't."

"Who booby-traps a front door with explosives?"

"Someone who has good reason to think she'll eventually have to go on the run. Someone who knows exactly what lurks in the dark." Ruri smiled slowly, her lips spreading off her teeth. The grin was predatory, and she didn't care. It's what she was, a predator, and one that humans did well to be terrified of. "There's worse out there than us, never forget that."

Cassidy shivered. "Let's go for that walk." She was only a few days removed from humanity. Her primitive hind brain must have been screaming warnings at her. One day, probably soon, the predatory side would be second nature. All Ruri had to do was make sure she lived long enough to get there.

"I suggest we take the back door."

"Good call."

Enough time had passed that the sun was well above the horizon, casting shadows through what trees remained to line the streets. The city's ash trees had been hard hit the past couple of years by parasites and were being cut down by the dozen. It was hard to tell if the trees still standing were bare because they slumbered in fall's grip or if they were dead, never to awaken again. Ruri supposed spring would tell. It was a melancholy thought, one she had practically every year. The steady trek of fall into winter always made her sad. She loved warm weather and couldn't wait until she could bask under a sky that warmed instead of one that chilled. Her wolf didn't understand. To her, summer was to be tolerated, while winter was time to play as the sometimes-bitter cold had no effect upon her thick pelt.

Memories of frolicking in the snow with Dean sprang unbidden to her mind. Her Alpha had loved the snow both in human and wolven form. The cold didn't seem to bother him at all. She'd seen him get into a snowball fight with pack young wearing nothing but a pair of pants as clouds from his laughing breath wreathed his chest and head. Would she hear the laughter of young wolven again? She hoped they had all survived MacTavish's usurpation.

"What's wrong?" Cassidy's soft question pulled her from her contemplation.

"Is it that obvious?"

"Your scent went low and blue." She shrugged self-consciously. "It seems like you're sad. You feel sad in my head."

There was no way Cassidy should have been sensitive enough to distinguish emotions, not yet. Her presence in Ruri's now-diminished web of awareness was only starting to coalesce. While she could have found Cassidy in a crowd, she certainly wouldn't have been able to make a judgment about how she felt, not without being able to smell her. Chalk up one more way she's different, Ruri thought.

"I miss my pack. My family." No point in burdening Cassidy with how different she was. She would learn soon enough. "I know some of them went with MacTavish." At Cassidy's raised eyebrow, Ruri elaborated. "The loner who killed my Alpha. He took over my pack then sicced his dogs on you."

If any of the pack members who had turned Cassidy had been there to hear the slur, she would have been attacked for sure. Calling one of the wolven dogs—implying they were domesticated by human hands—was about as mortal an insult as could be leveled at one of them, worse even than calling one a werewolf.

"Sounds like a great guy."

Cassidy's dry comment startled a bark of laughter from deep within Ruri. It seemed both sisters had a knack for making her smile: Cassidy by insisting on moving forward and getting answers, no matter the obstacles in her way. Mary Alice for…for what exactly? Ruri wasn't certain why she felt the way she did for her people's executioner. By all rights, she should have hated her. The human had kidnapped her and held her against her will. Her wolf should have been ready to rip her throat out, and yet she seemed like she wanted to curl up around her. She was so serious, so committed to providing for her sister, and without any support from those who mattered most. She labored alone in a very dark place. There was something admirable about her dedication, for all that it seemed sorely misplaced.

Sure, there *were* those who wreaked havoc upon their community, and they needed to be dealt with. MacTavish was case and point on that one. He'd broken their own tightly held rules and traditions and he was getting away with it. The wolven needed an arbitrator on occasion, both within their packs and without, against other groups of wolven and the vamps. And the other things that went bump in the night.

"So what are you going to do about him?" The question was uncharacteristically direct for someone so recently turned. Cassidy didn't waste time, it seemed. "What are we going to do? This asshole has destroyed my life. I'd like some of my own back, too."

"The pack might have been taken over, but not everyone stayed. I caught the scent of one of my packmates in the park last night. I didn't smell other wolven there, so I think he was alone, but I'm not sure. If he'd stayed with the pack, it's unlikely he would have been hunting alone so far from their new den."

Ruri stopped walking and stared into the distance. With one more they would be four, enough to start considering themselves a proper pack, though a small one. "I say we track him down and see if there are any more left out there. Let's rebuild the pack as well as we can from what's left, then we can go take back what's ours."

The more she thought about it, the more she liked the idea. Ruri was getting strong again, almost back to her original condition. With the strength of a pack around her, she would be in fighting form in no time. Cassidy was insanely strong, that much was already evident. Mary Alice would round out their little group and they would be formidable indeed. Her cheeks stretched and she realized she was grinning from ear to ear.

Cassidy stood in front of her, fists balled, a matching smile upon her face. "Let's do it."

Her wolf shifted in her breast, exultant energy washing through her and leaving a fading tingle behind it. Ruri had to hold herself back to keep from throwing back her head and howling her exuberance. The neighbors would talk surely if two women started baying at the clouds. She hoped that somewhere out there MacTavish felt the shift in the wind and was quietly alarmed.

CHAPTER TWENTY-SEVEN

The light streaming through the windows proved too bright to ignore any longer. Mary Alice opened her eyes and stared at the edge of the pillow. When was the last time she'd slept in her own bed? It seemed like she hadn't used it since before Cassidy had been bitten, but that couldn't be right. Could it? Since then, she'd been snatching bits and pieces of sleep where and when she could, most of them while seated and within eyeshot of the box. Groaning, she pushed herself up and glanced at the clock on the bedside table. Almost noon. Great.

"Not even six hours of sleep," she said aloud. The words echoed hollowly through the space. The loft felt empty, emptier than it had before she'd brought Ruri in. "Time to get to work." There she went again, still talking to herself, but it made the room feel like it had a little more life.

With a yawn that felt like it was going to pop off the top of her head, Mary Alice swung her legs over the bed's side and pushed herself up. The lure of warm covers tempted her. The room had gotten quite cool with all the windows open and the breeze rustling through. If any scent traces of lycan remained, she couldn't tell. She closed them all, which took a while. Walking the perimeter of the huge space she had up there only reminded her of how alone she was. Breakfast was a couple of eggs scrambled with green peppers and onions and stuck between two slices of bread. She devoured the sandwich on her way down the stairs.

She didn't need many lights for her sparring exercises. Darkness shrouded the rest of the first floor and Mary Alice stared through it as she ran through her forms with the practice blade. She lost herself in the flow from one stance to the next.

A change in the darkness brought her back to herself. It was nothing she saw. It hadn't been a sound either, more a change in the way the air moved. She flowed into a crouch, the wooden katana held at the ready. Somebody or something was in there with her.

A form dropped from the rafters to land behind her with a soft thump. Mary Alice whirled and lunged. She didn't come close to making contact. It was like trying to catch a cloud always drifting out of the reach of her sword.

Whoever it was had to be human or at least humanoid. It was almost impossible to catch a clear glimpse. They never stopped moving. All she could see was black clothes, tight to an androgynous body that was slender as a rail. Her visitor wasn't attacking and Mary Alice rapidly tired of the game.

"Can't you knock on the front door like a normal person?"

"I'm not a normal person." Her visitor came to a stop and folded her arms. "Neither are you, Malice."

"Would it hurt to act like it just this once?"

Mary Alice's grumbles didn't faze the other woman. She pulled the hood off her head to reveal close-cropped curls and dark skin. A wide smile split her face but didn't quite warm obsidian eyes.

"Then again, for you, it probably would. Hello, Stiletto."

"It's good to see you. How surprised were you?"

"Plenty surprised when I got word you were coming."

A small frown creased the skin between her eyebrows. "Uncle Ralph said he wasn't giving you the heads up."

"I have ways of staying up to date." Stiletto cocked her head questioningly, but she refused to elaborate. "What I don't know is why he saw fit to bring you on. Things are just fine here. I don't need your help." She moved to the side of the cage and placed the practice sword back in its holder, then grabbed a towel. On its own the workout hadn't been quite enough to work up a sweat, but her faceoff with Stiletto had perspiration rolling down the sides of her face and dripping along the small of her back.

"He seems to think you're not on top of the situation with that pack of lycans."

"That's insane. I checked up on them. They've moved to a different den location, but they aren't bothering anyone."

"But that's not the full story, at least not from what Uncle Ralph told me."

"What do you mean?" Mary Alice stopped toweling her face and stared at Stiletto, dreading what came next. Had Uncle Ralph somehow found out about Cassidy? She shifted her glance back to the practice blade. Stiletto was incredibly challenging to get a touch on with a blade, but if she could get the drop on her, Mary Alice could kill her with the wooden sword. It would be difficult, but she could manage. But only if she wasn't expecting anything.

"Your pack that isn't bothering anyone has taken to hijacking trailer trucks and stealing then selling the contents."

"What?" Her eyes shifted back to Stiletto in shock. She stared at the woman, hoping she'd misheard.

"You really didn't know?" Stiletto closed the gap between them and placed her hand on the practice katana. "How could you have missed that? They're being incredibly brazen about it. Uncle Ralph has video footage of them. Half of them were in wolf form. Fortunately, the local cops seem to think they're just large dogs."

"Of course I didn't know," Mary Alice said. She stepped away from her squadmate. "I would have put a stop to it if I'd known."

"He thinks you're being distracted. A new girlfriend or something. That's not a good idea. You know the program forbids it."

Mary Alice barked a dry laugh. "The program forbids a lot of things. You know, like getting blind drunk every night or shooting up. Let's not forget killing supras who haven't done anything?"

A lift of the shoulder was Stiletto's only response. "None of those are my problem, and I haven't broken any of those regs."

"I know." It would have made sense to assume Stiletto's handle had been given to her because of the way she looked. She was one of the most physically strong women Mary Alice had ever known, but there was no trace of it anywhere on her slender frame. Certainly, her slenderness had been a factor, but Mary Alice had always thought she must have gotten the name as much for her unerring aim and focus. She never missed a mark. She simply wouldn't allow it to happen. As far as Stiletto was concerned, the rules were there for a reason and should always be followed. She wondered what the woman would have done in her situation.

"Good." Stiletto rubbed her hands together. "Let's get your lycan problem under control."

"I can show you where they're staying, and we'll go from there."

"So a badass werewolf lives here?" Cassidy looked skeptical.

"Wolven," Ruri corrected absently. She understood Cassidy's disbelief, but this was where her nose had led. Lewis's trail had faded somewhat by the time they got back to the park, thanks to Ruri's hotwiring skills. Cassidy had been more than a little horrified about stealing a car. Only Ruri's reassurances that they would return it had mollified her, though she'd been nervous the entire drive up. It certainly wasn't Ruri's first time driving a stolen car, though the way Cassidy was reacting, it might be her last. She knew better than to stick out when driving a hot car. That meant acting like everyone else and breaking the speed limit. Being the slowest car on the road was almost as damning as being the fastest. If they did get pulled over, Cassidy would give them away for sure. Then they'd get to explain why Ruri didn't exist.

It had taken a while to retrace their steps once they got to the park. While the day wasn't far on by human standards, there were still enough of them in the park that Ruri hadn't felt it prudent to shift to wolven form. They parked not far from where they'd been the night before and watched as a trim human woman jogged past them down the trail. She paid scant attention to them, more interested in what she listened to on her headphones. She would have been easy prey if they'd been looking for a snack. From the voices that filtered out around the headphones, the jogger was listening to some sort of podcast then, not music. The brush with a human convinced her she'd been right to be leery of shifting, and they'd set off through the underbrush on foot.

The going was a lot rougher on two legs than it had been on four. Cassidy hadn't complained, but it was clear she still hadn't completely recovered from her days'-long ordeal. Her panting had sounded heavily in Ruri's ears, though she'd slowed their pace a few times to compensate. Still, when they paused to rest, Cassidy had recovered quickly enough.

Her human nose was no match for that of the wolf's and she chafed at not being able to shift. It took some doing, but by the time the sun had risen above the trees she had recaptured Lewis's scent.

He'd obviously been hunting the night before. His scent meandered through the woods until they happened upon his kill. What was left of a rabbit carcass had been stuffed into a hollow log, possibly for later. After that, he'd wandered the periphery of the trees overlooking expanses of lawn where even now, suburban men and women gathered for their morning exercise. What had interested Lewis so much the night before? Ruri had no way of knowing for sure, but she'd seen deer scat at the edge of the grass.

Not long before, he'd shifted into human form at the spot where they now stood. He must have stashed his clothes, as Ruri had gone from following paw tracks to bare feet for a few steps, then boots. She'd understood why when they'd scrambled over large rocks lining a narrow creek. It was the opening in the rocks that Cassidy stared at so dubiously now. It looked like they would have to climb inside a sewer culvert if they were to follow Lewis.

"That's what it looks like," Ruri said. "He's come by here an awful lot from his scent layers." She lifted her head and inhaled deeply. Lewis's scent was overlaid on the rocks, but she also got a noseful of rotting vegetation. It wasn't a sewer culvert then; it was probably for storm runoff. That was a relief, but not what she'd been searching for. There it was again. More than one wolven had used this entrance. Anticipation tingled through her. If she'd had a tail, it would have been wagging. "Come on."

Ruri clambered deftly over the rocks. From the scrabbling behind her, Cassidy followed along gamely though not gracefully. There was a grate over the mouth of the culvert but when she looked more closely, Ruri realized it was only resting in place. Someone had popped out the bolts securing it to the metal walls. She pulled on it, swinging it toward her and held it out for Cassidy. It was heavy enough for her, but Cassidy handled it without any comment or evidence of strain.

The entry yawned dark in front of them. Ruri could make out only shadows. They would need to enter and allow their eyes to acclimate before either of them would be able to see. Her wolf whined and shifted within her breast. She didn't like the idea of being effectively blind for the few moments it would take before they'd be able to really see again. Neither did Ruri, but there was nothing for it.

She slid through the gap between the edge of the culvert wall and the grate while Cassidy quietly held it up for her. As soon as she was clear, Cassidy followed her in and pulled the grate closed behind them.

"Let's go," Ruri said quietly. She started forward, Cassidy glued to her side. Their footsteps echoed hollowly on the corrugated metal, even with her best efforts at stealth. A few yards from the entry, the metal gave way to concrete or maybe stone. Her eyes hadn't acclimated enough to be able to tell. All she could really see were shadows stretching in front of them. The sickly sweet smell of rotting vegetation filled her nasal cavities, effectively blocking out anything other than the occasional hint of wolven.

They continued deeper into the black and slowly Ruri was able to make out shapes. There wasn't much to see, mostly piles of rotten leaves. Once she caught sight of what might have been a teddy bear sticking out of one of the piles. *How did that get down here?*

"Ruri," Cassidy whispered. She caught Ruri's elbow and pulled her to a stop.

"What is it?"

"We're not alone."

Ruri cast futilely about, trying to see more than vague shapes in the dark. Something moved against the far wall. Her wolf sprang to full alert, digging into the underside of her skin with her claws. She wanted out and Ruri's jaws ached with the effort of keeping her contained.

"No, you're not."

The voice was familiar and Ruri relaxed a bit, though her wolf did not. "Lewis." There was no response. "Come on, Lewis, it's me. It's Ruri."

"We know who you are." Rustling filled the passageway and more shadows slid into place around them. There was a soft pop and a sickly green glow lit the bottom of Lewis's face, throwing a stark shadow on the stone wall and ceiling. Half a dozen wolven surrounded them at a junction in the sewer pipe. "What we don't know is why you abandoned us."

CHAPTER TWENTY-EIGHT

"It looks empty," Stiletto said.

They lay side by side on top of the building from which she'd first watched the North Side pack's new den. Privately, Malice agreed, but didn't say anything. To do so would be to admit she'd fallen down on the job. If the pack wasn't there, they could be anywhere.

"They were here last time I checked on them."

"When was that?"

"Last week." It might even have been true; if not she wasn't off by that much. The days and nights hadn't meant much since Cassidy's attack.

"It's Thursday." Stiletto's voice held no emphasis, nothing to betray how she really felt. The lack of inflection carried enough indictment for twelve juries.

"They're not my only concern." *Is that too defensive?* Malice dialed back the heat. "Chicago's a big city, you know."

"So's Atlanta. You don't see me slacking off on my major lycan packs."

Malice stood and headed for the edge of the roof. A ladder led down to the ground. "Whatever. I'm going to go check it out."

"Finally." Stiletto was on her heels; she jostled past Malice to reach the ladder first. The woman had always been competitive, especially during training. She'd wanted everyone to think she was the best and had gone to some extreme lengths to prove it. Not that she'd ever broken any rules in her pursuit. There was no one more by the book than Stiletto. And of course, that hadn't ever prevented her from getting anyone else brought up on regs. It was part of what made her so dangerous. There was no way she would overlook Malice keeping Ralph in the dark about the werewolf attack on Cassidy.

The abandoned hub was at the edge of the industrial park, which was fairly active at this time of day. Large trucks rumbled to and fro on the park's winding roads. Fortunately, there was a lot of space between buildings and none of the civilians seemed to notice the two women. Even if they'd looked closely, it would have been difficult to make out their weapons, concealed as they were beneath long dusters. The wind wasn't making it easy. It tugged at the ends of their clothing, and Malice had to hold the end of her coat in place over the katana at her waist. Stiletto had no such problems, but then she didn't favor a weapon that long. Her preferred weapons were a pair of long knives for which the pommels doubled as stakes.

The chain-link fence around the long low former transportation hub was breeched in many places, and they easily found a spot to slip through. The closer they got to the main building, the more Malice became on edge. Her senses were open to their maximum, her eyes darting this way and that. It felt like nothing escaped them. Stiletto's company at her side was no distraction. Her presence faded into the background and didn't stand out in her mind like the other life forms around her.

There wasn't much else on her radar. Beyond the low-level energy she felt when in any area with wildlife and vegetation in it, she couldn't feel much.

"Feels pretty empty," Stiletto said, unconsciously echoing her own thoughts.

"Doesn't mean they've gone."

The sideways glance her companion leveled at her was damning in its lack of emotion. Stiletto knew she'd fucked up, but she wasn't going to say anything, not to Malice. No, she'd save that for her report to Uncle Ralph.

They got to a side door in the otherwise featureless side of the building. Three of the sides were almost completely featureless, while the far side held row upon row of loading docks. It was a strange place for a lycan pack to hole up. Each door represented a potential way in. It wouldn't have been easy if someone had decided to attack them. MacTavish obviously had something at work, and the building had been a part of it. Still, if he was robbing trailers, why wasn't he using the building anymore? Maybe she'd spooked him when she took out his wolves.

Malice pulled out her katana and held it at the ready. The doorknob turned under her hand. Stiletto readied her weapons on the other side. If there was anyone inside, they were well concealed and hadn't moved in quite some time. The chances were slim, but neither of them had survived this long without being cautious when warranted. Though caution wasn't the word she would use for sneaking into a possible pack den with only one other person. Yes, Stiletto was a member of the Program, but the only other time Malice had taken on an entire pack, she'd called in a squad of soldiers to help her handle the threat. The two of them could do a lot of damage on their own, but if they were wrong about the pack being gone, they would probably be torn to shreds. The unmarked pauper's grave at Homewood Cemetery beckoned.

Three, two, one, she mouthed, and yanked the door open. Stiletto burst through, making no more noise than a soft breeze through light curtains. Malice was right on her heels. She too was practically soundless, at least to human ears. Lycans were a different matter. Supras were always a different matter.

The hallway beyond was dark and locked in shadows. The light coming through the doorway allowed her to see well enough. The carpet had seen better days. It was stained and torn in places. Mustiness and damp were the first smells to reach her nostrils. There hadn't been any air moving through this hall in some time.

Stiletto led the way down the hall to the lonely door at the far end. It swung open under her touch, but not quietly. As it reached the end of its swing, it scraped on the concrete floor. The rasp of metal on cement echoed back through the hall, and Malice grimaced. If any lycans still remained, they knew someone else was on the premises.

Again, there was no sign of anyone. It seemed this had once been an office area. The only light in the room was what filtered in from the hallway and managed to make its way through a series of three filthy skylights high above. It was enough that they could see clearly. Cubicles took up most of the area, forming a maze of half walls around the periphery of the large room and in the center. Malice glanced into one and wasn't surprised to see a mattress along one side. It was heaped with dirty blankets. Something had made it into quite the nest. The cubicles were somewhat protected and enclosed; it made sense that the lycans might convert them to sleep in.

It seemed more like the actions of a feral, however. The pack members she'd run into had been more human in their behaviors. Ruri certainly was. This wasn't the sleeping place of a well-socialized lycan. She made a note to say something to Ruri about it. Maybe she'd have some insight.

Most of the rest of the cubes showed signs of having been inhabited. Some were neater than others, but all showed signs that their occupants had left in a hurry. Small belongings lay forgotten in the corners and the smell of spoiled meat lingered unpleasantly in the air.

It took them almost an hour to clear the rest of the old shipping hub. It was just as empty as the office had been. The signs all pointed to the lycans using the office area and portions of the shipping and storage areas, but other parts of the building looked like they hadn't been touched at all.

"They're definitely gone." Stiletto dropped any attempt at stealth. "Any ideas where they might have ended up?"

"No clue." Malice sheathed her katana. "If they're hijacking trucks, they'll need a setup like this. I'd start looking for more abandoned trucking operations."

"Maybe." Stiletto chewed on her lower lip thoughtfully. "Unless they figure this is the kind of place you'll check out first. What do you know about the new Alpha?"

Malice shrugged. "I know his name is MacTavish and he's nothing like the old one. He was a lone wolf before he decided to take over the pack. Based on what he's done since taking over, he's no saint, but the first time I heard about him was after that. So he's smart and knows how to keep a low profile."

"Great, that's just what we need. An intelligent animal. And he has a plan and the muscle to carry it out." Stiletto shook her head. "You are in so much trouble. It's a good thing I'm here to give you a hand."

"Oh yeah, it's great." *You're exactly what I need.* Still, if Stiletto could be kept on the trail of MacTavish and his pack, Malice would get some opportunities to peel off and check in on Ruri and Cassidy. All she had to do was keep the other woman occupied. "Let's go check out the scenes of the hijackings."

Ruri laughed, the sound raw in her throat. "Abandoned you? I've been trying to find you."

"It took you long enough." Lewis moved closer to them. He purposefully stepped in close enough that his body heat washed over her.

That deep inside her envelope of personal space, she fought the urge to push him back. That wasn't right. Lewis was pack, she should have welcomed his nearness, but her wolf prodded her to get him away from them. He might be pack, but right now he was a threat.

"Leave her alone," Cassidy said. She laid a hand on his shoulder and hauled him back.

"Don't," Ruri said too late. Lewis was looking for a confrontation, and Cassidy had just handed him one on a silver platter.

He whirled on Cassidy and lunged, snapping. His face lengthened into a partially furred muzzle that sprouted teeth as long as her thumb. They flashed in the shadows as he brought them together with a resounding clash mere inches from her face. Pinkish fluid drooled down from his jaws and his eyes glowed green in the dark.

The rest of the wolven moved forward, trapping them both in a tightening ring. Eyes of every imaginable shade gleamed menacingly at them. The telltale snap of bone rang out around them. Some of the watching wolven were shifting.

Her wolf savaged the underside of her belly with her claws. She demanded to be released, to protect herself and Cassidy.

No, not now! The pain was tremendous, as bad as anything the wolf might have inflicted on her skin. But if she gave in to her wolf and shifted, lashing out at the wolven around them, she would break whatever tenuous pack bonds remained.

Frustrated that Ruri wouldn't go after those hemming them in, her wolf growled. The sound escaped through her throat. Her jaws and hands ached. The change would be upon her soon if she couldn't calm down.

Her internal struggle seemed to go unremarked by the wolven, whose eyes never left Lewis and Cassidy. She had her hand wrapped around his throat and held him at arm's length. Lewis growled and slavered, covering her arm with saliva as he tried to reach her. No matter how he twisted, Cassidy kept him away from her. Lewis was an impressive figure in human form, and halfway to full wolf form, he was even more imposing. By all rights he should have been able to crush Cassidy, who barely came up to his shoulder.

The only sign of her wolf was in her eyes, one glowing brilliant azure, the other bright crimson. Aside from that, she seemed not to need the strength of her wolf to take on her challenger.

They were at a stalemate, Lewis unwilling to back down and Cassidy unable to. The second she gave an inch, the wolven would be at her neck for daring to challenge him. Cassidy's forearm had started to shake from the effort of holding Lewis at bay. The wolven realized it and redoubled his efforts, the nails on his back claws digging into the hard ground. Bit by bit, Cassidy was forced back, her shoes sliding on slime-covered concrete.

Ruri shifted around, ready to launch herself at Lewis should he get the upper hand. It broke every challenge rule she had ever known, and yet her wolf insisted upon it. Letting Cassidy die would be a far worse crime than leaving the challenge to the two wolven engaged in it. Cassidy was blood of Mary Alice. She belonged to the small pack Ruri had started to gather. The wolven around them now lay outside that pack.

Blood trickled down Lewis's neck and his thrashing redoubled. Cassidy's nails had transformed, piercing his skin beneath the fur obscuring his neck. He lashed out with a razor-clawed hand and caught Cassidy along the ribs, parting her shirt like paper and gouging four deep furrows into her skin.

She grunted, shock in her eyes, but her mouth tightened with what could only be resolve. Her mouth exploded in her own double row of razor-sharp teeth. She screamed in Lewis's face, a howl of deep and abiding rage that would have shredded the vocal cords of any human.

They toppled over in a blur of limbs and fur, rolling over and over until it was impossible to tell which had the advantage or was on top. The ring of wolven moved and shifted with them, and Ruri had to scamper to keep up. The combatants fetched up against the edge of the tunnel with a loud slam. When they stopped, Cassidy was astride her challenger, barely recognizable in her half-shifted form. Lewis lay on his back beneath her, in full wolf pelt. He didn't move a muscle and held himself so still his muscles quivered slightly. His eyes rolled to keep an eye on Cassidy, who had her teeth clamped around his throat. That crazed pattern of fur covered her, peeking out in multihued tufts through the rents in her clothes.

Lewis twisted, freeing his back legs. They kicked at her, his back claws digging into the flesh of her stomach; his front claws remained embedded in her shoulder. Blood streaked Cassidy's fur, and Ruri's wolf demanded she act immediately. By clenching her fists and digging the claws into her palm, Ruri was able to resist, but only barely. Slowly, imperceptibly, muscle by muscle, Lewis relaxed, pulling his claws free. Blood dripped down onto his pelt, mixing with his own, both liberally painting his front and sides.

Cassidy showed no sign of letting go. All it would take to end Lewis was a shake of her head, and he would be gone, neck broken and throat slashed.

"Cassidy." Ruri scooted forward on all fours, moving almost crablike across the cold floor. Lewis's eyes and those of the wolven surrounding them turned to her. Cassidy's did not. "Cassidy!" She reached out and touched the victorious wolven. "You beat him. He's done. You can let go now."

Awareness returned to her gaze, and she flicked her eyes up to meet Ruri's. A questioning whine made its way out, past her mouthful of flesh and fur.

"It's okay. You won. He'll be okay now."

Beneath her, Lewis carefully nodded his shaggy wolf head.

Cassidy relaxed her jaws slightly, enough that her teeth were no longer embedded in his neck. The rest of her stayed tense, poised for action should Lewis attack. When he didn't, Cassidy let go of his shoulders where her hands wrapped in his pelt. As she moved back, Ruri saw that just as his claws had been buried in Cassidy's skin, so too had her claws been buried in Lewis's. He rolled away with some effort and pulled himself up to all four paws.

The ring of wolven moved in toward them, and Cassidy whirled on them, her teeth gleaming threateningly in the shadows.

"It's okay," Ruri said, but her words were lost in the quiet voices of the wolven around them.

"Alpha," said one, then another until those still in human form chanted the word softly in overlapping murmurs. They reached Cassidy and touched her, running their hands over her pelt, those in full pelt rubbing their heads against her waist and thighs.

Cassidy stared at her, mute surprise evident on her face.

"Alpha," Ruri said quietly. She should have been as surprised as Cassidy, but she wasn't. Her wolf lay coiled quietly within her. She'd known all along.

Not sure how to feel, Ruri separated from the pack, slipping quietly through its ranks. No one noticed.

CHAPTER TWENTY-NINE

The safe house on Sayre Avenue was vacant. Mary Alice turned in a slow circle inside the kitchen, trying to get a sense of what she'd missed, if anything. She'd been through it top to bottom once already, and Ruri and Cassidy were definitely not there. *What the hell are they thinking?* Things hadn't quite started moving yet, but they were going to. Once they did, everyone needed to be ready to move at a moment's notice. There was a sense of urgency in the air; something was pushing her. Cassidy's transformation should have taken off the edge, but that didn't seem to be the case.

Stiletto was off checking out the final two hijacking locations. The first three had been useless for their purposes. Once again, Stiletto hadn't said anything to Mary Alice, but she was acutely aware that five hijacking incidents were four too many. She should have known about them days ago, and she had no excuses to offer. Instead, she'd slunk off saying she would look for leads in other areas.

"What is MacTavish up to, anyway?" This time she said the words aloud. It made the house feel a little less empty. For a second. Scent traces of the two werewolves still lingered, though they were fading rapidly. They hadn't spent enough time in the safe house to imprint their scent onto the place.

How long should she stick around, that was the question. Would they be back? If they weren't, Mary Alice hadn't the faintest idea where they'd gone. Or why. Her face colored slightly as she mentally amended the statement. She knew very well why Ruri would never want to see her again, though the werewolf had been less angry than she could have hoped. Cassidy was the one she couldn't understand disappearing. Hadn't she taken care of her? That she was still alive was thanks to her actions.

A rhythmic thumping sound pulled her out of her own head and she glanced at the back door before realizing it was her. She was tapping her foot. There was no point in sticking around any longer. Stiletto wasn't going to be occupied forever; she needed to get back to the loft.

Mary Alice reached for the door handle, but it turned under her hand and was pulled away from her. Ruri stood on the other side of the door. The look on her face was impossible to decipher and Mary Alice held her breath, wondering what was wrong.

They stared at each other for long moments before Mary Alice broke the silence.

"Where were you?" That was too accusing and she shifted tacks. "I was worried about you." That was no better.

"Worried?" The unreadable look on Ruri's face twitched into amusement. It was better than nothing, but not what she expected. She stepped through the doorway, pulling the door closed behind her. "Why would you do that?"

"I meant Cassidy." Why was she on the defensive? She'd done nothing wrong. It was perfectly reasonable that she should be checking on them.

Why is Cassidy always your second thought, then? she asked herself. *You can't stop thinking about Ruri and you know it. Can't stop thinking about how good she felt.*

Ruri's smile widened, and she stepped even closer, reaching out to lightly caress the edge of Mary Alice's collarbone where it peeked out of her shirt. "Sure you did."

The barest touch from Ruri was enough to send Mary Alice's heart hammering high in her chest. She was certain her cheeks were about to catch fire and a full breath was suddenly a major accomplishment.

When Mary Alice did nothing to stop or avoid the contact, Ruri moved so close Mary Alice felt the heat of her body scalding along the full length of her. It was all she could do not to lean in until they touched. A chance to be close to someone beckoned and she was tired of fighting it. This might be a werewolf, but she was no more a monster than Mary Alice was. In fact, in all the ways that counted, Mary Alice was the monster.

Tired of fighting a losing battle, she bridged the last of the distance between them. She covered Ruri's mouth with her own, molding her lips to the wolven's. After a moment of startled inaction, Ruri returned her kiss with interest. Arms came up and glided around her back, pulling her in tight. She moaned aloud at how good it felt to be held.

Ruri took advantage of her open mouth and gently slipped the tip of her tongue inside, teasing gently, almost questioningly. With a start, Mary Alice realized all she was doing was standing there like a lump. She was never the passive one, but it felt right to let Ruri take the lead. She skimmed her hands up over Ruri's hips, marveling at the coiled muscular power she felt, even through jeans. Her hands came to a rest at Ruri's waist for a moment before she took the opportunity to slide them beneath her shirt, touching soft skin she'd hungered after since seeing Ruri nude in the moonlight.

It was Ruri's turn to sigh at the contact, and Mary Alice pressed her advantage. A thrill shot through her at Ruri's arousal and she wondered if the wolven was as wet as she was. If this went on much longer, she was going to wish she had a change of underwear at the house. She moved her hands over silken skin, circling Ruri's waist; then moving back around to the front. Sculpted abs were hers to dance fingertips over. Ruri inhaled deeply in response to her touch.

Fingers tangled in her hair, pulling her head back and exposing her throat. Mary Alice bit her lip as a flood of wetness was released between her thighs. She was at Ruri's mercy. It would be the work of less than a second for the wolven to rip her throat out if she felt so inclined. It should have bothered her, but instead she yearned to be taken, to be wholly Ruri's, even if only for a little while. Warm breath caressed the sensitive skin along the side of her neck, followed by quick licks of Ruri's tongue. It was so hot that Mary Alice thought she would soon feel the pain of burning flesh. Instead, goose bumps broke out along her neck and down her left arm, spreading across her torso and all the way to the tips of her toes. She became aware that she clung to Ruri's waist and forced her knees to lock before she humiliated herself by collapsing in the kitchen.

"Maybe we should move somewhere more comfortable?" Ruri whispered the amused question in her ear.

Mary Alice quivered, trying to keep herself from flying apart. There was an appropriate response to Ruri's question, she knew it, but the answer was swimming just out of reach of her fogged brain's grasp. "Mm hmm," she finally managed.

"I'm so glad you agree." Ruri hooked her hands under Mary Alice's rump and squeezed.

"Oh god," Mary Alice said, throwing her head back. She was dimly aware of being lifted and wrapped her legs around Ruri's waist.

The wolven wasted no time once Mary Alice had limpeted herself to her. Ruri kept her safe within her grasp without any visible effort, and Mary Alice wondered if she could keep it up forever. *The rest of my life would be long enough.* The contact was thrilling, but the chance to rely on somebody else's strength for a while was more than she could resist.

She intercepted Ruri's mouth for a blistering kiss, one that probably curled Ruri's toes if her own reaction was any indication. Their tongues dueled and danced around each other as they each explored the mouth of the other. Mary Alice drank in the flavors of Ruri's mouth, savoring and memorizing each one. Ruri was breathing hard, matching Mary Alice's exhalations with her own. Finally, after what seemed like hours but still hadn't been long enough, Ruri pulled back reluctantly.

"Standing in front of the stairs wasn't what I had in mind for our first time."

"Then you'd better get us to bed quickly, or I'll have you right here."

"Pushy much?" Ruri laughed, a touch breathless when she met Mary Alice's eyes. She started up the steps as Mary Alice nibbled and sucked her way up one side of Ruri's neck and down the other. Mary Alice had no other thought except the warm skin beneath her lips and the arms cradling her securely, so it was a surprise when she was being laid down upon the woven cotton blanket on the house's only bed.

Ruri leaned above her, arms braced on either side of her shoulders. She smiled wickedly; then licked her lips. "You look good enough to eat."

Mary Alice couldn't stop the snort that escaped her. "Big bad wolf are you?"

"You have no idea." So quickly that she couldn't register the movement, Ruri was nose to nose with her. Her pupils were ringed with gold, but the rest of her eyes were still soft honey brown.

Realizing she was running out of air, Mary Alice forced herself to breathe. Ruri's eyes had drawn her in, guaranteeing delights she couldn't imagine, but she wanted to feel what was being promised. She wanted to feel Ruri. There were too many clothes between them.

"Maybe not," she whispered. "But I'd like to." Ruri's eyes flared fully golden as she reached beneath her shirt again and skimmed her hand up over Ruri's abdomen. She stopped just short of her breasts.

"Don't stop." Ruri's voice was rough. "Dear god, don't you stop now."

Mary Alice closed her hands over the soft mounds. They filled her hands perfectly, a little more than a generous handful. The points of Ruri's nipples poked into her palms. She ran her fingertips over the sensitive buds, coaxing a growl from Ruri's throat. Her hips ground into Mary Alice's pelvis and twin moans filled the air at the sudden friction. Mary Alice felt as though she were about to come alight or fly apart. Maybe both. Incredible heat and pressure had built up in her core and were still building.

Ruri fell upon her, hands roaming everywhere, mouth kissing, nipping, biting at whatever bare flesh she could reach. With each second that passed, more of Mary Alice's skin was exposed to the cool air. Stitches popped when Ruri yanked open her shirt at the shoulder, uncovering her left shoulder and upper arm. That too was pleasantly mauled; pools of expanding heat scorching her skin with each nip, bite and suck.

Before she knew it, she was almost completely naked from the waist up and Ruri was contemplating her bra.

"I'll get it," Mary Alice said. Or tried to say. All that came out was a soft rasp. She cleared her throat and tried again. "I'll get it."

"Not a chance" was the murmured response. With agonizing slowness, Ruri lifted first one side of the bra then the other, allowing each of her breasts to pop free of their fabric prisons. The sensation of cool air on her nipples was enough to send a fresh flow of liquid to her already dripping pussy.

Ruri quirked an amused eyebrow at her shuddering intake of breath and whipped off her shirt in one motion. Now her breasts were deliciously free and Mary Alice was free to roam. She ran the pads of her thumbs back across the buttons that still stood at attention on the peaks of Ruri's breasts. Ruri threw her head back and her hips jerked into Mary Alice again. The pleasure that rampaged through her groin was almost too much to be endured. She was so close and Ruri seemed determined to take her time.

Gentle hands removed her fingers from Ruri's warm chest. She made a small moue of disappointment.

"Don't pout, sweetheart," Ruri whispered. She lowered her head until her scalding breath caressed Mary Alice's nipple.

The tension that coiled in her belly was beyond belief. Never before could she remember being this turned on and this ready for release. She needed it more than she'd needed anything in her entire life. When Ruri finally closed her lips around the nipple that ached so much to be touched, it was more than she could bear. She flew apart, her consciousness fleeing in the explosion of light behind her corneas. For a moment or a thousand, she floated in blissful lack of awareness.

Bit by bit, she came back to herself. Her body was limp. It felt like her bones had drained out of her as she lay on the bed. Ruri was still there, hot along her body. She opened her eyes and Ruri smiled down at her before brushing a strand of hair back from her forehead.

"Welcome back."

"Thanks," Mary Alice whispered. "It's good to be here."

"Ready for another trip?" The gentleness was gone from her smile. What replaced it was wicked in the extreme.

Warm fingers combed through the curly hairs covering her most secret of places. With a shock, Mary Alice realized she was naked from the waist down. Ruri hadn't wasted any time while she was recovering from the massive orgasm.

She couldn't answer, couldn't say anything; her throat was too dry to be believed. Ruri's questing fingers reached slick flesh. The entirety of Mary Alice's universe was focused on the fingertips that parted her folds, sliding over the dripping flesh to skate over her proudly erect clitoris. She bit her lip in response to the exquisite sensation; saltiness filled her mouth. There was no time to dwell as Ruri gave up her thrilling exploration. Her magic fingers were poised barely inside the entrance to her pussy.

Her hips twitched, trying to force the fingers deeper inside, but Ruri just grinned and shifted with her. The groan that escaped her was sharp in her ears, but Ruri's smile only widened at the frustrated noise.

"Are you ready?" Ruri asked again.

"Damn it, Ruri! You know I am." The wolven didn't move a muscle; she seemed to be waiting for something. Mary Alice panted in desperation as her clouded mind searched frantically for what it could be. "Please, Ruri. I need you to take me. Oh god, Ruri. Please!"

Ruri's grin shifted from wicked to voracious. She had the upper hand, and Mary Alice knew she was hers. There was nothing she could do about it, and nothing she wanted to do. All that mattered was Ruri and the fingers nestling at the entrance of her pussy. Fingers that finally moved deliberately into her. She was being filled, but with such agonizing slowness that she couldn't stand it. She threw her head back and screamed, shifting her hips forward, drawing Ruri inside her. Three fingers slammed into her, filling her as completely as she needed. Her inner walls gripped Ruri, holding her deep within. Every inch of her being focused on those fingers, every twitch sent a shock through all that she was.

Ruri drew her fingers out with the same agonizing slowness with which she'd entered her. She penetrated Mary Alice again, faster this time, building speed with each thrust. Each repetition drove Mary Alice higher. She was dimly aware she was babbling, but what she said was lost to her. All that mattered was Ruri and the sensations the wolven was pulling from her.

Everything crested and for a moment Mary Alice was suspended at the top of that wave before it broke over her. A million points of light rippled across her skin and she was blind to everything except the golden of Ruri's eyes staring into her suddenly bared soul. The wave receded and left her, limp once again.

"I guess you were ready." Smugness understated the self-satisfaction in Ruri's voice.

"Mm hmm." Mary Alice didn't trust herself to talk.

"You don't have to say anything." Ruri pulled Mary Alice to her, cradling her in strong arms. They would keep her safe.

CHAPTER THIRTY

Cassidy's wounds were almost completely healed, with some livid scars where the gaping rents in her flesh had once been. She was starving and her inner wolf kept turning their thoughts to food and shelter. That had only gotten worse when they got to the house. Her wolf seemed equal parts ravenous and nervous. If a squirrel had dashed across the backyard, she wasn't sure that she would have been able to keep from going after it. As it was, she twitched at every noise.

The house was almost silent when Cassidy and the other wolven entered. She remembered to avoid the front door. She'd had a moment of pause when they got there. Her sister had only left one key. Ruri had it and she had gone ahead, claiming she needed to get things ready at the house for the rest of the strays, as she'd affectionately called them. No one had objected. One or two of the wolven had even laughed, though Lewis had seemed less than amused.

For a moment, Cassidy wondered if the house really was empty, though her nose told her that both Mary Alice and Ruri had been there recently. She could almost see their scent traces, gold and shadows. As usual, they wound around each other. It was funny how their scents seemed to seek each other out.

A gasp from upstairs perked her ears up, and hers weren't the only ones. Almost every head in the kitchen looked up at the soft noise.

"Ruri's blowing off some steam," one of the female wolven said. She seemed very casual about it. She might as well have mentioned that Ruri's eyes were brown.

Cassidy laughed lightly, though her insides clenched at the idea. "Lucky Ruri." Her answer was met with easy laughter. The wolven spread out. There were nine of them all told and they easily filled the first floor. There weren't enough seats for them all, but they didn't seem to mind, occupying floor space as willingly as they did the chairs.

She could feel them. All of them. They burned in her mind like bright stars, each one an individual. Cassidy didn't know all their names yet. The three who'd driven her over in their car had introduced themselves. It had involved a lot of smelling. She knew she'd be able to pick their scent out of almost anything going forward, and she'd gotten their names, but the rest of who they were was still a mystery. Naomi, Carlos and Harold. He'd been adamant that it was Harold, not Harry. The other two had seemed to be on the edge of giving him a hard time, but some remaining apprehension stopped them. Cassidy had smelled their nervousness and had worked to keep herself open and approachable. The approach had worked; by the time they were halfway back to the house, they'd started chatting amongst themselves.

The points in her mind pulled at her and cried out to be touched, to be brought closer. She reached out to one and pulled it in. It felt warm in her hand. Warm contact at her back surprised her and she looked back. One of the wolven she had yet to get to know had sidled up behind her and was standing close enough that they barely touched. She was hyperaware of his proximity; electricity seemed to arc between them. Her wolf wanted to wind herself around him, to feel his wolf against her. Inside her. Cassidy stepped away from him. She couldn't think with him that close.

"What is it, Alpha?" His voice was low and gravelly. It sounded much older than he looked. Until she caught his eyes. This was someone who'd been around for a long time, no matter how few wrinkles he sported. When he caught her questioning look, he smiled, the skin around his mouth crinkling slightly, though it never touched his eyes.

"Why are you so sad?" The whispered question left her before she could stop it. His scent was faded blue, like denim worn almost to the point of tearing. It was sadness so old it was a part of him, like the faded jeans that clung to every taut muscle on his legs.

"Alpha?" Sadness was momentarily overwhelmed by shock. His eyes gleamed silver for a moment before settling back to faded gray.

"Sorry."

"An Alpha must never apologize," he said. "You've gained a position of strength. You can't let it go now. Apologies make you seem weak."

"Oh. Sorry." Cassidy cringed internally at repeating herself.

"You're a cubling, aren't you?" He mirrored her nod. "That explains a lot. I'm Luther. You should stick by me. I can help you through this. Who turned you?"

"I don't know."

"Bastard should have stuck around long enough to get your feet under you." He shook his head and Cassidy's mind was filled by the face of a grizzled gray wolf. It competed with his face. The dual image was dizzying and she blinked a couple of times to clear it.

"It wasn't like that." Not sure how much she should say, she backed away from him. "I need to see Ruri." Something wasn't right. If the gray wolf showed any interest at all in her, he would find himself flat on his back while she climbed atop him, right here in front of everybody.

He said nothing but bowed his head in assent. The room suddenly felt much smaller and she had an uncomfortable flash of the horrid box Mary Alice had forced her into. No one was watching her, except Luther, and yet she knew everyone was aware of and tracking her. Ruri. She was upstairs and would explain exactly what was going on to her satisfaction, and she wouldn't leave until Cassidy knew what the deal was.

Suddenly angry, she stomped up the stairs. Her newly keen ears easily overheard the continuing sounds of passion that emanated from the main bedroom. Her nose told her who was in that room and what they were doing. How dare they get up to such things while she also burned to be touched.

Since those points in her head seemed to be able to draw those around her closer, Cassidy examined those that sparkled barely out of reach. Ruri's must be one of them, she reasoned. Carlos, Harold, Naomi, and now Luther were obvious to her. She couldn't have said how, but she recognized each twinkling mote. Lewis was probably one of those at a bit of a remove, but she felt she could have reached out to him had she wished to. Given Ruri's closeness, she should have been able to easily call the wolven to her, but she couldn't. Ruri's point was veiled somehow. Cassidy couldn't pierce the veil, and the inability to bring her in fueled the anger that had sent her up the stairs in the first place.

Screw this, Cassidy thought. I'm not going to swim through this mess by myself while those two amuse themselves! She pounded on the door once and stopped when the wood splintered under her fist.

Ruri wanted to howl in exasperation. Mary Alice's eyes met hers from her position between Ruri's legs. That agile tongue had ceased its ministrations as soon as the door had shaken in its frame.

"What the hell?" Mary Alice rolled to one side and strode toward the door, completely unfazed by her nudity. The human was almost wolven in her approach to the so-called baser aspects of life, it seemed. Ruri took advantage of the show and watched the play of ass muscles beneath her skin.

Cassidy's face on the other side of the door was priceless. Her sister might have been unconcerned by her lack of clothing, but Cassidy apparently didn't share the feeling. It was a human conceit; one that Ruri knew would fade over time.

"If you two are done, I have more questions."

"We'll be a while," Mary Alice said.

The smoldering tension between the sisters flared back to life. Ruri knew better than to get between them, but she wondered how much trouble she'd be in if she grabbed each of them by the scruff of the necks and shook them soundly. Both Nolan sisters turned and shot her a look. Ruri shrugged and stared unconcernedly back at them. *That's interesting.*

"No." Cassidy's voice was flat. "You're done."

"You don't get to tell me what to do in my own house."

Cassidy looked ready to punch Mary Alice in the mouth. Strain filled in the room, barely shy of snapping. Ruri had a corresponding knot in her stomach. Her wolf whined softly in her mind and urged her to get out of the way. Then the tension faded as if it had never been. Cassidy's frown wavered then reversed itself. She bent over, suddenly helpless with laughter.

"'In my house'? You're really going to go there?"

Mary Alice blinked down at her sister, confusion in her stance. She reached toward Cassidy, and then pulled back.

"You sound just like Dad did. 'Don't touch that thermostat! When you have your own house you can keep it tropical for all I care.'" Cassidy wiped a tear from the corner of one eye. "It only took fifteen years for you to turn into him."

"That's not fair!" Mary Alice's voice went up indignantly. "It *is* my house."

"Sure it is, sweetie." Cassidy actually reached out and patted her sister's arm. "That reminds me, I'm going to need a dozen sleeping bags."

"What?" Mary Alice turned around and stared blankly at Ruri. "What is she talking about?"

Ruri winced. She'd forgotten to warn the Hunter. It had been on the tip of her tongue until Mary Alice had looked at her with naked need on her face and in her scent. "We ran into some of my old pack. Not all of them went with MacTavish. Apparently some were able to escape."

"And they followed you home?"

"Something like that. Cassidy accidentally challenged their leader and now she's—"

"Alpha." Mary Alice whispered the word in a horrified breath.

"Alpha," Cassidy said. "Whatever that means."

"It means you're a giant target now."

Ruri bounded off the bed and crossed the room in a few strides. She drew Cassidy through the doorway past her naked sister. "It means you're the first and last thought of a group of wolven." She couldn't let Mary Alice pollute Cassidy against what had happened. It had been unanticipated, yes, but it was probably the best thing that could have happened to that group. They'd been barely holding on or they wouldn't have been hiding out in a storm drain. "It means they'll lay down their lives to keep your pack secure. It means you hold them in the palm of your hand and if you close your fist you'll crush them. But if you cup them gently, you'll shelter them from the worst this world has to offer."

She looked over at Mary Alice as she said the last. She'd meant it as an explanation, but Mary Alice clearly took it as an indictment. Her face closed up and she drew herself up to her full height.

"Excuse me for not wanting every lone wolf with his eye on a pack to look at my sister as fresh meat." She bent down, gathered her clothes and quickly pulled them on in economical jerks. "And don't tell me there aren't some of your *kind* who deserve exactly what I give them." Mary Alice jammed her feet into her boots and clumped out of the room without bothering to tie them.

"Mary…" Ruri reached out to her as she strode by, but the human shrugged her shoulder out of the way.

A strangled noise pulled her attention back to Cassidy. Her face had gone white, and her eyes wide. They glowed crimson and electric blue at her.

"What's wrong?" Ruri asked.

"I don't know," Cassidy mumbled. Her words were distorted by the sharp teeth that filled her mouth. She held up her hands, displaying the sharp claws tipping her fingers. "I feel like something's wrong. The others are scared. No, they're terrified."

"He's already here." Ruri snagged her pants and pulled them on then ran out the door. She wrestled her way into her shirt on the way down the stairs. If MacTavish had found them, it was better to face him clothed than naked. Cassidy would need her and Ruri knew they weren't at the point where her Alpha would understand the nonverbal cues of her wolves. Cassidy would be a strong Alpha, but her newness was a potentially deadly handicap for them all.

CHAPTER THIRTY-ONE

Mary Alice thudded down the stairs, still fuming. How could Ruri take Cassidy's side? Surely she saw how much danger her sister was in. Where had the wolven been when that whole disaster had unfolded?

A small part of her brain whispered that she was being unreasonable, but she brushed it aside. Righteous anger felt too good. It was something she could be sure of, something that wouldn't let her down. Now if only she had a target for it.

As if her thoughts had conjured the woman, Mary Alice came around the corner into the living room and stopped dead in her tracks. For all that the room was crammed full nearly a dozen or so werewolves, it was quiet enough to hear a mouse fart. To the last one, the wolves' attention was riveted to the slender woman who sat in a wooden armchair. They recognized a predator higher up on the food chain than they. It was likely a new experience for all of them.

She spread out her senses, trying to feel if any of them were about to shift. Werewolves in human form didn't register as strongly as those who had shifted. Those in the midst of a shift stood out in her mental landscape like a beacon. They all felt as if they were within moments of making the transition, and yet they hovered on the edge.

"Malice," Stiletto said, nodding slightly. Whether she was confirming something to herself or simply acknowledging her presence, Malice didn't know.

A low groan rippled through the room at her name, and a dozen glowing eyes quickly turned upon her. The boogeyman of their darkest stories was now made flesh in front of them. Malice smiled tightly.

"Stiletto." The code name had no discernible reaction to the assembled lycans. If they'd ever been on Stiletto's home turf, that would not have been the case.

The other woman looked perfectly comfortable, sitting straight-backed in the wooden chair. She looked as if she'd settled in for the long haul. Malice nodded toward the back door. This was bad enough already; she had to get Stiletto out of there before things deteriorated further. The room exploding in a fury of claws and fangs would be preferable to Cassidy or Ruri coming down those stairs.

Light footsteps at the top of the stairs heralded her worst fears.

"Come on, let's get out of here," Malice said, trying to bury her desperation in nonchalance. "I'll fill you in on the way."

"There are more lycans in this house. I want the measure of all of them." She looked disdainfully at the group arrayed around the room. "These are of no consequence."

A muted rumble swept through the corners of the living room. The lycans didn't like being dismissed, yet none of them moved so much as a muscle.

"This is ridiculous." Malice crossed the room in a flash and snatched at Stiletto's elbow.

Ever elusive, Stiletto shifted her arm just out of reach. In the same motion, she surged out of the chair and secured Malice's forearm in a crushing grip.

"Let go of her." The voice from across the room was unwelcome in the extreme. She had to look over to see who had said it, distorted as the words were. It sounded like they'd been pushed out around a mouthful of sharp rocks.

Both Cassidy and Ruri stood in the doorway, their eyes ablaze. Sharp teeth glittered in Cassidy's mouth, and her muzzle already protruded from her face. With frantic shakes of her head, Malice tried to warn them to stand down.

"They seem to know you pretty well around here," Stiletto whispered in her ear. "Have you been fraternizing?"

Before she could stop herself, Malice shifted her eyes over at Ruri. Sharp claws stood out in stark relief from the tips of her fingers.

"I see." Stiletto tightened her grip on Malice's forearm. "So one of them is your new girlfriend. Uncle Ralph said there was something off about her. Wait until he finds out she's one of the monsters you're supposed to have taken care of."

"She's done nothing wrong. No one here has. They're what's left over from the North Side pack after MacTavish took over."

"It's a matter of time. You know that as well as I do. They're monsters, Malice. They don't play nice, no matter how prettily you ask. You can only use them as tools for so long, then you have to put them down."

Cassidy was there beside them. Fur was filling in around her eyes and down the muzzle that stuck out even further from her face. "I said let go of her. Are you deaf or stupid?"

The pressure around Malice's arm ceased. When she looked down, she saw that Cassidy had one of Stiletto's fingers bent backward over her hand. This was bad. If Cassidy really was the Alpha to the lycans in the room, they wouldn't tolerate her being attacked and no way was Stiletto going to let this pass.

So fast that Malice almost couldn't see it, Stiletto shed her sister's grip. She spun Cassidy around in her grip and kicked her legs out from under her. Her sister lay face down on the ground, Stiletto's knee in the small of Cassidy's back. A chorus of growls and snapping bone filled the room. Ruri rushed forward, standing between where Cassidy was being held to the ground and the rest of the pack. Her eyes still blazed, but she'd kept from shifting any further, which was more than could be said for most of the others.

Aside from Ruri, one other lycan had managed to hold onto his skin. He watched closely, readiness to act coiled along his body but staying carefully in check.

"Stiletto, stop!" Malice lurched forward, horrified at how quickly everything had gone sideways.

"This thing attacked me, soldier." Stiletto's mouth was set in a grim line and she forced angry words through the harsh slit.

"She was protecting me."

"I saw that. This must be your new girlfriend." A twist of disgust writhed across Stiletto's lips.

"Simone."

Stiletto looked up at the quiet use of her real name, shock splashed upon her face. Her eyes widened and she drew in a deep breath to attack before getting a grip of herself. It was more emotion than Malice had ever seen on the woman's face, even during the most grueling portions of their training.

"She's my sister." Everything in the room ground to a halt. Though Mary Alice had uttered the words in scarcely more than a whisper, it was loud enough for each of the lycans to hear. Cassidy alone didn't stop. She continued to thrash and shift in Stiletto's hold. She was nearly in full fur-form now and in the stunned silence, she completed the transformation.

With a triumphant growl, Cassidy drew her legs under her and bucked while twisting. Stiletto lost her grip and fell to one side, catching herself on one outstretched arm. Cassidy threw herself at the woman, her long wolf body coiling and releasing like a hellish spring of fur and teeth. In the exhalation of the same breath, Mary Alice leaped at her sister, catching her around the neck, collaring her and holding her back. Wicked teeth scored the air and clashed together less than an inch from Stiletto's neck.

The lycan who'd managed to maintain his human form was suddenly at Cassidy's other side, murmuring urgently into one laid back ear. Mary Alice struggled to keep Cassidy contained. Her sister was strong, at least as strong as any lycan she'd ever encountered. Thankfully she hadn't picked up the moves a canny old wolf would know. She seemed to think she could brute force her way out of Mary Alice's hold. It was possible, but Mary Alice had years of experience in wrangling Cassidy's kind and knew where she could hold on and be reasonably protected from slashing claws and rending teeth. Letting go would be a problem, but she'd figure that out when she got there. What was that proverb about getting off a tiger? Odd how that seemed to perfectly describe her life.

Slowly Cassidy settled down. Stiletto took advantage of Mary Alice's restraint of her sister to slide backward and gain her feet in one motion. She surveyed the room, doubtless taking in the multitude of glowing eyes and dripping teeth. A large group of huge wolves stared back at her. She was good. Malice knew that from training. She'd only gotten better in the intervening years, but even she would have problems taking on a group this large in an enclosed space.

The man talking into Cassidy's ear sat back, and her sister relaxed slightly, no longer straining so desperately against her hold. Her muscles were still tight, rock hard beneath a layer of fur still sticking up in all directions from aggression, but they no longer quivered. When she loosened her own grip a hair, Cassidy relaxed even further.

"She won't stand down completely, not until she's free," the man said. His voice was rough, almost broken, but confident.

Mary Alice looked down at the crazily patterned fur she held onto. It wasn't that she didn't trust Cassidy… Actually, it was exactly that she didn't trust Cassidy. Her sister was as strong as the strongest lycan she'd ever come up against, and she had next to no control. She had neither the benefit of a strong sire nor the experience to keep herself in check. If Uncle Ralph had set her upon another werewolf in this situation, Malice would have eliminated the lycan without hesitation. But this was her sister. She had to believe that enough of Cassidy still remained. What she needed was time and experience. Mary Alice needed to make sure her sister survived long enough to receive it.

She opened her arms but managed to keep her hand wrapped around one hank of fur. If Cassidy lunged again, she would have warning and hopefully enough grip to at least alter her trajectory. Cassidy looked over at her, odd eyes glowing reproachfully. She couldn't read Mary Alice's thoughts, she knew that, but Cassidy definitely seemed to understand her struggle. *How could you?* those eyes seemed to ask.

There was nothing for it. Mary Alice stood up, letting go of her final handhold, feeling like she was letting go of everything she'd ever had with her sister. She grabbed Stiletto's elbow on the way by.

"Let's go," she pushed out through gritted teeth.

Stiletto said nothing and allowed herself to be drawn along in Malice's wake. She watched their six, making sure none of the lycans in the room made a move on them. Malice wasn't worried about them. The damage had been done. She knew exactly where she stood with her sister, and it hurt far worse than if one of the wolves had disemboweled her. The only solace she could take was in the way Ruri had placed herself between the lycans and Cassidy. Her sister was as safe as she could be if Ruri was around, probably safer than if Malice was there.

The two Hunters were finally gone from the house and silence reigned in their absence. Ruri had thought they would never leave. This was a disaster. A complete, unmitigated disaster. Things couldn't have gone more wrong if she'd tried.

"So you're sleeping with my sister." As if Cassidy's blunt words were a signal, the wolven flowed into action. Half peeled off to cover all possible entry points, while the rest stuck around. While Ruri approved of the instinct, she felt it was misplaced. The true enemy was MacTavish, not Mary Alice. That Stiletto could be trouble, however.

Lewis had regained his skin-form and stormed forward, completely naked. "You're fucking Malice? You really have turned your back on us."

Cassidy turned on him in a flash. "Back off. She doesn't answer to you."

He sneered at her. "And you. Malice is your *sister*." The word dripped with contempt, turning into something ugly. "Why should we trust you? How can we?"

Cassidy stalked up to him. The top of her head barely came up to his shoulder, but somehow she managed to loom over him. "Are you trying to make something of it?" Where his eyes glowed in the sunlit room, hers were dark. He should have been the dangerous one, but Ruri found herself far more worried for him than for Cassidy.

He opened his mouth to answer, but the wolven who'd held on to skin-form during the fracas got there first.

"Lewis." His voice was quiet, but the warning was clear.

Lewis looked over at him and the rage contorting his features smoothed out, leaving petulant disappointment instead. "Luther." He turned to leave, but Luther's hand shot out and grabbed him by the shoulder, forcibly turning him back around and holding him there.

"Alpha." The words were forced out through clenched teeth, but it wasn't until Lewis bowed his head in what someone with no social skills might have been taken as respect that Luther let him go.

Their little group watched him leave the room, a storm cloud hovering over him.

"It is a problem, you know," Luther said quietly.

Ruri closed her mouth with a snap. She'd been about to make much the same comment.

"Which one?" Cassidy asked.

"All of them," Ruri said quickly, pleased to get a word in before Luther could. He didn't seem overly discomfited, however. "Mary Alice is a problem for both of us. The pack needs to know what's going on."

"More importantly, they need to know you're still able to lead them. To protect them." Luther's voice dropped. "They're still shaken by what happened to Dean."

When Cassidy raised a questioning eyebrow at her, Ruri leaned forward. "Our old Alpha, remember?"

"She's my sister, not a monster," Cassidy said.

"No, she's just the boogeyman." Luther shook his head, shoulder-length hair brushing the tops of his shoulders.

"That's as may be. I'm not her. She has nothing to do with what I do. I'm my own person."

"So show that to the pack," Ruri said. "Or show them your relationship isn't a liability."

"Then I'm not the only one with that problem."

The point stung, and Ruri opened her mouth to deny it, but closed it without saying anything. It might sting, but it was also true. The fact was she simply didn't feel part of Cassidy's burgeoning pack. They were all wolven she'd known for years, though she wasn't sure she still knew who they all were. Lewis was being the same old asshole, but Luther? The wolven had been content to fade into the background before. He'd never been interested in a position of authority, though he certainly could have given most of them a run for their money. Probably not her or Dean, but the strongest wolven had always stepped warily around him. His lowly pack status had been his choice. Something had finally changed his mind.

"You're right, Alpha." Ruri bowed her head. Who was she to advise Cassidy? She needed to get her head screwed on right before she could act as Beta again.

Cassidy turned to Luther. "First things first. We need food and bedding. What resources does everyone have? I have some money, but I need to get to an ATM to get cash."

"Yes, Alpha. I'll speak with the others and see what they have. We only need enough food to get through the day. We can go for a proper run tonight, that should fill everyone's bellies."

They had everything under control and didn't need her. Ruri slipped from the room into the kitchen. She needed to do something. Her body fairly burned with the need to prove herself. Her wolf paced within, urging her on. There was only one gesture she knew that would be big enough to show she was still committed to the pack. It would also go a long way to demonstrating how advantageous an alliance with Mary Alice could be.

Confident she wouldn't be missed, Ruri closed the back door behind her. She had a Hunter to see about a wolf.

CHAPTER THIRTY-TWO

How had Stiletto tracked her down? Malice watched her comrade discreetly as she puttered around on her laptop in the living room. First things first, however. How did she keep Uncle Ralph from being pulled into their little drama? The last thing she needed was her government leash-holder sticking his nose into things.

"Your sister?" Stiletto neither looked up from the computer screen nor stopped typing. She might have been discussing the cool fall weather.

"That's right." Malice tried to match her tone for unconcern but knew she failed miserably.

"I assume you didn't report it."

"Of course I didn't!" There was no point in trying to hide her anger on that one. "You know as well as I do what they'd have done to her. I'm not putting my own sister through that."

"It's your loss." Stiletto actually shrugged. She looked back at Malice, the light from her laptop lighting the side of her face from below, giving her a slightly sinister cast. "It's ours also. The scientists could learn a lot from a tame werewolf."

"A tame werewolf?" Not able to believe what she was hearing, Malice moved to stand in front of the coffee table so she could see Stiletto's face clearly. "That's my sister you're talking about."

"I'm sure she would've been well-treated. Think what we could have discovered! New ways to kill the monsters that don't involve going toe-to-toe with them. Maybe some kind of nerve agent. Think about it, we could gas the things into oblivion without having to worry about civilian casualties." Her eyes glowed with terrible excitement. Malice had never seen her this animated without being in the midst of battle.

"That is the most obscene thing I've ever heard." The laptop jumped on the coffee table when Malice slammed her hands down on either side of it. "And it's not how we do things. We don't go after them all. Most of them haven't done anything wrong. We take down those that screw up and become a threat, that's all."

"Do you really believe that? Grow up, Malice." Stiletto's sneer twisted her face into an ugly facsimile of its usual bland mask. "Everyone's life would be better if we could purge those cancers from our existence."

"Fuck you, Stiletto." Her life wouldn't be better without the supras, not now. Maybe if she'd never heard of them. But then Ruri would be decades dead. And now... Now she'd be all alone. "If you report Cassidy, I'll—"

Stiletto leaned forward, her face right in Malice's. "Kill me? Why don't you do me a favor and give it a try." A fine spray of spittle misted the lower half of Mary Alice's face.

Malice grabbed her collar, hauling Stiletto across the coffee table. The laptop clattered to the floor along with a glass of water and half the books she owned. They landed in a heap on the concrete floor. The thin throw rug did little to cushion their fall, but Malice barely noticed. She kept their momentum rolling until she sat astride Stiletto. Her hands batted Malice's away from her collar and Malice gladly relinquished her hold. A shock ran through her arms as she boxed Stiletto along the ribs.

They'd never fought like this, not even during training. The gloves were off, finally and for real. A corona of light and pain exploded through her face, flooding her vision with brightness and snapping her head back. Stiletto took advantage of her head butt and dumped Malice onto her back. This time it was her turn to straddle Malice, her legs clamped around her rib cage, twin vises trying to force all breath from her lungs.

Blows rained down at her face, each one designed to kill or at least incapacitate if it landed. Malice intercepted or turned them aside. One grazed her temple, sending her ears ringing. With each exhalation,

Stiletto's legs tightened around her, making it that much harder to draw the next breath. She was running out of time. A knee to Stiletto's back loosened her grip so Malice could drag in a tortured breath. With the next kick, she nailed Stiletto in the back of the head, stunning her long enough for Malice to roll her over and bounce up. She dropped into a defensive crouch. Blood dripped from the side of her head, running down the side of her face from her temple.

Stiletto lay on the ground, her shoulders shaking. Shock stopped Malice from attacking when she realized the woman was laughing.

"What's so funny?" Her jaw was sore and didn't want to work properly. She had to work to get the words out without slurring. Stiletto must have snuck one past her defenses without her noticing.

"I don't think this is what Uncle Ralph had in mind when he sent me up here." She pushed herself over, moving as gingerly as Malice.

"I don't think there's any need to tell him."

"Absolutely." Stiletto rotated her left arm in its socket before reaching up to finger the cut on her lip. It oozed blood but only for a moment before Stiletto ran the tip of her tongue over it. Since the government injected them full of who knew what, their saliva had some mild coagulating properties. "The man's a creep."

"So I'm not the only one who thinks that?"

Stiletto barked out a short laugh. "I don't know anyone who can stand him. He treats us like we're a very small step up from the things he sends us after."

"Are we that different?" Malice's voice was soft, the question meant more for herself than for Stiletto.

"Of course we are." Stiletto answered anyway. She stood up and paced the length of the room. The more she moved, the faster her various aches and pains would subside. Malice knew she should be doing the same thing, but she didn't need another reminder of her differences. "We're still human. We control ourselves and don't go after civilians."

"No, just each other."

Stiletto's smile was almost warm. "No one else is a match."

"True enough." If only they were. Malice relaxed out of her defensive pose. Her ribs felt like they'd been used as a bellows, which they pretty much had been. "I need to get moving. I'm going for a run."

"Suit yourself." Stiletto leaned over to pick up her laptop. "Uh oh." Malice looked over at the expression of dismay, and Stiletto wordlessly tipped the laptop to one side. Water drained out of the keyboard.

"Ah, crap. I'm sorry."

"I won't be using this for a while. Do you have any rice? Like a lot of it."

"Sure, in the kitchen. There's a bag I just opened."

"Good, I'm going to see if I can salvage this. I don't want to have to requisition a new one through Uncle Ralph."

"Good call." Malice left the living room and stopped to change into her running clothes and clean up the blood that was already drying on the side of her head. From the waistband of her pants, she pulled the cell phone she'd lifted off Stiletto during their fight and stuck it in the pocket of her track pants.

"I'll be back in a bit," she called on her way out. From the noises in the kitchen, Stiletto was making good on her plan to dry out her laptop. It really was the best possible outcome. If the computer had been smashed, Stiletto would have needed to call in for a new one. This way, she had some breathing room. It wasn't much, but if she was careful it might be enough.

The run felt good; Mary Alice could already feel her battered muscles returning to normal. The more blood she moved through them, the faster they healed. The cut at her temple had been deep but had already stopped bleeding when she cleaned it. By the time she got back from her workout, it would look days old.

She stopped at a small park a few blocks away from the warehouse and pulled out her phone. The number she dialed went straight to voice mail and she didn't bother leaving a message. The sun shone weakly through a light haze, but it wasn't enough to warm her now that she was no longer running. The pants and light shirt she'd chosen were fine when she was moving, but fall's chill was definitely settling in. With a start she realized it was almost Halloween. The days had flown by.

To keep from stiffening up while she waited and to make sure blood kept pumping through those injured areas, Mary Alice dropped and worked her way through fifty push-ups. When that was done, she started on yoga. As she transitioned from a headstand to Chaturanga pose, Mary Alice heard the sound she'd been waiting for. The park was nice not only because it was one of the only green spaces for blocks in the area, but it was also home to one of the city's few remaining payphones. Every time this payphone was vandalized or destroyed, it was mysteriously replaced within a few days. Better yet, it only allowed incoming calls from one number.

"Hello." It wasn't a question, Mary Alice knew exactly who was on the other end. Rather, she knew who should have been on the other end. It didn't pay to assume in her line of work.

"Malice." TC's voice issued clearly from the speaker, reminding Mary Alice that there was no substitute for a landline when it came to clarity. "What's up?"

"I need you to route a number to a dummy voice mail box on this phone." She held up Stiletto's phone and read the serial number off the back.

"That's one of ours." He didn't sound surprised, merely matter-of-fact.

"That's right," Mary Alice replied as dispassionately. "Can you duplicate the voice mail message into the dummy box?"

He snorted lightly. "Of course I can. It's a lot easier when everything is in-house. Give me a second to…there."

"Thanks. Then the last thing I need you to do is route any of Uncle Ralph's incoming numbers to that voice mail. Give that about three days, then dump them back into her actual voice mail."

There was a long silence on the other end. "Malice, what are you up to?"

"The less you know, the safer you'll be. I wouldn't be doing it if I didn't have to."

"I don't know if I can do this." A heavy sigh came through the line. "I know I owe you, but—"

"You do owe me, TC." It wasn't fair and Mary Alice knew she was putting her friend in a bind, but she had no other choice. There was only one way she could see to unravel this whole mess, and she had to keep moving forward with it, no matter the cost. "Without me, your brother would have been dead or worse, in that vamp den. And how long do you think you'd have kept your job if I hadn't kept my mouth shut? You know as well as I do how the sins of the family overflow onto the rest of us."

More silence met her words, but at least it wasn't a dial tone. She pressed her case further. "Look, once this is done, we'll be square. If this is done right, the way I say, there won't be any blowback and we'll both be in the clear. But if it isn't, there'll be a whole lot of questions, ones I'll have to answer." She took a deep breath. "Answers our bosses won't like to hear."

"Damn you, Malice." Equal parts anger and resignation dragged down TC's voice.

Jubilation shot through Mary Alice. He was going to do it. A small part of her felt shame at pushing him so hard. She realized she'd likely lost more than an ally within the organization; she'd probably lost a friend. Still, if everything went according to plan, they'd all be safe. Hopefully he'd come around. *Would you?* the reproachful voice in her head asked.

"Thanks, TC."

"Don't mention it." Sarcasm dripped like acid from his words. "If there's nothing else."

"That's it."

The line disconnected, and Mary Alice stood for a few moments listening to the dial tone drone on in her ear. It needed to be done, and she'd done it.

When she returned home, Stiletto was still laboring over her laptop in the kitchen. Electronic pieces were laid out across the island, each one in a specific place. Stiletto dried each one meticulously with a cotton swab before depositing it in the bag of rice on the ground next to her. She didn't even look up when Malice cut through the kitchen on her way to the bedroom. The bruises on her arms had faded almost to nothingness, just as Malice's had.

She stripped off her workout clothes and detoured to the living room where she nudged the cell phone under the couch with her foot. A couple of books joined it for good measure, though not too close. She had to stage things carefully. There could be no question that the phone had ended up there by accident and not by design.

"What's with that giant metal box out there?" Stiletto asked as Malice reentered the kitchen.

"I needed somewhere to corral Cassidy while she was going through the change."

"You locked up your own sister?" Stiletto raised both eyebrows without looking up from the component she was carefully drying off with a Q-tip. "After all your talk, I didn't think you'd have it in you."

"I didn't want her hurting anyone. Or herself."

"It's not that much different from handing her over to our people."

"Hardly. There's a world of difference, but I guess there's no expecting you to get it." *Time to change the subject,* Malice decided. If Stiletto continued comparing her to the government, Malice would force feed that hard drive to her. "Looks like you've done that before."

"You could say that." Stiletto didn't look up from her task. "This is the first time I had help screwing it up, though."

"I had no idea you were so clumsy."

"I most certainly am not." Another piece went into the bag of rice. "I might have the tendency to multitask unsuccessfully."

"I'd say." Needling Stiletto probably wasn't the wisest thing to do, but she seemed to have come down from her earlier rage. With a heavy sigh, Malice lowered herself to a stool across the island from her counterpart. "We need to figure out our next steps with the pack."

Stiletto grunted in agreement. "Damn right we do."

"We should move now, before word of your presence in town spreads."

"And if it does, whose fault is that?"

"The way I see it, no one forced you to follow me." Malice glared at the top of Stiletto's head.

"You were hiding something, I knew it." Stiletto looked up to capture Malice's gaze. "Turns out I was right."

"And my business is my business. How I choose to deal with the supras in town is my deal. I get the job done and it works for me."

"Until now. Coddling them will get you killed. If you're going to work with them, they need to fear you or they'll take you down sooner rather than later."

"I don't plan on getting taken down at all. And since when do you work with supras? I thought you hated them too much to do that."

"Just because I know I'm going to kill them eventually doesn't mean they can't be useful until that happens. It's only a matter of time until they step a foot out of bounds, and knowing their haunts and habits makes it easier to hunt them down."

"That's cold. And isn't it against regs?"

"The regs aren't clear on that point. We're not supposed to fraternize," Stiletto's pointed look should have embarrassed her some, but it failed to raise the slightest bit of shame. "But they don't specifically forbid contact that's necessary to complete our mission."

"That's a great rationalization. Can you split hairs any finer?"

Stiletto held up her hand, and Malice bristled before realizing that she was looking toward the windows.

"What do you—?"

"Do you hear that?" Stiletto interrupted her again. Her eyes were intense; she looked like she was trying to see through the wall by sheer force of will.

Malice slowed her breathing and listened. Silence fell over the room and she made out quiet scratching noises. They seemed to be coming from outside. She opened herself up, but there was little to go on. The thickness of many layers of bricks muted her senses, but she couldn't deny that something was coming up the wall toward them.

"This is why you don't make pets of monsters," Stiletto hissed. She slid off her stool and slunk over to the wall of windows. The sounds were louder now, coming inexorably closer. Stiletto positioned herself by the open window.

It seemed a good idea to Malice, and she stopped only long enough to retrieve a couple of combat knives from her weapons drawer. She flipped one toward Stiletto, the knife turning end over end through the air. Stiletto grabbed it without looking and settled into a crouch. Malice took up her position on the window's other side, waiting for whatever it was that was crawling its way up the side of her home toward them.

The sound stopped only to be replaced by the tortured squeal of tearing metal. Malice gritted her teeth and readied herself. As soon as whatever it was came through that window, it was dead.

The silhouette of fingers made too long by the claws at their tips felt their way up the frosted glass of the window. They gripped the bottom of the opening left when the window had been opened. Small tufts of golden fur dusted the back of the fingers where they met the hand. An intimately familiar energy registered to her senses now that it wasn't being insulated by brick walls two feet thick.

Stiletto surged forward, her knife at the ready. She grabbed the nearest arm and yanked, pulling the intruder into the kitchen. The knife flashed, plunging toward the back of Ruri's neck. Mary Alice threw herself forward, pushing Ruri away from Stiletto and sandwiching her own body between her lover and her squadmate.

CHAPTER THIRTY-THREE

Ruri squawked in a most undignified way when a hand reached out from nowhere and grabbed her wrist. She flew through the window into a blur that even she had trouble following. The woman Mary Alice didn't like had a hold of her and was swinging a huge knife at her head. A weight like a wrecking ball smashed into her from the side, sending Ruri into Stiletto, knocking the breath from her in a thunderous whoosh.

The sound of a pop was followed by the smell of iron and salt. Blood, but she didn't feel any pain. Instead, she felt warm spots on her skin. Mary Alice's blood was dripping down on her from where she stood over her, protecting her from Stiletto.

Adrenaline surged through her veins and her wolf tried to break free. Fur and fluid flowed up her arm from her hands and a sharp pain rocketed through her jaw. Teeth burst from her gums in blood and agony.

Mary Alice still had one hand around her upper arm, and it tightened in warning. "Don't," she whispered.

Ruri looked up and caught the human's pain in the crease around her eyes. Fury flooded into her. The wolf would not be denied. She demanded to be fully let out, tearing at Ruri's belly and chest. More fur sprouted in the wake of her claws. The bones in her back legs broke and reformed in a series of loud snaps.

"Ruri, no!" The words were no request; they were an order. Surprisingly, her wolf took heed, stopping her internal rampage and retreating back inside Ruri with a whimper. Without the wolf's rage to sustain her, Ruri allowed the transformation to reverse itself. She came fully back to herself, crouched on the floor and pushed up against the cool brick of the exterior wall. Warm drops still splashed on the bare skin of her arm, dyeing it streaky red.

"What are you doing?" Stiletto's voice dug into her skull. Ruri rumbled a growl in response before realizing the question wasn't directed at her.

"I'm keeping you from killing each other." Mary Alice straightened, pulling Ruri with her. She shoved Ruri behind her. "What are you doing here?"

It took her a moment to figure out she was being addressed. She hid her pause behind an insouciant shrug. "You didn't give me a key. How else was I supposed to get in? I figured you'd booby-trapped your door, so I came up the side."

"For the love of all that's holy, Malice." Stiletto gestured toward them with the combat knife before turning away and running her free hand through her short hair. "It's a death wish. You have a total death wish."

"That's not it," Mary Alice said. "But I won't let you harm those under my protection."

"Just because you're sleeping with it doesn't mean it cares for you."

But this time it does, Ruri realized. *It means everything.* With a start she discovered her wolf had chosen a mate and she wondered when exactly that had happened. The wolf trusted Mary Alice completely and had for some time, even while she'd held them captive. As soon as she'd realized why Mary Alice had kidnapped her, the wolf had started becoming attached. So too had Ruri. Sure, she'd originally come on to her as a way to rattle the Hunter's cage and to gain an advantage, but the move hadn't been despite lack of interest. Someone who would give anything for family was someone Ruri understood, respected even.

But did she love her? It was possible, but how did she unravel that string of emotion from the tangle she found herself in? Her mate was supposed to be another wolven, not a human and certainly not one tasked with hunting them down. And her Alpha's sister? Something wasn't quite true about the last statement, though. Cassidy wasn't really her Alpha. Dean still held that position and her connection to Cassidy and the other wolven who'd been gathered under her protection was tenuous at best. She felt more connected to the woman in front of her than to them. The human woman who had kidnapped and held her there.

"That's not what's important here." The words were dismissive, each one falling on Ruri like a sledgehammer.

"This thing just crawled up three stories to get to you, and that's not important?" Even Stiletto seemed incredulous at Mary Alice's dismissal of Ruri's sudden presence. "What could be more important?"

"Taking care of the pack that's making a mess of my city, that's what." Mary Alice ground the words out. If her voice had been a weapon, holes would be smoking in Stiletto's torso. There was more going on here than an argument over her presence. "The sooner I get rid of them, the sooner things go back to normal. The sooner I can be done with you." The last was delivered through clenched teeth.

For a brief moment Ruri wondered if the last had been directed at her, but she decided it probably hadn't been. She focused on Mary Alice's back. The stab wound still oozed a sluggish streak of crimson blood. When she pulled her arm out of Mary Alice's grasp and stepped around her toward the kitchen, she couldn't help but notice how both sets of human eyes followed her. She appreciated being the target of Mary Alice's attention far more than she did Stiletto's.

Ruri opened the towel drawer and rummaged through until she found a particularly tatty dishtowel. She returned and pressed the towel against Mary Alice's stab wound. A slight intake of breath was the only acknowledgment she received.

"It knows its way around your kitchen. I knew one of them was your girlfriend."

"So what if she is?" Mary Alice turned her back to Stiletto and gave Ruri a small smile, but kept talking. "I'm done talking about my personal life. If you want to help me track down that rogue pack, then you can come along. Otherwise, do us all a favor and go back to Atlanta."

"That's what I wanted to talk to you about," Ruri said. She spoke quickly before Stiletto could get a word in edgewise. It sounded like they were picking up an interrupted argument. "You don't have to take out the entire pack. You *shouldn't* take them all out."

"So it's here to keep us from doing our jobs," Stiletto said. Ruri was starting to really hate the sneer in the human's voice whenever Stiletto spoke of her.

Stiletto subsided when Mary Alice held up her hand, though she tried to make it seem as if she'd had nothing else to say.

Mary Alice nodded to Ruri, encouraging her to go on.

"Most of the pack won't be involved in whatever MacTavish is up to. They're with him for the protection he affords, not because they believe in what he's doing. You want MacTavish and the top members of the pack. They're the ones who have choices in what they're doing. Let me have the rest of them."

"They could leave anytime, Ruri," Mary Alice said gently. "Why should I treat them any differently?"

"But they can't, not really. Don't you see? Dean would let anyone go if they really wanted to, but he had to break the bond with them. Somehow I don't see MacTavish letting go of anyone he's already sunk his claws into, not until they no longer have any use to him."

"Then what about you and the others?"

"Simple, we got out when he took over. The Alpha bond hadn't formed yet. Those under his thumb now aren't so lucky. If they try to get away, he'll be able to track them down. I can assure you he'll be less than kind when he catches up with them again."

Stiletto broke in, and Ruri felt a short burst of hot anger at her presumption. "How does he find them? What is it about the Alpha bond that makes that possible?"

Ruri just laughed scornfully, the harshness of her tone making Stiletto angry enough that red showed through her dark complexion. There was no way she would tell that woman any more than she had to. Stiletto would gain no advantage over her people from her.

"Mary, the rest of them don't deserve to be put down just because MacTavish is a murderous bastard." Surely she would see. Ruri held her breath as Mary Alice seemed to mull over her request.

"Anyone who had a hand in turning my sister is already dead." Mary Alice's face was unyielding, her lips set in a straight line. "They don't know it yet is all."

Even if Ruri had been inclined to disagree, she doubted she'd have been able to convince her otherwise. "I didn't expect anything less. Anyone who would do that to the unwilling deserves what's coming for them. I can point you in the direction of a couple of them. I recognized them in Cassidy."

"Thanks." Mary Alice's face softened slightly in gratitude before hardening again. "Let's get ready to head out, then. The sooner this is all handled, the better."

She strode out of the room, leaving Ruri eyeing Stiletto uneasily. The human glared back at her. She betrayed no outward sign of unease, but Ruri could smell her anxiety. It wasn't overwhelming, but the skittering stutter of mild fear colored her aroma. Like Mary Alice, Stiletto gave off very little scent. She too faded into the background of prevalent smells. Stiletto lingered a moment longer as if proving to them both that she had no reason to fear Ruri. She seemed to be having problems standing still, though, and followed Mary Alice out of the room after less than a minute.

Ruri perched on the edge of the kitchen island and waited. Voices floated to her from the far side of Mary Alice's home area.

"I can't believe you'll bargain with them," Stiletto said, her voice heated. "It has no claim on you, even if you are sleeping together."

"It's a reasonable request." Mary Alice's response was unruffled.

Something had changed; the Hunter no longer scrambled to find her feet. Somewhere in the time between when Mary Alice left the safe house and Ruri surprising her here, she'd gotten her bearings. In fact, she was more self-assured and in control than Ruri had ever seen her. Her wolf coiled around her in approval. The wolf may have chosen Mary Alice as her mate, but Ruri was still uncertain. There were simply too many complications for her to sign on, but how could she go against the wishes of her wolf? The stories of her people made it clear that it was a losing battle. Disagreement about the matebond was a recipe for unhappiness, but surely there had never been a situation like this one.

"This is a terrible idea." Stiletto's voice high and insistent. "Good lord, Malice, do you remember nothing from our training?"

"Our training hasn't exactly been good enough for what I've had to deal with lately. I'll take the best help I can get, and I'm not going to run a DNA test on who it's coming from." She laughed humorlessly. "Besides, if you have problems working with these lycans, you're going to like what I have planned even less."

If she'd been in fur-form, Ruri's ears would have pricked up in interest. As it was, she snickered a bit as Stiletto's voice increased in its register.

"What do you mean? What do you have planned?"

"I don't know where the lycans ended up, and neither do you. There's only one group I know of who knows whatever there is to find out about the supras in town."

"You don't mean—?"

"Yep. Vamps."

If she wasn't mistaken, there was a note of glee in Mary Alice's voice. As amusing as Stiletto's anticipated discomfiture had been, Ruri had to agree with her. Vampires made her skin crawl. The way the creatures practically licked their chops when one of her kind was around didn't help. Wolven blood was preferable to them than that of humans and easier to come by than fae or demon blood.

Her wolf shifted uncomfortably. She didn't like the idea of rubbing elbows with anything that thought itself higher up on the food chain. Still, if this could get her to the rest of her people, it might be a risk worth taking. When it came down to it, it was better by far that she should be the one going into the den of bloodsuckers than Cassidy. She couldn't see Cassidy sitting idly by if she knew what was going on, and her blood would be of special interest to vamps.

The two Hunters entered the kitchen. Mary Alice was dressed in what Ruri could only surmise were her work clothes. They were black and form-fitting without being tight. Pockets and straps seemed to cover every possible surface. She moved with purpose and without wasted effort. Ruri's mouth went dry when she saw her. Mary Alice was danger personified, and Ruri could feel herself being drawn to her. She wanted to slowly peel each item of clothing from her body and run her hands over the skin beneath.

"Are you okay?" Mary Alice asked.

Ruri came back to herself with a start. "Yeah, fine," she mumbled. She shook her head to clear it. "I'm coming with you."

"Are you sure that's a good idea?"

"Good idea or not, it's happening."

"It's your call." Mary Alice shrugged casually. She smelled relieved, however. It warmed Ruri to know she was wanted.

"I can help. I should help. These are my people. I failed them once. I'm not going to do so again."

"Good." Mary Alice looked her up and down. On the surface it was all business, but Ruri could smell the edge of arousal that crept into her scent. "You should shift. We're going to need some firepower for this one. Let's make it clear exactly what they'll be taking on if they decide to go up against us."

"If you say so." Ruri had no objection to taking on her fur-form, and neither did her wolf. They were a lot better equipped to protect themselves and Mary Alice with teeth and claws, and her wolf wouldn't let her mate go unprotected. "I'll shift now. Better to be ready to go when we get to the vamps."

Mary Alice nodded and turned a bland expression at Stiletto's inarticulate sound of disagreement. "If you want to try tracking the lycans down on your own, you're welcome to it. I'm doing this because I think it has the best chance of success based on what I know of my city. But by all means, if you disagree, feel free to do your own thing."

"I can't leave you with this monster," Stiletto said, her face ruddy. She clearly didn't appreciate being dismissed, no matter how backhandedly. "You need one of your own to watch back, especially since you're insisting on being insanely foolish. Lycans are one thing, vamps are a different kettle altogether. I hope you've proven yourself to them, or they'll eat you alive."

"Suit yourself." Triumph bled through in Mary Alice's scent. Ruri didn't understand how she could be so pleased that Stiletto continued to attach herself to them. In her way of seeing things, they would have been far better off without the interloping human.

Cool air hit her abdomen as she prepared to strip off her shirt. Ruri had it barely past her rib cage when Mary Alice laid a warm hand over hers.

"How about downstairs? I don't want to have to mop up another mess in here." Her eyes gleamed in amusement. Apparently she still remembered the gift Ruri had left in her bedroom.

"As you wish," Ruri said, laughing.

They were preparing to march into the belly of the beast, but she couldn't have been happier. Mary Alice was self-assured, at the top of her game. Ruri could tell by the way her lover had thrown back her shoulders. She seemed prepared to take anything head-on, and Ruri couldn't help but feel buoyed by her confidence. Things could still blow up in their faces—hell they probably would—but with Mary Alice at her side at least they had an even chance at survival.

Ruri stepped by to allow Mary Alice to lead the way, then cut in behind her, to Stiletto's obvious irritation. That was fine with her. She couldn't trust Stiletto with something as important as watching Mary Alice's back.

CHAPTER THIRTY-FOUR

Mary Alice's eyes slid right again. She couldn't help it. After all, it wasn't every day she rode around with a giant golden wolf in her passenger seat. Ruri lounged easily, head high enough that only her ears were visible from the outside. The fewer people who saw her, the better. Of course, most civilians wouldn't believe she was a wolf, let alone wolven, but Mary Alice wasn't going to tempt fate.

It was fortunate that her truck wasn't large enough for Stiletto to ride with them. She followed along behind in an old sedan, one as beaten up and innocuous as the truck Mary Alice called her own. She wasn't the only one who believed an old car was inconspicuous.

Her mind was inclined to wander and she allowed it. There was little point in dwelling on Cassidy. Her sister had to make her own way. It was clear their worlds were further apart now than they'd been when her sister had still been human. How much of that was because of what Cassidy now was, and how much of it was because of what Mary Alice had been all along?

She shook her head, which elicited a questioning whine from Ruri. Her eyes shifted right before she could stop herself. Ruri was almost as thorny an issue as Cassidy, and yet there was less regret there when she allowed herself to contemplate the wolven. Less regret…but what were they doing, exactly? How could anything they had together last? She'd killed more lycans over the years than she could count, and here she was screwing around with one. *It was only that one time,* she corrected herself. *Does that really count?* Still, the sadness that threatened to choke her at the idea of never seeing Ruri again was too intense for "just one time." When this was all over, Ruri would go back to her pack, to Cassidy's pack. Mary Alice would be all alone once more.

"Dammit," she swore under her breath.

Ruri shifted in her seat, and a cold nose touched Mary Alice on the back of her hand. Warm breath washed over the back of her hand before an even warmer tongue bathed it softly.

"It's okay," Mary Alice said. She dropped her hand and caressed the warm ruff around Ruri's neck, unsure how the gesture would be received. Quite well, it seemed, as Ruri leaned into it.

The contact helped calm her racing mind, and she focused back on the task at hand. The vamps would be a problem, but they were the least of the host of evils facing them. She needed them far more than they needed her, but the trick was making sure they didn't know that.

She pulled up behind the club. It was closed up tight. There would be no action here until night fell, but she knew they had human servants, humans who chased after the euphoria the vampire's bite gave them. They brokered their blood for pleasure and the chance to be part of something absent from their mundane lives.

She got out of the car and Ruri jumped down right behind her, head held high and nostrils wide. What danger the wolven thought she'd be able to smell with vamps involved, Mary Alice wasn't certain, but she was happy for her presence. Ruri was comfortingly solid by her side.

Stiletto pulled in behind them. Her car might have been a piece of crap, but it ran well, just as Mary Alice's truck did. Her counterpart's presence was much less comforting than Ruri's. Not for the first time, Malice wished Stiletto away.

"You both need to follow my lead in there," she said. She glanced down at Ruri and was reassured by the nod of her shaggy head. Stiletto was much less comforting. She set her jaw and said nothing. "I mean it, Simone."

As usual, the use of her given name had more effect upon the woman than threats of physical violence might have. "Fine, I got it. But if one of them looks ready to sample any of me—or either of you—they're not walking away."

"Unacceptable."

Stiletto cocked an eyebrow at her uncompromising tone but said nothing.

"I don't know what Atlanta vamps are like, but these are going to mess with you, try to get under your skin. It's what they did to me my first time here. If you let them push your buttons, you'll get us all killed." Malice pinched the bridge of her nose with one hand. It seemed like she'd had this headache for longer than she could remember. Stiletto only made it worse. Ruri stepped under her other hand and the pain behind her eyes lessened slightly. "I don't trust them any more than you do."

Stiletto barked a sharp laugh. "You have no idea."

"I don't. I want to get out of here with my skin intact too, you know. If I give the word, take out as many of them as you can manage, but if I don't, keep your knives sheathed." The katana across her back wasn't Malice's only weapon. There were also twin knives strapped to her thighs and the wakizashi at her waist. The trench coat kept them all concealed, more or less. Carla would know she was armed to the teeth and would expect no less. The company she kept would throw the vampire lord off more than weapons—or so Mary Alice hoped.

There was still no answer from Stiletto and Malice folded her arms and leaned against the truck. She wasn't moving until Stiletto agreed to play ball. They stood there for long minutes, Ruri shifting at their feet, swinging her head between them to watch each in turn.

"Fine." The agreement sounded like it might have caused her physical pain, but Malice was prepared to accept it. They didn't have the time to mess around, but since she was the only one who knew the deadline they operated against, she couldn't push it.

"Fine." She pushed herself up and led the way to an unassuming metal door. Cigarette butts littered the ground and the scent of stale smoke made her wrinkle her nose. Ruri sneezed and Malice smiled at her in commiseration. She pounded on the door hard enough that the sounds echoed hollowly inside. If that didn't bring someone running, there were other ways into the club, but she didn't want to risk putting the vampires on the defensive. She needed them too badly to get their backs up.

There was no answer and no sign that anyone was coming to the door. She waited longer as Stiletto drummed impatient fingers on the wide leather belt around her hips. Ruri's weight against her legs counseled her to patience, but this was not the time. She knocked again, louder this time. The door boomed beneath her fist.

It didn't take long for the sound of running footsteps to reach them through the thick metal. A few seconds passed and a slot shot open in the door. Dark eyes stared out at them.

"We're closed. Come back at sundown." The words were curt and delivered with dismissive bite. The human obviously had no idea who had come to call.

"I'm not here to dance." Malice stepped forward until she could see the veins in his eyes. "Carla will see me. Tell her Malice is here."

"Malice?" He was sneering; Malice could hear it. She itched to reach through the door and bash his head against the wall. This little man was slowing her down, and she couldn't allow that. "Never heard of you."

"If you don't open the door, you'll wish you never had either." When he started to slide the slot shut, Malice reached out and trapped it between her fingers. Try as he might, he couldn't move it. "Look, little man, I know who your masters are. I won't need to rip you into small pieces once they're done with you. They *will* want to talk to me, and if they find out you're the one who stopped that from happening, you will die long after you've stopped being able to scream."

He blanched slightly and stepped away from the door. There was a small in-ear receiver in his left ear, and he reached up to activate it. Apparently he was going to do the smart thing. She could hear every word he said, though there weren't many. In fact, he'd barely finished saying her name before he was back at the door. Tumblers chunked open, and he stood in front of them, one arm extended as if to welcome them into a grand palace. The front of the club might have been impressive enough for the gesture, but the back hallway certainly wasn't. A long hall of concrete and darkness opened before them. Malice caught a glimpse of movement further down the hall, well out of the possible reach of the sun's rays.

"You're to follow me. Mistress Sangre will see you as soon as she's able."

Malice said nothing and simply took his invitation to step into the building. Ruri was stuck at her side as if she'd been glued there. It didn't feel like she was frightened. Rather Malice got the feeling Ruri was trying to reassure her. Stiletto took up the rear, following soundlessly along in their footsteps. Malice didn't have to look back to know she was there, she could feel her, but without those extra senses, she would never have known.

"I didn't know," their reluctant guide was saying. He hadn't even batted an eye when Ruri and Stiletto filed in with her. "You won't tell them, will you?"

Malice ignored the man and his question. He was not her concern. A tall vamp met them around the next corner.

"You may go, Christian," he said to the doorman.

Christian gave a funny little bow and swiveled toward her before he was finished. He looked up before straightening, but whatever he saw in her face made him swallow hard and bow even more deeply. He waited until they were past before straightening up. She could hear him scurrying back down the hall.

"The Lord of Chicago will want to know who your guests are, Malice." The vampire watched her closely. The skin on his face was drawn tight over bones a shade too prominent. He seemed like he needed a good meal, but Malice suspected he had looked that way all his life. His color was good. Unless she was mistaken, he'd fed recently, and well. If he was up and about at this time of day then he was very old indeed, maybe even older than Carla. He also knew a wolven when he saw one. She hadn't missed how he'd asked for more than one name.

"You may tell Carla that Malice has brought Stiletto and Ruri with her." She didn't have to fill in the blanks for him; he was perfectly capable of doing so for himself.

He made no move to leave and stood there instead. A moment later he nodded and walked away. "This way" was all he said.

His grave manner was so stereotypical that Malice felt a laugh bubbling up from within her. At least he wasn't wearing a cape. No, his clothing was more suitable for a casual day at the office. Suit jacket and slacks were finished with a shirt buttoned up to the top, but no tie. He looked like an evil accountant on casual Friday.

A sharp pain in her right hand drew her attention down. Ruri showed her teeth in clear warning. If she couldn't pull herself together, she was going to get another nip.

With some effort, Malice managed to get herself under control. Nothing could distract her now. If this whole mess was going to be resolved, she needed to be at the top of her game. She reached down and touched Ruri on the back of the neck, taking reassurance in her strength.

CHAPTER THIRTY-FIVE

Chicago's so-called lord wasn't at all what Ruri expected. She was short, for one thing. Somehow, Ruri had assumed the vampire lord would be taller. She'd never had reason to interact with the woman before, but she knew Dean had at least once. The only time he'd spoken of her, he'd smelled coldly contemptuous. It only made sense that he would have some interaction with the self-styled leader of the city's non-human community. The word wasn't a good description for how the non-humans interacted. It implied a sense of cohesion instead of the shifting tapestry of alliances and feuds. Humans were a common enemy. That was about all they could agree to. The packs had more interaction with each other than they did with the vampires, but it was hard to dispute that the vamps knew everything that went on among the different flavors of non-humans. Still, it was difficult to trust them completely, especially given centuries-long feuds over territory and food.

For centuries, the wolven had done their best to shove vamps out of any communities they found them in. Vampires weren't able to blend with human society the way wolven could. Having a vampire in the area brought down scrutiny from humans and usually ended up tarring the wolven with the same brush. It wasn't fair. Humanity didn't have nearly as much to fear from the wolven. Generally, they were more interested in livestock than in humans. To vampires, humans *were* livestock. Vampires didn't trust the wolven, who returned the sentiment in spades. Apparently, not much had changed. Two vampires, including their escort, lounged in stiff-backed chairs next to a small table. They watched everything closely, as still as cats waiting for a foolish mouse to expose itself.

"Malice," the vampire lord said, pouting. "Why have you come to see me during the day? I really should be getting my beauty sleep." The excuse was pure crap. Ruri knew it and she was sure the Hunters did also. A vampire with the strength to run an entire city would have no problems staying awake during daylight. That ability was usually reserved for the oldest of vampires. This one didn't smell that old to Ruri, not that she could smell much. There was little of the mustiness of the crypt she tended to associate with the oldest vamps. They might not smell like much themselves, but they did tend to take on the scents of their surroundings, at least a little bit, which made ambushing them in their territory a chancy prospect indeed. When at home, vamps truly melted into their scentscape.

"Like you need any of that, Carla." Mary Alice seemed awfully friendly with the vampire. Obviously they'd met before, but Ruri wondered what kind of relationship they actually had.

"You're kind to say so," Carla said. She smiled widely, flashing tips of pointed eyeteeth against red lips. The smile disappeared as quickly as it had appeared. In its place was a small moue of disappointment. "But did you have to bring these…people with you?"

Stiletto shifted slightly on the other side of Mary Alice. Ruri agreed with her restlessness. The implied slight had hit home, for both of them it seemed. It was strange; the other Hunter didn't smell as uncomfortable as Ruri expected her to. If anything, she smelled of anticipation that bordered upon sexual. Stiletto certainly didn't smell as if she were readying herself for battle but for something far more carnal.

"I have some questions for you and they're involved in the worst of it." Mary Alice folded her arms and settled her weight back on her heels. If her posture was anything to go by, she would not be moved.

Ruri dropped her head slightly, tensing her shoulders and readying herself. The movements were infinitesimal, and she hoped no one would notice. Her wolf bristled in agreement. If anything attacked, they would have to contend with teeth and claws.

"Tell your pets to stand down," Carla said. "I'm not going to hurt them."

"Pets?" Stiletto's voice was mild, but she placed a hand under her trench coat. There was no doubt she gripped one of her knives.

"They certainly don't have much in the way of manners." Carla walked forward. Her steps were too smooth to be believed. She could have carried a stack of quarters on the top of her head without losing one of them.

Mary Alice turned to keep the vampire in front of her. Carla sauntered toward Ruri who refused to give ground. She recognized a play for dominance when she saw one. It was different than the way wolven took stock of each other, but she was being tested nonetheless. Carla had a presence that battered at her, trying to force the wolf and its protections out of her way. The wolf shifted and flowed around the vampire's probing, never meeting her head on but never offering an opening either. A head-to-head confrontation probably wouldn't end well for either Ruri or her wolf, but they hadn't forgotten the difficult lessons that decades of experience imparted. Some battles couldn't be won by a head-on attack. The vampire dropped a hand toward her, but it was intercepted before she could touch Ruri.

"Don't," was all Mary Alice said.

"I see I've been replaced in your affections."

"You were never in my affections."

A growl rumbled through Ruri's chest. Her wolf didn't like the competition the vampire alluded to. It seemed like it had been a couple of weeks since Ruri was in full agreement with her wolf, but on this one they were of the same mind. Mary Alice was hers. She didn't care how powerful the vampire thought she was. If this Carla thought she was going to take her mate away, she would find out how difficult it was to function without a face.

"Lord," one of Carla's bodyguards said. He stood next to his chair, though Ruri hadn't seen him get up. "That one is ready."

Carla looked down at her and Ruri saw a flash of scarlet in the depths of her pupils. She seemed delighted and negligently reclaimed her hand from Mary Alice's grasp. "You don't like me touching your mate, do you, puppy?"

"Mate?" Stiletto stepped forward.

"And your partner didn't know?" Carla clapped her hands. "This really is wonderful. How many more secrets are you holding onto, Malice?"

The vampire held her hand tantalizingly in front of Ruri's nose and though her wolf urged her to bite it, she tamped down the urge to snap. She had to trust Mary Alice knew what she was doing.

"I'm tired of playing with you, Carla," Mary Alice said. "I have business to discuss. If you're not interested, I'll find someone else who can answer my questions."

"Darling, really." Carla crossed the room and settled herself on a dark red settee. She crossed her legs demurely and regarded them with only the barest hint of mischief about her. "If it's that important to you, tell me what brings you here at this dreadful hour."

"I need a couple of things, maybe." Mary Alice abruptly smelled uncertain, though nothing about her demeanor changed.

Ruri leaned against her hip. *I'm here*, she thought at the Hunter.

"You know my policy, Malice. Payment comes first, then you can ask."

"Not this time." Mary Alice held up her hand to forestall the vampire's protest. "Technically you've already answered this question. I need to find the former North Side pack."

"Again?" Carla shook her head. "Darling, did you lose them already?"

"I've had things on my mind."

"Family is such a pesky thing, isn't it? Still, they do have their uses, especially when they become more."

Ruri kept herself from shifting at the dig. It was impossible to tell what Mary Alice thought of it, but the implication was clear. If her Hunter had thought she could keep the business with Cassidy a secret, it was already too late.

"Does that mean you don't know where they've ended up this time?"

"I didn't say that. Patience, my dear."

"That's exactly what I'm out of. Either we deal now, or I'm done with you. You know what that means."

Carla clearly did, but Ruri was mystified. They had some sort of understanding, that much was clear. Ruri would have given a lot to find out how far it went.

"Very well. I will tell you, but I'll be taking my payment from her." Carla's perfectly manicured fingernail pointed directly at Ruri, who stared at it as though it was a rattlesnake coiled to strike. It certainly carried the same amount of menace along with it.

"Absolutely not."

"There's nothing else you can offer me. Good luck finding out where they are from one of your other 'brokers.'" Carla's lips curled when she used the term. Even that looked lovely on her face. "The new Alpha has no compunction about eliminating what he perceives as a threat. I doubt you'll find anyone willing to put themselves on his radar."

"And you'll allow that kind of threat to your power base?" Stiletto's question was as pointed as it was surprising. Ruri didn't know how the Hunter could think that strategically, not smelling of arousal as she did. "It seems to me removing someone who can consolidate that kind of influence would be to your advantage."

"Your partner has a point," Carla said. She sat back and regarded the three of them over interlaced fingers. She looked Stiletto in the eye. "Very well, I'll tell you in exchange for your blood."

"Stiletto, you don't have to do this," Mary Alice said.

Ruri wasn't so sure. The Hunter's heartbeat was loud enough that she could hear it from ten feet away. It had picked up as soon Carla had pointed at her. Stiletto knew what she was doing. She'd courted Carla's attention on purpose.

"I know I don't, but this isn't my first tango with a vamp." Stiletto looked back at Carla. The sweet smell of anticipation practically dripped from her now. "It's a deal."

Carla patted the seat next to her. "Then come here, my lovely morsel." Her teeth protruded even further now, sliding over lips red as rubies. Carla didn't have to open her mouth for them to be visible. Her bodyguards were suddenly at her back. Like the vampire lord's, their pupils had swallowed the iris and most of the whites in their eyes. They stared at Stiletto as she walked slowly over to the vampire.

"She doesn't have to drink right from you," Mary Alice said loudly.

"For this information, I insist upon it," Carla said.

Stiletto shook her head and looked down her nose at the vampire. "No mind games. I want to be completely aware when you bite me. I won't have you clouding my thoughts."

"It's your decision, my sweet, and I certainly won't complain. You'll taste sweeter for the pain, though you'll enjoy it less." At Stiletto's shudder, Carla smiled. "Then again, maybe not."

Ruri's wolf paced back and forth in front of Mary Alice, agitated by the scent of Stiletto's excitement. Mary Alice smelled of purpose and a bit of vague concern. If there ever had been anything between her and the vampire, she gave no indication that any feelings remained.

Stiletto opened the front of her shirt and sat stoically as Carla ran her fingertips lightly over the exposed skin. She dawdled over the sternum, skirting delicately around the little bit of cleavage that was exposed. Slowly, lingeringly, she traced the outline of Stiletto's collarbone before lowering her head.

Her fangs sinking into the Hunter's flesh made almost no noise nor did the sucking sound as she drew forth Stiletto's blood. Iron and salt hung heavy in the air, as did the smell of Stiletto's excited sex. The bodyguard vamps hovered protectively over their lord while she drank. Slowly the smell of arousal abated, and all that was left was discomfort. Ruri whined uncertainly. The vampire had been feasting at Stiletto for a while, and Mary Alice didn't seem too concerned.

As if the mournful sound had brought Mary Alice back to herself, she shook her head and stepped forward.

"Stay back," their guide said. "She feeds yet."

"She's had enough. If she takes much more, Stiletto will be of no use to me."

"The lord will decide when she's had enough, not some half-rate dhampir."

"What did you just call me?" Strangely, Ruri didn't think Mary Alice's question was asked in anger. Rather she seemed genuinely curious. The intent had assuredly been to insult her, but she shrugged off the denigration.

Dhampir. It wasn't a word Ruri was familiar with either, but there were more important issues at hand.

"Stand down, Gunther." Carla sat back, sighing contentedly. Blood smeared her face and the front of her bare chest. Ruri had missed that; when had she opened up her blouse? "You may both clean me."

A strangled choke from Mary Alice betrayed her revulsion, but Ruri understood what the vampire lord was doing. Blood like Stiletto's was far too valuable to waste. Carla's vampires may have appeared subservient as they knelt to bathe her skin with their tongues, but they were being rewarded. Carla watched them over the two heads that lavished her with attention. The look on her face was that of ecstasy, though it was impossible to tell if it was from the blood or the ministrations of her minions. If Ruri had to guess, she would have said both.

"The pack you seek is working out of a warehouse in the Armitage industrial area." She threw back her head, eyes closed, and cried out in the final pangs of pleasure. The spasm that wracked her frame lasted for long seconds to the observers. Finally, she pushed her attendants back and sat before them, breasts bare and still heaving in the blood-streaked blouse. "They're living in abandoned row houses on North Mayfield."

"Then I have something else I need to ask of you," Mary Alice said.

"What is it, darling?" Carla stretched like a cat waking up from a long nap. Her bodyguards stood behind her again. They paid no attention to Stiletto as she moved away from the settee, her movements slow.

"I need a favor."

Carla's laughter filled the space until the shadows seemed to pulse with her delight. "A favor? How delicious. You will find those don't come cheaply, little Hunter."

"I know what I'm doing and what I need. It's to your advantage as well." Mary Alice paused and Ruri heard her swallow before she continued. "We don't have the numbers to take on MacTavish alone. I need to get him out of his den and to a place where we can take him on and soon. He's a loose cannon and is going to expose his people and yours if he isn't stopped. On his own turf, he'll be too hard to kill, especially with his pack around him. Unless you want a mess of government special forces running around your city, that is. If we can't get him alone, I'll need to call in the cavalry and risk exposure."

"And if the only way I would do that was with a drink from your little pet there?"

"It's not going to happen, Carla. You will not touch her. If that ever happens, I will forget every understanding we've come to."

"You would never survive attacking me." Not the least bit concerned, Carla lounged back on her seat.

"Neither would you."

The vampire watched them both. Her eyes had returned to their normal state, though her bodyguards were still in a state of heightened awareness. There was no hint of fang on her either. For all her words, she wasn't worried.

"Very well, but only because the rogue's actions can't be permitted to continue." She chewed delicately on her lower lip. "I need to think on it and will contact you with the details."

"Sooner would be better."

"So hasty. And yet, MacTavish has been allowed to flourish long enough. One of my people will reach out to you soon."

"Thank you."

Carla's face split with a wide grin. Though her teeth no longer extended beyond her lips, the smile was predatory in the extreme. "You may not be thanking me when I call in your favor."

Mary Alice nodded, her face betraying nothing to the vampire. Her scent was no help to Ruri either. She didn't smell worried, though by all rights she should have been. If anything, she smelled resolved, like she'd been loosed at a target and would damn well make sure she took it out.

"Let's go." Stiletto stood by the door. She'd shaken off her mild stupor and the only thing that betrayed what had happened was a lingering odor of uncertainty.

"You'll call and soon?" Mary Alice wouldn't let Carla off the hook.

"We got what we needed. What does it matter when they call?" A tapping foot betrayed Stiletto's impatience and the scent of mild uncertainty was growing stronger. If Ruri hadn't known better, she would have said the Hunter was on the edge of a panic attack.

The finger that Mary Alice held up to forestall Stiletto didn't assuage her. Mary Alice had locked eyes with the vampire lord and refused to look away.

"Yes, Malice," Carla finally said. The small smile still lurking around her lips made a mockery of her easy acquiescence. "You'll hear from us within twenty-four hours, if not less."

"Very well." Now wearing a veneer of unconcern, Mary Alice dipped her head.

Their guide appeared by the door. Ruri had been watching for him this time and was able to track his movements. They were quick in the extreme, and he seemed to blur around the edges. There was more to vampires than insanely quick reflexes, and she wondered if they were a little out of phase with reality. It would explain the lack of scent.

With no further word to Carla or amongst themselves, they headed back home.

CHAPTER THIRTY-SIX

It was very warm in the bed, and Cassidy tossed, trying to push the blankets down from her shoulders. They didn't budge and she pushed on them harder and was rewarded by the sound of tearing fabric. That roused her all the way. She sat up and blinked blearily around her. The bodies surrounding her definitely hadn't been there when she went to bed. It seemed half the pack had decided to nap with her.

Somehow, she'd managed to find a whole new family. How would her mom react to that? she wondered. Her eyes moved from one form to another, not really seeing any of them. *Mom.* How would she explain any of this to her? How could she even try? Mary never had, and the more she thought about it, the better the idea sounded.

I can't lose my mommy. Cassidy pulled in on herself, tucking her knees up under her chin. *I can't lose my new family either.* There had to be an answer there somewhere. She reached out and placed a gentle hand upon the nearest furry shoulder. Instantly her racing thoughts slowed. It would all work out. She would see to it.

The wolven slept soundly about her, dead to the world. Most of them were in human form, but a few of them had opted to shift and slept with tails tucked over muzzles in tight balls between their packmates. She cocked her head, listening for sounds in the house. All was quiet or at least nearly so. They'd eaten a lot before she'd decided she needed to lie down for a bit. Her bank account was now hurting from the cost of feeding ten hungry wolven mouths. That definitely wasn't sustainable and Cassidy wondered how a pack of wolven stayed fed.

She extricated herself from the crowded bed, taking care not to jostle or wake anyone. She was successful and they slumbered along without her. The house felt like it slept with them, as if they all breathed with the same steady exhalations. Everything felt as if it was one. Cassidy stood in the doorway to the bedroom, soaking it all in. If she'd wanted to, she thought she could have reached out inside her head and touched any one of the sleeping wolven. They glowed as soft points in her awareness. Those must be the sleeping ones. A few of them glittered in sharp contrast, and she assumed those were still awake.

Cassidy couldn't share in their peace. Every brush of her finger on bare skin ratcheted up her internal thermostat. What was wrong with her? There hadn't been the time to ask Ruri, and she didn't know who else she could trust. How was she supposed to tell someone she'd just met that she was ready to jump on pretty much anyone who looked at her sideways. If only she had someone to talk to. The glowing points in her head made that a cruel mockery. She was never by herself, but in that moment she felt acutely alone.

Luther was one of those points, she could tell by the feel of it. He seemed to be pulling at her from the general area of the kitchen. That was as good a place to go as any, and she padded softly down the stairs.

"Alpha," Luther said. He drank from a glass of water as he gazed out the window over the sink. From there he had a great view of the depressing back yard. Mary Alice had kept up the front yard enough that the house didn't look abandoned, but she hadn't done the same for the back.

Something to drink sounded like a good idea. Cassidy joined the grizzled wolven. As she filled a glass, she looked out over the same dead overgrowth he stared at. A small garage took up half the yard. It wasn't falling down, but one window was missing a couple panes.

"We'll need to clear the grass and weeds," Luther said. "Too many hiding places."

"Are we going to stay here long enough to make that worth the trouble?" Cassidy took a long gulp of her water, trying to distract herself from the way his ass looked in his jeans. "I don't think this place is going to work very well over the long run."

"If you say so, Alpha." He sounded politely doubtful.

"What do you suggest?"

"Have some of the wolven clear it anyway. It'll give them something to do while you figure out our next move. It really does need to be chopped back."

"I wanted to talk to you about that anyway. My next move, I mean." Cassidy paused, unsure how to go one. Was she going to look weak in front of him? That was a big deal for him.

"What are you thinking?"

"More wondering, right now. How did your last Alpha figure out how to provide for you all? Was he independently wealthy or something?"

Luther looked down at her, his eyes wide with disbelief. The laugh that issued from him surprised them both. Cassidy had yet to see a smile cross his face, let alone a full belly laugh. It was the hottest thing she'd ever heard.

"I don't think Dean had worked in decades. He certainly hadn't come into a large inheritance."

"Did he find buried treasure, then? There has to be something he did to keep you all fed. Lunch almost tapped me out. I'm not sure what I'll do for dinner."

"The members of a healthy pack contribute their own earnings and food for the good of the whole." All trace of amusement disappeared from Luther's face. "We haven't been a healthy pack since Dean was murdered."

"That's a relief." Realizing how that had sounded, Cassidy hastened to clarify. "That I won't be expected to support everyone, I mean. I haven't even finished my degree, so that wouldn't happen any time soon."

"We can always stretch our food supplies by hunting. That'll also help bind the pack even tighter to you. Lead them in the hunt a few times, and they'll follow you anywhere."

Cassidy lowered her voice and leaned in toward him. "I don't know if I'm cut out to be Alpha."

"You defeated Lewis in challenge, you are the Alpha." A muscle jumped in his jaw, but his voice never changed. "You are the strongest, therefore you lead."

"I don't know how. I've never done anything like this before."

"Then keep your eyes and ears open, and ask questions of those you can trust."

"Can I trust you, Luther?"

"With your life, Alpha." His face never changed, but she knew he was telling the truth. He smelled and felt…solid. Cassidy had no other way to explain it, but she knew he would lay down his life for her if that was what the situation required.

"Hopefully it won't come to that." She thought her voice was a match for his in dryness. One corner of his mouth lifted slightly.

"Right now we need to be careful, concentrate on rebuilding and stay under the radar. If MacTavish finds out we're regrouping, he'll do a much better job of wiping us out the next time."

"That's not going to happen." The idea of all the points of light that accompanied her going dark was more than Cassidy would contemplate. "I won't allow it."

"And you say you're not cut out to be Alpha." Luther shook his head at her. "Only an Alpha would have the temerity to try rolling back the tide and the strength to accomplish it."

"We'll see about the strength."

"Indeed we will." He smiled at her again, the corners of his eyes crinkling adorably.

Unable to stop herself, Cassidy leaned forward and laid a light kiss along the line of his jaw.

"Alpha?" Luther held himself still as if worried he might spook her. "Do you understand what you're doing?"

He smelled so good, like dark loam and old growth. The skin of his neck beckoned her and she ran the tip of her tongue over it; then sank her teeth lightly around the pounding point of his pulse.

"Cassidy." He stepped back. "You're too new."

"I'm too nothing," she said, matching his steps until he was trapped against the kitchen cabinets. "And you don't tell me what to do."

He looked away and lifted his chin, offering his neck to her. His silent submission was the most erotic gesture she'd ever experienced. This time the bite at his neck was anything but light. She pushed him to the floor and he went without protest. He was ready for her and she for him.

"What the hell was that?" Cassidy asked thirty minutes later. She gathered the torn shreds of her clothes to her before stopping ruefully. The shirt was never going to be much more than a holey tank top, and the pants were beyond saving.

"You don't know?" Luther's clothes weren't in any better condition, but he didn't seem to mind lounging nude on the kitchen floor. "I thought Ruri would have passed that along."

"She passed on the important stuff. Things have been… complicated."

"Very well." He sat up and regarded her levelly. "That was your heat. Your wolf drives you to mate every moon when you're at your most fertile. You're bound to find a wolven and mate with them."

"Heat? Like an animal."

"Yes."

His simple answer took Cassidy aback. She wasn't sure what to make of someone who was so sanguine about being compared to a beast. Her head whipped around to stare at him when the rest of what he'd said sank in. "Most fertile? Am I pregnant?"

Luther shrugged and tucked a strand of hair back behind his ear. "Maybe. You won't know for a few weeks. It's unlikely, though. We're not the most fertile bunch. Natural wolven births do happen, but it seems to take a lot for one of our women to catch. Without you being mated, I'd be surprised if you had."

"Thank god." Like many women, Cassidy had always assumed that eventually she'd get married and have kids. The events of the past couple week were not at all what she'd had in mind for her life, and adding a kid to the mix seemed like a really bad idea. "If I'm going to have to do this every month, how do I keep from getting pregnant?"

"You could mate with a female wolven." At her shrug, Luther went on quickly. "If you mate with a wolven who is much more submissive than you are, chances are better you won't conceive. Even Alphas don't tend to breed successfully unless they've found themselves a mate. Until that happens, your chances are very low."

"But it could still happen."

"Yes."

"Well, that's just great."

"There's always the standard protection. Only don't bother with birth control pills, they won't work for you."

Two wolven padded quietly into the kitchen. Lewis didn't bat an eye at the two of them sitting on the floor surrounded by the ruins of their clothing. He gave them a wide berth and pulled open the refrigerator instead. Lewis had to stoop to look inside; Cassidy marveled that she'd been able to fight him to a standstill. Her wolf disagreed. They hadn't fought him to a draw; they'd demolished him. Reluctantly, Cassidy agreed, which assuaged the wolf somewhat. She continued to be on her guard with Lewis, however. If the wolven decided he wanted to be Alpha again, who knew when he might attack next. The wolf seemed much less worried and was confident he would stay in his place.

The other wolven had left the room but came back quickly. She padded over to where Cassidy and Luther sat and handed them a small stack of clothing.

"Thank you," Cassidy said quietly. The wolven smiled shyly at her, and then moved to the sink to pour herself a glass of water.

Cassidy pulled on the T-shirt and sweatpants. Her nudity didn't bother her so much as remind her that she was at a disadvantage with Lewis. He hadn't noticed, not that she could tell, but she felt more vulnerable naked.

"There's not much food left," Lewis said, removing a Styrofoam carton and peering dubiously inside it. He shut the door with a little more force than was necessary.

"Lewis." Luther's voice overflowed with warning. He said nothing further, but apparently he didn't have to. Lewis flushed angry red and sulked over to the counter where he stood and gobbled his way through the contents of the box. He might have complained about how much food was left, but from where Cassidy stood, it appeared the carton was almost completely full. With the way he chowed through it, however, the rest of the food wasn't likely to last long, maybe through dinner, if they were lucky.

Cassidy wondered if she should do something to show her dominance over Lewis, but Luther wasn't giving her any kind of sign, and her wolf continued to lounge.

"Someone comes," Luther said suddenly, head snapping up. His eyes glowed silver and he shifted to face the door.

Cassidy felt it also, like a pressure along the side of her body, almost but not quite pushing into her skin. It was a pressure that felt familiar. "It's Ruri."

"That's just what we need," Lewis said around a mouthful of food. He didn't move toward the door, but his eyes glowed also. Luther said nothing to reprimand him this time around, and Cassidy wondered what their problem was with Ruri.

The back door swung open to reveal Ruri silhouetted against the late afternoon sky. Fall sunlight filtered around her, somehow weaker than that of the summer, but without the chill edge of winter.

"Oh good, you're here," Ruri said. She grinned at the group, not seeming to notice the wolven who regarded her with glowing stares. "Boy, do I have some good news!"

"You're leaving town, never to return?"

The growl that erupted from Cassidy's chest surprised them all, even her. Lewis turned surprised eyes upon her. He seemed shocked at the rebuke but subsided, the light in his eyes dimming slightly.

"What are you talking about?" Cassidy asked once Lewis was back in his place.

"MacTavish." Ruri's grin widened until she looked maniacally gleeful. "I know where he's holed up. I also know that he's going to be away from his den soon. It's perfect."

"How do you know that?" Luther demanded.

"What's perfect?" Cassidy asked at the same time.

"Apologies, Alpha," Luther said. He gave her a significant look, though Cassidy wasn't sure what he was getting at. His scent had softened, but not in a pleasant manner. It seemed shifty, as if he had problems trusting Ruri.

"What's perfect?" she asked again.

"Taking back the pack."

A shattering of glass on the linoleum floor caused them to turn as one and regard the other wolven. She'd dropped her water glass and a puddle of water widened at her feet. "I'm sorry," she murmured and bent to pick up shards of broken glass with trembling fingers. It wasn't long before she cut herself, though she didn't seem to notice.

"Beth, let me give you a hand," Lewis said. He bent down and gathered up the remaining pieces before throwing them in the small trash can under the sink. "I'll just take her out, if you don't mind." He stood there waiting until Cassidy belatedly realized he'd been talking to her.

"Of course," she said. He drew the female wolven out the door and into the living room. Cassidy could barely hear what he said to her, but his hushed tones seemed to be having the desired effect. Beth's fear was flattening out, to be replaced by the unpredictable peaks and valleys of anxiety.

"MacTavish is no good for those wolven, Cassidy." The ragged edge of Ruri's voice tugged at her. The anguish in her voice was echoed by the miasma of despair her scent exuded. "He may think he's a criminal mastermind, but most of the rest of them aren't that way. These are people I've lived with for a long time, most of them. All they want is someone who will take care of them, who will keep the pack strong. I thought all that mattered was killing MacTavish, but it's not. Someone has to draw the rest of our people away from him. That's more important than getting to be the one to kill him."

Lewis reappeared in the doorway. Arms folded, he leaned against it and watched them closely.

"How do you know he's going to be away?" Luther pressed back in with his original question.

Ruri's eyes shifted left before looking back at them. "Malice is setting it up."

"Malice?" Luther slammed both hands down on the edge of the counter. The chipped laminate caved in under his fists. "The Hunter? You'd trust her enough to work with her on this? Ruri, she kills us for sport."

"Actually, she kills us for her job." Ruri ran both hands through her hair. "I know you don't like her, but she's not the way you think."

"A job. Hunting down our packmates is her job, so that makes it all right." Luther vaulted over the counter to stand toe-to-toe with Ruri. She didn't flinch and looked right at him, even when he thrust his face so close to hers that if she'd shifted a bit, their noses would have touched.

"Enough!" Cassidy leaped over the counter before she realized what she was doing. Her wolf was fully engaged, all sign of complacence gone. Ruri was the closest thing she had to a sire, and she would be damned if another wolf was going to take her out. She grabbed Luther by the elbow and hauled him back. He grunted with the effort of resisting her, and she shook him sharply.

"Why are you protecting her?" Luther's eyes glowed even brighter. His teeth were pointed and his jaw was shifting to make room for them. Cassidy looked down to see claws sprouting from his fingertips. "She didn't protect us! She ran. MacTavish killed Dean and she ran. How many more of us would have survived if she'd stuck around? Would Beth be jumping at every sound because that bastard took her mate out in front of her? Mouse and Skippy might still be alive instead of being slaughtered in each other's arms. And now…Now she wants us to go along with her on the plan of someone else who wouldn't mind seeing us all dead. Someone who preys upon us the way the humans think we stalk them. Whose *job*—" an ugly grimace split his face "—is to wipe out as many of us as possible, then she can go home and put her feet up."

"That someone is my sister." Cassidy dragged him close to her and wrapped her other hand around his throat. She was dimly aware of the claws that now adorned her own fingertips as well as the ache in her jaw as it flexed to make room for more teeth. "And this woman is the only reason I'm standing here. Without her, I'd be a drooling vegetable or worse. You will apologize to her."

"It's all right, Cassidy." Ruri placed a hand on her shoulder. As it had back in the box in Mary Alice's loft, the touch calmed her, allowing her to think straight. "He's right, as far as it goes. I did run. I was injured and Dean had just been killed in front of me. I thought I could draw MacTavish and some of the others after me, but it wasn't enough."

"They did go after her," Lewis said. "If Ruri had stayed to fight, I don't know if any of us would've gotten out." He shrugged. "Sorry, Luther, but she's here now and it sounds like there's a plan to get at least some of our packmates back. We should listen to her."

"It isn't prudent," Luther said. His eyes rolled as he tried to get a look at the hand around his windpipe. Both hands were wrapped around Cassidy's arm now, but it felt to her more like he was steadying himself than trying to pull her hand away. "We need to keep a low profile and rebuild."

"I tried that, remember?" Lewis said. "We were living in the sewer, Luther. Besides, if MacTavish is out of the picture, we don't need to keep our heads down, we just need to reclaim our old den before someone else moves in on it. I think we should hear out her plan."

"So do I." Cassidy released her hold on Luther. "What does my sister have in mind?"

CHAPTER THIRTY-SEVEN

"Have you seen my phone?" Stiletto asked immediately upon their return to the loft. "I need to let Uncle Ralph know about the plan."

"So now that you think it might actually work it's *the* plan and not *my* plan?" Malice shook her head. The grousing was all show, of course. She would be happy when this was all over. "I haven't seen it. You probably lost it when we had our…disagreement."

"Maybe." Stiletto seemed unconvinced, but she headed toward the living room anyway.

"I'll call Uncle Ralph," Malice called after her. There was no response and Malice waited a second before heading over to the bag of rice. With deliberate care, she dug into the bag, exposing the components inside. The rice around them was damp. She poured the rest of the bottle of water in her hand over the laptop pieces, and then covered them back up.

When Stiletto came back into the kitchen, Malice was seated at the island waiting on hold. Uncle Ralph hadn't been immediately available, but apparently he wanted to talk to them badly enough that he'd set someone to answer the line. Malice had been informed in no uncertain terms that she was to wait to talk to him.

Stiletto held up her phone and Malice nodded with approval. *I'm on hold*, she mouthed, pointing at her own phone.

Okay, Stiletto mouthed back before becoming quickly involved in checking something on her phone.

That was fine with Malice. The less she had to interact with the woman, the better. It would all be over soon. The mantra was supposed to reassure her, to get her to relax, but it had the opposite effect. It might all be over soon, but would it be over because things had gone the way she hoped? With so many moving pieces, so many things could go wrong. She wasn't used to having to rely on others as part of her operations. Usually the only other one who was involved was Uncle Ralph, and he only because he was giving her the target.

"What's going on, kiddo?" When her handler finally came to the phone, Malice had already contemplated hanging up three times. She'd been stuck cooling her feet for thirty minutes. At least there had been no sign that Carla or her people had tried calling. She would have dropped him like a four-day-dead fish for that. Stiletto still sat across from her, the pieces of her laptop spread across the table.

"Nothing much. Just checking in to let you know that Sissy and I will be making a move soon."

Across the island, Stiletto wrinkled her nose at Malice's mocking nickname for her. Ralph laughed unpleasantly.

"Good, and I'm glad to hear she's been helpful. I knew you could use the hand."

"Yes, well. I'm forever grateful." The sarcasm was obvious. She made no attempt to hide it. He didn't care. In fact, he would be less suspicious if she continued to be bitter than if she suddenly changed her tune.

"So when is this all going down?"

"In the next day or so. A few things need to fall into place, then we're golden."

"Do you need any backup or cleaners?"

"Keep the cleaners on standby. I think Sissy and I can handle anything that comes our way until mop-up."

"Exactly right," Stiletto said without looking up from the components she worked on with a cotton ball and rag. She'd been irked to find out the pieces weren't as dry as she'd expected and was methodically working them over by hand again.

"We'll let you know when we head out," Malice said. "If we need the cleaners…"

"Give me a call when everything's squared away," Uncle Ralph said. "I'm glad you finally came to your senses, Malice. I have to say, I have no idea what the hell you were thinking with this one."

"Just trying to do my job."

"So long as you keep doing it. Let me know when you're heading out. Just leave me a message." Without any kind of pleasantries from either of them, her handler ended the call.

"What did he say?" Stiletto still didn't pull any attention from the work in front of her.

"You heard." It was unlikely Stiletto hadn't been able to hear his side of the conversation as well as her own. "He's pleased, or as much as he ever is."

"Fine." Finished with the component in her hand, Stiletto laid it down on the table and looked up at Malice. "You didn't say anything about your sister."

"Why would I do that?"

"Regs, if nothing else. Because it's a bad idea to keep this to yourself."

"It's not going to happen. I don't care if Jesus himself comes down out of the clouds to tell me to do it, I'm not telling Uncle Ralph or those asswipes at the CIA about my sister."

Looking slightly pained at her choice of language, Stiletto shrugged. "That's certainly your decision, but they need to know. Your MacTavish probably had more innocents corrupted. Your sister isn't the only one, but she's part of it."

"I will include a full report on MacTavish's activities to Uncle Ralph, but Cassidy won't be anywhere in it." Why wouldn't Stiletto drop it? All they needed to do was take care of MacTavish, and then everyone could go back to their lives. Well, almost everyone. Cassidy's life was going to look a lot different than it had. Malice wished she could do something about that, but there was no going back now.

"And I'll have my own report to file." Stiletto picked up another piece of her laptop. "There may be some discrepancies between our accounts." She bent her head over it, dismissing Malice.

"I have some things to handle before we move out." Malice pushed herself away from the island and headed to the elevator without waiting for a response. If one even came, it was so quiet she didn't hear it.

While it was true she had things to do before they went up against MacTavish and his crew, Malice mostly needed to distract herself from the wait and from Stiletto's' veiled threat. If Ruri had been there, that would have been a lot easier. Her belly tightened pleasantly as she remembered their time together at the safe house. The wolven was hot as hell; that was for certain. *Mate.* Unbidden, Carla's word came floating back to her. What did that even mean? Ruri had decided they were mates now? How could that be?

She stepped out of the stairwell and into her studio. The organized riot of materials and tools barely registered as she tried to pull apart what it might mean to be the wolven's mate. Maybe. There was no way that was a for-sure thing, right? She could have said something in the car—should have said something in the car—but she'd held back, afraid of what Ruri's response might be. The wolven had shifted back to human form right after they'd left. Somehow, she'd managed to get dressed so quickly Mary Alice barely had time to gawk, which was good. Ruri's body was more than a little gawk-worthy, but not while on the Tri-State.

What if she'd asked and Ruri had confirmed Carla's claim? Worse yet, what if she'd blown it off? There was no denying that she enjoyed Ruri's company, though she had no right to do so.

This line of thought was no help at all. Mary Alice shook her head to clear Ruri out of it for a bit. It wouldn't last long; it never seemed to. Golden eyes were there every time her mind wandered. She pulled on a thick leather apron and gloves. The pile of scrap metal in the corner was exactly what she needed. Determined to kill some time and stop worrying about everything, Mary Alice got to work.

It was hours later when the phone rang, startling Mary Alice, who was deep in the middle of a new sculpture. She'd finished what she'd come down to work on, but the urge to start something new had been impossible to resist. It was different than a lot of her other work. Gone were the harsh edges and uncomfortable joins. This one was all soaring curves and fine lines. She had no idea what the gallery would make of it. She wasn't even sure if she wanted to sell this one.

She dropped the tools with alacrity and shook off one glove to fish the phone out of her pocket before it stopped ringing. "Malice."

"I thought you were going to let it go to voice mail, darling." Carla's voice issued through the speaker in a crackly burst of static.

"Hold on, I need to get upstairs. Stiletto will want to hear this, and I need a better connection."

"I'm afraid the connection won't be improved. For some reason, we don't work well with cell phones."

"Huh." That was news to her, but then she'd never before had reason to speak with a vamp over the phone. "Hold on anyway."

She took the stairs two at a time and burst out into the loft. Stiletto wasn't in the kitchen when she arrived, but she stepped through the opening to the living room, almost running into Malice who'd had the same idea. "It's Carla."

"About time." Was it her imagination, or had Stiletto's face reddened when she'd said Carla's name. She was probably still remembering being fed upon. Malice wondered if the heightened color was from anger or arousal.

"Is my little snack there?" Carla asked. "How delightful!"

The red was definitely from anger now. Stiletto didn't like being anyone's little anything. If Carla had been in front of them, she might have had a fight on her hands. The idea that someone might claim her was the only thing Malice had ever seen her snap on. Most of the rest of the time, Stiletto didn't allow her emotions to goad her into action. She might run hot under the collar, but she kept herself under such iron control that she almost never acted upon it.

"What's the news?" They didn't have time for Carla to goad her former squadmate.

"MacTavish has agreed to undertake the retrieval of an item for me. He will be at Liberty Savings and Loan in Hoffmann Estates tomorrow night. What I need is in a safe-deposit box in the vault."

"At Liberty?" Malice mulled it over. It felt all right. It was a bank so there would be one way in, which should make it easy enough to keep the lycans bottled up. It would be the perfect site for an ambush. "But tomorrow night?"

Stiletto nodded approvingly.

"That's right, darling. I'm sorry if the timing isn't everything you'd like it to be. However, my people will be able to disable the alarm system for the night. I doubt you want the police arriving too early to this little party of yours."

"It's fine. I guess this gives us more time to prepare. Thanks, Carla. I owe you."

"You certainly do, pet." Carla terminated the call in a final burst of static. Malice was left to hope the final endearment was simply a nickname and not an indication of how Carla thought she would be paid back.

"We can make a bank work," Stiletto said. "Where's your laptop? I want to take a look at the area."

"It's on the first floor." Malice stood up and headed toward the stairs, Stiletto right beside her. "I know the area. It should be far enough from where MacTavish's new den is."

"Even better."

"If Ruri and Cassidy can keep the rest of the pack occupied, we'll have plenty of time to take him out." In fact, according to her plan, they needed to interfere with each group at the same time. The remnants of MacTavish's pack at the den would be distracted and weakened by Malice's attack upon him, while he would be laboring under the same disadvantage while they attacked him. It was handy to have another group working toward the same goals, one they could coordinate with.

"As long as they can be trusted to hold on until we need them to move. If they allow their emotions to get the best of them, they could blow this whole thing."

"Ruri will handle it." If the wolven was anything, she was cool under pressure. The way she'd handled Mary Alice while being held against her will was nothing if not proof of that. Admiration filled her, warming her to her toes and not for the first time. Ruri was exactly the kind of person she wanted by her side.

Stiletto didn't bat an eye at the fact that Malice's laptop was behind a biometric lock in an enclosed cube of chain-link fencing. Her setup on her home turf was probably similar. Still, Malice wished Stiletto would show some other emotion than cold disinterest or anger. It was impossible to read the woman. She waited patiently enough while Malice unlocked the laptop before trying to take it over. Malice scooted the computer out of her reach and brought up the Internet browser. It was the work of a few seconds before they had an overhead view of the area around the bank.

"It's secluded enough. That's nice," Malice said.

"We won't have to worry too much about civilians bumbling into our operation." Stiletto chewed on her lower lip as she examined the screen. "Nowhere high to set up an observation post, though."

"There's some cover in those trees." Malice pointed at the upper right corner of the screen. "Looks like a creek that runs through there. It'll be a good enough place to set up and wait for the lycans to arrive."

"Sounds like a plan. I'd rather be up high, if we can." Stiletto tapped her fingers on the table while looking over the bank building. "If they're heading for the vault, their options will be limited."

"Nothing we can't cover if we set up over there."

"We need building schematics."

"I'll get them from Uncle Ralph. I need to let him know what the plan is anyway."

"Good." Stiletto grinned suddenly, her whole face lighting up. "It's finally coming together, isn't it, Malice?" She stretched hugely, all the way to the tips of her fingers. "I can't wait to give those things what's coming."

Malice smiled back. If her smile came across as little more than the baring of teeth, that was fine, too. They were almost done. The hardest part still lie ahead, but at least she could finally see it coming.

"I'll call Uncle Ralph, then we can really get down to prepping," Malice said.

CHAPTER THIRTY-EIGHT

The moon bathed them in more than enough light to see by. It waxed just short of full, reminding Malice of what was at stake. Cassidy. A few days ago they'd been racing this, and now she wasn't certain she even recognized her sister. But this was all for her. If they were to be rid of MacTavish, she needed to get her mind back to it.

The corner where the bank stood was as deserted as Malice had hoped. The little stucco-sided building was soaked by the streetlights in the parking lot. It didn't look like it was about to be the site of an epic showdown. From their little blind halfway up a tree in the woods that skirted the property, she surveyed the area again. All they knew was MacTavish would be there that night. Exactly when he planned to make his move, they didn't know. Not knowing made her twitchy.

Stiletto had insisted on setting themselves up high. It seemed unnecessary to Malice, but her partner had pointed out that the lycans might want to case the bank and they'd been planning to set up in the best place to do so. That there was no sign of the lycans had Malice on edge. What if they decided to go after Carla's package another night? There had been neither hide nor hair of the vamps who were supposed to disable the security system either. If she'd seen them, she might feel a little better about sitting and waiting. At least then she'd know the plan was still on. She gave in to the urge and checked her watch. The barely glowing numbers told her it was a little after two a.m. Twenty minutes from when she last checked it. Great.

"They'll be here," Stiletto said quietly. Malice smiled a little bit at the attempt to make her feel better. "Or they won't. There's more than one way to skin a cat."

The smile sloughed off her face and the tension that had momentarily abated returned with a vengeance. Malice forced herself to relax and lower her shoulders. They felt like they were up around her ears.

"This is our best chance. Even you have to admit Cassidy's pack helping out is an asset." At least she hoped it would be an asset. When she'd spoken to Ruri, the wolven had seemed anxious. She hadn't been willing to go into much detail, but the remnant pack wasn't allied as strongly with her as she'd expected. Fortunately, it sounded like they'd accepted Cassidy's leadership. Now if only Mary Alice could have a normal conversation with her sister that didn't turn into a shouting match. It was better to go through Ruri for now.

When had Cassidy gotten so contrary? Sure, she'd sometimes chafed at Mary Alice's role as the older sister, but she could usually be brought around to see things the way they were. Ever since the revelation of Mary Alice's real life, Cassidy seemed to question everything she said. Maybe Cassidy felt like she'd been betrayed, but she had to know Mary Alice had her best interests at heart. There was danger in mixing the two worlds she lived in; Cassidy's current status proved that.

And there she was again, in the same vortex of blame and doubt she'd already spiraled into more than once. The only things that derailed the cannibalistic spiral of her thoughts were action and Ruri's presence. If only MacTavish and his lycans would show up. She tried to get back to the task at hand and to quiet the thoughts that chased themselves in circles, devouring each other and growing larger and harder to ignore with each passing moment.

Her phone buzzed spitefully, reminding her that Ruri was also waiting.

"You're really going to check that now?" Stiletto whispered when she pulled the phone out of one of her jacket's pockets.

"What if they went off plan? Of course I'm going to check it." There was no way she would turn on the screen. Even as concealed as they were, it wouldn't take much light to betray their position. Instead, she plugged her ear bud into the phone and played it as an audio message. Relief washed through her when the message proved to be a query about whether there was any sign of MacTavish.

"There's no sign of him here. Must be on his way." The mechanical voice reading the message conveyed no emotion, but Malice thought she felt Ruri's tension all the same.

"Nothing yet," Malice murmured into the crappy microphone on the cheap headphone's cord. "You'll hear when we see him."

"What does your girlfriend want?" Stiletto surveyed the area through a pair of binoculars. She covered the bank; then stood up to get a better view of the road. The branch she was on barely rustled.

"Says there's been no sign of MacTavish at their end. Hopefully that means he's on his way."

"We'll take him out tonight or another night. It's all the same, Malice. A dead lycan is a dead lycan." She leaned forward a bit to get a better look at something on the road.

"What do you see?" As the words left her mouth, a new sound hit her ears. The area had been quiet so far. The only noise was the very occasional car passing on the stretch of Highway 72 that went past the little corner where the bank was located. A large engine was coming their way and at speed. She could hear it laboring as it came into her unassisted view.

"Looks like some crazy person in a semi."

"The lycans have been knocking over semis."

"Yep. Seems we have company."

The truck's lights flashed suddenly into high beams, illuminating the side of the bank in sharp relief.

"Holy crap, he's going to—"

A tremendous crash shattered the night. Chunks of masonry rained down on the paved parking lot. Even those were hard to hear over the tortured twisting of metal as the front of the truck bent back on itself. The hood cover slid into the windshield, which exploded into little squares of flying safety glass. Silence fell over the parking lot, punctuated only by the hiss of air escaping the semi's large front tires and the tinkling of falling glass.

"—ram it," Malice concluded softly.

"That's one way of breaking in," Stiletto said. "Come on." She swung herself out of her perch and started down the tree.

"Right behind you," Malice said. First things first, however. She pulled out her phone and dictated a short message to Ruri. "We're on."

Ruri's phone finally vibrated. It felt strange to have one, but Mary Alice had insisted. How else would they stay in contact? *Not necessary,* her wolf whispered disapprovingly. *She is bonded to us, she will know.* But the mate bond didn't work when only one of them believed in it. She turned it on to see the words they'd been waiting to hear.

"We're on," she said to Cassidy.

The Alpha inhaled deeply, and then exhaled a huge puff of air through her muzzle. Ruri was the only one not in fur-form yet; everyone else had shifted. Sadly, the phone required thumbs to use it, so she was still in skin-form. Opposable thumbs would also come in handy to get that door open so they could get into the row houses. Not that there were many of them. Surprisingly, Lewis had been the first to volunteer to come along, before even Cassidy. Some of the wolven had stayed behind at the safe house, those who were too damaged by the events of Dean's death to fight, and Luther.

Someone had to stay back with the others. Luther hadn't been very happy about letting Cassidy out of his sight, but he had grudgingly agreed to watch the rest of the pack. Ruri knew Luther thought the whole operation was a bad idea. He didn't want to bet his new Alpha on what he saw as a desperate gambit, and maybe it was. Luther had always struck her as being pretty levelheaded, but she'd been unable to convince him this was their best bet. His idea of dealing seemed to be hiding in the shadows until MacTavish forgot they existed. Ruri had met MacTavish's type before, and she believed he would never forget about them. Sooner or later, he would have darkened their doorways to finish what he'd started those weeks previous.

She was glad for the opportunity and for the chance to partner with Mary Alice. Stiletto she could have done without, but there was no such thing as a perfect plan. As much as she wanted to be the one to rip MacTavish's throat out, she would happily leave it to Mary Alice if it meant getting some of her family back. Giving up the chance to take down MacTavish had been difficult, but the other wolven were the more important piece. If she'd been the one to go after MacTavish, the Hunters would have been responsible for bringing the others out. Mary Alice would have done it, but that Stiletto? There was no telling what she would have decided.

There was no sign of life in the row houses that squatted before them in the moonlight. It seemed everyone inside was asleep. That, in itself, was sloppy. MacTavish should have set someone to guard. His skills as Alpha were lacking in the extreme, and contempt added another layer to the raging hatred that pulsed molten inside her whenever she thought of the lone wolf.

The dark wasn't enough to hide the neglected aspect of the buildings. They'd obviously been abandoned for years. The city's glacial reputation for taking care of blighted properties was well earned, it seemed. On the other side, chipped concrete steps led up to front doors barricaded by large sheets of plywood. Boards had been nailed over most of the front windows but had been removed from some in the back, which was why they huddled in the alleyway. The four adjoining units with accessible back doors were the objects of their interest.

At Cassidy's signal, the rest of the wolven rose to their feet. Ruri feared seven of them wouldn't be enough. Cassidy was their most decided advantage. Still, a large part of the plan hung upon the hope that the opposing wolven would be easier to overcome once MacTavish came under attack. Mary Alice's message had let them know things were moving on her end, but it didn't let them know when MacTavish himself was engaged. He hadn't been attacked yet. If he had been, the row houses would be boiling with activity. But if their little group failed here, his wolven would descend upon Mary Alice and Stiletto and tear them apart. She had to trust that things proceeded apace at the other end. They had to, or she and her wolven would be annihilated.

As silent as a night breeze, Ruri slid forward from one shadow to the next, Lewis and Cassidy hot at her heels, Harold trailing along behind them. They would work their way through the row houses, while the other three stayed outside and dealt with anyone who came out. The most submissive wolven would be allowed to escape; they were little threat. Given a few days, they would turn up again and could be welcomed into Cassidy's pack. The wolven who were strongly in MacTavish's camp were the ones they wanted—those who'd helped MacTavish overthrow Dean and those who had turned Cassidy. They couldn't be allowed to live.

Working on the assumption that the wolven had opened passages between the houses, they planned to start at one end and work their way to the other. Ruri wrapped her hand around the doorknob and turned. It was locked, which was surprising. They'd never bothered to lock anything at the hotel. Locks couldn't keep out wolven, and little else would have been stupid enough to attack them. Apparently, this lot wasn't quite so sanguine.

The locks on the doors at the hotel wouldn't have stopped her, and this one was no match for her strength either. It gave under her hand with a loud snap and she pulled it open, stepping back to let Lewis and Cassidy by. She dropped to all fours on the concrete stoop and called her wolf to her.

Fluid burst from her and ran down her skin as it was swiftly covered with fur. Her bones snapped and shifted in a hurry, sounding like someone throwing a handful of gravel at a window. By the time her tail sprouted at the base of her spine, she was ready to go. Ruri panted at the exertion; forcing the shift into such a short amount of time was difficult and exhausting. Adrenaline and stubbornness would carry her through what she needed to accomplish, but after that, she would need a couple of days' sleep. If she was still alive.

She bounded through the dark hole of the back door into chaos. Fighting wolves surged around her. As they'd anticipated, someone had knocked a hole in the wall to connect the two units. Lewis engaged two wolven in front of the door. He snapped and circled, keeping them at bay. There was only enough room in the narrow hall for one of them to approach him at once, and he was taking full advantage of that. Already, both wolven facing him were bloodied; one had lost the better part of an ear.

The sound of fighting down the hall demanded her attention. Ruri charged through the hallway and skidded to a stop in front of the stairs. Two wolven rolled by, one partially shifted and the other in full wolf-form. Neither of them was Cassidy, and she spared a moment to wonder which one was on their side. With no way of knowing, she let them be. They seemed more concerned with each other than with her. There would be time to sort out the victor later. That fight was going to end in the death of one or both or so she surmised from the bloody puncture wounds around the throat of the half-shifted wolven.

There was only one place Cassidy could have gone. Ruri galloped up the stairs, her ears open for sounds of disturbance. The air was rank with the smell of unwashed bodies, blood and despair. No one had been happy in these rooms. Cowering wolven avoided her eyes when she stuck her head through the doorways of the upstairs bedrooms. These were of no moment and she backed out. They might be frightened, but she knew better than to stay too long in the doorway or to turn her back on any of them. As long as they knew there was a way out if they wanted it, they wouldn't attack.

Overlapping snarls filtered down the hall to the bedroom at the very front of the house. It sounded like at least two wolven. A low growl caused her to up her estimate. Three, then. She surged forward, not caring who heard her coming. The last growl belonged to Cassidy.

Two wolven were backed into a corner and Cassidy stood in the middle of the room. One of them darted forward, heading for the door, but Cassidy snapped at him. Her teeth clacked shut on empty air, but not for lack of trying. The young wolven retreated back into the corner. He wasn't happy about being on the attack. Deep gouges lined the side of his neck. Ruri wondered if he'd tried to submit to Cassidy. She hadn't accepted it, if that was the case. This was probably one of the wolven who'd attacked her. Ruri hadn't been certain if Cassidy would remember them; Cassidy hadn't been sure either. It seems their question was answered.

Her presence in the room's doorway hadn't gone unnoticed by any of the room's occupants. It took only a split second for the confronted wolven to realize she wasn't attacking Cassidy. They were now well and truly cornered. As one, they tried to surge past Cassidy, one high and the other low. With breathtaking speed, Cassidy snatched the high one out of the air with her jaws and slammed him down onto the lower one. They tumbled to the ground with twin yips, one of which was cut short when Cassidy's closed her jaws around his throat. She shook him vigorously. The snap of his spine reverberated through the small room and the other wolven scrambled to his feet. Blood poured down his neck, staining his rusty pelt bright red. One front leg was likely broken; he put no weight upon it and scrabbled to present his uninjured side to Cassidy.

Ruri stalked into the room, cutting off his escape route. He backed up slowly, paws slipping on the hardwood floor. Cassidy matched her pace on the other side. They backed him into the corner. Light gray eyes rolled wildly, from Ruri to Cassidy and back again. From the way his eyes darted around the room and how he shifted his weight back and forth, he was going to make his move and soon. No one was coming to save him, a fact that seemed finally to dawn upon him. Maddened and with foam dripping from the side of his the mouth, he broke and lunged at her.

Ruri danced to one side, then rammed the crazed wolven as he tried to get by, body-slamming him to the floor. He screamed as he went down, his injured leg taking all his weight. She followed in, grabbing his exposed throat in between her jaws. Blood filled her mouth where she broke the skin. It was hot and sweet like the exultation that filled her and the wolf upon their victory. His whine stopped when she tore out his throat in a gout of blood and gore. The wolven's legs churned for a moment longer before his body gave in to death.

Cassidy pulled at her mind from the doorway. Ruri looked up and met the odd-eyed stare that pierced its way through the dark. There was work yet to be done.

CHAPTER THIRTY-NINE

The message had only taken a couple seconds to send, but Stiletto was already halfway down the tree. Malice followed along quickly and smoothly. There was no point in alerting anyone to their presence by dashing through the bushes like a couple of bull elephants.

There was still no movement in the parking lot when they took up assault positions at the edge of the tree line.

"What's with the wait?" Malice asked Stiletto. "Why haven't they moved?"

"The lycan in the truck is probably out. I imagine the rest of them will be along any moment now."

True to Stiletto's prediction, another truck rumbled around the long curve and into the parking lot. Unlike the one that had just mashed itself through the side of the bank, this one kept to the road and had a trailer attached. The hiss and the squeal of air brakes drowned out the sounds of the crash's aftermath. The truck creaked to a stop next to the smoking mass of the first semi.

Lycans in human form leaped out of the cab and from the back doors of the trailer. There were eight of them. One of the lycans directed his men with shouted insults and cuffs to the back of the head. That must be MacTavish.

It seemed the biggest problem was that the ruined truck was blocking the hole they'd punched in the bank. Fur sprouted along MacTavish's arms while his muzzle elongated. The muscles in his legs shifted and popped, but he halted the transformation halfway through. A couple of other lycans had managed a similar transformation. The others watched and waited with poorly concealed impatience.

"Move it," MacTavish shouted, the words somewhat distorted by the shape of his face.

As one, the eight lycans took up positions around the semi. They heaved and slowly the truck moved. The wheels were trashed; there was no way those would turn again. Instead, the lycans dragged the truck back about six feet. It wasn't much and even for them it took a few minutes, but they finally had unrestricted access to the inside of the bank. By the time they finished, the driver had recovered enough to scramble out of the cab. He was a mass of blood. At least one limb was bent at an unnatural angle, but it straightened as they watched.

MacTavish clapped the lycan on the shoulder. Even with the amount of pain the man must have been in, he still straightened under the gesture of approval. He seemed young, even from where they watched. His limbs were gangly, slightly too long for his frame.

"Wait inside," MacTavish said. "We'll be done soon."

The partially shifted lycans dropped to all fours and completed their transformations. The remaining lycans still in human form filtered into the bank and the Alpha joined them, two large wolves taking up the rear. The young driver headed to the back of the trailer.

"I'll get the group of them," Stiletto said. "You take care of him, then come help." She indicated the driver with her chin.

"Got it. Flashbangs?"

Stiletto nodded and took off across the parking lot at a silent sprint. In the dark and against the parking lot blacktop, she was almost impossible to spot. Malice waited a couple of heartbeats, then headed to the trailer.

The lycan had closed the doors most of the way behind him, but one was slightly open. She slipped between the metal doors, causing one to swing open a little further. A metallic squeal echoed through the trailer, and she froze just inside the door.

"Who's there?" The voice sounded even younger than the lycan looked. It was surprisingly high-pitched, like he had only recently started going through puberty.

Malice gave no answer, instead ghosting her way down the central passage between two sets of deep metal shelves.

"Alpha, is that you?" The sound of boot heels against metal reached her ears. "Do you need me?" Soft clangs accompanied his steps. It was very dark in the container, but if he got much closer he would see her.

Without the slightest whisper of sound, she swung herself to the top of a nearby shelving unit. Her feet hooked to the edge of the shelves on either side of the aisle, and holding on with both hands, she waited for him to walk beneath her. Slowly he came closer. He wasn't moving quickly; he definitely knew something was up. As he passed underneath, Malice let go to pull a short metal baton from the back of her belt. With a flick of the wrist, she deployed it, and then released her grip to drop on top of him, striking him to the ground with a loud clang. Before he could get his feet under him or his bearings, she raised the baton and brought it down on the back of his head. He collapsed instantly, all movement gone from his limbs at once.

Quickly, Malice brought two fingers to his throat and checked for a pulse. In the light from the partially open door, he looked absurdly young. There was little way to tell how old a lycan was. They tended to look on the young side until shortly before they died. It seemed the transformation rejuvenated them until their bodies simply gave out. Even older humans who were turned tended to gain a youthful demeanor to themselves, but not as young as this one. He seemed like he'd been turned recently. If he was older than seventeen, Malice would have been shocked.

She hesitated for a moment, knowing she should kill him but loathe to do so. Finally, she pulled out a handful of flex cuffs from an inner pocket in her jacket. Jesus, he's heavy! Malice thought while maneuvering him into place. Quickly, she cuffed him to the metal shelves before giving him an insurance rap behind the ear. He shouldn't be waking up anytime soon. The metal doors on the back of the container squealed in protest as she muscled them closed. Fortunately, it was unlikely anybody in the bank heard it. The noise of the fight reached all the way over to where she was. With a loud clunk, she engaged the external lock and approached the bank.

Across the lot and revealed by the lights of the intact semi, a shaggy figure staggered out of the gaping hole on two legs. He bled from half a dozen wounds along one side of his torso and appeared to have lost an ear and part of his hand. He stood with his uninjured hand pressed to his side and stared back into the bank. Blood matted the fur on his chest and abdomen, but it wouldn't slow him down for long. Malice froze, trying to evade his notice.

His head lifted, muzzle tracking back and forth, tasting for scents in the air. It was unlikely he'd be able to smell her. *The young lycan,* she realized. *That's what he's smelling.* With an oath that would have gotten her a disapproving glare if her mother had been around, Malice rushed forward and lowered her shoulder. Before he was all the way around, she collided with him. They went down in a tangle of limbs, his pained yelp hanging in the air and ringing out again when they hit the ground.

Malice used the momentum of the tackle to bounce to her feet and turn back toward the lycan to finish him off before he completed the transformation. In his in-between state he was much easier to handle than as a wolf. He got his feet under him and bounded up faster than she could react and she stared at him for a split second as he swung his hand at her, fingers splayed and claws gleaming. She ducked under his reach at the last second and felt a slight tug when his claws snagged on her hair, pulling strands out at the roots. She snatched the knife from the sheath on her leg. His look of surprise when she slipped his grasp was almost comical, but it was quickly replaced with agony when she buried the blade up to its hilt in his armpit. It went in easily at first before grinding up against one of his ribs. She yanked it out, sending a gout of blood bursting from the wound. He fell heavily to his knees as his energy drained from his body along with his blood. He cast a questioning look over his shoulder, and then pitched forward onto the asphalt.

Malice wiped the blade of her knife carefully on her pants, then slipped it back home in its sheath. The battle raging in the bank called to her. There was plenty of work yet to do.

Ruri backed up foot by foot, giving ground but making the wolves who had her cornered work for it. She snapped at the muzzle of the nearest wolven and made brief contact. Blood spattered onto her own muzzle, adding to the layers of speckles already there. The first row house had been easy enough to clear out, and the four of them had forced their way into the second one, but things had rapidly gone downhill since then. There was no way these wolven were dealing with the effects of an injury to their Alpha. Instead, Ruri, Cassidy and Lewis were in a corner, snarling and snapping at the wolven who harried them mercilessly. She had no idea where Harold had ended up.

The wolven she'd gotten a piece of shrank back but was quickly replaced by another. White fur and brilliant blue eyes filled her vision; nothing else existed around her. *Britt.* Her wolf growled, and she joined in, the sound rumbling through her chest. The woman she thought had loved her grinned wolfishly at her, tongue lolling out of the side of her mouth. Ruri's growling increased in intensity until she fairly vibrated with the force of it. At her side, Cassidy glanced over for a brief moment before returning her attention to the two wolven who pressured her with teeth and claws. Seeing Cassidy's electric blue eye, the one that matched Brittney's eyes so closely, sent a bolt of rage jangling through Ruri's nerves. Inside, her wolf howled and demanded complete control, throwing herself against the tethers of self-control Ruri had built up over a century and a half.

"Get her, you mangy curs!" MacTavish's rough voice split the night as he urged his lycans on. The snarl at the edge of his voice grated and made his words almost impossible to understand, but the urgency was unmistakable. "Take her down, we need to get out of here! Someone is attacking the pack!"

This was it, the point of no return. MacTavish could not be allowed to overtake Stiletto.

Malice pulled two flashbang grenades from her pocket and armed them. "Fire in the hole!" she hollered, and sent them spinning sidearm, one after the other, through the gaping opening. Despite her tightly squeezed eyelids, light still bled through and crimson filled her vision for a second. Sharp reports filtered through the hands she'd clapped over her ears.

She was already moving, vaulting over the partially collapsed wall, when the lycans realized they were under attack from behind. A lycan on his knees looked up at her blindly as she descended upon him, katana extended. He didn't have enough time to raise his arms before she sliced through his neck, shearing his head from his body in one stroke.

An agonized roar shook the small space. It was hard to make much out—dust still floated through the air and it was dark. The light from the parking lot didn't penetrate far into the shattered vault. Even with her enhanced vision, Malice could barely make out shapes that were only now starting to move after being stunned into inaction. They were gathered around one corner where two slumped bodies gave mute evidence to the ferocity of the fight so far.

The lycans attacking Stiletto were big, each easily a hundred and eighty pounds if not more. Those still on two legs topped Stiletto by almost a foot, and she wasn't a short woman. They easily had the advantage on her, in reach and in strength, and yet time and again she slipped their lunges, disappearing like mist in one grasp after another. It probably didn't seem like it to them, but she was tiring. She was as fast as ever, but Malice could tell her motions were starting to lose their efficient crispness.

Five lycans still stood. She'd downed one on the way in, and two were on the ground, though it was impossible to tell if they were dead or merely incapacitated. With the one trussed up in the trailer, it was still too many. If MacTavish were to prevail now, he would be able to get back to his pack and destroy Ruri and Cassidy.

Malice rushed the nearest lycan, katana held in front of her like a spear. He turned and reached toward her, claws ripping through the air. They passed nowhere near her; he was probably still blind from the grenades. He had no way of knowing she'd dropped to one knee and pivoted. Her blade opened a long gash in his belly and blood poured from the wound, staining the fur around it bright red. His whimper was drowned out by another roar. MacTavish wasn't happy. Malice grinned. *Good.*

The lycan fell forward, landing on his hands and knees. He'd been halfway to his wolf-form, and now it seemed he was trying to finish the transformation. It couldn't be allowed to finish. The process of shifting would hasten the lycan's already insanely quick healing abilities. It was a desperate gamble. He was completely unable to defend himself when she thrust the katana through the base of his neck, severing the spinal column. He collapsed, beyond the point of regeneration. There was no coming back from having the spinal cord severed, not even for a lycan.

She fell back into a recovery stance, the katana blade down and off to one side. She had company. Three lycans closed in on her, their eyes glowing steadily at her from the shadows. Her blood pounded in her ears, filling her head with exultant pounding. This was what she lived for, to surf the edge of the adrenaline rush. Pressure filled her chest, demanding she surge forward, insisting she take the fight to them. Experience told her to stay put, to let them come to her. The smile on her face widened.

Ruri came back to herself in a puddle of blood. At the sight of Brittney, her wolf had overwhelmed her completely. It had been almost a hundred years since she lost herself in the wolf when it wasn't a full moon. The results weren't pretty. Brittney's body lay mangled and bent below her. She licked her chops, her long tongue removing blood from her muzzle, blood that tasted of the woman she had once loved, the woman she'd thought had loved her. The dead wolven had already undergone the final shift back to human form. Her head was bent at an unnatural angle; in her blind rage, Ruri had snapped her neck.

The amount of damage Ruri's wolf had inflicted upon her was insane. Hardly an inch of her looked as if it had escaped her angry jaws, and yet Britt's face was almost completely untouched. At least she still looks good, Ruri thought. She'd like that.

Now that she was dead, Ruri could no longer summon her blazing anger toward her former paramour. All she felt was sadness and disappointment. She wondered again why Britt had seen fit to betray Dean and the rest of the pack. She doubted she would ever know.

Nothing moved around her and she looked up to see a ring of shocked glowing eyes surrounding her. Lewis and Cassidy were behind her. She could feel their presences solidly at her back without looking, but they weren't moving any more than those facing them. All seemed to have been stunned into stillness by the ferocity of her attack upon Britt.

Have I even been hit? Ruri wondered. *It doesn't feel like it.* She would probably feel every bump, bruise and laceration when this was finished, but for now she felt nothing but the need to keep moving. Every second they let up on the wolven in front of them was a second MacTavish wasn't feeling pressured by their attack.

She growled and moved forward. The grouped wolven skittered away from her. Lewis and Cassidy sprang away from her flanks, heading the wolven off. They'd have to harry them, drive them even further apart before they could regroup, but the wolven she tracked scattered in different directions. She hesitated for a moment, torn about who to go after. Lewis was taking on the bigger group, but her first priority had to be the Alpha. Cassidy was facing a group of three wolven who seemed more interested in avoiding her than in confrontation.

Ruri crept up on the group while Cassidy had their attention. Given an opening, there was one who would turn and run—she could tell by the wolven's shifting eyes and twitching ears. She was looking for her chance, but she was the furthest of the three from being able to make a break. Ruri lunged forward and snapped her jaws around the hind leg of the closest wolven. A surprised yip met her attack. She twisted, dragging the wolven across the floor as it struggled to flip around and bite her.

Cassidy took advantage of Ruri's distraction and rushed the middle wolven. She dropped her shoulder at the last second and bowled it over. They rolled together a short distance, smashing up against the near wall with a resounding thud. Wooden lath snapped inside the wall and plaster rained down from the ceiling to dust the struggling tangle of wolven below.

As Ruri had anticipated, the female wolven took the opportunity to run. She'd had enough. Ruri was happy to allow her to take off. One of those outside would take care of her. If they didn't, she would disappear into the night. Maybe she'd show up again and maybe she wouldn't.

The wolven she'd pulled down had managed to regain its feet, though the leg she'd grabbed no longer held his weight. He wasn't too slowed down by his injury, however, and lunged at her. Ruri dodged to one side, then shouldered back into him as he flew past her. He went down in a tangle of limbs and she pressed her advantage, grabbing another leg and crushing the joint between her jaws. The shatter of bone beneath her teeth pulled an agonized half-howl from his throat. He tried to get up, but with two legs that wouldn't bear his weight, he flopped around on the floor instead. Satisfied the wolven would be no immediate threat, Ruri turned to look for Cassidy.

Her Alpha looked up at her from where she crouched over the body of the wolven she'd demolished. Blood flecked her muzzle, fading into the crazed stripes and speckles of her coat. Satisfied that Cassidy was all right, Ruri looked round for Lewis, but he was no longer with them. The fight had boiled into the next room and, by the sound of it, was still raging.

Cassidy's ears pricked forward, and her entire body stiffened for a second. She shot out of the room as if from a bow. Something had happened to one of her wolven and she'd felt it. Ruri had seen the same response from Dean on more than one occasion. The link between Alpha and pack went both ways.

Ruri flew after her, right on her tail. Somebody had to watch her back.

What furniture had once graced the adjoining room was little more than toothpicks now. Two wolven were down, but four more had backed Lewis into a corner. He bled from half a dozen wounds and his right ear had been torn clean off. Try as they might, they weren't quick enough to get past his flashing teeth and raking claws. The wolven who faced him were as bad off as he was, but there were four of them and Lewis was tired. His tail was down and his reactions sluggish, allowing a graze here and a swipe there.

One of the wolven got in a lucky bite as Lewis dodged away from one of her companions. Ruri and Cassidy bolted across the room in a flash, but not in time to stop the side of Lewis's face from being laid open to the bone, taking his eye with it. Though he must have been in terrible pain, Lewis pivoted and lunged in one motion, taking his attacker by the throat and bearing them both down to the ground.

Before he could regain his feet, the other three were upon him and he disappeared under a pile of blood-soaked fur and ripping teeth. Cassidy bellowed and flung herself at the pile, but Ruri was there first, grabbing her by the scruff of the neck and pulling her back. Lewis was done for, and if Cassidy went in there, she would be, too. Cassidy roared again, but the sound died in her throat, swallowed by a pained whimper.

The wolven turned toward them, leaving their prey behind. Lewis didn't move, but neither did the wolven he'd taken to the ground. The three paced toward them, wounds closing before their eyes as they took sustenance from Lewis's blood and flesh. His physical essence boosted their metabolisms and they benefited fully. As she and Cassidy backed up, Ruri realized they'd miscalculated, and badly. The wolven they fought against had no compunctions about devouring their flesh for the energy it gave, while Cassidy's pack members were foregoing the opportunity. Though they fought for their lives, Ruri still thought of the wolven as family and the idea of consuming them was repugnant to her and her wolf. Cassidy might not be so sentimental—certainly she had no attachment to these wolven—but she didn't know. And there was no way to tell her.

More wolven were coming; she could hear their claws scraping against the hardwood floors of the row houses' narrow halls, coming ever closer. They were cornered and badly outmatched.

CHAPTER FORTY

The lycans took their time getting to Malice. One lifted his head, sniffing deeply, likely trying to determine if there were more of her. It would have been nice, but the day she couldn't take on a handful of lycans was the day she needed to hang up her katana. She wouldn't hang it up, though. It would be torn from her hands and her head separated from her body. Her enemies would rejoice, but no one from the human world would ever know what had become of her. She would simply disappear; all trace of her activities would be wiped from existence, traces which now included Cassidy. Malice firmed her grip on her blade and bided her time just a little longer.

One lycan bumped into the lycan next to him and was rewarded with a snarl and shove for his trouble. Good, they weren't used to working together, at least not like this. She could take advantage of that. It was funny. Pack structure should have meant that working together was second nature, but these lycans seemed more like they happened to be fighting her at the same time, not that they were there to support each other. *Has MacTavish been bringing in new weres?* If that was true, that was bad news for Ruri and Cassidy. They could be facing far more lycans than they'd bargained for.

She glanced past the three lycans at the rogue Alpha. They had to take him down and soon. Her training still told her to wait while her brain and heart, in perfect agreement for once, screamed at her to move. The katana quivered in her hand from the tension of not giving in to her instincts.

More eyes glowed at them from the dark than Cassidy had thought possible. They were well and truly outnumbered. She knew she was strong, far stronger than she ought to have been, at least according to Ruri and the others back at the safe house, but there was no way the two of them could take on all those now gathered against them. At her side, Ruri rumbled threateningly. It was an impressive display and some of the wolven seemed cowed by it.

Harold still battled somewhere in the house, but he was weakening. Aching emptiness yawned within her where Lewis's point of light had been. His presence in her heart was more conspicuous for its absence. Another point had disappeared, this one when Ruri had gone berserk and savaged the white werewolf to death. She'd known wolven fought and knew they sometimes killed each other, that much had been easy to surmise, but Ruri's ferocity had taken her aback. Her own ferocity had taken her aback at first also. Letting her wolf take the lead had helped and she'd quickly lost her hesitation. It seemed she had a knack for this.

The other point that had gone out still troubled her and she gnawed at it while they did their best to keep the wolven at bay. From what she'd been told, she could only affect those in her pack. If that was true, how had she felt that wolven's death?

Cassidy snapped at a wolven who dared to get too close. She mostly missed, but still managed to graze a bit of ruff. She dug into the thick fur and pulled, coming away with a hank that bled at the roots. The wolven pulled back, only to be replaced by another.

This wasn't going to work. They would soon be buried in hostile wolven. Her packmates outside were all alive, but being pressed. She could feel the distant echo of wounds on them, each one a spot of cold fire upon her body.

If her sister had been successful, they should have been able to overwhelm these wolven, or so Ruri had said. Cassidy should have been able to step into the void and assume the mantle of Alpha. Mary Alice was either dead or things weren't working out well for them either. There was no time to wait. She had to do something.

New points of lights numbered among the stars of her pack. These outnumbered those of her people by quite a few, but they didn't flicker nearly as strongly. It was as though they were stars light-years further away than her own. They corresponded to the lives of the wolves they fought. Maybe she could do something about them.

Her wolf rumbled in warm agreement. She paced on the outside of their skin, rippling along the edges of her fur.

Can you take over? Cassidy asked the wolf. *Is that even possible?*

The wolf's assent was palpable, and Cassidy stepped back within herself. Her body kept moving, more purposefully now. It was strange to be a passenger in her own form, but she had more important things to attend to—like saving their collective asses—than to worry about which of them would disembowel the next wolven.

The pinprick points beckoned to her and she reached out toward them. There was something there after all, something she could hook into. Maybe. They slipped through her fingers on the first try. She could almost grasp them, but they felt fragile as if they might crumble to dust in her fingers if she grasped too hard. With deadly concentration, Cassidy reached out again.

Her body moved beyond her field of concentration. She was barely aware of her wolf bringing down another wolven, riding him to the ground. That meant nothing if she couldn't succeed.

Some of the points twitched, quivering as she reached one hand toward them. Four of them seemed more solid than the rest and she concentrated on those. It wasn't all the wolven facing them, but at this point, even four might sway the battle their way. Cassidy screwed her face up into a mask of utter focus. Her nose scrunched and her mouth pulled back from clenched teeth. Her jaw ached from grinding her teeth together. It reminded her of the faces she would make when in kindergarten, trying to force her recalcitrant fingers to trace unfamiliar letter shapes.

The points vibrated more now, moving faster and faster. She dragged them slowly toward her, yet another power held them back and they oscillated back and forth between her and the other force. She reached out with her other hand and pulled mightily, hauling at the points with the entire weight of her body. Finally, after what seemed like hours, they moved smoothly forward into her orbit. They matched the other stars she saw in intensity and warmth. They were hers!

She threw her head back and howled in triumph. Eyes closed, she reveled in the feeling of her conquest. Her gambit had worked; the struggle had paid off. She opened her eyes to a ruined room, walls spattered with blood. From the lines of fire that lined her rib cage and one haunch, some of that blood was hers. She had no idea how much time had passed since she handed control of their body over to the wolf, but she was still alive. From the sound of fighting, Ruri was still kicking also. A wolven lay on its side in front of her, ribs heaving as it tried to draw breath. One back leg was ripped open, hamstrings shredded and dangling. It was no longer a threat and Cassidy turned to confront the next one.

Ruri was forced away from Cassidy a step at a time, one wolven snapping at her from one side and another inserting his body between her and the Alpha when she recoiled. What had started out as a few feet widened until they were on opposite sides of the room. Cassidy was a dervish of teeth and claws. She fought without regard for herself, doing her best to take down the wolven that harried her cautiously. Ruri recognized the all-or-nothing approach most wolven couldn't achieve unless they'd given themselves over fully to their wolves.

Her own style of combat was more conservative now. She bled from a dozen or so wounds, some had partially healed, but at least one was still actively bleeding. Beyond that, one knee ached, though she hadn't been injured there. It felt like the memory of a wound, which was no surprise as it came to her over a long distance. Somewhere, Mary Alice had been injured. There was also a stitch in her ribs. She couldn't tell if it was from exertion or if her mate had been wounded there as well.

The clash of teeth by her right shoulder was kept from being more only by her frantic dodge to one side. Then she was in range of a wicked raking of claws from another wolven. Three more lines of fire joined those that already burned at her. She was surrounded on three sides, her tail in the corner. There was nothing to do except keep them at bay as long as she could. They were going to take her down.

I'm sorry. Ruri sent the thought winging to serious eyes peering out from a strong façade. Would Mary Alice feel her fall? She would have felt it if the Hunter had gone down, she knew that. Something had gone wrong. Had it been her fault? Ruri fended off another wicked bite and received a shoulder to the ribs for her trouble. Stars burst behind her eyes as she slammed into the wall, then slid down it to land in a boneless heap.

Her wolf howled at her, urging her to stand, to continue the fight.

I'm trying, she thought fiercely at it. The thoughts were the only point of clarity in her mind. Everything else shimmered and wobbled.

The wolf's only answer was to howl louder and louder.

That's not my wolf. Ruri blinked her eyes, trying to see through the fog of her head injury and the legs that blocked her way. Confusion reigned as the wolven attacking her paused to look over at Cassidy whose howl was not one of pain or despair, but rather that of victory. She disappeared from Ruri's view again as the wolven dismissed her and stalked ever closer to where Ruri lay, desperately trying to get her legs to move. All she could see were teeth smooth and sharp against muzzles slick with her blood.

First one wolven then another looked back. Snarls rose to a high crescendo, punctuated by the concussive snap of jaws breaking bone and piercing skin. A wolven skidded into Ruri's view, turning to present its back to her. As she watched, unable to comprehend what was happening, one of the wolven who had tried to tear out her throat was snatched between the jaws of this new arrival and smashed to the ground. Ruri struggled to her feet, though her legs wouldn't work quite right. Getting all her knees to lock was still a bit of a problem.

The wolven, a charcoal-colored male slightly bigger than average, was taking on all comers. The other wolven seemed reluctant to confront him, trying to get past him to get at her, but he wouldn't allow it. He was familiar, and Ruri was fairly certain she'd just seen him in the group that was trying to take out Cassidy. His scent rolled over her and it was familiar. He wasn't one she'd known in the pack before Dean, but she'd smelled him before. The aroma tickled something in the back of her mind, but she didn't have time to track it down. There would be time enough for that when she wasn't a hair from dying.

She moved forward to stand shoulder-to-shoulder with her defender. One side wasn't responding well, and she moved as close as she could for further protection. Across the room, Cassidy had picked up a partner as well. A blond wolven darted out from behind her to hassle the wolven who faced them. They were now four against a dozen, but they had the upper hand, Ruri could taste it. The wolven were confused and had lost all confidence. One whimpered and stumbled before righting herself. Her tail between her legs, she slunk from the room. Another tumbled to the ground right at Cassidy's feet and received a sharp buffet to the head. It didn't get up.

The dark gray wolven growled in the face of one of his packmates, displaying impressive teeth. Ruri snapped on the other side, and the wolven's nerve broke. With a shrill whine, it turned tail and fled. Maybe they could survive this after all.

CHAPTER FORTY-ONE

MacTavish was frothing with rage. Large globs of white spit drooled from his mouth to splat loudly upon the ground. He'd torn open the back of one of his lycans to get at Stiletto, who fought to the very edge of her abilities to keep the rogue Alpha away from her.

Malice kept three lycans at bay with broad sweeps of her katana. Every time one of the lycans tried to duck under the blade, it was met with an abrupt chop or lightning-quick lunge. They bled in more than one place, but so did she. One had gotten around and almost hamstrung her while its mates kept her busy in front. Her right leg wasn't functioning quite right, and she couldn't trust all her weight to it. Her ribs were one large mass of pain, but the left side sent agony stabbing deep within her whenever she tried to take a deep breath.

What she needed was a break, one small thing to go her way. So far such things had been few and far between. The lycans had figured out how to work together and her single edge over them was gone. So, they were capable of attacking together. Were they able to do the same on defense?

She took a deep breath, doing her best to ignore the pain in her side, and raised her katana over her head with one hand. With her left hand, she slid the wakizashi from its sheath at the back of her waist. The extra blade would give her the advantage on the attack but would open her up to their assaults. There was one who was a little shorter and slower than the others. He would be her first target. Once he was down, she would only have the two others to contend with.

She flowed from one foot to the other, never stopping, giving away none of her intentions. The lycans swiveled to follow her, not letting her get out of arms' reach, always on the edge of closing on her. She feinted to one side, slashing the katana at the eyes of the biggest one. He raised a hand and flinched away from her, then roared a challenge when she dropped back. Malice whirled and darted toward the other two lycans, the big one on her tail. He dragged himself along on powerful forearms, sprinting on all fours after her. As soon as she cleared the small ring of lycans, Malice leaped straight up, flipping backward to land between two of them. Her ribs screamed at her, not to mention what her leg had screeched when she pushed off. Her landing was off and she stumbled to one side. Fortunately, the lycans had been bowled over by the big guy and were only beginning to get back to their feet.

The little one was slower than his buddy and barely had time to lift one claw-tipped hand to defend himself. The katana sheared through it as easily as it took the head from his shoulders.

The wind of something passing right behind her ruffled Malice's hair. She turned in time to see the large lycan take down the remaining one. They tumbled end over end and crashed into a heap by a wall of safe-deposit boxes, some of which were open. The larger lycan ended up on the bottom and was having problems avoiding the teeth of the other. It ripped large chunks out of his arms.

Stunned at the turn of events, Malice stared for a moment. Cursing pulled her attention away from the two lycans mauling each other.

"You fucking bulldagger!" MacTavish heaved a chunk of masonry out of the way, exposing Stiletto to his attack. "How did you do it?" His words were almost impossible to understand, rage rendering nearly indistinct the sounds he forced past his muzzle. "How did you take my wolves?" He picked up a huge section of wall and raised it over his head. "Give. Them. Back!"

Stiletto dropped to the ground, flattening herself as the huge piece of concrete and rebar flew over her head and exploded into a cloud of dust. Smaller chunks rained down on her where she lay. When the dust cleared, Stiletto looked at her, eyes wide. A large chunk had landed across her leg, pinning her to the ground.

"Malice!" She reached out toward her, and Malice swore in her head. The last thing she needed was MacTavish's attention, but there he was turning toward her.

"More of you?" He sneered, lip curling to reveal wicked teeth, yellow and jagged. "Cockroaches you are, scuttling out from under the toilet. I'll crush you like I crushed her."

"You never should have gone near my sister, MacTavish," Malice said. She held the blades in front of her, ready to fend him off should he rush her. "That was your first mistake."

"Mistake." He grinned; then ran his tongue over his top teeth. "Not making her myself was the mistake. She would have been mine then. I would have watched while she ripped out your throat with her teeth."

Malice took a careful step to one side, being careful not to show how much her bad leg hurt. She laughed. "There's no way that would have happened. Blood is thicker than…whatever it is you have."

He mirrored her movements, careful not to let her flank him. The crazed grin didn't change. It remained pasted on his face with drool and froth dripping from one side. "That's adorable. Your puny family bonds are no match for the bonds of the pack. I've seen it, I've used it."

"And you don't know my sister." The trick was to keep him talking, but not too much longer. If he was allowing her to delay things, then he was probably nursing his own injuries. Her own wounds were healing, blood had long since stopped dripping down the back of her leg. It was the only reason she could still use it. Because of the knowledge and training drilled into her by her creators, Malice knew she could withstand almost anything and it would heal. She could come back from just about anything short of the loss of a limb. But where her healing was off the charts for a human, his would be far better than what she could manage. In a waiting game with a lycan, she was at a serious disadvantage.

"I know them all," MacTavish said. "I've turned brothers and sisters, parents even. They all became mine."

Malice kept moving. "Then where did they all end up? Why did you have to steal yourself a pack, if those you turned were so closely bound to you?"

His grin cracked, shifting to snarl and back to the grin so quickly she thought maybe she'd imagined it. "They get ideas eventually. Then they need to be taken care of. Still, some of them were around long enough to help me break down that weakling Dean's defenses." He kept moving with her. "Don't think I don't know what you're doing."

"And what am I doing?"

"You're stalling until the rest of your friends can arrive. I'll hear them coming long before they can help you, and you'll be dead in less than a second. The rest of those weaklings might be scared of you, but I know you're all flash."

"That's an interesting theory." Malice stopped sliding around in a circle. "But you're wrong."

He came to a stop across from her and tilted his head, manic smile still in place. Behind him, Stiletto levered herself up on one arm and drove her knife through the back of his ankle and down into his foot.

MacTavish roared and swept his hand down behind himself, catching Stiletto on the side of the head and pivoting her body to one side. Her pinned leg didn't move, but the rest of her was brushed aside like a child's toy.

It was the opening Malice had been looking for. She'd hoped Stiletto would realize what she was doing, and her squadmate hadn't disappointed. Her leg protested but didn't slow her down, and she took off toward the rogue Alpha. She covered those the three paces in less time than it took to blink an eye, and yet he was already turning back toward her when she came within reach. The claw-tipped hand was easy enough to dodge; she'd seen that move coming. She dodged to the inside, leading with the katana, piercing his pelt as if it were paper. The katana slid through him with little resistance, but she still felt it when the tip exited through his back.

MacTavish closed his jaws around her left shoulder with a snap that shivered through her entire body. Agony overwhelmed her, centering on the shoulder that he pulped by shaking his head back and forth. More than one tooth ground against bone, and the wakizashi dropped from her nerveless fingers. She wasn't going anywhere, and there was only one way she would survive.

Malice put her weight behind the katana that protruded from his abdomen, pushing it up, seeking out a vital organ. Without momentum behind it, the blade didn't cut as cleanly and she had to saw it back and forth to move it. He growled around his mouthful of shoulder and Malice became dimly aware that she was screaming.

She pulled back on the katana, drawing it out of his body. Both of his hands were wrapped around her, claws piercing the skin of her back, rending deeply. The pain would stop; it was simply one more sensation like hunger or cold. It could be ignored as easily. She winced at a particularly savage tear. Maybe not that easily. By some miracle, he hadn't hit any major blood vessels yet. She could fight until she bled out or until she lost a limb or two.

The katana shook in her hand and she steadied herself; then thrust the blade forward, straight at his heart. Her aim was true and

MacTavish stiffened when the katana burst through his fur-covered skin and sought out his most vital organ. His claws dug even deeper, and her shoulder was ripped to tattered shreds when he ripped his head free in an agonized howl. The sound was drowned by a gout of blood and he coughed. The claws slid out of her skin as his grip slackened. He looked at her blankly for a moment, then his eyes glassed over and he toppled backward, landing on Stiletto. She didn't move at all.

Malice stood dumbly without any weapons in her hands. Her katana stood proudly in MacTavish's chest and her wakizashi was somewhere on the ground next to her. Something scraped over concrete behind her and she whirled or tried to. She ended up stumbling in a circle. She'd completely forgotten about the two lycans who'd been fighting in the corner. The big one was pulling himself across the broken floor, heading for the hole the semi had punched in the side of the vault. He ignored her completely. Behind him, the other lycan lay in a bloody heap. Rather most of him did. His head was a little way beyond the rest of his body. That was one who wouldn't be getting up again.

She turned to consider MacTavish for a second. He was down, but until his head was removed from his body, she couldn't be certain he was dead. It was possible to kill a lycan through massive trauma, but the best way to be sure he wouldn't come back was destroying or separating the upper spinal column.

Wearily, she picked up the second blade and made her way over to him. Her left arm was useless and her torso a mass of pain, but there was still work to do. There was *always* more work to do. She put the blade to his throat and pushed down. His pelt resisted the blade before his head parted with his body and rolled over. The eyes stared accusingly at her, but she paid them no mind. What had happened to MacTavish had been necessary.

She pulled her katana out of MacTavish's chest and cleaned it off on a clean patch of fur before sliding it home in its scabbard. She stepped around his corpse to contemplate Stiletto. Her squadmate was still alive. Her chest rose and fell, though slowly.

Malice squatted next to her and cleaned the wakizashi before stowing it as well. A terrible thought had occurred to her when she saw that Stiletto was down. The woman was a threat to her family. Given the opportunity, she would run straight to Uncle Ralph and his superiors, she'd said as much. Before Malice could do anything about it, they would take Cassidy. If she ever saw her sister again, she would be a government guinea pig, and that was if she didn't die on some surgeon's dissection table.

Stiletto was a comrade, but she was also a threat. Covered as she was with still-bleeding wounds, it was unlikely she would survive without some help. If Malice had died taking out MacTavish, Stiletto would have died also. Malice took a deep breath and lifted her hand. It wavered slightly. Try as she might, she couldn't stop it shaking.

There might be some discrepancies in our accounts. Stiletto's not-so-veiled threat rang in her ears. She paused; then reached forward, closing her hand over Stiletto's nose and mouth. She held it there, but for how long she had no idea. There was no struggle for breath, there was nothing at all. Stiletto was dead. There could be no discrepancies now. Cassidy was safe. Was the price too high? Could she even put a price on keeping her family safe and whole?

Suddenly sick of the small space and the carnage and death inside it, Mary Alice stood. Everything shifted to the side and she put out a hand to steady herself. The walls felt like they were seconds from toppling over and burying her. She had to get out. Now. She scrambled over the pile of rubble at the lycans' improvised entrance, paying no attention to the blood splattering down on the debris in her wake. It was no more than she deserved. The parking lot smelled less of death, and she took a deep breath. The skin on her hands was torn to shreds from her climb over chunks of concrete and rebar. She gazed down at her trembling fingers. The ache in her hands was nothing compared to the desperate agony that threatened to hollow out her heart. She pulled out her phone and smeared her way through the touch interface, pausing to rub blood off the screen. She took a deep breath and shoved the emotions away in that little compartment in the back of her brain. They were in good company back there.

"Uncle Ralph?" Malice's voice was all business. "It's done. I need a cleanup crew." Mary Alice paused and allowed some pain to seep back into her voice. "And I need a body bag."

CHAPTER FORTY-TWO

The hotel no longer smelled like death, and for that Ruri was thankful. It didn't smell like home either. The mix of scents was different now, and it had sat empty long enough to lose the vitality she associated with a lived-in place. She pushed aside a treadmill to clean shattered glass out from under it. She'd broken the window, after all. It only made sense that she be the one to clean up the mess.

Plenty of things still needed fixing, and the other wolven had been busy scrubbing the place down. Even with her sensitive nose, she was no longer overwhelmed by the stench of decay. Ruri had been hesitant to come back to the hotel, but the Sayre Avenue house was much too small for all the wolven who had decided to come with Cassidy.

She'd known the exact moment MacTavish died as they fought for their lives in those filthy row houses. A few of the wolven they'd been facing had continued to battle, but most of them had become disoriented, almost delirious, before breaking off. Once it became obvious their Alpha was gone, they'd lost all will to fight. At that point, Ruri still had no idea that Cassidy had managed to pull away the allegiance of that handful of wolven. It was something she was in no way supposed to be able to do, but somehow Cassidy had managed. Ruri chalked it up to one more thing that made Cassidy different than any other wolven she'd met.

Cassidy had given the other wolven the choice to come with her if they wanted to. Ruri suspected that she'd sealed more of their loyalty with that one choice than she would have by forcing them to submit. Most of them had pledged themselves to Cassidy, but a few had decided not to.

"That's fine," Cassidy had said. "But you can't stay around here. I won't have you threatening my people. You have two days to get what you need, then move on. After that, you know how you'll be dealt with."

They'd known, even if Cassidy hadn't, though Ruri was sure she had an inkling. Territory was of utmost importance to wolven, and blood was shed over it more often than not. Ruri wasn't sure what Cassidy was going to do about the remainder of the wolven who'd turned her. Brittney and one other wolven were dead, but the other three had survived. Mary Alice had no idea what Cassidy planned for them either. They'd turned Cassidy, but she seemed to hold little animus toward them for it. They'd also helped turn the tide at the end; maybe that had earned them their reprieve. Those three hadn't gotten the option of leaving. Cassidy seemed to have bound them to her more tightly even than the others.

All the broken glass had been swept up, and Ruri's sharp eyes didn't make out any more pieces. It was time to bring out the shop vac and give the place a thorough once-over. Instead of heading down to the basement workshop to get the vacuum, Ruri stood there. She was going through the motions; she could feel it.

Maybe it had to do with the way the other wolven treated her, even the ones from her original pack. She didn't feel a part of this new family. She felt like the friend of a friend who was grudgingly tolerated at Thanksgiving dinner. This wasn't how it was supposed to be. They'd taken care of MacTavish, the pack had a new Alpha; everything should have been better. And maybe it was, but not for her.

Laughter preceded a group of three wolven into the exercise room. As soon as they saw her, the merriment dried up.

"I'm heading out," Ruri said lightly. There wasn't a whole lot of point in pretending it didn't hurt; they'd be able to smell her upset almost immediately. There also wasn't much point in making things awkward, which is what her continued presence seemed to be doing. "I'll see you around."

"Sure," said the closest one, a young female whose name she didn't yet know. She was one of MacTavish's additions, but she had chosen to stick around regardless. The other two were wolven she'd known from before, but they barely acknowledged her. Beth's refusal to look her in the eye hurt most of all. They'd been friendly before Dean's death, but Consuelo's death seemed to have changed all that.

The trip back to her room was uneventful, though too quiet. She could hear people chatting and laughing together, but the sounds petered out as soon as she came near. It was a little crazy, but she really wished Lewis had made it out. She had the feeling they would have gotten on. At least she could have counted on him to give it to her straight.

Maybe that was the problem. Most of the wolven left now were fairly low on the dominance scale. They mostly avoided confrontations at all costs. The more dominant wolven had been taken out by MacTavish when he took over the pack. They'd returned the favor when they wrested control of the pack back from him. Short of Cassidy and maybe Luther, there was no one to challenge her, so they avoided her instead.

Ruri stopped in the door to her room. She'd insisted on keeping the same room MacTavish's wolves had defaced, even though there were many open rooms in the hotel. It had been cleaned to within an inch of its life, but she imagined she could still smell excrement. Everything had been removed, including the furniture. Nothing had been salvageable. The new furniture was fine and of similar quality to what she'd thrown out. It wasn't hers. It didn't smell like it belonged to her. None of it did.

Standing there, Ruri made up her mind. In that moment, she realized she'd been moving toward the decision for days. Not even the pack's run during the full moon had helped. Cassidy certainly seemed to have benefited from it. The rest of the wolven had bonded even more strongly to her, but not Ruri. Again, she was right outside the circle of this new pack she wasn't even sure she recognized. It stung. She'd worked so hard to re-form the pack, and she wasn't a part of it. The thrill of the hunt and her wolf's relaxation hadn't been enough to stave off tears when she'd finally came fully back to herself. That had been two days ago, but nothing had changed since then. It was time.

She pulled a small duffel out of the closet and stuffed her meager belongings into it. Clothes made up the bulk of what she packed. They were about all she had left. The one thing she really wanted was the tintype of her family, the one that had been completely destroyed when MacTavish's wolven had trashed her stuff. Someone had taken the time to scratch the faces off her family members; then crushed the little piece of metal into a ball. She'd discovered it in a corner when cleaning the rest of the trash out of the room.

It took a little hunting to find Cassidy. That shouldn't have been the case either and was just one more indication of how she wasn't fitting with this new pack. She'd been able to point unerringly at Dean when he'd been Alpha no matter where he'd been. Cassidy hadn't claimed her in the same way. She was aware the Alpha was nearby, but she didn't have that close bond. Mary Alice now, Ruri could have found her way to the Hunter blindfolded. Even now she could feel her somewhere to the south.

As usual, Cassidy was wrapped up in conversation with Luther. They made no attempt to keep the discussion private, and Ruri could easily hear them talking about the pack's situation. Cassidy had chosen well when it came to her Beta. Ruri couldn't begrudge her that. Luther knew what he was about and had seen it all. He'd seen more than most of the rest of the pack combined. It still hurt, however. She knew what she was about also, but she was the one at loose ends, the one cut out of the decision-making process.

"How did MacTavish manage to keep so many wolven bound to him without anyone knowing?" Cassidy asked. "From what I've gathered, he shouldn't have been able to. Didn't Dean think he was a loner?"

"He certainly acted like one." Luther's voice was halting as he mulled over Cassidy's question. It wasn't the first time Ruri had heard it. MacTavish had been an enigma, even to the wolven he'd created. "Some of his wolven have said he could reclaim his Alpha-bond with them even after he abandoned it."

"You don't believe them?"

Luther was no fool to have doubts. Ruri didn't believe it either. That wasn't how the Alpha-bond worked. Once an Alpha claimed a wolven, the bond could only be broken by the Alpha holding it or by death. If it was given up, there was no reclaiming it. There were no backsies.

"I wish I didn't. It's unprecedented. I've never even heard rumors of such an ability."

"Huh." It was Cassidy's turn to sound troubled.

Ruri shifted where she stood, her feet scuffing softly against the floor. This is it, she thought, but she made no move to enter.

"What's up, Ruri?" Cassidy finally called out.

"I need to speak with you, Alpha," she said, stepping through the doorway.

"You going on a trip?" Luther asked, voice studiedly neutral. He tipped his head toward the duffel in her left hand.

"That's what I want to talk to Cassidy about," Ruri said. She stepped to one side and gestured one hand toward the door. This was something for which she needed no audience, especially not him.

He cast a glance toward Cassidy and waited for her assent before leaving. He got a little too close to Ruri for comfort. She refused to move; he had plenty of room to get by. For a second, it seemed like he might push it. Ruri raised her chin, daring him to do something about it, but he passed by without comment instead.

"What's on your mind?" Cassidy asked. She waved a hand at the overstuffed chair next to her.

Ruri dropped into it and placed the duffel on her lap. "This isn't working. I need to go."

"Things have been a little tense, I know. I'm sorry for that. The others don't seem to trust you."

"I know. That's been made abundantly clear." Ruri chewed on her lower lip, unsure how far to proceed. Finally she shrugged. She might as well get everything out there. "You don't either."

"I've had you at my back. I know you're there for me." Cassidy tilted her head in silent disagreement. "Without you I'd be dead more than once."

"And yet you haven't claimed me. Why not?"

"I can't."

"Can't or won't?"

"I've tried, but there's something stopping me."

"Is it Mary Alice?"

"It might be, I don't really know. I'm not sure if it might not be your attachment to her that is stopping it. I think if I really pushed it, I probably could, but that doesn't seem fair to you." It was Cassidy's turn to pause. "Besides, one of the reasons some in the pack don't trust you is because of her. I'm not sure if I ever really knew her, not once she left home. But I know you have my back."

"It's complicated. What about MacTavish's three? Do you really think you can trust them after what they did to you?"

"They've been taken care of." Cassidy's scent was prickly, warning her not to poke her nose too close. "I'm as sure of them as I am of you."

"If you say so." Ruri nodded. She didn't need the details. If Cassidy was certain, that was good enough for her. Besides that, Luther would be there to keep an eye on them. He was a good Beta and would watch her back, even against those Cassidy trusted, something Ruri had failed to do with Dean. "Things are too complicated to work out right now.

I think everything's too raw yet. I'm going to take off for a bit, give things a chance to settle down here. They don't need me reminding them what came before. You don't need that either."

"I'll miss having you around, you know." Cassidy was telling the truth. Ruri could smell the conviction on her, like bedrock warmed in the sun.

"I won't be far. I'd like to stick around the city, if you'll allow it."

"Of course. Are you going to be with her?"

Ruri shrugged. "If she'll have me."

Cassidy nodded. "Good, Mary needs you. I never knew how alone she was. I think you'll be good for her. Let me know if she needs anything. I'm not sure she'll ask me."

"I won't spy on her for you."

"And I don't expect you to. Take care of her, that's all I ask. Keep her safe, keep her sane. And come back to us when you think it's time."

"Thanks, Cassidy." Ruri got up and hovered awkwardly in front of the chair. There were too many things left unsaid, but it didn't feel like the right time either.

"For crying out loud, Ruri." Cassidy bounded out of her chair and enveloped her in a huge hug. She held Ruri for a long time, and Ruri reveled in the feeling of closeness to her Alpha. "I mean it, I want you to come back," she finally whispered in Ruri's ear before letting her go.

"I will," Ruri said, wondering as she did if she'd be able to make good on the promise. She picked up the duffel bag from where it had fallen on the floor during the hug and left the room.

Luther leaned against the wall a little way down the hall. It was far enough away that he might not have been able to hear what they'd said. He nodded to her, face giving nothing away, though unease swirled in his scent. It was traced through with what might have been disappointment, but Ruri couldn't untangle the complicated emotions he exuded. Likely he couldn't either.

"Luther" was all she said. She walked down the hall and out the front doors.

CHAPTER FORTY-THREE

Mary Alice glanced at her phone as it buzzed insistently at her from next to the laptop. Her mom's face filled the display. At least it wasn't Uncle Ralph. She didn't really want to talk to anyone. She hadn't left the loft since taking out MacTavish. And Stiletto.

Still, there was no getting around it. She'd been avoiding her mom since Cassidy was attacked, speaking to her only as much as was absolutely necessary. They weren't the kind of family who spoke even weekly, but it had been a long time since they last chatted. If she kept ducking Sophia's calls, she was liable to have her turn up on the doorstep.

"Hi, Mom." Maybe the phone would drop the call, then she'd have an excuse to continue being antisocial.

"Hi, sweetie." Unfortunately her mom's voice came over the line loud and clear. There would be no avoiding this unless they had a sudden solar flare. Wiping out all electronic devices on earth would be a small price to pay to avoid this talk. "It's been a while. How've you been?"

"Oh you know, same old." With unconscious ease born of many years of practice, Mary Alice kept her voice light. "What's going on in your neck of the woods?"

"Pretty good. Work was crazy there for a few weeks. Suddenly we had all sorts of people needing language sessions. I think I clocked more air travel since visiting you and Cass than I have most years. I think I've been pretty much everywhere in the US, except Chicago."

"That's nuts." Mary Alice sent a silent *thank you* to TC. He'd done a good job. It was too bad she'd had to repay him by twisting his arm. She hadn't heard from him since then, and she hoped she hadn't burned that bridge. Given the same set of circumstances, she would have made the same choice again, however.

"I know! But the travel bonuses were nice, so I'm not complaining." She laughed. "Well, not too much. It's nice to be home again. It sounds like things are settling back down again."

"Glad to hear it."

"How's your sister? I haven't been able to get hold of her yet."

"Good, I think." Mary Alice made a mental note to tell Cassidy to get a new phone and get the number to Sophia. She could offer some pointers in keeping their mother from being the wiser about what was going on if Cassidy would accept them. "She's been busy with her new thing. You know how she gets when she has a new project."

"I know it. And I wouldn't take that long-suffering tone. You're not that different, sweetie."

Mary Alice let the conversation pull her away from the dark thoughts that had overtaken her for the past five days. As much as she hadn't wanted to go through with the call, she was feeling better. Family could do that, it seemed. When it wasn't being the source of misery, that was. By the end of the call, she was smiling again. It felt like it had been years since she laughed and when she disconnected the call, she felt a lightness that had been missing for weeks. The only other time the heaviness of her life had been lifted off her had been when Ruri was around.

A tap on the metal door caught her attention. She looked over at it, but she heard nothing more so she went back to the laptop. The rundown of that night's activities was something Uncle Ralph still waited on and not very patiently. He was willing to cut her some slack because of Stiletto's death, but his tolerance was wearing thin.

Another tap pulled her away from the report. This one was followed by a rattle. Was someone throwing gravel at the door?

Mary Alice got up and left the cage, closing and locking it behind her through force of habit. She stopped to take a look at the security monitors and recognized the figure standing outside immediately. The displays were crap and the cameras even worse, but she thought she would recognize Ruri anywhere.

She stuck her head out the door next to the large garage door in time to see Ruri wind up with a large brick in her hand.

"I'd rather you didn't dent my door."

Ruri looked over and blushed. She dropped the brick in the gutter. "I was trying to get your attention."

"Consider it gotten." This was beyond awkward. What she wanted to do was wrap her arms around Ruri and bury her face in her hair, but what was coming out was stupidly formal. "You can come in if you want."

"I'd like that." Ruri picked up a small duffel bag and walked toward the door.

"You going on a trip?" Mary Alice wasn't sure what to make of the grimace she got in response to the question. She also didn't know what to make of the disappointment that sat like an icy ball in the bottom of her stomach at the prospect.

"Maybe not."

Ruri didn't seem inclined to elaborate, and they headed toward the elevator in silence. The ride up to the third floor was as awkward as everything else. Mary Alice glanced over at Ruri, drinking in her profile and the way her hair barely brushed her shoulders, a curtain that moved like a living thing with every twitch of her head. When Ruri looked over, Mary Alice pretended to be looking down at the ground. The diamond-plate bottom of the elevator wasn't nearly as fascinating as she made it out to be. The third time she looked away, Ruri let out a small sigh. She reached past Mary Alice and pressed the stop button. The elevator ground to a halt between the second and third floors.

"What did you do that for?" Mary Alice asked.

"We need to talk and I want to do it somewhere you can't walk out on me."

"Where are you going?" The question burst out of Mary Alice before she could stop it. "When will you be back?"

"Why do you want to know?" Ruri studied her seriously. She seemed to be trying to look *into* Mary Alice.

"Because…" Mary Alice trailed off, suddenly anxious. Why did she care? Why did it feel like there would be a giant hole in her life if this woman she'd only known for two weeks was suddenly gone from it? "I shouldn't want to."

"Why not?"

"Because of who you are. Because of who I am."

"But you still want to, don't you?"

"God help me, I shouldn't."

"But you do."

Ruri stared at her like she was willing Mary Alice to say the right thing. She didn't know what the right thing was, and if she did, she probably shouldn't say it. And yet... "I do."

Ruri's smile broke upon her, warming her like the sun coming out from behind the clouds in deepest winter. She turned toward Mary Alice and reached out her hands, taking Mary Alice's arms right above the elbows. Ruri's hands were hot on her skin. It was her turn to blush, remembering how good those hands had felt on another part of her body. What if that's all they were? Just pheromones and animal lust. Panic chilled her to the bone and stole her breath away. She inhaled deeply, trying to get her breathing back under control.

"I can't," Mary Alice said. "I want to, but I can't. If things were different, then I'd..." She couldn't finish the thought. Her eyes prickled and she blinked rapidly to keep tears from overflowing down her cheeks. She tried to twist out of Ruri's grasp.

"Maybe we can pretend things are different." Ruri ignored her weak struggle and pulled her into a loose embrace. She nestled Mary Alice's head under her chin and held her, one hand rubbing soothing circles over her back. "And if we pretend long enough, maybe one day we'll realize we aren't pretending anymore."

The hug completely undid Mary Alice's resolve. The sense of belonging was suddenly so strong she felt it like a physical sensation wrapped around her. Home wasn't a place, or at least not one made of brick and mortar. Home was in this woman's arms. She leaned back and allowed her eyes to roam over Ruri's face, blurry though it was through the tears that fell without constraint from her eyes. Golden eyes stared back at her, achingly open, urging her to say yes.

"God, yes." She leaned in and covered Ruri's lips with her own, drinking her in, memorizing how she tasted. She never wanted this to end, though chances were good it would. If there was even the tiniest slice of a possibility that they could make it work, she had to try.

"Then I guess the only place I'm going is here," Ruri said when they came up for air. "We'll pretend for as long as we need to."

"Forever would be long enough."

Ruri laughed and released the elevator before taking her mouth again. The elevator shuddered and ground to a start, taking them up.

Bella Books, Inc.

Women. Books. Even Better Together.

P.O. Box 10543
Tallahassee, FL 32302

Phone: 800-729-4992
www.bellabooks.com

Printed in the USA
CPSIA information can be obtained
at www.ICGtesting.com
JSHW082152140824
68134JS00014B/191